Be Brave. Love Hard.

Baggage

A Firestone Brothers Hot Hockey Romance

Mar Mills

Published by Girl Time -IGFT Soul- Publishing, 2024.

Baggage

Publisher: Girl Time -It's Good for the Soul- Publishing

Editor: Wizards Publishing

Image: Deposit Photos

Cover Design: Fantasia Frog

Dedicated to my husband, the believer of all my dreams.

Chapter One

Karis Hill glared at the yawning entrance of the ice rink. Fogged with humidity, the sliding glass doors mocked her with each open and close. For the past eleven years, she'd worked hard to shut the sport out of her life, yet one week back home in Florida, and here she was facing hockey's front door.

Literally.

The mess of it all weighed a ton, but she held tight to her determination to keep her niece's life as normal as possible. Such a tiny summer task, and the one thing Karis and her mother, Iona, had ever agreed on. With everything Lindsey had gone through, and with an uncertain future peeking over the horizon, how could Karis waltz in and deny the girl her true love?

Karis despised hockey.

Lindsey loved it.

It didn't matter how or when she entered the hockey rink. She'd still have to trudge through the doors and confront the broken promises hockey dangled in front of her. No time like immediately.

Coughing on the recirculated air of the rink, trying like hell to ignore the memories the stench of hockey gear brought back, Karis scanned the faces of beer-holding hockey parents clogging the doorway. As a practicing psychologist, she assessed every one of them, and as a brand-new substitute parent to a moody teenager, she understood why they each nursed a beer.

Pulling in a desperate breath, wishing it would actually do what it was supposed to do—*damn lying yoga coach*—Karis steadied herself, pushed past her anxiety, and swam through the masses, hunting for Lindsey.

The place was all white ice bordered by scuffed rectangles of plexiglass. Black-and-blue carpet butted up against rubber mats and painted concrete. Nothing glamorous. The rink hadn't changed since her high school days, but not much in Edge View had.

Spotting Lindsey through glass doors labeled Rink One, Karis studied her niece with the calculating eye of the therapist she'd promised herself she'd lock away for the summer. Out with the shrink, and in with the aunt. Fingers crossed because shrinking was easier than aunting.

Convinced she was the absolute wrong person for this job, Karis tried another cleansing breath, and wished her niece had someone in her life better suited to take care of her. The poor girl scraped the bottom of the barrel in the family department.

Lindsey stared through the glass, watching the hockey world carry on, like it was normal for a mother to disappear, to have an estranged aunt show up, and to live with a grandma losing her mind.

A teenager had to be terrified. Karis was thirty-two, and the reality scared her to death. No kid deserved the shitty upbringing Karis and her older sister had lived through, but Lindsey's life skirted the edge of history.

Pondering it all, like she'd told herself *not* to do, she attempted to console the teenager who had more than her fair share of dysfunction. "Lindsey." She steadied her breathing, taking control of her self-doubt. Hard to do with a teenage glare scorching her to the bones.

Lindsey's ponytail swished across the back of her jacket. "I changed my mind. I want to go home."

Not buying it. Karis never met a hockey player capable of denying the lure of the game. Even her own niece didn't seem convinced of her tight-lipped words. Watching the players, the ache to skate was plastered across her face. Dreams didn't burn out on Aunt Karis' watch.

"I think you should stay," she mumbled, sliding her arm across her niece's tense shoulders. Lindsey's tall, slim body, a replica of what Karis could remember of her older sister and Lindsey's mother, Leah.

Lindsey shrugged out of Karis' affection and snagged her stick and gear bag. "Can we just go? I changed my mind. Grandma needs me."

With a nonrefundable thousand dollars spent for two weeks of hockey camp, there was no changing minds. Maybe slide a couple of days to adjust, but not coming at all? No refunds? A thousand dollars was difficult to overlook with a pile of merciless medical bills stacked on the desk at home. Leaving would be so easy and put them both out of their misery. But dodging problems never solved them, and they were both stronger than running away.

Stepping close, Karis did her best persuading. "Grandma's fine. I'm going back to check on her, so she won't be alone." She ignored Lindsey's headshake and plowed on. "You can't sit with Grandma all summer. It's not healthy."

"Yes, I can," Lindsey countered. "What do you know? You haven't been here. What if I'm at the rink, and she needs help?" She banged her stick on the rubber mat. "This is a waste of time." Her words flew out fast and final, as if rehearsed or ingrained from a disgruntled adult unworthy of having a child in their life. "I'm not good at this anyway," she finished quietly, curling into herself.

A counterargument would be weak against the truth. No one had wanted her around, but she was here now, ready to pick up the scattered pieces of her niece's heart. "Nice try, sweets, but Grandma says you're an outstanding hockey player—" She made her words light and playful. Something she had never experienced from her own mother.

Lindsey cut her off, slinging her bag over her shoulder. "Wrong. I *was* outstanding, but I'm done now." She leaned forward, supporting the weight of her gear.

The hurt and fear laced in Lindsey's words punched Karis smack in the heart. Not giving up, she reached for the bag. "How about you just give it a shot today?" A reasonable compromise.

"No!" Lindsey's voice carried up to the rafters, and everyone in Rink One gawked their way.

Awesome.

"Come on, Lindsey," she whispered, holding back her own tears. Her stomach twisted into knots, imagining the scene playing out in Lindsey's mind. Her grandma, at home, withering away while she spent hours doing something she loved. "It's okay to feel this way," Karis attempted.

"Oh God. Don't even try to therapy me. You don't get it, just take me home." Another brilliant teenage eye roll.

"I'm not taking you home." Although that would be easy.

"I'm only good at this if Grandma's here."

Before Karis spoke, a shift in the universe, smelling of salt and woodsy soap, invaded her resolve.

Only one man possessed that power.

"That's an inaccurate assessment of your skills, Linds." His voice. Deep. Dark. Commanding. Confident. Capable of saying the right thing at the right time, breaking her heart into a million tiny shards. She'd listen to it on repeat if it put a hint of hope on Lindsey's face. Steadying herself, Karis stole a look at the man she'd left years ago.

Ty Firestone was still beautiful.

Tempted to reach out and touch the skin she had touched a million times, she forced her nails into the sweaty lines of her palms instead.

The skates he wore added inches to his already six-three frame, and, of course, he was in great shape for a retired professional hockey player. Catching the glint of his stormy gaze, she prepared herself against a possible disaster.

His large, calloused hands reached for Lindsey's bag. Thinking about the things those capable hands had done to her body, a rising blush heated Karis' cheeks.

Lindsey released her duffle. "Hey, Coach."

"Hey, Linds." He flung her bag over his shoulder. "Welcome back." His words were cautiously tender with a clear sign of familiarity.

Lindsey's face darkened. "I'm not staying."

His concern kicked Karis in the heart. He'd always excelled at pulling her apart. She sucked in a breath, ignoring the burning effort it took to keep her feelings in check and off her face. Rapid-fire emotions swamped her judgement, and Ty's sizzling stare made her skin hot and her brain work overtime. He could always read her, and their time apart had done nothing to diminish the skill.

Within a beat, Ty did what he always did. He took care of the issue.

"Smith'll be thrilled you're here. Your team needs you, big-time." He tried to make light. Never one to give up, he leaned over and whispered, "I know it's hard to be here without your grandma." In return for his efforts, he received a lip curl and silence. "Listen," he persevered, ignoring Lindsey's slumped shoulders and distant demeanor. "It takes a lot of courage to move forward with a dream when you've lost your support." He glanced at Karis. "Isn't that right?"

The air thinned with the accusation in his tone. Disappointed in her slipping shield, Karis met his gaze, her heartbeat a face-off to the fury in his eyes. The clench of his square jaw and the squeeze of his perfect lips confirmed her theory. After all this time, he still hated her.

"Support can come in different ways," Karis snapped, caving to her anger. She'd produced a million explanations. He bought none of them. But this wasn't about her, him, or them. It was about Lindsey. Lindsey. Lindsey. Lindsey.

She sealed the angst pushing against her rib cage and focused on the reason she was back home. "It's up to you, kiddo. It won't hurt to stay. If you still feel like you can't do it, we can cross that bridge when we get there. If it doesn't collapse first." Karis mumbled the last part, flying by the seat of her unworthy parenting pants.

"Oh, I can do it," she corrected, stubborn like her grandma, and every other female in the Hill clan.

Poor girl.

Karis tried again. "Stay today. I think you might surprise yourself, and maybe Grandma will feel like coming with us tomorrow."

Lindsey's solid stance didn't waver. Damn teenagers and their hardcore convictions.

Ty nodded toward the locker room. "All those mixed emotions you're having right now, take 'em on the ice. You'll be unstoppable."

Oh, he was laying it on thick. Message clear. What more did he want? Her heart ripped out and thrown on the ground? A bloody, pooling mat for him to stomp on?

"Oh God, Coach. You sound like my aunt." Lindsey faced the ice. "It's weird being here without Grandma. She's home alone."

"Put your anger to work. There comes a time when you feel like you have nothing else to lose; put that in your game," Ty urged.

Karis stifled a groan and stared at the front doors letting people in, and teasing her with glimpses of freedom. Somehow the world continued its steady hum, while she contemplated choices she'd made years ago, young and lost in the shuffle of trying to become who she needed to be with something to lose and nothing to give.

Like now.

No one would ever convince her she'd made the wrong decision, and Ty had the successful hockey career to prove it. He thought they could have it all. He acted first and thought later. She never had such an admirable luxury.

The ability to be so confident, like everything in the world was his, and he deserved it all.

Didn't he?

In college, he'd worked out all hours of the night. Paid for the ice at midnight, so he could get it cheap. Willing to do anything to land his dreams, and so was she.

For him. Anything.

She would not be an excuse.

But here he stood inches from her, with the hands she'd loved shoved in his pockets, hiding the strong fingers that used to slip into hers. Years ago, touching was as necessary as breathing.

Her thoughts collided. Too many years had passed, and the raw emptiness she'd learned to live with buzzed to the surface, reacting to his tenderness toward her broken niece.

Time to go.

"Lindsey," Karis uttered. "I'm going to go check on Grandma. I'll come back early to check in on you, but if you need me, text me, and I'll be here." She landed a peck on Lindsey's cheek and darted out the doors. An abrupt and irresponsible parental move but come on. She needed air, needed to breathe, needed out of Ty's spell.

Stopping outside the exit, fighting through her panic, the morning's heavy humidity clouded her sense of direction.

Left or right?

Right or wrong?

The blinding Florida sun reflecting off the white brick of the old building made the wretched Buick impossible to find. Tall palm trees lined the tiny parking spaces filled with oversized trucks. An old fountain gushed in the center of a small pond glorifying Florida hockey. Money wasted.

"Karis."

His harsh tone zipped up her spine, releasing the dormant need her body had neglected for years. If she turned around, the hurricane building between them would blow her to her knees.

One step was all she took before his strong fingers gripped her arm, heating her skin through the fabric of her jacket. Her knees buckled, and his hold tightened, sending her thoughts in a million different directions. All of them impossible.

She pried his fingers from her arm and stepped away. "I'm not doing this." Her heart kicked into high gear, demanding the stability of his nearness, but her mind held strong.

Scratching his jaw, he looked away. She almost laughed at the familiar move, his pinched lips and stern jawline a prelude to the argument forthcoming and the hurt he was trying to hide.

His black wavy hair still brushed the back of his tan neck, and the long sides remained tucked behind his ears. He was always too busy for a cut. Squinting against the sun, his scruffy cheek lifted in a smirk. His wide shoulders blocked out the world around them. She used to count on that. On only seeing him.

"Are you ever gonna do this? You ever gonna talk to me?" His gaze dug into hers, his words soft, deliberate, and unrelenting. So very Ty.

"No," she sighed. "It's been too long." He'd break her.

His index finger hovered over her heart. "Not fair." Hurt flared across his face.

Fair had nothing to do with them.

Fair didn't belong in her life.

"What?" She batted his accusing finger away. Doused in high emotion he was always combative. It was the hockey living inside of him.

"Eleven years later and you're still playing dirty. Cryptic. Like I should know more than I do," he spat.

Karis dodged. "Eleven years later, and you still have to be reminded not to walk outside with your skates on." She was a master at avoidance.

Breaking their stare, he studied the sky, an annoyed slip of a grin on his lips. "Some things never change."

"And they never will." Her mended heart tore wide open.

***

Zoning out while coaching forty kids laced up in boots with blades on a slippery wet surface promised a high level of danger. Ty had to clear his head and get back into practice before someone got hurt.

At the whistle, the kids raced to the bench, sucked down water, and waited for the next drill. Ty wracked his brain for said drill, but the only thought snagged starred Karis' dark, thick hair falling down her bare back, brushing her waist, the silky waves heavy in his hands and threaded between his fingers.

Would it be the same?

It had to be.

The memory of her half-lidded green gaze preyed on him from the inside out. With a gloved hand, he gripped the side boards, steadying himself against the heated memory. He dropped his gloves, removed his helmet, and doused his face with freezing water.

It didn't help.

An unwanted wave of desire curled low in his belly. He didn't need to care how she felt in his arms. How she would *still* feel. They were over. She'd made sure of it, and he'd worked the hell out of his mind and body to forget her. Work erased the minute he spotted her in the rink.

Truth be told, he'd deal with Karis if it meant having Lindsey back. He'd feared her grandmother's illness would keep her from playing hockey and crush Smith in the process. Kind of like what Karis had done to him in their college days back in North Carolina, cementing his mission in life. His nephew would never experience such torture.

Some men never recovered.

A million stressors pressed him as he explained the drill to the group of antsy eight-to-fourteen-year-olds. He blew the whistle with no recollection of one word he'd said.

"Aaaa, Uncle Ty, you good?"

Ty smiled, facing the reason he worked with the Edge View youth hockey program.

Smith.

Tall and lanky, with crazy curly hair refusing to be tamed by his hockey helmet. The kid had great hands and a mature hockey sense, making him a standout in his age group, but he still cut up with the best of them. Humble as hell, too.

Ty patted Smith's helmet. "Yeah, I'm good. Why? You good?" The boy's wide smile grounded Ty tight to the life he'd created.

"Yeah, I'm good, but you spaced out." Smith tapped his stick on the ice, unconvinced and rarely able to be still longer than a millisecond.

Having Smith in his life for twelve years, there wasn't much Ty could hide from him, so he stopped trying and offered life unfiltered. Every second of the day, outside of school, they were together. So much time together made hiding emotions impossible. Ty couldn't imagine his life without the kid, and he would do whatever it took to keep him in it.

"Lindsey's back." Ty snapped his helmet strap.

"She's quiet today. Most of the time, you can't shut her up." Smith laughed at his own sarcasm.

Ty chuckled, batting Smith's skate with his stick. "Be nice. She's had a rough go. We all know what that's like, right?"

"Yes, sir." He glided to Lindsey. There were worse kids to flock to. It wasn't her fault her mom sucked, her grandmother fell ill, and her dad jetted before her birth. Idiot.

Parents held an unexplainable power over their children. He was living proof it was a gift and a curse. Manipulative and lovely all at once. Ty's short summer stint as head coach for the U14 hockey team often ended with driving Lindsey home because her mom had vanished for the night, or her grandmother had forgotten.

"Tyson!"

Jesus. "What?" Ty glared at his younger brother. Ryan guaranteed a good time on the ice. Good and unfortunate because it meant their professional hockey team missed the playoffs. On the flip, they were both home for the summer, not something an assistant coach should confess to enjoying. Ryan, the ultimate player, despised an early summer and sulked for a good week when the season ended without playoffs.

"You got music in your helmet? I've been calling you for fifteen minutes." Ryan smiled behind the plastic shield. A plastic shield. Really? With kids?

Ryan was a wuss.

"Bullshit. What do you want?" Ty scanned the ice. Short, fit bodies maneuvered through the drills. Ryan had the practice for both age groups running like clockwork. A vast improvement from past summers. Building muscles and reading *O, The Oprah Magazine* could only go so far. The man had come a long way. He didn't care for the younger group of skaters, but he handled it for the love of Smith.

"Stop thinking about Karis. These kids didn't come out to watch you mourn the love of your life." Ryan grinned, all too happy to tell it straight.

"I'm not mourning the love of my..." Why bother? Ryan leaned on his stick, bouncing his bushy brows up and down, taking nothing seriously, ever. "Shut the fuck up. Don't you have a drill to run or a kid to torture?"

"Nah, man, practice is over. It's one o'clock."

Ty checked his watch and blew the whistle. "Let's go, guys and gal. Off the ice. Grab your water. Time's up. Lindsey and Smith, move the nets for the Zamboni."

Ice shavings hit his waterproof pants from every kid trying to stop before smacking into the boards. The runny red noses of the seven-year-olds glistened behind helmet cages.

"So, how is Karis?" Ryan teased, shoving water bottles into outstretched hands.

Ty glared down the boards, preparing for the assault of questions that he'd leave unanswered. His brother's smile flashed wide and condescending over helmeted heads.

He wouldn't give in.

"This is not up for discussion. Not with you anyway." Reaching behind the boards, he felt around for stray water bottles.

"Ah, come on. You've been in la-la land all day. She's got your mind reeling."

He squirted water at his brother's face. It didn't matter. Nothing ever shut him up.

"Shit, that's cold." Ryan shook his head, flicking water every which way.

"Serves you right. Mind your own business." With the water bottle tucked under his arm, he grabbed two forgotten hockey sticks and skated to the locker rooms.

"You are my business." Ryan caught up. "She shook you, huh?"

Ty spun on his blades. "Shook me? Listen, I do not, and just in case you missed those words because of my wicked snarl, let me repeat, *I do not* want to talk about Karis. Stop asking me. Go help your kids get undressed."

He would never be ready. Ready didn't exist when it came to her.

"Fine, but did you ask her?" Ryan pushed.

"Enough," he warned.

"Ty?" Ryan gripped his shoulder, all kidding gone. "You have to talk to her about it. Especially if you're going to be seeing her. Not knowing is going to kill you. It *did* kill you."

Ugh, emotional hockey players. Ty flung his brother's hand away. "Wrong. I haven't known in almost eleven years. I'm not dead yet. And who said I was going to be seeing her?"

"Dude, you can see her right now. She's standing over there." Ryan lifted his chin toward the glass.

"I swear to God, I'm going to knock that grin right off your face and take whatever teeth you have left with it."

"No chance, bro. You can't hurt steel." They stepped off the ice.

The metal handle slammed into place. "Man, where did you get that confidence from?"

"You." Ryan shrugged.

Ty put his hand over his heart, faking faint. "You slay me."

"Good. Now trade locker rooms with me."

"Not on your life."

"Oh, come on."

The closer they got to Karis, the more fascinating the worn floor mats became. "No way. When you're a retired player, you can have the older kids' locker room."

"That's a hundred years from now."

"Again, the confidence is just extraordinary." His body tightened with each step closer to her. She leaned against the glass, her wavy hair curving against her breasts, stopping at her waist. He sucked in a worthless breath. Ryan's incessant talking and Karis' feminine curves had his nerves shredded.

"Shut up," Ryan tossed. "We should refuse kids who don't know how to tie their skates. I have blisters from pulling laces. Maybe we shouldn't take kids under seven in this camp."

He rounded on the diva. "You're a professional hockey player. You weigh well over two hundred pounds—"

"Two-ten. It's summer. Give me a break."

"Whatever," Ty continued. "You're six-three. Six-six with skates. Men bigger than you pound you against the boards ten months out of the year, and you're bitching about tying hockey skates for little kids."

"Yes. I am. My fingers hurt. I've got lace burn. You ever had lace burn? It's worse than a paper cut." He held out his hands. "So, can we switch?"

Ty shoved his brother's hands. "I think you need to grow a pair. I'm telling your coach what a whining baby you are off-season, *and* I'm requesting you tie all your teammates' skates."

"You are my coach. Trade with me. Just for a day," he whined.

"Assistant coach," Ty corrected. "I could never be fully responsible for you," he said with love. He'd been happily responsible for Ryan for many years.

Ty headed for his locker room, refusing to slide his gaze down Karis' jean-covered legs. Sweet lavender and a smell as soft as melted butter filled his nose, clouded his thoughts, and infringed on his focus. He dared his eyelids to close and his nose to soak in her fragrance. Thank God the Zamboni's grinding covered the moan pushing past his lips. His body always had a mind of its own when it came to her.

"You suck," Ryan shouted over the chatter coming from his kids' locker room.

"Only in the good places." Giving a wink, Ty headed to his locker room, with Karis' sweet gasp echoing in his ears.

Chapter Two

Hoisting the heavy bag over his shoulder, Ty escaped the coaches' locker room before the walls pressed him like a buttery Cuban sandwich. Laughter tumbled from locker room 3, planting a smile on his heart. Behind the door, Lindsey strummed her hockey stick like a guitar. Smith rolled on the floor, laughing straight from the belly.

He soaked in the sweet sound. Every summer, Lindsey became a part of their family, and every summer, Ty waited for her to disappear.

Back to breathing, the duo lofted a bright-orange ball from tape to tape, their sticks scraped the floor with whacks, bangs, and one-timers. The small square locker rooms fitted with wooden benches along the walls were ill-equipped for play. A calculated design to keep the roughhousing to a minimum. Smith had direct orders to stay out of Lindsey's locker room. At least they were dressed.

"Smith, five minutes. I'll meet you out front," he called out. "Lindsey, you did great today."

She shrugged and whacked the ball. "Thanks, Coach."

These two. They had to have something going, but every time he brought it up, Smith yucked and gagged like death had him by the throat. Lindsey was just one of the guys. *For now.*

Adjusting his gear, Ty pinched the bridge of his nose. Where did the time go? Yesterday, Smith was a baby today, a teenager tomorrow —Christ— he couldn't think about it.

He couldn't think about her, either, but his thoughts blew in sideways, leaving him no choice. His body scouted her out. Searching for her flowery scent and riddled with angst until it could angle up against her. His mind knew the rules, but his body refused to entertain them.

Spotting her in the atrium, waiting for her kid like every other hockey parent, a light hum buzzed beneath his weak composure. He wanted nothing more than the right to sidle up hip to hip and swing his arm around Karis' shoulders.

Submitting to habit, and wanting her as close as possible, he dropped his gear beside her booted feet. The same boots he'd slipped off a million times after a grueling practice. His hands needing to be on her the second he left the ice.

He struggled with it now.

"Hey, Coach." Hockey dad, Josh Morrow, spoke with his usual arrogant enthusiasm, and slithered into their space.

Ty shook the outstretched hand, happy for the interruption but ultra-aware of Karis' posture going rigid and the ridiculous effect it had on him. She'd seeped into his core without a fucking clue. His body tightened. She liked her space.

"Mr. Morrow, good to see you." Ty smiled through the lie. This man was a douche.

"You, too, Coach. How'd he do today?" The man's clothes were tucked tighter than a military-grade bed.

Mr. Morrow ranked within the top ten reasons Ty preferred to grab Smith and sneak out the back. Most parents didn't bother Ty or Ryan about their superstar status, and he had a pretty good grasp on how to handle it when they did. But Mr. Morrow lacked all social graces. It didn't matter. Ty had to mingle in the lobby while Smith lingered with Lindsey. Leaving him no choice but to engage with Josh Morrow. Hardcore hockey dad and first-class asshole.

Ty put his coach face on. "Joe did great, as usual." What good would it do to elaborate in front of all the parents, waiting to pounce on a tidbit? Coaching youth hockey on the off-season was the best; dealing with the parents was the absolute fucking worst.

"Give it to me straight," Josh urged.

"No, really. He did great. It's just the beginning of the summer season." Time to wrap this up. He rested his hand against the small of Karis' back, stopping her getaway. "Josh, have you met Karis Hill? This is Lindsey's aunt."

Ty didn't miss her smirk or the way his goddamn hand lingered.

Karis shook Josh's hand and eased away from Ty's traitorous fingers.

"Good to meet you." Josh pumped her hand until she jerked it away.

"Yeah, you, too." She flashed him a smile.

"Lindsey's back. That's great." Josh wiped a sweaty brow. "She been keeping up with her privates? I noticed she struggled on her edges a little today."

See?

Douche.

Ty narrowed his gaze, ready to intervene on Karis' behalf, but as usual, intervention was unnecessary.

She tilted her head, sizing up Josh the douchebag. "I'm not sure if she has been keeping up with her *privates*. I'll have to ask about that, but her grandmother's been sick, and her mother bailed, so hockey really hasn't been a priority."

Josh got smaller and smaller. "Yeah. Sorry about that."

Karis plowed on, aiming her venom in the guy's direction. "And I'm not sure what you mean by edges. I stopped being interested in hockey years ago."

Her witty tongue, still impressive, sliced the smile off Mr. Morrow's face. "Coach." She leered Ty's way. "Thanks for the help with Lindsey today. I appreciate it." She flung the words, leaving the men in her wake.

"See ya, Josh." Instinctively, Ty followed her, blocking the view of her swinging hips from anyone but him. When Smith and Lindsey entered the hallway red-faced and chuckling, her pinched shoulders relaxed, and the smile on her lips had his heart hammering and his stomach muscles clenched too tight for his liking. Lying on the ice wouldn't keep his body from burning. His hands from twitching. His mind from spinning to memories of his fingers sliding over her bare skin. His body hardened. The treadmill would get the worst of his frustration this afternoon. "Smith," he called, getting the boy's attention, a hard task with a ball and stick in proximity.

"Can Lindsey come to lunch with us?" Smith asked, batting at an orange ball.

As if seeing her curves didn't kill him enough. As if touching her back didn't send enough heat into his veins to melt all the ice in Canada. Now his nephew expected him to eat with her. Where was the bro code?

Ty swallowed the growl crawling up his throat. Every which way, this was a bad idea, but she deserved to be on the hook for a bad idea. The prospect of her looking him in the eye for about an hour suddenly held great appeal.

"Sure," Ty agreed. "You ladies want to come to lunch with us?"

He didn't expect her hesitation to stab him like it did. *Please, just push the knife all the way in and put me out of my misery.* How, after all these years, could he still feel this way?

"Um." Karis bit her lip, and he threatened to bust his kneecaps if they hit the floor.

"Listen, no worries. No big deal. Just lunch. I thought the kids might want to hang out. It's been a while." He swung his hockey bag onto his shoulder and reached for his stick, trying to leash his agitation.

She shook her head and reached inside her purse. "Um, I'm not sure."

Ouch. "Smith, let's go. Maybe another time."

Both kids moaned, bodies sagging on cue.

She called after him in a tone only she could get away with. His name on her lips. Again, he threatened his knees. Nothing should sound so sexy.

"Just let me call my mom and see if she's all right to stay home by herself for another hour." With the phone to her ear, he watched every stretch of her long legs carry her to a quiet corner. His jaw ached to be popped. How bad would it look if he banged his head against the glass?

"Roll your tongue up and close your mouth. Kids are asking me why you're drooling." His brother eased up beside him, all healthy, confident, and untouched by love.

Love?

"Shut up. We're long over."

Ryan chuckled and held onto three hockey sticks. "I got news for you. You're far from over."

"You're wrong. I want her. No question. Look at her. You want her. And if that happened, your professional hockey career would be over, along with every other bodily function you hold dear." Ty gripped his brother's shoulder. There weren't many men he could stand head-to-head with.

"Easy, Coach, I get it." Ryan shrugged out of his grip.

"I'm glad you do because I don't," he sighed. "There's no room in my life for her again. I have to be able to take care of Smith." Panic snaked up his spine.

"Relax. You *do* take care of Smith." Ryan stared down at a seven-year-old clinging to his leg.

"Coach Ryan." The voice rang out small and giddy. Hockey happy.

Ty welcomed the rug rat. The last time he let himself dive into memories of him and Karis, he couldn't shake it.

"What's up, Mikael?"

"That's my stick, Coach." The kid tugged a stick from the bunch.

Ryan bent down, leveling with the little player. "Mikael, you can't leave your stick in the locker room."

"I know, sorry, Coach." The kid grabbed his stick and ran off.

Ty subdued his proud smile. "You love these kids."

Ryan shook his head. "You really think he's sorry? He doesn't look sorry."

"He's eight. He doesn't have to be sorry for anything he does for another ten years. Leave him be." Ty glanced over at Karis standing in the corner, gripping her phone. Her brows scrunched together, and red blots bloomed on her cheeks. His brain scrolled through every possible and impossible solution to replace the worry. That's what she did to him. He couldn't allow it. Not anymore. She'd passed on her chance to matter to him.

"Smith, let's go," Ty called, a bit more curt than necessary. "Ryan, we'll catch you later?"

"Yep, see ya." He moved into the fray of young players and searched for stick owners.

"We're all set for lunch." Karis slipped her phone into her back pocket.

Bullshit.

"Listen, if you need to go, I can drop Lindsey home when we're done." He captured a breath and watched her teeth sink into her plump bottom lip. Glossy and no doubt tasting like coconut. Just kill him.

"Am I uninvited now?"

He pulled his gaze away from the trance her mouth had him under. Control slipped and confusion rushed in, tearing him between making Smith happy, making himself somewhat happy, and wondering what made Karis *un*happy.

How could he deny Smith and Lindsey a simple pleasure? It was lunch, not moving in together. "Of course you're still invited." He didn't have to sound so convincing. "Everything good with your mom?" Ty moved to the front doors, shouting across the rink. "Smith. Lindsey. Let's go. Lindsey, you can ride with us." Both kids moved with no urgency whatsoever.

"I think so." The words more question than confirmation.

Suspicion crept between his shoulder blades. "You *think* so? Is she having a rough day?" Soft black lashes fanned with stubborn determination. She started a slow inquisition. "I feel like you know a little more about my mom than I do."

If he told her the truth, she would push him away. Frustration roared through his veins. Outside, squinting against the sun's blinding heat, Ty focused a little too hard on ignoring her, until her icy fingers wrapped around his forearm.

He took the safe route. "Leah was frustrated with your mom, is all."

Karis' sister, Leah, when she did show up at the hockey rink during her brief flybys, spoke blatantly about her distaste for their aging mother. He could have made a profession trying to keep Lindsey away from the trash talk.

"Yeah, my mom's a master at fueling frustration." She pulled a tube of lip balm from her bag and swiped it over her lips. "Leah and I never talked much, so I'm kind of learning as I go."

He hated himself for twisting through ways to ease her pain. Ways to make it better. He'd moved on. But standing inches apart, sharing air and sun and life again, Ty battled the urge to demand answers of his own. Pushing her to the brink would do more harm than good.

Smith and Lindsey bounced out of the rink without a care. The luxury of youth.

"What do you want to eat?" he asked her, following the kids to his truck.

The sun doused bright rays on her hair, highlighting touchable coppery-red streaks. Temptation had him by the balls.

"I'm not really hungry," she said.

"Me, neither," Ty mumbled.

Chapter Three

Karis' stomach looped and rolled like a carnival ride. She didn't want to leave Iona alone any longer than she had to, but expecting Lindsey to sit home all summer with an aging grandmother and an aunt she knew no better than a stranger was unreasonable.

A quick explanation, and Iona tossed out easy permission for lunch. No convincing necessary. Anything for Lindsey. So far, Iona proved to be a much better grandmother than she ever was a mother.

Now, Karis needed to convince *herself* lunch would be fine. Impossible.

Ty hated her.

She could see it on his face, clear as day. He cradled the feeling like a puck nestled in a glove. But she'd never regret her decision to let him go. She'd had to. All he'd wanted to do was take care of her, and all she wanted to do was take care of herself.

Years ago, his career had been ready to take off, and hers remained in college. He understood college meant her survival, and still acted shocked and hurt when she chose independence over following him around the country like a puck bunny.

Even Ty's older brother, Wes, had agreed with her. He'd been in the league a few years and knew what it took to play professionally. Ty deserved to go pro but would have held himself back if she remained in the picture.

She'd kept up with his career until her heart couldn't take much more of seeing him on social media with a different woman draped over his arm for each snapshot and post. Through all the posts and print articles, no one mentioned a son.

Karis took a deep breath before meeting them at the table. The diner smelled like fried food and syrup. Ty must have loved it. Their first date had been at a diner.

"Aunt Karis, they have the best Greek salad." Lindsey scooted to the window, giving Karis room to slide into the booth.

"Greek salad it is. Do you think this will take long?"

Ty studied the menu like it was a captivating novel. "If you don't want to stay, I can take Lindsey home."

The hitch in his voice scratched down her spine, but she refused to get into it with him. "It's not that I don't want to stay."

"Here, go play foosball." Ty handed over a five.

"If you want us gone, just tell us," Smith teased.

"I want you gone."

Lindsey stood and snatched the money from Smith. "See ya."

Smith grabbed her hand and pulled her to the game room. Karis' heart stuttered. Two weeks in Lindsey's life and the girl mattered more to her than most people.

The tension hovered above the table, forming an indestructible wall. A wall she had no interest in destroying by venturing down memory lane. As happy as it had been, and as horrible as it ended, it deserved to stay buried. She steeled her nerves and searched his questioning blue stare.

"Spill it." His menu landed on the sticky table.

"Spill what?" If he pressed her, she'd crumble.

Ty propped his thick forearms against the table. "Don't do that. I may not have touched you in years," he whispered, "but I can still and always will be able to read your face."

How far was she willing to go? His hushed voice ignited a spark buried in the ash of an old flame. "They're good friends, aren't they?" She nodded toward the game room.

"The best of. Now tell me why I had to get rid of them." He leaned closer, comfortable in his skin, ignoring the gawkers from nearby tables.

"Hey, Ty." The waitress butted up to the table, all flared hips and batting lashes.

"Hey, Stacey, give us one more minute." Intensity rifled across the table and the waitress slipped away.

"I didn't ask you to do that." *He knew the waitress' name?*

"Your eyes did." His lips were still perfect, and for a moment, they tempted her to reach over and brush her fingertips across their heat.

Ding-ding. This match went to Ty. She didn't have it in her to fight, and it had been so long since she had confided in anyone. "My mom's not well," she started, her throat clogging on the words.

He stared a beat. "I know." Leaning back, he folded his arms across his chest, growing defensive.

"You know?" A hard pounding surged at her temples. Her senses sprang to high alert. The waitress buzzed around the counter, her humming raking against Karis' nerves.

Ty reached for her hands, but she jerked them against her chest. "I don't understand." The pieces wouldn't connect.

A curse escaped his lips, and his stubbled jaw twitched. His thick fingers tapped the table. "Tell me what you know, and I'll fill you in."

Tension tugged at the back of her neck. He would fill her in? About her own family? Humiliation had no shame.

She picked at the chipped Formica. "I'm—" She coughed, clearing her throat. Once again, Ty's hand slid across the table, landing inches from hers. Her fingers twitched, accustomed to linking with his, but they settled on fiddling with the flatware. A meager alternative.

"I think my mom is in the beginning stages of dementia." She let the words settle in and absorbed the relief washing over her. Releasing pent-up worries was a huge part of healthy living, of course. But, always guarded, and way too private for her own good, worries stayed in the vault. "But you knew that already?"

He hesitated. "I know a little and thought the same thing." His voice dropped tiptoe quiet.

Elbows on the table, she dug her thumbs into her forehead. If he thought the same thing, there had to be obvious evidence, or— "How'd you know? Leah?" She coughed on the question. He'd never liked her sister. There wasn't much to like.

"Leah," he admitted.

Confession didn't include pity; it included releasing a buildup of emotions, brewing since returning home to find things worse than she imagined. "I took a leave from my job in North Carolina to help my mom with Lindsey for the summer. Which, of course, is a constant battle because most of the time, she doesn't think she needs help. But there's something wrong." The last few phone calls with her mom dipped past concerning, so she jumped on a plane and headed south.

"What do you mean?"

"You know what I mean. My mom's been taking care of Lindsey on and off for a couple of years now. I don't talk to Leah. My mom doesn't want my help. She's glad I'm here, but resents it, I think. You know we never got along."

He nodded.

"There's a stack of doctor bills a mile high in the kitchen. I found them a week ago when I cleared all the clutter." She paused, fidgeting with the paper placemat. The words poured out too easily.

"Where's Leah now?" he questioned through clenched teeth.

Karis clutched her fluttering stomach and swallowed hard. "She's somewhere up north working."

Ty laughed and signaled for the waitress. His deep voice scraped across her heart.

"Exactly. You and I both know that's not true."

He rubbed the back of his neck. "I've had to deal with her over the past two summers with hockey."

"You did?" Taking Lindsey to hockey must have hedged too close to mothering for Leah's liking.

"Don't get too wrapped up in trying to figure that out." He still knew her brain ran a mile a minute. "Most of the time, Iona brought Lindsey to practice. Leah stopped by to flirt with Ryan."

No surprise there. "Of course. Same old Leah. Money and men. Just like my mom when we were growing up." She brushed a smudge of lip balm across her mouth.

"Why do you think dementia?"

"She started calling me Leah and forgetting conversations we'd had. I could never get ahold of Leah, and when I realized she wasn't around, I knew I had to come home. Check on Lindsey, at least." She shrugged and took in his concentrated stare.

"Why did Leah need to go up north? What's wrong with getting a job here?" His hand stretched flat on the table. Those masculine fingers tempting her once again.

"Apparently, her company offered her buckets of money to work in their New York office for three months." She swallowed hard. "It's a nice thought considering the number of medical bills my mom has, but—"

The flirting waitress reappeared and took Ty's order for water with a little too much perk.

"Listen, let me—" he started.

"Don't." She held her hands up and fought off the warning signals flashing inside her head. "Don't offer, please."

Of course he'd offer, but she had her own money. And, as bitchy as it sounded, it wasn't her responsibility to pay for hockey or medical bills. She'd worked and saved for years to not be in the same financial mess she grew up in. And why should Leah be off the hook?

"Let me make it easier on Lindsey at least." He cut into her thoughts. "It's got to be hard seeing Iona declining and living with an aunt she doesn't know."

Ooh, a punch in her already bruised heart. "Thanks for that reminder." It wasn't entirely her fault they were strangers. No one ever wanted her to come home for a visit.

Ty raked his hands through his hair. Talking about her family could do that to a person. "Listen, you were busy." He tried to gain momentum and drummed his fingers on the table.

She ignored his effort. "My mom's just as stubborn as she's always been about taking help, and it's just going to get harder as the disease progresses. If that's even what it is. Her independence is a little unsettling for me."

"That trait runs hard in your family." He cracked a tight smile.

She didn't appreciate the jab at all the work she'd done to make something of her life. Something, at this point in time, he knew very little about. "Shall we talk about the traits in your family?" she shot back. After sixteen years, maybe he and his dad were on the mend. His tight lips and flared nostrils said no.

"Karis." The topic remained off-limits.

She held her hands up, surrendering. "Sorry." She respected the line in the sand. "I've been here for two weeks, and Mom's forgetfulness has increased. It comes and goes. It's been from losing her glasses and keys to leaving the front door open, or not remembering she was cooking dinner."

His brows knitted together. "Are you planning on taking her to the doctor?"

"I think that's a good start. Leah's off the grid, and who knows when she plans on showing up. If at all. My mom struggles to explain what all the bills mean, and I feel like an idiot asking her, but I'm going to have to head back to my own life eventually, and I want to have it all straightened out for her."

"You think Leah will come back?"

Great question. "I would hope so. Her daughter's here." A sad silence hung between them. Leah didn't care about her daughter, and Lindsey deserved better.

"So you took a leave?" he fished, aligning his fork with his spoon.

"Yes." She'd succeeded in claiming her independence but refused to elaborate on how lonely it was.

"And baseball being shitty baseball," Ty quipped, "they don't have a need for a psychologist right now? Funny, I'd think baseball players would need a lot of therapy just to get through the boredom of the game." He flashed a smile.

Her heart lightened. "Still a hockey snob, I see. How do you know I work for a baseball team?"

"Your mom," he said a little too quick. His jawline angled just right. Tight, clenched, and most of the time covered in two-day growth. The foundation for perfect lips and a crooked nose. Broken three times, maybe more.

Iona always had a soft spot for him. He was the perfect make. Gorgeous with lots of money. In her much younger years, Iona Hill would have never let a guy like Ty out of her bullseye.

Karis tucked her hair behind her ear. "My mom told you?"

Ty sighed and rubbed the heels of his hands over his lashes. Stalling.

"Here we go," the waitress sang, throwing four straws on the table and banging red plastic cups in front of each setting.

"Thank you." Karis pulled the paper off her straw and took a long sip of water.

"You guys ready?" The server flipped open her ragged notebook.

"Yes—" Ready for a reprieve.

"Not yet." Ty dismissed the server and locked in. "I've coached Lindsey for two summers. I've seen your mom's decline and the toll it's taken." His blunt fingers jabbed at the table.

Karis countered, "If you thought something was up and you were that concerned, you should have called me. You knew where I was."

He shoved his glass to the side.

"Call you?" He choked out a frightening laugh. "Let's get square here, darlin'. You left me. Why would I call you?"

The chatter in the room fell to a low buzz. Karis counted the diners and the chairs, hoping to dampen the adrenaline racing through her veins. "Because, I—" She turned away, unable to acknowledge what she'd lost. As usual, indulging in the selfish act of survival.

Ty moved quick, sliding onto her booth bench and sitting way too close. "It murdered me when you pushed me out of your life and now you want to know why I didn't call you to let you know how your family was doing? That your mother was deteriorating, and no one was here but Lindsey?"

She covered her mouth, catching her gasp. She gave in to the weight of her shoulders, curving into herself, and shutting out his words.

Relentless, he angled his head, catching her stare with his. "You left me. You didn't want me." His fingers jabbed into his chest. "The only thing I could do for you was stay away because that's what you wanted."

Tears rushed down her cheeks. "I never wanted that." She flinched at the admission. He could always strip away her defenses.

"Then why?" His whisper echoed between them, covering the shatter of her heart. His heightened heat rolled off his body and landed on every inch of her skin.

The rehearsed reason rolled off her tongue. "You had to start your career, and I had to finish school." Her words jittered with deceit, exposing her rationale.

"Liar. We had a plan."

She tore her gaze from his burning glare. The energy to spar with him disappeared. Laughter from the game room broke past her barrier. Lindsey's chuckle sparked a swirling warmth, confirming how critical the girl's happiness had become in such a short time.

"We can't do this." She pushed against him.

He inched closer and laid his arm across the back of the booth. She wanted to fall against the secure wall of his chest.

"What can I get you guys?" The gum-popping server appeared, and, after digging deep into her apron, pulled out a mermaid pen, banged it against her unicorn notepad, and prepared to take anyone's order. Perfect timing.

"I'll have the Greek salad." Karis inched away from him.

"What can I get you, Ty?" The words floated from the woman's mouth like she'd said them a thousand times in a more private setting.

Karis glared at him, hating the way her stomach knotted at the intimate tone.

"Chicken sandwich, side salad, and onion rings."

"Thanks, I'll go get the kids' orders." Winking, she grabbed the menus and dashed off.

Unwarranted hurt burned deep. "You slept with the waitress." She dug through her purse. Was it so hard to put lip balm back in the same pocket?

"What?" He sat back, shoulders squared.

"You brought your son to a restaurant where you're sleeping with the waitress. Classy. Super Classy." Leaning back, the cold booth jarred her temper.

"Judge much?"

"I'm not judging. You turned into one of those gigolo hockey players you said you'd never be. And now with a kid. I expected more from you." She lashed out, and so what if she was judging?

"Back at ya. What the hell makes you think I give a shit about what you think of me?"

"Ty," she interjected. He wouldn't let her get a word in, but it wouldn't be because she didn't try.

"I could sleep with the whole fucking town, and it wouldn't be your business. Remember? You walked." His whispered words blared in her ears. "I would have killed to share my life with you. You don't get to ask about it now."

What would it take to make him believe it was all for him? "I told you. You needed to focus on you."

"Bullshit," he spat.

Dropping her head, she inhaled a deep breath. It had to work sometime. The stench of grease fryers filled her nose and nausea swept in, playing with her stomach. Her heart would never survive this. She overestimated herself when she agreed to lunch.

She glanced at the kids crowding the foosball table. The vision of them laughing blurred as she searched for the restroom.

"Karis?" The edge in his voice softened. "Smith is not my son."

"What?" Her voice quivered in a pathetic wave of confusion.

"Smith is Wes' son."

"Wes has a son?" she stammered, clearing her throat. His older brother, Wes, played hockey, but played women more. So no shocker about having a kid, but it hurt not knowing. She had been close to Wes at one time.

"How is Wes?" She pulled at her collar, still searching to escape.

Ty flinched. "Not good. He's dead."

Chapter Four

A fierce urge to bolt drummed through her veins. Desperate, she itched for a place safe from his scrutiny. Regret held hands with escape and squeezed hard. A million questions set up shop in her mind. She scooted to the edge of the bench, ready to run.

"No." Ty's hand shot out, blocking her escape. She gripped his wrist. Heat burned between them.

How could so much time be gone?

He caged her in, bending close to her ear. "You had to have known."

So typical. So egotistical. She covered her mouth with a shaky hand, controlling the need to scream. "How would I know?"

Her head lightened with every unsatisfying breath. Releasing his wrist, she wrapped her arms around her stomach, squeezing the nausea growing there. With no escape, she scooted back into the booth and let the diner swirl around her.

"Take a drink." Ty held the plastic cup to her lips. His attempt at comfort only made the world tilt more. He slid back to his side, giving her space. But the world still rolled.

How had she missed a death? A child? A lifetime had gone by without her. She wanted the time back. Did she think everyone would stop and wait until she was ready to get back on the train of life?

No one waited for her.

What if all this time she'd chosen the wrong thing? Made all the wrong choices?

"Are you all right?" Lindsey's concern cracked through her thoughts.

No, she wasn't all right. Everything she'd ever valued and wanted in her life proved inconsequential to all the things she'd missed. Unfolding herself, she stood, and allowed the kids to slide into the booth.

"I'm fine," Karis said, snapping back to responsible adult, trying to look the part. From across the table, Ty's stare remained steady with hers, reading too much and understanding it all. Smith gave her the same Firestone assessment, adding to the pile of *what the hell is happening right now?*

"I didn't know about Wes—" she breathed.

"My dad?" Smith questioned. His gaze shifted from scrutiny to curious.

Ty looped his arms around the boy's shoulders. "Karis knew your dad, too."

"Oh." Smith threw her a suspicious glance. All the Firestone boys possessed that same look. They'd jump through fire for each other. She had never understood that kind of loyalty.

Ty reached for her hand.

"I think we're just gonna go." She dug into her purse, searching for keys. One day, she'd use the outside pockets. She pushed up from the table, and a hard muscled arm blocked her path. He snagged her hand and shuffled her into the empty game room.

"Don't go. Not yet. Not like this." His words were soft and airy. Private. Concern tugged at his brow. "I need you to be okay, and you are not okay."

He reached out to touch her again.

She wasn't strong enough for this. "I'm fine," she lied, stepping back.

"You don't look fine."

"Thanks," she quipped.

"You know what I mean. I'm sorry. I didn't mean to drop Wes' death on you like that. That was shitty. I know you two had a bond." He cleared his throat. "I guess I still hate how close you guys became."

"I can't talk about this right now." *Or ever.*

His calloused fingers brushed over her skin, leaving a trail of heat no other man had ever replicated.

"What's there to talk about? He's gone."

She wanted to tangle her fingers into his hair. Pull his mouth to hers and let the ever-loving embers rising between them, explode into sparks and ignite her past decisions. He had the power to make her forget.

"Is there something else?" He tilted his head. Black hair fell over his creased brow. He deserved the answers he wanted, but she wouldn't do that to Wes' memory. The brothers had been inseparable at one time, causing her to evaluate her own relationship with her sister many times. A Firestone was loyal to a fault. Hills left each other face down in the mud.

"There's nothing else." She pressed against her temples, hoping to kill the forming headache. "I think it's best if we just go." She marched back to the table where Smith and Lindsey sat like conspirators, with their heads close together and their voices breaking in a husky whisper.

"Let's go, kiddo."

"But we haven't eaten," Lindsey smarted, not budging.

"Right."

Eat and leave.

Easy.

She almost laughed out loud.

Nothing with Ty was ever easy.

***

"Why didn't you tell me Smith was Ty's nephew and not his son?" Karis pulled into the driveway, inspecting the shabby two-story.

Lindsey kept her head down and tuned into her phone. Her thumbs jabbed over the keyboard. "Why would I? I didn't know you thought he was his son. Well, he kind of is. Smith's been living with Coach since he was like two. I think."

"Lindsey," Karis said, sharpening her tone. Damn cell phones would be the end of all decent civilization.

One huge, uncalled for sigh later, Lindsey's phone plopped into her lap. "How long are you planning on staying?"

"Not sure. A month. Maybe." She hadn't nailed down a return time. Her mother needed to get to a doctor. Until then, things could go either way. Trying to decipher her mom's prognosis through bills and letters amounted to zilch.

"And then what?" Lindsey played with a seam on her jeans.

She shrugged. "I'm not sure."

"Well, I'm not sure I'm going to play hockey this summer." A sad silence filled the car.

"And why not?" Karis tiptoed, unsure if she *could* play hockey over the summer. A thousand bucks for one camp? These kids better be NHL bound for that kind of money.

She could pay, but it burned her to foot the bill while Leah paid nothing. Most of Karis' money had to be earmarked for medical bills and keeping her apartment in North Carolina. Pulling money out of her savings sent her straight to a panic attack faster than a room packed with people. She'd spent years hoarding money not to be strapped.

Lindsey fiddled with the entertaining hole in her jeans. "I think Grandma needs me to stay at home with her."

Well, wasn't this the never-ending, heartbreaking afternoon? Karis needed a whiskey and a bath. The tension in the car soaked into her bones. A thirteen-year-old giving up something she loved to stay with her ailing grandmother sailed beyond depressing.

Exhaling, Karis glanced at her niece. "I think Grandma would want you to play hockey instead of staying home." The price tag of that statement flashed like a warning on a Jumbotron.

"What happens when you leave?" Lindsey stared out the passenger window.

Mother of everything holy.

Why in the world did Ty pop into her mind when Lindsey asked that question? He didn't care if she came or went.

She gripped the steering wheel and leveled with Lindsey. "I think you guys might have to come with me."

"No, I don't think we will."

Of course.

"Well, my job, which might come in handy to pay for hockey and bills, is a necessity. Giving it up would be irresponsible."

"We've made it this far without you," Lindsey scoffed.

A true mystery.

"My mom sends us money, and Grandma gets her social security check." Lindsey cleared up.

"Oh, Lindsey." Karis hid her gulp.

"What?" she choked. "Don't feel sorry for me. We've been fine without you and without my mom."

A smart cookie like Lindsey would figure out, eventually, that her plan to take care of her grandmother with social security and inconsistent checks from her mother would dwindle fast.

Lindsey perked up. "Maybe you could work here. We have sports. I'm sure some team needs a sports therapist. Then you could stay."

Karis rolled the back of her aching skull across the headrest and landed her focus on the hopeful girl. "I can't leave my job. They've done so much for me, including giving me the month off. Plus, the pay is way too good."

Up and leaving wasn't easy, but a teenager's mind didn't have the barriers and hang-ups of bills, mortgages, food, and gas.

Ever hopeful, or plain stubborn, Lindsey countered, "Yeah, but can't you be a sports therapist anywhere?"

This kid, fighting tooth and nail. Karis could relate.

"Yeah, but—" She stared out the windshield. The truth bundled up in the unknown of what could come. They needed a plan.

Lindsey stilled. "Wait, I get it. You don't want to pay for me. You don't want to take care of us."

It wasn't a matter of not wanting to.

Karis tried the usual breath. "It's a little hard to get a job as a sports therapist."

"You dated Coach. He can help you."

"That was a long time ago." He wouldn't help her, and she would never ask.

"If you weren't staying, why'd you come?" Lindsey snipped.

Great question. "Because believe it or not, Lindsey, I care about you and wanted to check in on you and Grandma," she answered, leaving out Iona's worrisome spells of forgetfulness.

"Grandma can take care of me. We don't need you to stay." Lindsey faced Karis. A fighter. A Hill woman.

Karis agreed. "Of course, Grandma could take care of you, but summer is long, and I'm just here to help."

A quiet understanding filled the car. Lindsey fiddled with her braid and finally asked, "Is Grandma okay?"

Lying would make things worse, and Lindsey deserved better. "I'm not sure, but we're going to find out."

"Are you two gonna sit in that car all day?" Iona's stern voice stretched from the front door across the shell driveway.

They stared at Iona through the windshield. She stood on the porch, feet spread wide, hands planted on her hips, ready to give 'em the business.

"Oh, boy." Karis scanned her mother from head to toe. A chuckle escaped her lips.

Smiling, Lindsey grabbed her water bottle and opened the car door. "Grandma, what did you do?"

Karis took two breaths. It would take more than a month to fix these people. Slamming the door, she slung her purse over her shoulder. "Hey, Mom. What's the white stuff all over your apron?" *Please don't be flour.*

"It's flour, honey."

Awesome.

"What'd ya cook?" Lindsey skipped up the steps and clasped her grandmother's small hands.

"Mom, you're not supposed to cook unless I'm home." Keeping her tone light, Karis charged for the front door.

"Leah, I can bake cookies for my granddaughter if I want to."

Karis froze. Lindsey whispered into her ear, "She called you Leah."

"I know," she answered from the side of her mouth.

"You're not Leah."

"I know that, too." She took her niece's empty hand. Calling the doctor would be the first thing she did in the morning.

"The kitchen is going to be a mess." Lindsey giggled.

Karis sighed. "Yep."

"I gotta get my hockey stuff out of the car and lay it out to dry."

"Yeah? How long does that take?"

"About as long as it'll take you to clean up the kitchen."

She threw her arms around Lindsey's shoulders. "Smarty pants." She chuckled and placed a kiss on the side of the teenager's sweaty head. The powerful scent of hockey hair caused a slight kick to her sad heart. No time to dwell on memories.

Flicking her wrist, Karis popped the trunk and headed to kitchen duty.

"What cookies did you make?" she asked, ushering her mom into the house.

"I didn't make cookies." Flour didn't lie.

"You said you made cookies." A better person with a mind not so wrung out by a tattered heart would have skipped the accusation.

"I did?" Iona stared, blank faced, into the house. Lindsey lugged hockey gear into the garage and out of earshot. Thank goodness.

No amount of training, in any field, prepared someone for the demise of their mother's mind. "Wanna help me clean the kitchen?" Awards would never be handed to Iona for her parenting skills, yet manipulative redirection, the kind used for small children, didn't feel right. Even Iona deserved better.

"Sure, dear. Who made a mess?" Karis held open the front door with a smile and a quiet count to ten.

"I'm not sure." She gasped. White powder stuck to every countertop. Every drawer. Every cupboard. How in the world did making cookies turn into this?

The daughter in her wanted to fall to the floor and cry. The psychologist in her wanted to sit her mother down and ask a million questions, and the aunt wanted to hose down the place as fast as she could to hide the mess.

Iona stiffened in the doorway. "Karis, what in the world did you do to the kitchen?"

It was the most frightening question ever asked.

Chapter Five

"I want to see my goddamn grandson, Tyson."

Ty pinched the bridge of his nose. "I know, Pop, you've made that clear. Let me make myself clear. Smith is not up for grabs. You don't get to beat him down like you did your own sons."

Silence.

It took one minute to regret answering his dad's phone call. The guy was still mean as hell.

"Today's my day. Bring him over." Fucking new cars and their hands-free bullshit.

Ty jabbed a button and grabbed his cell from the stand. Talking while driving sucked as far as setting a stellar example, but letting Smith listen to his grandfather rant and slur words didn't meet parent-of-the-year standards, either.

"Yeah, Pop, today is your day, but..." He glanced to the passenger seat. Pain strained his nephew's face.

"But nothing. It's my day with my grandson." One startled jump from Smith, and Ty's mind raced back to his younger days. Wilson Firestone always had a shaking effect on his family.

He pulled the car roadside, shifted into park, and jumped out before the engine conked.

"Listen to me, Pop. You've been drinking. The rule is you don't get Smith when you've been drinking." He shouldn't even get Smith when he wasn't drinking. The tyrant.

The gravel cracked beneath his boots and panic shot from his bones. Smith stood behind him. Concern wrinkling his face. The knife of unworthy parenting twisted a little deeper.

Across the cell connection, Pop cleared his throat.

"Bring the boy to me. I've got the entire day mapped out for training. He's gonna love it."

Training? Try torture. Taking Smith to his grandfather's for so-called hockey training was a hard no. Breaking the news to a delusional Pop would initiate a new level of rage. If he didn't get his way, he'd take it out on Smith next time, and there was always a next time.

"Not sure that's true, Pop. Is Ryan home?" How Ryan could stand to be around the man who created super athletes through wicked pain and mind-numbing torture proved Ty and Wes' plan to keep their younger brother free from the obsessive clutches of their father actually worked.

The one thing they did right as a family.

"Ryan doesn't need to be here," he snarled.

Ty scratched the back of his neck. Hockey season couldn't start soon enough. His father left him alone about Smith during the season. He bothered him about other things, like how shitty his team played, and how he could get his team, meaning Ryan, to the next level. All trivial things compared to the well-being of Smith.

An assistant coach for a professional hockey team didn't need his father contributing his two cents. But Wilson Firestone always had change to spare. Telling him to fuck off would only hurt the people Ty loved. Ryan had a soft spot for the old drunk, and Smith clung to family.

"Uncle Ty. I'll go. It's fine." No child should have to listen to their uncle yell at their drunken grandfather. Smith had been through enough.

"Smith, get back in the car." Ty held the phone away from his mouth and pressed the words through tight teeth.

"Tyson," his dad yelled, but it didn't instill fear like it used to.

"Enough. He's not coming over today."

Smith trudged back to the car.

Ty hung his head and stood, baking in the Florida heat.

"You forget yourself." A sobering reminder.

"How's that?" He waited for the usual threat.

"You forget who made you into the man you are today. The hockey player you are today. The coach you are today." Demeaning words. Typical conversation between father and son in the Firestone house.

Ty released a caged breath, counted to ten, and steadied his heartbeat. "I pay you a lot of money for the so-called services you rendered to me as a kid." Not his proudest moment.

"You pay a few people, don't you, Son?"

He squeezed the phone. The crunch of the case, a mental release of the stacking tension, echoed in his ear. The man played dirty and did it best after a few rum and Cokes. Ready to end this, he did what he had to do to protect Smith. He swallowed hard, added an hour to tonight's workout agenda, and surrendered.

"I'll bring him over when Ryan gets home." Ty jerked the car door open and threw the obnoxious phone into the backseat. Who in the hell wanted access to people 24/7?

Smith covered his head, protecting himself from the bouncing block of technology. "Holy shit, Uncle Ty."

"No, on the holy shit. Rink only." Smith grew up in a locker room but knew better.

"Yes, sir."

The car hugged every curve. Neighborhoods flew by in a hazy blur. The usual haunting thoughts, post-Wilson rant, pushed him to the edge of sanity. Regrets and poor decisions poised to give a nudge.

Telling Smith the truth skated through his mind, on sharpened blades, at least twice a day, with or without Pop's bullying. But the deceit remained a secret. Hard conversations had too many ways to go wrong, and Smith had more than his fair share of gone wrongs. Taking down two-hundred-pound men or reprimanding a locker room full of over-intense hockey players, didn't compare to the gut punch he took when the past bled into the here and now.

A buzz vibrated from the backseat. The light of the exposing glow saved him from another dangerous thought.

"Uncle Ty, want me to get that?"

"No. Don't unbuckle your seat belt while the car is moving. Whoever it is can wait. You wanna be dead for a phone call?"

"No, jeez, just trying to help, and you don't drive that bad." Smith chuckled at his own joke, cracking the tension.

"It's not me you have to worry about. It's the other drivers. Haven't we had this conversation?"

"A million times," Smith sneered. His eye roll palpable.

The BMW turned into the lit-up gated community. Hockey player turned coach wasn't a bad gig as far as the paycheck. The travel schedule took a toll. So he owned a beautiful house he stayed in four months out of the year. The leather couch stood stiff as wood and the fridge shined showroom new. Smith and Ryan deserved it. One day, Ryan would give up on his fairy-tale family and leave the piece of shit they called a father to move in with Ty and Smith. Period.

"A million times, huh? And that wasn't enough?" Ty stared ahead, maneuvering through the landscaped road leading to the house.

"It was enough, thank you," Smith smarted back.

"Apparently not. This is why you won't drive until you're eighteen." Ty rounded the driveway.

Smith huffed. "Eighteen. The driving age in Florida is sixteen."

"Yeah, well, the driving age in Uncle Ty land is eighteen."

"Eighteen. That sucks," he mumbled. "I'll just go live with Pop and Uncle Ryan. They'd let me drive now."

"Listen." Ty put the car in park and twisted in his seat.

"Sorry." Smith held up his hands and did his best to hide unshed tears.

A knife straight to the heart. Ty absorbed the usual exhaustion that came with a long day of parenting. "Smith." He swallowed. "How about we talk about cars and driving when you're close to it actually happening?"

"Fine, but you won't change your mind."

Smart kid. "Probably not, but I'm willing to negotiate. Cool?"

"No one says cool." He reached for the door handle.

"I do. Cool?" He grabbed his shoulder.

"Cool," he chuckled.

"Okay, now get your smelly gear out of my car." How could he love someone so much, and with such abandon? The world began and ended with Smith.

The phone buzzed again, and Ty snagged the intruder. Stepping out of the car, he relaxed when he saw Ryan's stupid grin light up his screen.

"Smith, empty your bag and get in the shower," he called over the car.

He complied, easily. Thank God. The boy may have grown up in chaos, but his manners were golden. Ty smiled, happy to take the credit, but he couldn't. Smith was a naturally cool kid. Chill to the bone.

"Ryan?" Ty ventured down the driveway away from Smith's earshot because *he* was not chill to the bone.

"Hey, I'm home, and thanks for warning me about the mood Pop's in. Appreciate that." The trademark Firestone sarcasm, ripe and efficient.

"Sorry, yeah, super busy doing coach stuff."

"Yeah, I know what you were super busy doing. How is Karis?" Ryan chirped.

"Not talking about Karis right now."

Doubled over with gear, Smith slammed the trunk and made his way to the garage.

"Yeah, so that must have gone well." Ryan could dig all he wanted. He'd end up empty.

"Is there a reason you're calling your coach on the off-season?" Best part about coaching? Busting Ryan's chops. *All the time.*

"Yeah, is my brother around? I need to talk to him and tell him the next time he has a bitch fight with Pop to call me so I know what I'm walking into." The sentence ended with agitation. Good.

Ty dug his fingers into his hair, scrubbed his scalp, and pressed the back of his neck, massaging with force. For what good it did. Before summer's end, he'd get a real massage. Upstairs, Smith's bedroom light flicked on, and Ty's body reset. With the light on, the six-bedroom monstrosity presented like a home. Warm, comfortable, and safe. Something he never had and was damn certain Smith would always have.

"You're right, sorry." Ty pinched the bridge of his nose, waiting for Ryan's lecture.

"Ty, you have to let Pop see Smith. That's what Wes wanted." Ryan spoke soft and reasonable.

Damn it.

"No. Wes wanted Smith to be safe." Round and round they went.

"Yes, and he is safe, but he also has a right to know his grandfather and build his own relationship with him."

Ridiculous. The cell phone case wouldn't make it through the night.

"You're kidding, right? What kind of relationship would that be? Misery? Do you remember that movie? Did you forget about all the late-night workouts Wes and I told you about? The physical abuse. The verbal abuse. How we sucked. How we would never make it pro. How fat we were. How skinny we were." He could roll on about the abuse he and Wes, his older brother, had lived through. Hiding it all from their baby brother, until he reached an age to understand what had actually gone on in the motherless Firestone house. Through all the truths, Ryan remained a relentless defender of their father. Pop must have done something right to create such elite hockey players. Yeah, tell that to Wes. In his grave.

"I'm home now," Ryan continued, unphased and as smooth as black ice. "Bring Smith over and I'll stay with him and Pop. It's all right."

"We just got home." He ambled up the driveway, each foot slow and heavy.

"You can't keep Smith from Pop." He paused. "If you're going to honor Wes' wishes, we have to figure this out."

Ryan scored with solid reasoning, as always, and Ty's state of mind failed to block the shot. Wes' will stipulated if something were to happen to him, Ty was to take care of Smith and Smith's mess of a mother. Sadly, the will also spelled out, *more like demanded*, for Smith to have a relationship with Pop. Insane. No question. All three brothers agreed. Wilson was an asshole, but he could create rock-solid hockey players, and for some reason that ranked important to Wes. Plus, Smith needed a family because everyone needed backup. A team. Wilson demeaned the very men he created in his home, but he drove family into their very souls. A tough shot to handle.

"I know what you're saying. But Pop's going to shove his skills into Smith's head. He's been calling more and more, wanting Smith, and I have fucking nightmares about what's going through his head. He plans on training him, and we both know what Pop's training's like. Smith will have to endure therapy like the rest of us. Can't we have one of us without a talk doc?"

"Ty," Ryan charged, "I will not let Pop screw Smith up like he did us. Like he did you and Wes."

"I don't understand your soft spot for him." Truth be told, Ryan was not as strong as he thought he was when it came to Pop. None of them were. Kids had a weakness for their parents. If Ty learned anything over the years, it was that.

"Because he's Pop. He's an abusive alcoholic, but he's our Pop. Our family, and he needs us."

"Christ, we need a mother." Ty's chest tightened.

"Yeah, I know," Ryan swore. "Bring Smith over. I'm home. Let him get his visit over with so I don't have to hear about it for the rest of the week."

"You wouldn't have to if you moved in with me." He double locked the car.

"For the last time, I am not living with my coach. No way."

"You'd rather live with Pop?"

"Yes, I would. You're a tyrant when you get into training mode. At least Pop lets me eat what I want," he joked.

"No, he doesn't."

"No, he doesn't, but he's old now. I can hide it from him easier than I can hide it from you."

"If you have cookies in that pantry—" He liked cookies too much to have quick access.

"See, this is why," Ryan shot back.

In the garage, Smith's hockey bag stood upright and still packed.

"I get it. You're a little baby when it comes to cookies. I'm out. I'll bring Smith over when he's out of the shower, and you'd better be there." Ty stalked to the door.

"Wow, you're listening to me? Look at me, taking the lead."

He could feel Ryan's smile through the phone. "Yeah okay. I was coming over anyway. I want to talk about the fundraiser coming up."

"Sure you do," Ryan sang.

"No girls at the house while Smith is there and throw Pop in the shower. He may sound like a drunk, but he doesn't have to smell like one."

"Fine."

"See ya in a few."

Inside the house, the upstairs shower pounded full throttle, and Metallica ripped up the quiet. The hammock on the back porch promised a breakaway and ten minutes of shut-eye under the dusky stars.

The hammock's cords moaned. The damn thing better hold. Between his father and Karis, Ty's shoulders would never relax again. So much for rejuvenation and pressing reset.

Two weeks into summer, and Ty itched to be back on the ice with his team, working through shifts, personalities, and salary caps. Strategic plays and money jumbling through his mind left room for nothing else.

Calculations and rookie relationships were cake compared to dealing with his family and downtime.

The sun settled low in the purple sky. The lull of the hammock quieted his mind and sent it drifting down a path of memories and what-ifs.

What did he expect? Her mother and sister still lived in Edge View. Did he think he'd never see her again? Her hair? Her legs? Her smile? At lunch, he fell deeper with each blink of her lashes, and hated her admission.

She let him go to live his dream.

Liar.

She let him go to protect her independence, thinking he'd rob her of it. An insult to him and everything they'd been.

"Uncle Ty?"

A squeaky-clean Smith pulled at the macrame. Poor kid had no idea. In a matter of an hour, he'd be sweaty and smelly again. That's what visits to Pop's house were like. Smith claimed to love it, and Ty had no recourse. He squeezed his fist and stretched his legs, hoping for a Charlie horse. Anything to get his mind right.

"What's up?"

"I took Lindsey's hockey bag by mistake." Smith grinned.

There goes his nap. "I was wondering why your bag wasn't cleaned out. We can bring it to practice on Wednesday for her."

"No dice, Coach. She wants it now." Smith held up his phone, revealing a million texts. The last one ended with *Now!*

Ty laughed. "Demanding, isn't she?"

Smith threw himself in the wicker chair next to the hammock. "She's always been like that about her stuff." He scrolled through something on his phone, oblivious to the setting sun.

"Smith?"

"Yeah?" Smith's focus remained on the screen.

Dread joined the pounding in his head. "You okay to go to Pop's house tonight?"

"Yeah."

Unconvincing. "You sure?"

"Do you want me to go?" Smith asked cautiously. His head tilted. The phone forgotten.

Ty's heart sank. "No way. You know the answer to that. You know the rules. If he ever does anything to you, that's—" Jesus, hard conversations sucked.

"I know. I got it. He's fine when I'm there. We do hockey stuff. We work out. Watch games. Eat carrot sticks. It's not bad."

"I hate carrot sticks." Ty stood and stretched his arms over his head. The empty hammock swayed. A sad sight.

"I do, too. Now."

Life held too much promise for sad. "Break's over. Everybody wants us." He spread his arms wide and soaked in the freedom.

Smith jumped up. "I know, right? It's summer, chill people."

"We'll take the Princess her stuff and then we'll go by Pop's. Good?"

"Yeah, good. Is Uncle Ryan at Pop's?"

The older Smith got, the more intense his visits with his grandfather would become. Ty doubted Smith would ever say one word about it. The kid never complained, and Pop's drills had settled down. Ty gripped the handle to the slider, cracked opened the door, and let Smith inside. "Uncle Ryan will always be with you when you visit Pop. That's how we do this. Get me?"

"Got you," Smith replied.

"Give me fifteen minutes to shower and then I'm ready to go. Put something gross and disgusting in Lindsey's hockey bag."

He had to find fun somewhere. There's more to hockey than just playing it.

"Good idea."

"Yeah, cool, right?"

Smith snorted. "Yeah, cool."

Chapter Six

"What the hell happened?" Ty's gaze roamed head to toe.

"What do you mean?" And who the hell did he think he was knocking on her door demanding to know what happened? He didn't get to care anymore.

"Why are you crying?" He clutched the doorframe, angling closer. All strong and put together.

"I'm not crying." Karis wiped her cheeks. Super inconspicuous. "Why are you here?"

Crisply clean and showered to perfection. A dangerous combination of masculinity and seacoast soap filled her nose and obstructed all reasonable thinking. She widened the door, inviting him over the threshold, and waited while he surveyed *the out of control, what the hell am I doing here, chaos of her life.*

From the entryway, he scanned the kitchen from corner to corner, his jaw hardening with each turn of his head. When his stare landed on her, she itched to run and hide. She crushed her bottom lip between her teeth. Another default function of nerves.

"So help me God, Karis, if you don't stop with that lip, I will not be responsible for my actions," he whispered into her ear, and entered the kitchen. "You were never a cook, but Holy Gretzky." His hands hung on his hips, fingers loose and casual. No nerves whatsoever. His perfect lips slipped into a curious line.

After an hour of cleaning, the kitchen still looked bakery gone wild. She swallowed her tears and chalked it up to exhaustion. "You're not funny, just like I remember." She tried to lighten the nightmare. He didn't buy it. So, she went for a cover-up and leaned against the sink, blocking the pile of dirty towels and rags.

His hard stare softened, matching the release of his tense shoulders. She stretched her fingers, controlling their natural inclination to reach up and massage his tight neck after floating through his soft hair. Old habits. Cherished habits. The crack in her heart deepened.

He shoved his hands into his jean pockets. A thousand questions lined every inch of his face. The squint at his temples. The understanding purse of his lips.

A quick glance out the window confirmed her mother and Lindsey were still sitting on the back porch. The dim lights hazed against the fading sunlight. Smith had joined them, concern on his face and a hockey stick in his hand.

As much as the extra hands would help, she preferred to clean up alone and skip the explanation, giving her heart and emotions a chance at survival. Worse loomed closer than getting better.

"Tell me what happened?" he asked with the sincerity of someone who knew her secrets and cared about every single one of them.

"My mom baked cookies." She gripped the sink behind her, scared to let her hands within an inch of his skin.

He shook his head. "No, I've seen your mom bake cookies and I've been here many times eating them. Never once did it look like this."

His right brow lifted higher than his left, a true sign of his processing.

"Things change?" She flashed a plastic grin and lifted her shoulder.

"Not baking cookies," he challenged.

His messy hair and capable confidence weakened her determination. The kitchen closed in around her, pulling her into a blurry spin. She wanted to forget everything happening and sink into him, letting his arms wrap around her waist and shield her from the uncertain future.

"Ty." The airy word dripped with desperation, but she didn't care. The urge to melt into him throbbed and threatened to crush her.

"So..." He inspected the powdery mess, absently cupping the back of his neck. "I'll wipe the counter." He reached around her and grabbed a dishrag. His arm brushed her side, and she pulled in a breath. He froze. Their skin touching. Her's tingling. His head low. His lips inches from her ear.

She fit against him. Tight. Snug. Perfect. At one time, they were made for each other, but life stepped in and kicked them both in the heart.

He shifted closer. His arms locked her against the counter. She wanted to want to move away, but for the past hour she'd been on her knees vacuuming the floor and wiping baseboards, pondering life and all the wrong turns she'd made morphing her into a much more vulnerable version of herself. Nothing made every vivid memory, every regret, and every touch come to life like scrubbing.

Every disinfected-smelling thought featured him and then he came knocking on the door, all heroic and strong. She could only take so much, for crying out loud.

"No, I got it." Her fingers wrapped around his thick wrists, trying to take back her space. He didn't budge.

"Come on," he whispered.

"No, really." She tore away. The sound of breaking glass coming from outside cut her off. She ran to the sliding glass door, threw it open, and stepped onto the porch. The energy crackled in all the wrong ways. "What's wrong? What happened?"

Lindsey sat frozen. Tears rolling down her cheeks. Shock and confusion blanketed her face.

Panic struck from gut to heart. No matter what, she had to clear the fear from Lindsey's face.

"Aunt Karis." The words trembled.

"Don't call her that. She's not your aunt. Leah, that's your sister. You've gone far enough." Iona stood in the middle of broken glass and splattered tea, glaring down at a withering Lindsey.

"Mom, what's going on? Here, get out of that glass." She reached for her mother's hand and guided her to a glass-free zone. "What happened?"

"Leah's making me crazy, just like she always has." Iona jerked her shaking hand away and anchored it to her chest.

"I don't think—" Ty eased up behind her, and for a moment, she soaked in his heat and support. His large hand rested against her back, and she almost sagged with relief.

But dementia doesn't pause.

"I know my own daughters," Iona spat.

With a renewed strength, Karis inched closer to her mother and wrapped her arm around her shoulders. She flashed Ty a small smile. He understood without a word.

He corralled the kids in a loose hug. "Let's go get Lindsey's gear out of the car."

Lindsey wiped her red nose and blinked at her grandmother. Nodding, she followed Smith through the sliders.

"Mom, that's Lindsey, not Leah. Leah's not here. It's me, you, and Lindsey." Karis steered her mom into the living room, cataloguing the house's breakables. "Sit down and tell me what happened." Iona complied, sitting down next to her on the worn sofa.

"Nothing happened. Same old Leah. Trying to convince me she plays hockey." Iona sucked in her cheeks and studied her fidgeting fingers.

"Mom, that's Lindsey. Your granddaughter. Not Leah. Lindsey is Leah's daughter." Karis reached for Iona's hand.

Iona pursed her lips, scanning the room from wall to wall. "Impossible. How could I not remember my granddaughter? And I certainly don't need any help from you taking care of my family."

There's the Iona she remembered. Snappy, cruel, and always ready with a vicious jab toward her daughters. Out of all the things her mother could lose, why couldn't she lose the mean?

"Did you break the glass?" No psych course could prepare a daughter for testing her own mother's mind.

"The glass?" Confusion settled onto Iona's aging face. Karis waited for realization to strike. The longer the wait, the harder the thump of her heart.

Iona's small, wrinkled hands covered her mouth. Tears overflowed, falling in waves. Karis wiped her sweaty palms onto her jeans and witnessed her cold, hard mother go soft with fear and remorse.

"I threw the glass down. Why would I do that?" Her chin quivered beneath shaking fingers.

Karis rested her hand on her shoulder. "I think you were upset."

"I was that upset?" She sagged.

"Sometimes dealing with a thirteen-year-old can make you do crazy things." The joke fell flat.

"I forgot my granddaughter." On a sob, Iona crumpled in half. Karis wrapped her arms around her and rubbed her back. Tiny shivers vibrated beneath her fingers.

"It's okay." Karis stroked in circles. Surprised and uncomfortable with the pain swirling through her at the sight of her broken mother.

"There's something wrong with me. I can't get a grip on it."

Karis bit her lip, glancing at the motion across the room. Ty, Smith, and Lindsey stood in the doorway, staring at the scene. A crippling fear she had no idea how to handle clogged her throat. A protective surge roared through her. Lindsey didn't need to see the reality of their situation.

"Let's go finish cleaning up the kitchen," Ty suggested with a gentle push.

"I can't." Lindsey started for the stairs, Smith right behind her.

Iona startled at Lindsey's voice. She rose from the couch, blocked Lindsey's escape, and took the girl's hands.

"Lindsey, I'm not sure what's happening to me, but I promise I love you and I know you, no matter what comes out of my mouth."

Tears fell down Lindsey's face, and Iona pulled her in for a hug.

"I love you, Grandma."

"I love you, too."

"We'll figure this out," Karis said. Determined now more than ever, she relished in the need to take care of her family.

"Have patience with me." A small, but heavy, request.

"I will," Lindsey squeaked, still holding her grandma.

"I'm so sorry." Iona swiped at a falling tear. Lindsey kissed her cheek and made her way up the stairs with Smith.

"I can't do this to her. I've ruined so much. I won't ruin her. I can't torture that little girl, who already has a whack job for a mother." Iona smoothed down her gray bob.

Karis choked on a laugh. Past Iona would have never called Leah a whack job, but it fit. "We're doing what we can."

"I know, but—" Iona swallowed. "I don't want Lindsey to watch me lose my mind. I can't put her through that. I won't. I can't put you through it, either." Her hands trembled, but she spoke with an edge, leaving no one guessing who was in charge.

"We'll talk to your doctor and do what he says we need to do."

Iona sighed, looking more than her seventy-three years. "We don't have the money to take me to doctors, and you shouldn't have to take care of me. My health is none of your business," she sassed, wielding her authority.

Karis caught Ty's eye. His cute grin melted her like it always did. They both recognized Iona's down-to-business tone. The same tone she'd used on them more than once when they were college students visiting and trying to sleep in the same room. The one time Iona's mothering side sprang out.

"Your health is what we *do* have money for." Karis ignored the hot panic in her heart and the lightness in her head. Savings accounts were for emergencies. Breathe in. Breathe out.

Ty cleared his throat.

"Don't you dare," she threatened.

"Come on." He stepped forward, bringing the size of the room to tiny proportions.

"No," she hissed. He would not pay for a thing.

He threw her his usual *this isn't over* glare and moved into the flour-doused kitchen.

"Don't spend money on me. We have to have money for Lindsey." Iona surveyed the room like the money would appear. If only it worked like that.

"We have money for Lindsey. Don't worry." *Not "we." Me.* Karis had spent years training her mind to protect the money she'd made. Money she'd socked away, never imagining spending it on healthcare and hockey. Spending the money on anything didn't fit into the plan. How sad and almost pathetic, but the idea of spending her savings unleashed a suffocating pain and an urgent need for a paper bag.

"Don't let her tell you she wants to give up hockey to stay home with me like I'm some kind of invalid. She loves hockey and needs to play." Iona sat back on the couch. Each word snapped at the edges. "That girl," she sighed, "has been through the wringer. A mother in and out of her life, and now this. Damn it." She clasped her shaky hands and folded them onto her lap.

Karis curled her fingers around her mother's. "Don't worry. I've got it covered. You worry about you, and I'll worry about the rest." Skepticism crossed her face. "Listen to me. Lindsey will play hockey. I'll make sure of it."

"Promise me." Iona gripped her hand.

Independence flittered away. The shabby house around them was a stark reminder of why she'd worked so hard and saved so much. "I promise."

Cookie sheets and oven drawers banged from the kitchen. Ty lacked grace with breakables. Like a heart. Or dishes. Totally dishes.

"Mom." Karis scooted to the edge of the worn-out couch, needing to salvage what remained of their kitchen.

The loud crash made both women jump. How in the world could he be cleaning?

"Sorry," he yelled.

Karis stood and assessed her mom. Her once-piercing glare had softened. Exhaustion lined her face. She was a long way from the reckless mother Karis grew up with.

"I'm going up to take a nap."

"A nap? It's almost time for bed."

Iona sucked her teeth. "Oh, Karis, so much to learn. You always were so innocent. I'm not napping. I'm going upstairs to spy on Smith and Lindsey. Never let them into a bedroom by themselves. They're teenagers, for goodness' sake. You know what I was doing at thirteen?"

Karis stiffened and turned her mother toward the stairs. "Yeah, go check on them."

Iona climbed the stairs one at a time. Happy to see she didn't need help, relief washed over her, but damn if she was struggling to keep it together. No matter how hard Iona had made Karis' childhood, it still hurt to watch dementia take over her once-vibrant, ornery mother. Karis attempted her best box breath before moving on to her next dilemma.

Which she found on hands and knees scrubbing her kitchen floor.

***

She'd been crying, and it tore through him like a Florida hurricane, blowing him over and filling his lungs to the brim with salt water. It burned. He wanted to do everything in his power to take her hurt away, and that made him want to beat the shit out of himself. Taking care of her wasn't his problem anymore. She didn't want his care, and yet, here he was, on his hands and knees. Sucker.

He hadn't scrubbed floors since his rookie days. With his assistant-coach responsibilities and raising Smith, he never once considered cleaning the floorboards in his kitchen a necessity.

It was damn near therapeutic.

Sure, his thoughts lingered on Smith going to Pop's, and he wanted to fling a chair through the wall. Sure, he replayed the hurt and pain in Karis' eyes. Again, another chair through the wall. But it felt good to mindlessly scrub something. Get the flour off the floor and the cookie dough from between cabinets. Good hard physical labor. Cleaning. Who knew?

"You don't have to do that."

Scrubbing stopped. He ignored her comment, but not her nearness.

His tight-leashed frustration surfaced, taking over every *nice guy* thought he tried to have when it came to her. *Give her time. Let her handle her family.* No matter how many times he tried, he couldn't control his emotions and refrain from demanding the answers he needed in order to survive the next minute. Fear for Smith and witnessing the despair in Karis' face had him raw inside his own skin.

Her red-rimmed eyes hid her family demons, and she didn't deserve the twist of his temper, but all the built-up anger and years without her crashed into him.

All the battles he'd started on the ice against unsuspecting players had never relieved his fury. He wanted to battle with her. Demand reasons she ignored his calls. His texts. The doors. He needed to know why she didn't trust him with their future. Because if he knew why, he could start not wanting her.

This must be the downfall of cleaning. Deep thoughts and revelations. Jumping up from the floor, he pounced, catching her off guard. Surprise had her shoulders squared.

"Why'd you do it?" Flour everywhere, and he didn't care. All he saw was her.

"What?" she questioned.

"Why'd you quit on us?"

She shook her head. The color drained from her face. "That was eleven years ago. I'm not doing this. It's gone."

"Not for me, and you know it. I want to know why. I deserve to know why." Her flowery scent destroyed the remaining threads of his composure. Her dark hair curved to her waist. She made a white T-shirt and jeans the sexiest lingerie.

"*Deserve* to know why. Deserve?" Her teeth clenched and a spark flashed in her eyes.

"Yeah, deserve." Heat bounced between them. He stepped back and his body tensed with refusal.

"Oh, like you had no clue what was going on? I let you go, and you ran with it. You were all in to go our separate ways. Remember?" Her voice grew louder, fueling his frustration. They were both way too tired for this.

"I was all in for you." He jabbed a finger in her direction.

Shock deepened the puzzled dip of her brow. Her plush lips gaped open. "Bullshit. You loved that I let you go. Wes told me all about it." Her long fingers slapped over her mouth.

Silence.

"What do you mean, Wes told you all about it?" His heart thrashed. The room swam sideways, and his lungs pumped double time.

"Nothing." She turned her back to him and reached for a dish towel.

"Fuck nothing." His fingers clasped around her forearms and readjusted her to face him. "At least look at me when you throw me a lie." He held her stare, waiting. His phone buzzed, cutting through the air. Even off the ice, his brother had impeccable timing.

"Yeah, Ryan, we're on our way." Ty snarled and followed Karis across the kitchen, his body on autopilot, needing to be next to her at all costs. Cornering her between the counter and his body, he pressed the phone to his ear. He tried to listen to Ryan, but the lip pulled between her teeth stole his attention.

"Ryan, not now." His blood pulsed. Hard. "Jesus Christ. Shut up. Remember when you told me to find out? Yeah well, hang the fuck up so I can." His temper teetered, and his fingers twitched to reach for her. To just hold on. All he wanted was to know what he'd done, and how she'd lived without him when living without her had ruined him.

Phone back in his pocket, he tried again. "Start talking or I will not be responsible for the way this kitchen looks when *I* leave."

She rubbed her lips together and surrendered. "When you left school, I kept in touch with Wes. I needed to make sure you were good."

She said it like the entire population of ex-girlfriend land checked in on their ex-boyfriends. "And why didn't you ask *me* if I was good?"

She hesitated, and he knew her family was on her mind, but seeing her so vulnerable opened his wound like a filleted fish. He wanted answers. Answers to why he still felt so compelled to help her and make everything right, when she made his anger too hard to control, and his hurt impossible to contain.

"I called you a million times. I took flights back to North Carolina on every single fucking day off, only to find you gone." He paced the small room, spilling his guts and praying he could keep his voice from coach level, but damn, remembering the crush of finding her gone still hit like a slash to the hands.

"It was better that way." She wrapped her arms around her body.

"Not for me, but maybe for you and Wes." He moved away from her, hoping she said something to shift his brain *into I don't care* mode.

"What? There was no me and Wes. Ty, look at the career you had. The career you have."

She'd talked to his brother but blew him off. Wes never mentioned Karis. Why would he? When they weren't playing hockey, they were partying with girls. Fuck. Lots and lots of girls.

The world swirled around him so fast he couldn't grab a solid thought and connect the pieces.

"I've got to go." He pulled the fob from his pocket.

"Please wait. Let me explain," she pleaded.

Ty stalked to the door; overcome by a desire he'd fooled himself into thinking he could handle. "I did wait. Time's up. I will never understand why you threw us away, but it hurts like hell to even *think* Wes knew. Smith," —he yelled up the stairs— "let's go."

Her sob shot him straight in the heart.

He didn't care.

Who the fuck was he kidding?

Of course he cared.

That was going to be a problem.

Chapter Seven

"I'm not going." Iona waddled around the kitchen, organizing air and mumbling to herself. Ignoring the morning chaos, she tinkered in a motherly way she'd never done before.

For the one hundredth time, Karis pulled out every kitchen chair, searching for her purse. "Of course you're going, Mom. Please, get ready." The day just started and her brain was already spongey.

"Lindsey, let's go." She yelled up the stairs.

Her purse had to be somewhere.

Karis preferred easing into the day, reading with a cup of hot coffee. Checking out the latest research, or baseball stats. Chill stuff like that. Not yelling or shuffling around like a lunatic. What more did these people want? What else did they need? Going from Miss Independent to complicated family didn't align with her life plan, and she had a plan. Relied on it on a day-to-day basis to function. A character flaw for sure because plans changed. Frequently and fast.

Iona and Ty made committing to a plan impossible. An annoying spark of a habit they both shared. They were both barging into her life. Making her remember things better left forgotten. Especially Ty.

The anguish pouring from him a week ago still tugged at her heart and haunted her restless nights. Across the kitchen, his hot blue stare had held doubt and distrust after she confessed to keeping tabs on him through Wes. Desperate people did crazy things.

Wes had been her only link to him. Ryan wouldn't speak to her, and talking to Ty had the potential to undo everything he'd accomplished. Everything *she'd* accomplished. She refused to entertain the thought. The hurt in his eyes may have gutted her, but she'd do it again.

Her one selfless act.

Ty always thought so much of Wes, Mr. Hockey Star, the one who reached the highest hockey status, and never returned home. Wes took the first plane to his professional hockey career way before he even graduated. Like Wes, Ty wanted it all.

Karis ran her fingers through her wet hair, letting the guilt of leaving him roll over her. Abandonment, he'd say. But a hockey star didn't need his ex-college girlfriend to make him feel better. He had money to do that for him.

Remorse flared, but time ticked on, and reflection would have to wait. In the middle of the kitchen, she tried to gather her wits and find her purse while Iona shuffled around. Her slippers scraping the yellow linoleum. It took them hours to get moving. How did things get done around here? Oh, right. They didn't.

"Linds, let's go. Hockey practice started an hour ago. If you want to play, you need to be on time. Tomorrow, start getting ready two hours before it's time to go." *There we go, problem solved.*

"It's fine. The party doesn't start until I get there." Lindsey posed in the kitchen doorway, snapping her fingers in time with her words.

"Yeah, but it's not a party. It's practice and, if I know anything about Ty, I know he doesn't do late."

Iona placed her hands on her hips like a mother on a mission. "I'm not going and I'm not talking about the doctor."

Karis froze between her mother and her niece, counting to ten for the hundredth time. They were ganging up on her, pushing her to crazy the minute her feet hit the floor.

"What are you talking about, not the doctor?" Her patience waned. *In through the nose, out through the mouth.*

Iona searched the kitchen. She wasn't giving much away these days. Any sign of confusion, and Karis pounced, unintentionally, and Iona had picked up on the routine. Karis blamed it on cognitive curiosity. The more she read about dementia, the more questions she had, and the more symptoms she noticed.

"I'm not going to North Carolina." Iona crossed her arms. "I'm not leaving my house." Her mother stood ramrod straight, defiance carved in the corners of her pressed lips.

"Wait. We're going to North Carolina?" Lindsey's question shot through the kitchen.

Karis steadied herself, placing her hands in front of her as if she were dealing with wild animals, which could describe a thirteen-year-old nicely.

"It's an option. I haven't discussed it with anyone." One stinking idea and her roommates were up in arms.

"Obviously you discussed it with Grandma."

Karis regarded her mother, who continued to avoid responsibility, as much as a teenager.

"Mom?" Karis stepped closer. "Were you listening to my phone call with my boss yesterday?"

"How dare— Oh what the hell? I have nothing to hide. This is my house, for heaven's sake."

"You have no right to listen to my conversations. They're confidential." Her mother had been eavesdropping since Karis' teenage years. "I went specifically to my bedroom for privacy."

"A lot of good that did you." Lindsey smirked. "I'm not moving to North Carolina, either. I'm staying here with Grandma."

Karis slouched over the counter, and in one gigantic useless gush, blew the air out of her lungs. "Well, see, here's the thing. Thirteen-year-olds don't get a vote on where they live. We adults"—she signaled to herself and kind of at her mother— "get to make these decisions."

"You don't get to decide for me," Lindsey snapped.

"Lindsey, that's enough." Iona dropped into her chair at the table, worn out, but her voice still carried the authority of a no-nonsense mom.

Three weeks into a hot, painful Florida summer, taking care of hormonal and forgetful, Karis needed stock in aspirin.

"If we can't afford hockey, I won't play, but I'm not moving." Lindsey shrugged and pursed her lips.

They rallied against her but needed her to have a job, and her job was in North Carolina.

"My mom will be home soon. She'll have money," Lindsey tried.

Of course, that's the answer. Leah will ride in and save the day. Just like she never did. But the hope on Lindsey's face pushed Karis' anger to the edge.

Time to sprinkle the kitchen with reality.

"Lindsey, you're playing hockey." She turned her accusing finger on Iona. "And, Mom, you're going to the doctor. This has closed the open opinion portion of our morning. Thank you both so much."

They were clueless about the angst they caused. All night, Karis' finger hovered over her banking app. At two a.m. she tapped confirm, transferring money from her savings into her checking. Another week of hockey paid with one lousy too-easy-to-do click.

"Now let's go." Neither one of them moved. Perfect.

Flopping down in the chair next to her mom, she tried reasoning. "You guys, listen. Moving may be our only option, because I need to collect a paycheck to maintain our sparkly lifestyle." She blew a rogue hair away from her face. "Right now, I can Skype sessions, but that's temporary. I can't imagine the players digging that for long."

Iona's chair scraped the floor. "I'm not going," she yelled from the living room.

"Ignore her," she said to Lindsey, pushing the chair under the table.

"They're baseball players. What do they have to be uptight about?" Lindsey questioned.

Karis lightly hip-checked her into the counter. "You sound like your coach. Hockey snobs. The both of you." The morning stress melted. "I don't want to move you away from everything you love, but North Carolina is where my job is, and I can't give that up."

Lindsey pondered her situation as any thirteen-year-old can. It was over within seconds.

"Fine."

"See, was that so hard?" Karis questioned.

"Painful." Lindsey clucked.

"One more thing, I don't mind paying for hockey as long as I can but be ready on time especially if Grandma has a doctor's appointment. They charge if I'm late, and so does the rink. Those precious seconds you are late are costing me big bucks."

Lindsey flashed a half-hearted smile. "Oh God, Aunt Karis, it's four dollars for fifteen minutes of ice. Even I have four dollars."

"Well, get it out, sista. We need all the help we can get."

Chapter Eight

A person moving through the stages of dementia required a lot of patience. A box Karis couldn't check. Especially for her mother.

Angsty moods plagued the car. She was all for quiet but not for eerie. Iona slumped in the passenger seat, staring out the window. Her slim fingers fiddled with her handbag. Lindsey, with her brooding teenage disapproval, occupied the back seat, her head in her phone. Fine. Fume and sulk away. But the day's checklist would be reconciled.

Unanswered questions appeared in her mind like cartoon speech bubbles. If she wasn't thinking about her mother or Lindsey, she was thinking about her job and how to have virtual meetings with baseball players and ensure the meetings mattered. In person, the players hardly engaged because they were so resentful about needing help, virtually could be a nightmare. But, to stay in Edge View, she had to make it work.

A quick curbside hockey drop-off led to a long day of worrying about Lindsey. Did she feel loved? Wanted? Worth the trouble? So, even with a mile long to-do list, Karis hauled herself into the rink, Iona in tow, to settle Lindsey in for practice. The chances of running into Ty had to be super slim and had absolutely nothing to do with her rapid heartbeat and laser focus. The rink had enough room for both of them. She didn't have time to hide from an old boyfriend who hated her guts.

Inside, true to hockey-mom form, Karis rubbed her hands together and studied the whiteboard, detailing locker room assignments.

"Okay, Linds, you're in number seven." Without a word, Lindsey marched away. Karis yelled across the rink, "Bye, Lindsey, see you this afternoon!" Fellow parents offered sympathetic, *right there with ya*, nods.

Teenagers.

"I'm going in the pro shop," Iona quipped, adjusting her handbag onto her arm.

"I think we should get go—" and her mom was gone. Awesome.

"Hey, Karis," Ryan called from down the hall. The man looked the same. Long hair, white teeth for days, and a build beyond compare. A good guy. Squeaky clean.

With a silent groan, she bent her knees and pushed her hands into her pockets, only because her entire body wouldn't fit. Was it too much to ask to just swing in and drop off?

"Hey, Ryan." Her teeth ground against each other, and her voice hit a high note.

"Where's Lindsey?" He flashed a winning grin, but she had his number. Danger lurked in those good looks. Karis inched closer to the pro shop's glass door and spotted Iona shuffling around the goalie sticks. Safe and sound.

"I'm guessing she went to the locker room. We're kind of in between conversations right now." She bit her lip and caught Ty coming her way. Goodness gracious, she'd never survive both Firestones, not with the morning she'd had.

"Why is Lindsey late?" He halted in front of her, all tensed up with a sexy stare and a tight jaw. Karis prepared to spar, but his piney, laundry-soap scent was a sucker punch straight to the heart. Slightly registering the smile Ryan threw at them, she reclaimed her composure.

Tried to anyway.

She didn't owe him an excuse —and yet— "I called the rink. We had some trouble getting things together this morning," she rattled off, not bothering to hide the struggle. She was too tired, and he'd see right through it anyway.

His brows deepened to canyon depth. "What's wrong? I saw her fly into the locker room. She looked like hell."

A direct hit.

"Why don't you ask *her* what's wrong?" Karis pushed her hands deeper into her pockets.

Ty unzipped his jacket. "No thanks. I know that look. She's pissed about more than being late."

A furious twitch started at her temple.

"She hates being late, and it costs the team practice time."

Seriously?

"Why does it cost them practice time?"

"Because now we all have to do laps."

Was this parent guilt?

She clenched her teeth. "Jesus, Ty. She's late. We had issues this morning. I'm sorry. I didn't realize there'd be mass consequences."

A rogue jaw muscle jumped. "Karis." He moved closer.

"Stop." She stepped back, cleared her throat, and peeked into the pro shop.

Ryan coughed. "I'll go see if Lindsey needs help with her skates. You good?" He cupped Ty's shoulder.

Ty's gaze held tight to Karis'. "Yeah, I'm good. Give me five minutes."

Every inch of her body heated from the closeness of his guarding frame. Leaning into him would cause a parental uproar for sure. Plus, she no longer had the right to sink into him and release everything tearing her up inside.

"Karis." His voice slipped past tired and well into concerned.

She shook her head, dreading her next drop of disappointment. "Lindsey can't stay the whole time today."

He reached for her elbow, but she backed away. If he touched her, she'd lose it.

"Talk to me." The whisper splintered her heart.

She wouldn't survive another attack from him. "I can't—" Her words stuck in her throat; she regrouped and tried her sentence again. "She can't stay."

He tilted his head to the side. "But she just got here."

Deflated, she attempted an explanation. "I have to take my mom to the doctor." She paused, loosening the words lodged in her throat. "I am not sure how long it will take, so I told Lindsey she could only stay for a couple hours."

"What doctor?"

Just like Ty. Right to the point. Strong and capable. Everything she was missing. Her shield collapsed. She gripped her hips with white-knuckle pressure. "A neurologist."

His head dipped low over her ear. "How's her week been? Worse?"

He didn't give her time to answer.

"Karis?" His touch warmed her skin. She needed to pull away and begged her arm to move.

"Worse than what? What do you know?" His tight shoulders sold him out. Shame on him.

He pulled her away from the door and blocked her view of Iona, who stood in the store, holding a hockey stick, chatting up the sales guy.

Karis jerked her arm free and plastered him with her best death stare. He talked now or never.

"I know she's forgetting things." Pulling off his hat, he pushed back his wet hair. His normal nervous twitch.

"Forgetting things?" The cloud inside her head thickened.

"Yeah. Her keys. Her purse. The stove," he hesitated.

She might be sick. Her vision blurred, doubling the people in the lobby. A sinking weight hit the pit of her stomach. Heat rose from her neck and sprawled onto her cheeks. She covered each globe with shaky fingers, scanning the room for a quick escape. Too many people and too many emotions collided, creating one imminent meltdown.

Ty grabbed her hip and blocked the stares coming from his usual audience.

"The stove? She made a mess baking. I never considered the stove." She broke his grip and took off. She needed space. Room to breathe. Room without people and judging stares.

"Karis, stop," he called. His skates banging on the carpeted ground behind her.

Entering an empty arena, the cold hit her skin, darted into her nostrils, and stabbed at her lungs. She rounded on him. "Why didn't you tell me?"

He backed away, like a good man should when under attack by a crazy woman with little sleep, little coffee, and too many tears.

"How in the hell would I tell you, and why don't you know all ready? I thought you spoke to your mother."

"I do speak to my mother. You know we have a messy relationship. She's not going to tell me she's losing her mind. She wants Lindsey. I'm trying to put the puzzle together and, all this time, you had pieces."

"You're yelling at me because of what you don't know about *your* mother? Maybe if you came out from under your independence, you'd know what's going on," he shot back, and turned to leave, showing her the back of his dark-blue hockey jacket with the word COACH scrawled across the shoulders. The same jacket she bought for him when he started coaching youth hockey back in college.

Taking a play from Lindsey's playbook, she leaned her forehead on the glass and let the cold shift her thoughts from emotional to physical. She held steady, closed her eyes, and forced her body to stay in place and suffer the cold.

Seconds into the pain, his powerful body leaned into hers, nuzzling her hips against the boards. Her heart broke wide open at the familiarity of his secure arms holding her in their frame. His large hands gripped the boards on both sides of her hips, and she dug her fingers into his wrists. This couldn't be right. His body hunched over her, trying to get closer than he should.

"What can I do?" His words were a breeze against her skin, breathy in her ear.

"Don't ask that." She squeezed her eyes shut. Her body zeroed in on their touching hips and the light pressure connecting them.

He turned her around, his arms still locked, keeping her in place.

"What can I do?" Intensity coiled around them. An old knit hat covered his dark-brown beautiful hair. Thank goodness.

This man.

"Nothing. There's nothing you can do." Even if there were, this wasn't his problem. She would take care of it.

He tilted his head. Reading her. "You're still not going to let me in?" His mouth tightened.

"Ty. We're getting on the ice," Ryan's voice echoed from the side hall of the rink.

Ty sighed, rubbed his cheek against his shoulder and pressed his forehead head against the glass above her shoulder.

She counted at least two deep breaths before he spoke. "I can take Lindsey home," he offered in a surrendered whisper.

"No, I can stay and take her with me. Mom wants to watch a little anyway." She really should let Lindsey stay longer. After all, she was paying for the entire day, and Lindsey needed the outlet.

"Just let her stay. I'll bring her home when camp is over. She can stay and help me clean the locker room as punishment for missing this morning, and I'll nix the team laps."

A choked laugh escaped. "I think what we went through this morning may have been punishment enough."

"Probably." His cheek lifted in a small smile.

She sighed. Control of her situation surfaced, replacing the awakened need to let him lead. He backed up, giving her the space she needed.

"Ty, come on," Ryan called.

"I'm coming. Jesus, you're worse than a girlfriend."

"How would you know?" Ryan smarted. "I'll get them started but hurry up."

He cringed. "I'll take Lindsey home. Take your mom to the doctor, and I'll see you later."

And just like that, he took control. And just like that, she let him.

***

"I hope you know what you're doing," Ryan spat.

"Not up for discussion." Ty adjusted himself and made his way down the hall. The smell of her hair haunted his nose. The heat of her body seeped into every bone.

"Well, maybe it should be," Ryan retorted.

Ty stopped before stepping into the rink for the afternoon practice. For a second, he thought about tossing Ryan through the door, but he'd be the one to clean it up. Not to mention, it wasn't very coach-like to toss a player into a glass door just to get him to shut up. His brother, yes, but as long as Ty remained one of Ryan's coaches, he stayed pretty safe from glass doors.

Ty reached the door, but Ryan blocked his exit. Gripping the pull bar, every one of his muscles flexed, keeping Ty from heading into the rink and out of the issue at hand.

"Why can't you be this strong and steady on your feet when you're on the ice?" Ty said in all seriousness.

"I am this strong and steady on my feet when I'm on the ice." Ryan pushed his hand into Ty's chest.

He ignored the push and spotted his U13 players waiting as patiently as boys with sticks could.

"I meant with players your own age," Ty tossed back.

Ryan stepped into Ty's bubble, determination set on his face.

"She ruined you."

A fair reminder.

"We're not talking about this, Firestone." He tried his best coach's growl.

"Shut up with the Firestone, right now, you're my brother, and I'm telling you, I will not be there to pull you out of bars, beds, and God forbid you ever do this again, haystacks." Ryan jabbed at his chest.

Ty broke away, laced his fingers behind his head, and began the deep-breathing bullshit Ryan was always trying to get him to do. Did Ryan think he wanted to feel like this? All knotted up? No matter how much time passed between them, Karis would always possess the power to knock him down. The minor revelation didn't sit well. He needed to move fast before he climbed out of his skin.

"I need to get through that door."

"Ty," Ryan warned.

Ryan's hand didn't move, but the faltering determination in his blink gave Ty the edge. They were great friends. A strong family. And, although it hurt to admit, Ryan was right. Karis killed him and always would.

"I get your concern." Ty pushed against the door. Ryan's strength, an amazing force, held it closed. "I will not lose myself again, and we are dropping this right the fuck now. We have kids to coach, and I need to get out there quick and sling some pucks before I put my hand through this glass."

He tried to unhinge his jaw. It wouldn't budge.

Ryan cracked the door and pushed his hand into Ty's chest. A warning. "Just remember the Ty you are now versus the Ty you became when she left you. And think of Smith. That's all I'm asking." Low blow pulling Smith into the conversation.

"She won't consume me again."

Ryan sighed. "I'm not so sure you have a choice."

An unfortunate truth. She weakened every steel resolve he possessed. Ty stepped into Ryan, forcing him to open the door wider, and giving him a sprawling view of the rink.

A familiar face with the beady eyes of a scout glanced through the glass, waiting for skaters to hit the ice. Unbelievable. "This just gets better and better. What the fuck is he doing here?"

Too honest to lie, Ryan offered a sympathetic look. Ty leashed his fury and fought the urge to punch his brother square in the face. He stormed through the door instead.

"Shit. Wait," Ryan called.

"No." Ty took Ryan head-on. "Open the ice and get the kids started. I'll go see what the hell you did."

Firestones toe to toe.

Ryan played it safe and did exactly as ordered, but not without one last jab. "Ty, it's Pop."

Pushing past the sap, Ty darted to the end of the rink, dodging parents asking about their kids and bitching about the second session's practice starting late. When he reached the man standing against the boards behind the goalie net, he attacked full force. "You're not supposed to be here. We made a deal."

Pop kept his eyes on the ice and chewed his gum with deliberate grinding. Ty couldn't remember the last time his father came to the ice rink. The man usually liked to do his demeaning in private.

"I know we made a deal, Son, but I was invited." His rusty voice struck suspicion.

"I'm gonna kill Ryan." Ty glanced through the glass. Ryan had gone too far this time. He kept trying to make a family out of broken pieces that didn't fit together. The guy was too softhearted, and family oriented for his own good. Across the ice, Ryan's playful attempt at rounding up the skaters made it so hard to stay mad.

"You can't kill Ryan. He's the best player on your team this upcoming season. And from the looks of this Peewee team, you better get out there. Smith looks—"

Ty dug his fingers into his father's coat and jerked the old man close. Their identical stares collided.

The skid from the ice hardly registered, but Ryan's large body stopped in front of the scene, blocking it from the young players on the ice. Ty ignored the stick tap Ryan gave against the glass.

"Listen to me, Pop. You do not, do not"—Ty tightened his grip—"get to comment on Smith's play. Your invitation's been retracted."

The man smirked at his son, liquor-deprived shaky hands heightened Ty's disgust. Pop needed a toss against the boards and a punch in the throat. But he'd probably like it and then tell Ty how he could do it better.

"Ty, let him go," Ryan shouted through the barrier. The vibration buzzed in Ty's ears, but his focus shored up on the man who had controlled his young life. Ty would kill him in front of everyone before he let his venom soak into Smith.

"You forget yourself, Tyson. Get your hands off me." Wilson worked his wrists trying to get free, but Ty's hate prevailed.

"Go home. You can't stay here. I will cancel this practice before I let you stay here." Ty dropped his hands, pounded the glass, and focused his fury on Ryan. "We'll discuss this later."

"Yeah, put it on the list. Now come on." Ryan held his stare for a second before skating away.

"You know, Son, one of these days you're gonna have to forgive me for making you the hockey player you were and the coach you are."

"You think you made this?" He gestured from head to toe. "The only thing you did was fuck this up." Ty pointed to his temple. "Hockey fixed me. You and your evil ways of training had nothing to do with it."

"I made you."

"You killed Wes."

Father and son faced off. Pop still loomed well over six feet. Ty stopped himself from taking a step back. He didn't have to do that anymore.

"Wes' death had nothing to do with me."

"Keep telling *yourself* that, Pop," Ty spat.

"Ya know, Smith's mother's gonna want more money, and then she's gonna come strolling back into your life and want to see that boy you paid her for." Wilson Firestone always had the ace.

"Not a problem. I'm used to dealing with assholes. Now get the fuck out of my rink."

Chapter Nine

Between the heat from Karis' body and his father showing up at the rink, Ty edged closer to crazy. His only savior?

Smith.

All practice, he watched him, soaking in the needed reminder of the good in his life. His family. The fractured, fucked-up one that it was. The reason for all of it. Pain. Happiness. Tears.

Losing Wes created a new reality. Family first. Hockey was hockey. You played and you played and you played some more, but the game would eventually be the exact reason you couldn't play anymore.

Not a problem. A relationship with hockey, full of breaks and bridges, couldn't compare to the love of family. The game tied them together. As much as he hated to admit it, his father had started it all. The dick. The man loved hockey and passed it down to all three of his sons in heavy-handed force, but Ty refused to be grateful. He would have found the sport and excelled regardless because it lived inside of him, not because his father kept him up all hours of the night running drills in the garage.

Ty slammed his fist against the steering wheel. His BMW had seen its fair share of pissed off, but the passengers in the back seat witnessed it for the first time.

"Uncle Ty, you good?" Ty's stomach churned at the fear in Smith's voice.

"All good."

"Coach, you and my aunt have a thing, huh?" *No words from her all day and now this.*

No surprise Smith and Lindsey took to each other. Both broken, together they made a whole. They found family. Fixed each other. Which sent another roll through Ty's stomach. Their attachment connected him to Karis.

Smith smacked Lindsey on the leg. Ty gave her points for punching back.

"Nope. Not a thing," he denied.

"We can tell there's a thing." Smith chuckled.

The laugh put a slight crack in Ty's wall. "Whose side are you on?"

"Lindsey's," Smith said with the huge grin Ty lived for.

"Traitor." The tension in his shoulders released.

"It doesn't matter, because she's moving us to North Carolina," Lindsey chimed in.

Ty jacked up the AC and pulled at his collar. "What do you mean, she's moving you?"

It's not moving. It's running away from him again.

He rubbed at the pain clinging to his chest. The heat from pressing into her body hours ago burned through his veins. His head swam in confusion, and his body lit up knowing she still fit him perfectly. Tall, long, and curved. No woman he'd ever been with trying to forget her, made the match.

Lindsey coughed. "Her boss gave her a leave, but she has to go back. She needs the money. We need the money," she finished in a whisper.

Jesus. Karis had her hands full. The last thing she needed was his interference, but he wasn't sure he'd watch her walk away as easily as he had before. He'd learned the lesson. But now, he had more to lose than his heart. He couldn't afford to break again. The smart thing to do would be to wish them well, but spotting Smith lost in thought, gazing out the window, blew the idea to pieces.

"I guess I could quit hockey. I mean, if we can't pay for it, we can't pay for it. Right?" She stared out her own window, her words a mindful mumble.

"Lindsey, do you want to quit hockey?"

Her glare met his in the mirror. "No, but I don't want my aunt to stress about it, and I don't want to move. I'd rather stay here and watch you guys play than leave, and—" She peered down at her lap. Smith gave her a shoulder bump.

"And what?" Ty asked.

"I don't think my grandma would do well with a move."

A quiet agreement filled the car. A move could be detrimental to an Alzheimer's or dementia patient. Moving went against everything he had read about the disease. After finding Iona the first night she took off, scaring Lindsey to death, Ty, following a hunch, spent the rest of the night glued to the web, devouring everything he could find on dementia. People with dementia did better with structure and boring routines. Moving to a different state didn't scream rigid schedule.

"I wish my mom would come back."

During the past two summers, Lindsey's mom hadn't been home for more than a couple of days. She was incapable of settling down. Exactly the way Karis had once described her mother.

With Iona in her seventies, it was hard to picture her sleeping with an array of men to get her bills paid. Not mother-of-the-year material. Certainly, Iona had been a looker in her day.

He'd met her during a rare visit home from college. The tension hung puck-thick between mother and daughter, and neither one of them was thrilled to see the other. Iona made Ty feel right at home, and not in a cougar way but more of a mom way. But what did he know about mothers? Still, he liked Iona from the very beginning and would never hold someone negligent for doing what they had to do to survive.

The Hills were a hockey family, and when Ty returned to Florida to play pro hockey for the team he'd cheered on as a teenager, he couldn't wait to see Iona. She didn't blow him off when Karis dumped him and rearranged the life they had planned. Mother and daughter had always been at odds, and Karis' decision to stay in North Carolina to finish her degree never sat well with Iona. At least that's what Iona told him, but whether for money or love, he didn't know.

Iona loved hockey, so naturally, Lindsey came out for Ty's U13 team. The Hills would always be a part of his life; Ty learned to live with it.

It made him a believer in the whole "meant to be" thing. Karis and Ty, two kids from the same town, found each other at an out-of-state college, both trying to escape their families. Twenty years later, here they were again. He didn't know whether to thank the universe or put his head through a wall.

"Fuck," he whispered, pulling into Lindsey's driveway. Karis sat on the porch's run-down steps, slumped forward, head in her hands. Glancing up at him, she said it all with one look. His body kicked into gear. He wanted to make it better. His heartbeat thrashed against his rib cage, and every muscle blazed to move as his stomach knotted with a deep twist. He was not making it out of this a sane man.

***

They arrived too soon. Karis checked her watch and tried to calculate the time as if it mattered. Practice ended at five thirty, and she needed to pull herself together.

She wiped beneath her eyes as if that could erase two hours of crying. After Ty had angled up against her at the rink, reminding her of all the ways they'd fit perfectly and highlighting all the reasons she was angry with herself for letting him go, the day never recovered, going from bad to God-awful.

Throughout the day, her brain toggled between memories of her mom and memories of Ty. By the afternoon, her nerves were good and shot. Convinced Karis was taking her to North Carolina instead of the doctor, Iona took more than a backbreaking hour to get in the car, leaving Karis no choice but to call the doctor and cancel their much-needed appointment.

Thank goodness, disagreeable patients were an everyday occurrence for Dr. Simonette, and the accommodating receptionist said they could arrive anytime within a certain window. An hour later, at the doctor's office, Iona was out of the car within ten minutes. Progress.

The prognosis sucked and was exactly what Karis expected, and, according to Dr. Simonette, exactly what he'd already explained to Leah. Iona presented with early stage Alzheimer's. The disease would progressively worsen. The doctor rattled on about good days, bad days, medicated days, offering pamphlets and websites, laced with large, sad, expensive words. She processed it all, bouncing through every concerning question, growing more livid with Leah, who'd learned everything in one of her short flybys, but shared nothing, and took care of less.

Karis squeezed her eyes shut, holding back the tears and anger best saved for her worthless sister.

Ty unfolded from the car, and Karis stopped herself from running into his arms. Lindsey needed her to be strong, but everyone had a breaking point. She teetered on the edge of hers.

He stalked straight for her, and she stepped into his open arms. He held her against his chest. Tucked into him, his woodsy scent rolled through her. He was still the wall she needed. Rogue sobs shook her body. His hold tightened. Her fingers dug into his shirt, grazing thick muscles and soft skin. She couldn't get close enough. She needed him, and it hurt. It all hurt.

His fingers slid into her hair and cradled the back of her head. "You want to talk about it?" he whispered.

"I'm not sure I can." Everything the doctor said shuffled inside her mind, pushing her beyond her limits. At the brink of her capacity, she filled her lungs to their max and focused on the rhythm of his chest.

"Where's your mom?"

She choked back a sob. Bending at the waist, she rested the crown of her head against his stomach. The ground swirled beneath her, and she slid her fingertips over the soft fabric of his shirt, searching to be anchored.

"Karis." His fingers caressed her elbows, her name a breath on his lips. Her hands lay at his waist. Hesitation weighed heavy on her tongue. The words weren't coming. Only fits of crying. Her mind circled, trying to grasp what was happening. She could fix it if she could just nail down a thought and concoct a plan.

He backed away. His caress ran featherlight over her skin. What a sight she must be? He leaned down, and she burrowed farther into him.

"Karis, look at me. Where's your mom?"

"She's upstairs, Coach. Sleeping." Lindsey didn't need to see another adult in her life falling apart.

Reading her mind, Ty shifted left, taking a protective stance. "Why don't you and Smith go in and order pizza? We'll be there in a minute."

The kids trudged into the house. Sad hockey sticks dragging behind them, scraping the splintered wood.

With a shuddered breath, she followed him to the steps. They sat thigh to thigh. His strength seeping into her, leveling her thoughts from echoing roar to slight hum. The pink-and-purple twilight sky hovered above them. An ignored beauty amid pain. Thick fingers entwined with hers. The link more mesmerizing than the sky. Painful and pleasurable all at once.

"Talk to me," he whispered, rubbing her palm with his thumb.

"Um, we were right." She pulled her hand away. "My mom's sick. Early stages Alzheimer's."

He stabbed his fingers into his hair, balanced his elbows on his knees, and clasped his hands together. The whiter his knuckles, the more control he tried to get. There was no controlling this.

She gulped against the burn in her throat. "Hearing the doctor say it confirmed what we knew all along. I never wanted to be wrong so much in my life." Her voice cracked and wavered. He hung his head. When he grabbed her hand again, the tears tumbled down her cheek.

"We can talk later if you need to." So kind and caring.

"I won't remember any of it by then." She lifted her shoulder, swiping at the falling tears. The world in front of her a colorful blur of a haunting future. "My mom has been in this stage for about three months. Leah knew, sticking around long enough to go to a doctor's appointment, but not finding it important enough to stay or let me know what was happening."

He swore.

"Agreed." She rubbed her lips and took a breath. "Dr. Simonette called and said my mom missed her appointment, which is what got this ball rolling in the first place, thank goodness. I don't know why I'm surprised or so upset, but I know I could be in over my head here."

The fear overwhelmed every good intention she mustered up. Antsy, she stood up on the step above him. He followed her lead.

Concern flickered behind his lashes. Dark stubble shadowed his jaw. He looked way past his three-day limit. His overgrown hair covered his forehead, grazed the tips of his ears, and curled around his neck, still wet from a post-hockey shower.

His fingers stroked her cheek, and she leaned into the touch. Her strength wavered, and her resolve melted like ice on the beach. Endless tears slid down her face.

Closing the gap between them, his warm mouth hovered over hers.

Secure and familiar.

She inched close, needing him more than she wanted to admit. He slipped an arm around her waist, and the soft skin of his lips met hers with tender reassurance. A deep growl vibrated from his lips to hers. The heat between them gave her something to clasp on to, and they smoldered into a gripping embrace.

Amongst the muddy waters, she ached to fall into him and forget it all. But a woman responsible for a teenage girl and an ill mother didn't get to forget it all.

She wouldn't do this.

Their touching lips stirred a hibernating want she couldn't allow herself to have. Her want for the kiss, a mind trick. A game to focus on something other than the demise of her fractured family. She'd been fooled before and swore it would never happen again.

He would consume her, and one delicious kiss could ruin them all. Her. Iona. Lindsey. Too much happiness lay at stake, and most of it wasn't hers. A weighted responsibility, but when he kissed her, all the heaviness melted away.

Ty crooked a finger beneath her chin, erasing her doubt with one sincere gaze. "You make me weak," she confessed.

"And you kill me." His soft lips pressed against hers again, and his tongue went to work, stripping her of responsibility.

With one long groan, she stepped away, rubbing her lips with nervous fingers. "Stay back." She crossed her arms and moved away, her body protesting the entire inch.

He waved a gentle gesture. "Okay." But he took a step closer, slowly, as if calming a wild animal.

"I should go talk to Lindsey," she blurted, and pushed the heated want back into its locked corner of her heart. "You and Smith don't have to stay. We'll be fine."

So not true.

He stepped in front of her. "Don't do this."

She attempted to sidestep him, but exhaustion controlled every cell in her body, and all she accomplished was some incoherent shuffle.

"Don't push me away," he tried, adding another log on the blaze burning inside her.

She'd never be strong enough to push him away, and that's what made pulling him close so dangerous. "I have to go talk to Lindsey." She sighed, angry at herself for opening the door to their past with one kiss.

He moved behind her like a breeze floating through a palm tree. "Smith and I will go get the pizza." Of course they would.

"Ty," she attempted.

"Come on, everyone has to eat. At least let me take care of dinner."

She faced him before going inside the house. "Fine. Pizza." Eat? With her insides strung tight and legs like jelly. Not happening.

His mouth lifted at the corner, flashing a small winning grin. "You're letting me help." He sang it like a hit song.

She opened the door. "It's pizza, not a million dollars."

"It's a start." He called for Smith and headed out the door.

Before heading to Lindsey's room, Karis peeked in on her mom. Sound asleep, Iona lay on the bed with her quilt pulled up to her chin, a peacefulness resting on her face.

The caveat to a late nap was the inability to sleep at night. A major issue for dementia patients. Iona's soft T-shirt floated with each inhale. A small smile rested on her lips. The room, so small and tidy, stretched with a calm demeanor. Outside, two doors slammed, and a car cranked. Content, she made her way down the hall.

After two knocks and a shimmy to the locked door, she tried her luck through the flimsy wood. "Lindsey, we should talk."

Silence.

"Lindsey, please." She flattened her palm against the door.

"I already know what you want to talk about. I'm good. Go away. Go back to North Carolina. Leave us alone. I'll take care of Grandma. We don't need you."

Ouch.

Karis rested her head against the cold wooden door. "I'm not going away. Open the door."

"When my mom comes back, she'll stay, and you can leave." But even if Leah came back, Karis wasn't so sure she'd leave.

Her fingers tapped on the door. "If only it were that easy."

"What?" she yelled.

"Open the door. I don't want to wake Grandma up."

Dark circles hung beneath Lindsey's eyes, a complement to her wet and runny nose. A surging ache to take the burden and make it better clenched Karis' soul. How did parents deal with this?

"Listen."

Lindsey stood firm at the door. "I know what the doctor said. It's what they've been saying, so are you gonna leave?"

"What? No." She stepped inside. Everything hinged on this moment. She couldn't mess it up. She couldn't succumb to the need for escape.

Chapter Ten

With an upturned lip, Lindsey plopped onto her bed. Challenge accepted. The bed creaked under Karis and her fingers anchored into the mattress. In less than a second, Lindsey dashed to the window. Her straight back and defiant shoulders a telltale of pissed off.

"I was fine with Grandma before you came. We were fine." Her gaze stuck to whatever fascination lay outside, but her soft words exposed tenderness. "I can take care of her."

"You're thirteen. You shouldn't have to take care of her. She wouldn't want that." Panic flared to life inside her chest, the type of panic that gave deep breathing the finger. She gripped the iron footboard, exercising her resilience. If she got up, she'd pack her things and jet back to her well-maintained life in North Carolina. Flight, fight, or freeze. Those bitches had returned.

Flight won every time.

Willing Lindsey to at least turn around, Karis waited, clinging to the glimmer of hope persuading her to stay put. Her heartbeat, a frantic soundtrack in her ears, reminded her how careful she had to be in this fragile moment.

"You want us to move?"

It wasn't the end of the world. Adjusting herself on the bed, Karis answered with the truth. "It's possible."

"So when my mom comes back, we'll be gone."

Leah had to come back for that to be true.

"We need to do something now, Linds. We can't wait for your mom." She swallowed and wiped the sweat from her armpits.

"Grandma shouldn't move," Lindsey retorted.

Fair enough. "Yes, you're probably right." Trusting her aunt side, she approached Lindsey, and a shock of protectiveness burst from her heart.

"I'm not moving with you. You don't know me, and you don't know Grandma." Lindsey backed into the corner and slid down the wall, landing in a frail un-hockey-like ball of mush.

The room began a slow spin. How in the world was she supposed to protect this young girl from the perils of life? She wanted to go on a rampage until a smile lit her face from chin to hairline.

"You're right." Karis shrugged. "We don't know each other, but I can't leave you and Grandma here, hoping your mom will come back. Grandma's going to need a lot of care."

Dusk settled over the neighborhood and the outside streetlight flashed on, seeping through the draped windows, coloring Lindsey's cheeks a light shade of pink. Beautiful.

Karis slid down the wall and wrapped her arms around Lindsey's shoulders.

"I'm too much for Grandma to take care of. Am I why she's forgetting everything?"

"No. Look at me." Karis lifted her chin with a gentle finger. "What's happening to Grandma is not your fault. It's no one's fault." The doctor had told her the same thing.

"The mind is fragile, and nothing we did or didn't do made this happen." Karis glanced around her old bedroom. Nothing had changed. Not the décor. Not even the paint color. A sad sight. Rubbing Lindsey's hair, she whispered whatever reassuring mantra she could think of.

"We're back. Pizza's here," Ty knocked and spoke through the door.

"We'll be out in a minute," Karis called. She took Lindsey's forearms and met her stare for stare.

"Do you understand what I am saying to you? Not. Your. Fault."

She needed more than a nod, but the healing had to start somewhere.

"Go wash up. We'll have pizza and then we'll just hang tonight. Me, you, and Grandma."

"Is she going to be okay?"

The heart of the matter.

Karis bit into her lip and helped Lindsey up from the floor. "This is going to be a big change for us. Grandma's not going to get better." The information settled. "It may be years before she gets worse, and we're going to have to keep things as structured as possible for her, and we, especially me," —Karis blew out a breath— "are going to have to have a truckload of patience."

"I can do that."

Karis chuckled, "Then I can, too."

"So structure, like a routine?"

"Yep," Karis confirmed.

"So not moving to North Carolina?"

Knife in the heart.

"Lindsey, I have to consider it, because there is this thing called money that we need in order to live. But that's a conversation for another time."

Lindsey deflated, but lying to her about their chances of staying in Florida wouldn't do any good. They had to stick together.

"I'm going to go scrub the cry off my face. If Smith sees me like this, he'll never let me live it down."

"You guys are close?"

A smile broke across her face. "Not like that. We would never make it as boyfriend and girlfriend. We've known each other too long. He knows too much about me. Plus, he's a wicked wingman, and I'm not giving that up."

"Wicked wingman, huh, so was his uncle Ty." Karis caught herself smiling at the memory. "Downstairs in five?"

"Yeah." Lindsey darted to the bathroom.

If they stayed, this bedroom would have to change. Her lungs wanted to heave from the dust living amongst the old fabric and unwiped walls.

"So you coming down to eat?" Ty strolled through the door, shrinking the faded room.

"Yep," Karis said.

"Your mom's downstairs. She seems good."

"She's downstairs?" How had she missed that?

"Yeah. Scarfing pizza as fast as Smith."

Karis laughed through her tears, welcoming the lightness.

Concerned blue eyes searched hers, leaving her vulnerable and exposed.

"Her memory's going to come and go. It's not going to get better. It may take time before it gets worse, or it may get worse tomorrow and just work its way to awful." She ended on an airy cry, cutting through a forced smile. He looked away and shoved his hands into his pockets.

Her heart thumped, and the room took another spin. "Ty, what am I—" Her hands reached for him, and he caught her before her bones turned to jelly.

"I got you," he breathed, dissolving her into a frightened woman, desperate to curl up and hide inside of him. But to stand on her own, she'd forfeited her right to him years ago.

"I wish you did."

His hands froze on her hips. The air in the room stilled. One beat. Then two.

"Your mom?" Controlled as always, Ty moved the topic back to the issue. Calculating and precise to a fault.

"She needs structure, routine, and patience," she stuttered. "All the things I'm running low on. Maybe a facility depending on my ability or inability to take care of her." Her past relationship with her mother was shaky, but things had to change for Lindsey's sake. For everyone's sake.

"So no North Carolina?" his voice rumbled.

"How do you know about— Lindsey?" She guessed.

"Yeah, Lindsey." His hands still cradled her hips. A grimace fell across his lips.

"I don't know what I am going to do. My mom has two more doctor's appointments next week, so we'll see after that. I can't make these decisions right now."

"Aunt Karis, let's go—" Lindsey moseyed into her bedroom, like any teenage girl would, and ignored the semi-embrace in front of her.

"Right. Pizza. Let's go." Karis disregarded Lindsey's oblivion and stepped away from Ty's solid embrace. She raced downstairs, eager to check on her mother and forget about Ty's hands on her hips.

Centered at the kitchen table, her mom sat scarfing cheesy pizza, Smith a slice behind.

"Mom, tell me you're saving some for the rest of us?" Karis reached for paper plates and handed one to Lindsey.

"You snooze, you lose. I can't remember the last time I had pizza this good." Iona wiped her mouth and took another bite of her favorite food. They'd had it for dinner last week, from the same place.

"Grandma," Lindsey tried, but Ty intervened.

"I could have pizza every night." He grabbed a slice and passed a handful of napkins to Smith. "Eat over the plate, Smith, I'd hate to make you mop these floors, especially since I just did it last week." Ty ruffled Smith's hair and sat down next to him.

When did he become so fatherly? So family?

Ty's rocky relationship with his father had placed family on the back burner. A philosophy she understood. Years of grueling travel hockey schedules and brow-beating training sessions built a strained foundation between father and son. Many times, Ty swore up and down he'd never have kids because chances were high, he'd parent the same way. A valid theory, and one most adults indulged in if they grew up in a house with an abuser. But he was strong enough to beat the odds.

In college, she'd spent many nights holding him. His arms squeezing her waist. Doubled over, his head pressing into her stomach. His entire body shaking with frustration after one phone call from Wilson Firestone. Seeing a man the size of Ty break down from a few curt words solidified her own family theory.

Not much help in the family-is-great department. She had tried her damnedest to get him to think differently about building a family of his own. He always said let family happen to someone else, but whenever his brothers were around, he automatically took on the fatherly role. It fit him. All the years they dated, he never brought her home to meet his father, but they always hung out with his brothers.

Looking around the kitchen, Karis' heart swelled with tangible joy. With Iona smiling, Lindsey shoving pizza in her face, and stealing Smith's drink, the room looked like a family. The family she'd always wanted to belong to.

And Ty was here, in her kitchen. Certainly, he had a million places he needed to be. She never remembered seeing him sit so still or look so content.

In a glance, her mind erased it all and regret churned, ready to choke her with every tendril of a memory.

What had she done?

What could they have been if only she had been brave enough? Trusted him enough. Loved him enough.

She slid her chair away from the table, knocking the buffet covered in bills and holding her laptop. The entire contents on the table a perfectly timed reminder of her sad reality. She needed a job and money to chip away at the medical debt. Without a word, she grabbed her water and studied Iona, sitting with Smith and Lindsey, all grandmotherly and normal.

"Aunt Karis, you okay?" Lindsey wiped her mouth. Her head tilting like a curious puppy, able to sniff out any lie.

"I'm good." She told one anyway.

The room squeezed and her thick hair stuck hot and heavy against her back. Mechanically, she grabbed the hair tie from her wrist and twisted strands onto her head. The cool air hit her neck, but it wasn't enough. Jumping up, her foot caught on the chair and a loud attention-getting thump echoed over the happiness going on around her. Without her.

"Hey." Ty's calm voice drifted into her ears. One word stuffed with sweet concern. So unnerving. He knew she wasn't okay. A brief glance around the room ended with a swift gaze into his eyes. Solid remorse for every decision she'd ever made set into her like wet cement curing for the long haul. Her heart ached too much to hide her pathetic self-induced shame. She didn't trust what would come out of her mouth.

With a single, "I'm good," she carried her plate to the trash and escaped from the suffocating room. The front porch had air to spare and no Ty. She leaned against the rail, ignoring the creaking reminder that, like most things in her life, the railing needed repair.

Get in line.

One second of pity, that's all she'd allow herself.

"I'm gonna need more than an 'I'm good.'" He stood close. As close as he used to when he belonged to her.

Her hands tightened on the crumbling rail. The humid air filled her lungs like thick billows of rain clouds. Hidden in the bushes, the cricket's usual calming theme scraped against her nerves. Anxiety rifled through her in massive waves, and she wanted to grab him and hold him hard while the world exploded around them.

How did she get here? He should have belonged to her forever. Together, they had a chance at happiness, but the drive to accomplish their dreams and goals diminished their ability to capture it. The balancing act of having it all proved impossible, and now here she was coming in to save the day for a family she'd fought so hard to get away from. She knew nothing about saving the day. About saving her family. She was a one-woman show.

Sadly, by her own design.

Family closed in, threatening to sabotage independence, stability, and money. Family meant a long list of responsibilities topped with a beast of a man she didn't know what to do with. How could a girl fighting for her own life be pulled by so many people stay true to herself?

Chapter Eleven

"You don't need to be here." Her hips shifted against the rotting rail. She folded her arms, covering the quick pump of her chest. Hiding herself from him.

The need to reach out and assure her burned beneath his skin.

She wasn't leaving him again.

"Don't do that." Ty chipped at the paint on the rail, making particles fly to the ground and Karis' demeanor drop another inch. Goddamn it. He'd fix the porch tomorrow. Right now, he either grabbed the splintered rail or her, and the way she left the kitchen, all in her head, if he pulled her arms away from her chest, and curved his fingers around her waist, she'd take off.

"It's better if you go."

Her words were edgy and clipped, rightfully so. She'd been at odds with her mom for years. To see Iona like this had to be a mind bend. Growing up, Iona had been difficult for her to deal with, especially during high school. Men frequented the house, and once her sister started high school, the number of men doubled. Karis longed to escape and would take with her the devastating lesson that men equaled control. Ty knew the story. She needed space when she started thinking like this, but he still couldn't give her up.

"Nope. Not going," he quipped.

"I know you mean well."

He faced her, trying to tamp down the desire to do whatever it took to erase the sadness inside her. In two seconds, his lips could lock on hers, soft and warm and consuming. Her height, an easy fit for him, made her mouth hard to refuse, but he stepped back.

"This is more than mean well. What's on your mind?" She kept her feelings vault-tight. Killing him with every fight they'd had until he left exhausted from trying to pry things out of her. Things he had no right to know, things he shouldn't want to know, but fuck him, he wanted to know it all.

She shook her head, and anger zipped up his spine.

"Not going to go down that road with you. And you shouldn't want me to." Her quiet voice combatted the screaming inside of him.

"What does that mean?" Her delicate features twisted in confusion.

"Why are you here?"

He questioned his ability to muscle through an answer. "I'm here." He swallowed, giving himself time to conjure up an answer that didn't push her away. His hands itched to grab her, and he fisted them against his thighs. Why *was* he here? It's not like he didn't have his own family drama to deal with.

She released her hair and let it twist down her back, distracting him speechless. His body waged war with his mind, winning on every front. Sweet, perfected imagery seized him. In his mind, she lay naked beneath him, sinking into his mattress. Her lavender scent muddled his brain and her silky strands slid through his fingers, tangling around his wrists. He released a ragged breath. Anchored in trouble.

"Please go. It's hard enough to deal with all of this, but with you here, I can hardly stomach myself. And that won't help Mom, Lindsey, or me." Her hand settled on his chest and his body hardened. If she wanted him to leave, touching him was not the way to get it done.

He cleared his throat. They stood face-to-face. Body to body. It was everything to him, and nothing but a complication to her. He wanted to run and lean in at the same time.

"I can't."

She would always shake him.

The air between them thinned as his lips landed hard on hers. Her warm mouth tasted like all he'd missed and more, slaughtering him with each wet swipe of her tongue, but he refused to stop. Catching her moans, he licked the inside of her mouth, searching for what they'd lost.

It was better than ever and right where she'd left it. An excruciating pleasure. A feminine vibration rolled down his throat and into his pants. He spread his fingers wide, drawing circles on her hips, searching for skin. She stiffened before backing away, her hands clapped over her lips.

Stepping forward, he reached out to her, still wanting her in his arms. Her head shook, matching his body.

"Don't," he begged. Too much thought would ruin it.

"Please go," she cried. Weak and pleading.

He raked his fingers through his hair and dug his fingertips into his scalp. How in the hell did she expect him to leave with tears pouring down her face?

"I'm not going anywhere."

"I can't do this again. Can't you see that?"

"All I see right now is you."

"Don't say things like that." Her eyes slid closed. "I ruined us so long ago, and I can't get it back." She doubled over at the waist, her arms wrapped around her stomach, layers of soft dark hair fell around her face.

Her deep sobs rattled his brain. What was she saying? Did she have regret? He didn't do regret. He couldn't. He had too much of it in his life. Regret wasn't entertained; it was recognized, and locked away to rot.

When her knees buckled, he guided her to sit on the steps. The taste of her still in his mouth and the smell of her drifting in his nose tortured his slipping composure. His fingers roamed over her back, turning him into a man he didn't trust. Sitting next to her, his mind twisted, and his body burned.

"I can't do this," she breathed.

His greedy fingers continued their stroll, outlining the printed letters of his name on her T-shirt. His mind stumbled sideways with impossible thoughts, starring her hips and the soft dip of her waist.

Hearing her limp confession, he calmed his breathing.

"I'm in over my head," she said, dropping her head into her hands.

"Bullshit. You can handle anything." She flashed him a piercing look. He leaned back, hands in surrender, and buried all skin-on-skin thoughts.

"I don't understand how you can say that. I don't know how to do this."

"Do what? Be a part of your family?" He'd pull his fingers away any second.

"As horrible as that sounds, yes." She was breathless. Scared. "I've never been needed like this before."

Yes, she had.

His heartbeat jacked up, pounding at the walls inside his chest. He gripped the step beneath him. She'd kicked the switch. Standing, he landed heavy steps on the cement in front of her.

"I know you have shit going on, Karis, but fuck," he yelled. Stopping in front of her, he hardened his heart against her red, swollen eyes. Her long hair covered her chest, ripping his sanity. He jabbed his hands into his pockets. Touching her would torch the entire house.

Looking toward the sky, he searched for control. When she was his, he would have done anything...anything to make those tears go away. Now they just burned and confused him. No one ever *needed* her before. Was she out of her mind?

"Jesus, Karis, *I needed* you."

"No one needs me." She jumped up, darted down the steps, and into the middle of the darkened driveway between her car and his. She leaned against his beamer; her arms locked in a fold across her body.

He barely fit in the tight space but would have moved both cars with his bare hands to get to her.

"I needed you, and you left anyway, but you can't walk away from Lindsey and your mom. Not now." His patience waned, toggling between convincing her that Iona and Lindsey needed her and needing her to admit he meant nothing to her. His old, wounded ego prevailed.

She looked everywhere but at him, and his jaw snapped and crunched with the effort it took to hold himself in check.

"I can't do this now. My mom—" Her sobs caused another trip up in his mind, but not for long.

"Your mom is in the kitchen, happy as can be, with the best two kids in the world. It's all she needs right now."

Her face softened under the moonlight, and realization dawned.

Her bottom lip slipped between her teeth. "You're right. I can't leave them, and I didn't leave you." Surrender slumped her shoulders.

"Not true," he tried.

"Please, let me get this out." Her voice strained with serious desperation. "I needed to finish my degree, and you were offered your dream. You had to go. We had no choice."

Same old story.

He erased the space between them. "Yes, and we had it all worked out, but you quit. It was going to be hard, but it was going to work, and you gave up." His accusing tone, a bit more than he expected, sliced through him with every flinch of her lashes.

"I never gave up on you. I believed in you and let you go live your life the way it was supposed to be lived."

Jackhammers worked overtime inside his skull. "Wrong." He stepped closer. "My life had you in it. You left me in a nightmare. You left." He paused, considering how much she could take, and went against his better judgement. "You left because you couldn't handle it." Or he wasn't worth the effort.

Her brows knotted together. "I couldn't handle it? What the hell does that mean? I couldn't handle what, exactly? Away games? Girls? Drinking? Partying? Drugs? Yeah, that's awesome, Ty. If that's what you mean, then you're right. I couldn't handle it."

That's what she thought of him? "I was never that guy."

"Bullshit. You became that guy."

There it was.

He stared hard. She'd been waiting for him to screw up, and deep in his psyche, he knew why, but damn, it still irked him. Not all men were the cash cows Iona brought home. "After you left me, I had no one but Wes. All he wanted to do was party, and he ended up dead. You left me in good hands, so no worries for you." Every woman he ever cared about left him with insane father figures, and if he dissected that chunk of knowledge, he'd be committed to his shrink for the rest of his life.

His stomach quaked like a rookie. He reached for her before she could turn away. His fingers had never yearned to touch anyone like they did her, and he was weak enough to let them. "You're not running now." He pulled her in, and his lips crushed her protest. Her tongue slid into his mouth, and ardent desire fueled their flame.

Her head tilted back against the car, and he went in for it all, licking the soft spot beneath her ear, catching her moan, and loving her fingers pushing through his hair.

He fused his body to hers, needing her to feel what she did to him. How rock hard he'd become with every hair she touched, and every moan she released.

Their touching bodies added a complication they didn't need. A blip of conscious thought. "Tell me to stop," he demanded. His lips stamped a moist trail down her neck and across her silky collarbone.

He paused, dropping his forehead to rest between her shoulder and neck, soaking in her smell. Her heat. Her. His breathing came hard and restless, matching hers and dwindling his reasoning.

"Karis," he whispered. Her body shivered against his.

"I can't—"

Ty jerked his head up, his struggle reflected across her face. Their mouths held inches from touching. Sharing breath. He leashed his desire.

Her burning gaze pleaded for him. But her silent headshake muddied his interpretation of what she wanted.

A feather-soft touch landed on his chest, but she didn't push him away. Swallowing, her pink tongue peeked out, dampening her lips. "I can't tell you to stop."

With a gentle finger under her chin, he tilted her face, giving him the best angle to get inside her mouth and let her know what she'd given him permission to do. In no time, his impatient fingers invaded her waistband, gripping her tight, in a torturing combination of satiny skin, rough jean fabric, and a sliver of lace.

Sweet fingernails dug into his back.

"Jesus Christ, baby. Still so hot for you."

Her hands reached between them, cupping him through his hockey pants. He clenched his teeth and hissed with need, ready to lower her to the ground and dive into her wet center.

He slid his hand between her thighs, palming her warm mound. Her head fell against his shoulder. Her fingers curled around his wrist. Her legs widened. Her fingers covered his as he massaged her through her jeans. Pushing his hand against her heat, every bit of his control slipped away.

"Please," she begged, melting into his arms.

"That please was so unnecessary." He reached past her panties, sliding one finger into her wet core. The heel of his hand pressed against her swollen bud, and her sweet smell drifted into his nose, lighting him up.

"Ty," she sighed, arching her against him.

"You want more?" he whispered in her ear.

"Yes." She clawed at his shoulders.

"What do you want me to do?"

A sweet moan escaped her lips.

"This?" He slipped another finger between her folds. The jeans made it hard to maneuver, but nothing was going to keep her silky wetness from clenching his fingers.

She worked her fingers beneath his waistband. Her light touch slid over his skin and her hand encircled his cock. "Christ," he seethed, locking his knees and soaking in every graze of her touch.

Her core tightened around his fingers, and he withdrew quickly. The desire to be inside of her, turning him savage.

"We have to—"

He sucked in a breath awaiting her next words, because it would take everything he had to stop. "Karis, I couldn't stop right now if my life depended on it," he warned.

Her eyes brewed with lust and the need for release. He loved it.

"Ty?" she whimpered.

"You ready?" He spoke right outside her ear, and before she could say another word, he sunk three thick fingers inside her. She dug a hard score down his back. He fused his lips to hers, swallowing a sexy whimper as her body pulsed in his arms.

With her release, her tongue drank from his welcoming mouth. Her muffled scream sent him spinning. He'd drown in her if she'd let him.

Ty tore his mouth away and rested his forehead against hers. Slowly, he pulled his fingers from her contracting heat, and, staring into her, he slipped them into his mouth, and licked them clean.

"You were so wet for me." His lips blazed above hers. Her lithe body draped over his forearms. He held her with possession.

"Always," she whispered. Her lashes rested against her pink cheeks.

"Always?" The one word had him twisted. Aching to make her his.

Her delicate fingers brushed his waist. A spike of hope and need for a spelled-out explanation enveloped his brain.

"Always, and never another."

Was his brain still muddled with lust and, Holy God, wanting to be inside of her and live there until he died?

"What about Wes?" He didn't want it to be true and, reasonably, he didn't think it could be, because when Wes had been alive, they were together more often than not.

"Wes?" Karis moved out of his reach and buttoned her pants but didn't turn around.

He eased behind her, afraid to touch the very body he'd once devoured, and almost did seconds ago. Frustration held him hostage.

Her arms circled her waist, and his stomach twitched, aching to have her locked in his embrace. The air stilled, and she sucked in a shaky breath. Whatever she said next could break him.

"I let you go because Wes told me to." The words barely left her lips before fading in the air between them, but he heard every single one.

No way. No matter how many times he processed her words, they still didn't make sense. In any order.

Wes said to leave him.

Leave him, Wes said.

Said Wes to leave him.

The air clogged his breathing, and the night boxed him in. He clenched his fist tight enough to shatter bone. Even from the grave, Wes was still ruining him.

Karis shot him a watery look. Her swollen mouth, red from the pressure he'd happily put there, turned down at the corners. He jabbed a quick punch to the roof of his car. The smell of her lingered on his lips and fingertips. Her scent. Her words. All of it knocked him to his knees.

And no one knocked him to his knees anymore.

"This must be a fucking joke." He looked back at the house. The kitchen light burned a yellow haze through the pollen-covered windows. Smith and Lindsey stood at the sink. Iona sat at the table, smiling at the two punks washing dishes.

With everything locked up and looking as normal as possible, he cleared his throat and stole a second glance at Smith's smile. Losing Smith because of a stupid mistake on his part couldn't happen. Conversations about Wes stayed clear of Smith's earshot. Seeing the boy through the window was the wake-up call he needed.

With her scent covering his fingers, and clouding his mind, he guided Karis down the driveway, farther from the house. He didn't take chances where Smith was concerned.

"Ty, stop."

With each step, anger hooked into his core. All these years, he thought she'd abandoned him. He thought he'd done something wrong. That he wasn't enough for her. That he wasn't worth making hard decisions or conquering difficult situations.

He released her hand. "Explain. Now." The fewer the words, the less yelling.

She studied him, trying to get a read, like she used to after a game with her fucking psych bullshit.

"You do not get a minute to size me up and figure out how this is going to go. Talk to me."

Her perfect lips pursed ready for words. Her eyes, still moist with imminent tears, weakened the bubbling fury moving through his veins. He squeezed the waistband of his hockey pants, because, God help him, he needed to grab something and, for his sanity, it couldn't be her.

***

She recognized the stance. Feet wide. Shoulders, fresh from her hands, tight with tension. Her body pulsed with the memory of his fingers deep inside her, stirring up a longing for him she didn't deserve. He was right. She didn't expect to make everything better, but she didn't expect to melt in his hands, either.

He stepped closer, reducing her world to a muscled chest and adamant demands. A weakening combination.

She held her hands up. If he wanted to have this conversation, he couldn't come any closer.

The carved muscles beneath his T-shirt twitched. "What the hell, Karis? My fingers were just inside you and now you want me to stay away?" He slid into her space.

She backed up, defense stiffening her spine.

"Fuck!" he yelled, plowing his hands through his hair.

"Ty." She despised her shaky voice, but the words had to come out. "I ruined everything for us. All of it, and now seeing my family"—she looked toward the house, a suffocating regret curled within her—"I gave up everything I wanted."

"Karis, it can be—" Shadows filled the contours of his face, and her heart ached knowing she was hurting him all over again.

"Just let me finish." There was more to it than whatever black-and-white scenario playing in his head. The Florida night didn't have enough air to fill her lungs or calm her nerves. She concentrated on every word as best she could, trying to block out the feel of him slipping his fingers inside of her. The pure feeling of home his touch incited.

"So many years have gone by, and I can never—" She cleared her throat, forced her tears back, and glanced away from his grim frown. "I lost so many years because I thought I was doing the right thing. I was told to make you go without me." Swallowing her hesitation, she stole a look his way.

He'd never forgive her.

"I hate myself for giving you up. I hate myself for hurting you and hurting me, but I did what needed to be done. I had this life set up in my head about what I wanted, or more like, what I didn't want, so I did what you needed. Wes agreed. Staying at school was easier than going with you." She folded her arms over her stomach. A pathetic attempt to alleviate the pain.

"Karis," he whispered, killing her with sincerity.

"I just wanted you to have everything you had worked so hard for. And Wes," she tried, but watching Ty flinch at hearing his brother's name gave her pause.

His hurt and confusion jabbed at her heart. "For me, college meant independence, but from the beginning, I found you. And your future happened so fast, but I needed to support myself. I didn't want to rely on you for my future. Like my mom relied on so many men to make her happy, to pay her bills, to feed her children." The usual shiver rumbled through her core. "I would not turn into my mother, and I would not hold you back. Wes said a true pro had no room for a committed relationship anyway, and I wanted you to be a true pro. Didn't you deserve that?"

"No." Shaking his head, he took a step forward.

She pressed on with her conviction. "But you did. You deserved it all, and so did I." She wrapped her arms around herself and squeezed. "You deserved it more than anyone I'd ever met. From day one, you worked tirelessly to play professionally. We would hold each other back."

His brows knitted together, and his lips lay in a disappointed line. Defense flashed across his face. He squared his shoulders. "Did it ever occur to you I worked so hard for *us*? I knew exactly what you had grown up in and I wanted to make that better for you? I knew you needed to be independent, but you didn't trust me, and you took stock in what Wes told you. Jesus, Karis," Ty spat.

She stumbled over her thoughts, wanting to take back the insane conversation Wes had cornered her into having years ago.

"Wes just made so much sense, and confirmed my theory," she offered.

"He made sense, or he made it easy for you to have a life all your own? Were you ever all in with us?"

"Yes," she pleaded.

"You bailed on us. On all the long nights we spent planning and talking and crying and promising." Anger rang in every word.

She spoke fast. "Wes said you needed to establish yourself in the league. You needed to start building a career and that I would keep you from leveling up because you were so invested in me." She grimaced at the childish tone outlining her words.

"And you believed that shit?" He moved in, aligning his warm body close to hers, forcing her to look him in the eyes.

A desperate need to repair everything seized her, but where would she begin? Forgiveness didn't come easy. "I didn't know what to believe. He was your brother. Didn't he want you to make it? He knew the league. Knew what it took to be great, to be where you wanted to be."

"Yeah, he knew what it took to get a party buddy. To get leverage with a brother who put up enough points, no one would consider kicking his drug-addicted older brother out of the league for fear the superstar would quit."

"What?" *No, that's not how it went.* The dark world swayed. The fractured moon hung in the sky. Another weight ready to drop.

"Jesus, Karis. You know how this goes. I thought you followed hockey?"

"Not after—" Defeated and confused, she couldn't bring herself to say it.

"After what? You slayed me?" He wasn't holding back, and she deserved it. It hurt like hell.

She twisted her shirt and pushed her fingers into her stomach. Something had to stop the panic. "I couldn't watch you," she lied. "It was too hard."

"That's a pity because I did great."

"I know. I spoke to Wes, almost every weekend." Phone calls she swore to take to her grave.

"What?" His hard stare cornered her.

"I couldn't stomach the tabloids and hockey sites. In the pictures plastered everywhere, you didn't look broken up at all." Wes was her only access to him.

"Believe what you want. When I wasn't on the ice banging heads against the boards, I was pushing myself to injury in the weight room or wasted drunk with Wes. You should have had the balls to call *me* if you wanted to know how *I* was doing?" He jabbed a thick finger into his chest, driving his point home.

He had to understand. Mercy had to lie somewhere inside of him. "I didn't want to shake your game. Wes said you were thriving, and I couldn't look at you on the arm of some supermodel redhead. *Who was the new rookie dating? Rookie turned twenty-three at strip club.*" She quoted haunting taglines.

"So, you believed the tabloids and Wes. Great combo." He released a wicked laugh. "Do you have any idea the hell he was to live with? It was like living with my father again."

She cringed. "It couldn't have been. He was looking out for you."

"Please. How the fuck would you know?"

"He told me. He told me you were breaking records and making a name for yourself, just like you always wanted."

"Jesus. I could wring your neck. When did you ever start believing my family cared? Wes was a drug addict. Seriously addicted to speed because he never thought he was good enough and it killed him." His voice quieted, leaving the tension hanging in the air. His stance was so slack, Karis wondered how she could hold him up. Which would not have been a first. Ty's family was the one thing capable of cutting him to the knees.

"Wes and I fought nonstop. He wanted to go out night after night, after every game, on our off days, and I didn't."

Drinking was usually out of the question.

"No, you didn't," she offered.

His hard stare softened. "I'm surprise you remember."

"Of course, I remember," she whispered. His sleep schedule was for kindergartners, and his diet rivaled any nutritionist's, but it worked for him, and Karis respected it.

"Yeah, well, hockey players can put down some beer, and Wes was no exception. We started on separate teams, then he got traded to my team with a hush-hush condition. I needed to straighten him up. And you know how that always went."

"Wes didn't do anything he didn't want to."

"Right. When we were on the same team, I'd get calls from the coach to go find him. He'd be wasted in some bar, under a stack of women, and the payoffs were unbelievable."

"What?" she questioned.

"In my defense, half the time the coach would offer to pay and that was a hard no."

"My God, you guys are nuts. All this for a game."

"Damn right." Passion and commitment for the game ran deep among all players.

"So, the girls?"

"Yeah, the girls." He grabbed her hand and absently played with her fingers. She soaked in the feel of him and zeroed in on the tension rising.

"The last night he was alive"—Ty paused and squeezed his eyes shut— "I was trying to get a girl out of his hotel room, and he wouldn't open the door. I banged on it for twenty minutes. Finally, she came out and said I could have him. When she escaped, he locked the door and I never got in."

She laced her fingers with his, hoping he wouldn't stop talking.

"He screamed for me to leave him alone. He didn't need my super stardom glaring in his face. I was a piece of work, taking all the things he'd taught me and outplaying him. Making him look bad. Look weak." He swallowed and looked out over the dark yard.

"You know that's not true." All three Firestone boys were a mental mess, but this was brother to brother and not at all how they usually behaved. They had each other's back, no matter what. But life changed people.

"Those were my father's words." Exhaustion crept into his face. He rubbed his square jaw. "Pop and Wes spoke after each game, which continued to fuck Wes up. Anyway, that night he infuriated me, but he wanted me to leave him alone, so I told him to fuck off and left. Two hours later, I returned with the concierge. Wes lay on the floor, dead. Drug overdose."

"Oh, God." Without hesitation, she wrapped her arms around his waist and pulled him to her. His shoulders tensed beneath her touch, but she didn't care.

"I lost my mind trying to reconcile why I'd left him." His arms snaked around her waist, tucking her tight against him. He lodged his face into the crook of her neck. His quick gasps warmed her skin.

"Look at me." She looked up and into his face. He dodged her stare until she maneuvered herself where he had no choice but to meet her gaze. "You can't take the blame for this."

"Too late. I have and I do. Daily." His muscled arms bunched with each sweep of her fingers. So much hurt and sadness floated in his voice.

"He can take the blame for this, not you." She shifted her head to fit beneath his face. They were the only two people in the world.

Not quite.

"Uncle Ty? My dad overdosed?"

Panic flashed in Ty's widened eyes.

Her mind sorted through words, trying to land one or two powerful enough to ease his panic. Her brain refused to cooperate, and all she could do was watch Ty's world unravel around him.

Chapter Twelve

Ty was up to his frontal lobe in complications, and they continued to pile up one fucked-up issue after another. What happened to Wes was to never hit Smith's ears. Why work so hard to keep his father's mouth shut about it when Ty himself couldn't?

Goddamn it.

Not all Firestones needed to have a fast pass to therapy. He lived to keep Smith's life normal and happy. But she blinded him. Made him drop his guard, and he was about to pay the price. How could he be so stupid? They weren't in college anymore. They weren't young and free, if they ever were, with all their family baggage tucked into each crevice of their lives.

An alcoholic father who beat two-thirds of his sons into hockey greatness and a bed-hopping mother who slept with men to pay the bills. Ty Firestone and Karis Hill. A match made in constant dysfunction.

He crossed over to Smith, testing how close he could get before the boy bolted. Lost trust and all that. But Smith stood stiff. Lines of confusion ran across his forehead. Ty pressed fingertips into his chest. A pathetic attempt to erase the pain stabbing into his heart. For years, he'd kept Smith from the horrible truth of his father, and in one slip, one Karis-induced slip, his world tumbled head over ass.

"Uncle Ty?" he questioned.

His withering trust a dropkick to the gut. Ty held his breath, waiting for the fog to lift.

Smith backed away from him. The movement more painful than any hit Ty ever took on the ice. A clawing desperation worked its way up his spine, burning him from the inside out. There had to be a way to make him understand.

"Smith, listen to me." He spoke every deliberate word gently and sent a silent prayer straight to anyone who could help him explain his deceit.

"You told me my dad had a bad heart. You said it was a heart attack. You never talked about a drug overdose. My dad was a drug addict?" Smith's rapid-fire questions hit him like a goalie, with no saves.

"It's not that simple," Ty tried again.

"No," Smith yelled. "Answer the question. Was he a drug addict? Is that how he died? He was a junkie?"

His head raced with too many lies. Life didn't run linear. It was jagged and crisscrossed. Complicated. But the lies were crushing. "There's more to it than that. You can't just—"

"Yes, I can. Answer the question," Smith shouted. His posture became more rigid with each word. A wild rage churned behind his eyes, edging him toward total anger.

Ty stretched his brain for a way to make him understand. "Your dad had a heart attack"—he paused and swallowed hard— "but it was drug induced."

"What does that even mean?" Smith's tall body folded, his arms circling his slender frame. A broken child.

"It means—" Ty released a breath. His heart pummeled the inside of his chest. He deserved it. Smith doubled over, in pain, mutilated his reasoning. He couldn't let that happen. "Your dad had a big life. He played his ass off, and was a huge success, and yes"—Ty clenched his teeth and grounded his molars close to dust—"he started drugs to enhance his game, which if the league were to find out while he was playing, he would have been suspended or kicked out."

"But he used drugs?" Smith reached for exact answers with a tone unlike the teenage-cracking, semi-deep puberty voice he'd had since last year.

Ty surrendered. "Yes." Smith's face crumbled and Ty rushed to explain. "I had no idea how much or how often." He pinched the bridge of his nose, wishing this conversation was happening ten years from now.

"Didn't you try to stop him?" Smith pleaded.

Did a thirteen-year-old have the mental capacity to figure this shit out? Jesus. At thirty-eight, Ty struggled to figure it out. He held Smith by the forearms, desperate to reach him with the truth. "Yes. Yes. Every day. Every game. Every minute."

"All this time, I was so scared I would lose you and that was all a lie?" Smith asked. His gaze drifted. His voice faded.

"Why would you lose me? You're not going to lose me." He stood up, trying to piece together Smith's comments.

"You told me my dad died of a heart attack. All the research I've done says heart attacks run in families."

Another blow to the stomach. "You've researched heart attacks?" Fucking Internet. He scrubbed his jaw. The sandpaper too dull to put him out of his misery.

Smith gave a shy shrug. "Yeah, I researched it. I needed to know. I needed to know what might kill you and what might kill me."

He'd never survive raising a kid. Smith meant more to him than breathing. How was he supposed to cope with the sadness and the mistakes?

"Ty." Karis' hand warmed his biceps, leveling him back to reality. He wanted to drop to his knees and pull her close. Smother his face against her stomach and let her scent clear his conscience. Lift the fog. The warmth of her touch soothed him, and that was a problem. He wouldn't allow his weakness for her to ruin Smith. Not again.

"Smith, listen." He knocked the rust off his voice.

"You lied. My dad killed himself, and you lied to me about it." Anger and disappointment outlined each word. "I've been freaking out for so long about what killed him and is it going to kill me, you, Uncle Ryan, Pop? But what do you care? You have a dad."

"Stop right there." Everybody had a breaking point. An unknown line drawn in the sand. Invisible until crossed.

"Ty, don't." Even Karis couldn't stop him.

What the hell did she know about how to talk to or reason with a teenager? His heartbeat spiked. He clenched his hands into fists, angling for control. Smith didn't dare look his way, a quick elbow to his already bruised heart. But, if he was going to dish it out, he was going to have to take it.

"Yeah, lucky me. I have a dad. A dad who ruined me and my brother with his competitive psychotic torture. You want a dad so bad, Smith, take mine. I did what I thought was right by you. No kid wants to know their dad died of a drug overdose."

"Ty," Karis pleaded with one look.

He distanced himself and glanced up at the stars. Anything else he said would, for sure, morph into regret. He steadied himself and met Smith's lock-hard stare. "You want the truth? Here you go. Your dad thought he wasn't good enough. He competed his way through life, and it took him down. Why did he do that? Easy. It was how Pop raised him. Hockey ruled, and he had to be number one. His body hurt with unimaginable pain. He took pills to enhance his performance on the ice and he took pills to kill the pain off the ice. And if you ever do that to your body, I'll kill you myself."

He loved Smith more than life, and he would not let him venture down Wes' path. The message had to be clear.

Without a word, Smith dredged back to the house. Taking a body against the boards or blocking a puck was cake compared to fathering. He'd been trained all his life, but never for this.

"What about my mom?" Smith stood on the porch, with Lindsey on wing, ready to protect.

Karis eased up behind him. Her presence, a cursed comfort, required a great deal of concentration to stay focused. "What about her?" Ty steeled himself and waited for the next question. He had several swift, acceptable answers. Each one a lie.

"Did she leave me?" Smith asked.

It's for his own good. It's all for his own good. At thirteen, Ty would have loved Pop out of his life. He sucked in a breath and steeled his guilt. "We've talked about this, Smith."

"Answer the question," Lindsey demanded.

"Lindsey," Karis warned.

Ty reached behind his back, and her hand fell right into his.

"Yes. She did, and I am so sorry. If I could change all of this, I would. In a minute. In a heartbeat."

He pulled Karis up the porch steps. Dropping her hand, he faced his shattered nephew. "I'm not going to apologize for doing what I think is right for you."

"You think lying to me about my father is right for me?" Smith asked. Hurt and defense structured every syllable.

Later, after they left Karis' house, Smith would ask to stop at the rink so he could shoot pucks and Ty would comply. It was Smith's way of handling stress and working off frustration. He'd pay a million dollars a year for ice time if that's what Smith needed. Anything to steer him away from the path his father had taken.

Ty chose his words carefully. "I think doing whatever I can to keep you safe is right for you."

Smith stared. "That's a safe answer."

"That's my answer."

"That's weak," Smith countered.

"And so am I on most nights these days." Ty glanced at Karis. His biggest weakness of all.

Chapter Thirteen

"You know he's only thirteen, right?" Ryan shot the basketball, scoring another basket. Nothing like getting your ass handed to you by your little brother and getting sucked dry by early evening mosquitoes at the same time.

"He's been my responsibility since he was two, Ryan. I'm well aware of how old Smith is."

Ty shot and missed the basket just as beautifully as Ryan had nailed it.

Every early evening for the past three weeks, in front of no one else —thank goodness— Ty humiliated himself on his home basketball court. If he didn't think about how much he sucked at it, basketball could actually be his therapy. A sick, twisted therapy where he got in his head and wrapped around his thoughts, discovering no answer to any of his issues.

Since the night Smith overheard the truth about Wes overdosing, sunset basketball had been Ty's outlet of choice. It would take years to rectify the worst night of his life, followed by the longest silent treatment known to man. But at least by then, perhaps he'd be a stellar b-ball player.

The nasty hangover of disappointing people was nothing new. He'd been chipping down rosters and eliminating players for years, but nothing compared to the cut-him-to-the-core sadness he saw in Smith. Their communication trickled down to a few grunts and some jaw-grinding nods. Luckily, Smith was still chatty-chatty with Ryan, so Ty relied on him for updates on mood and disposition.

"So what did you and Smith talk about at lunch today?" Once in a while, Smith and Ryan ventured to lunch without him. Fine. But today it burned in his stomach and had him working out in the rink's gym like a young professional player with too much to prove. No thirty-eight-year-old needed to be lifting the amount of weight he'd lifted, but until Smith decided he wanted to reconnect, Ty had to live with old man body aches.

He needed Smith to talk to him like he needed air, and pushing his body beyond its limits took a bit of the edge off. Plus, it was better than the normal self-pity Firestone pastime.

Ryan snatched the ball from Ty's missed shot. "You know I can't tell you that."

"You can, but you won't. You're no help." He reached for the ball.

"So not true."

Swish.

Dammit.

"Then tell me." Ty dribbled with no shot in sight.

Ryan grabbed the ball, and they squared up. The man was enormous. Shoulders wide. Intimidating to any player in any sport. Except for his older brother.

Ty snagged the ball and took a shot. The net laughed at him. "Fuck me," he cursed under his breath. Could he get a sliver of mercy?

"Ah, no thanks." Ryan held the ball and sat down on the driveway gulping water and swatting mosquitoes.

Resigned to defeat, Ty snatched his water bottle, squirted Ryan in the face, and plopped down next to him.

"Basketball will not fix your problem with Smith." Ryan wiped his face with his T-shirt.

"Don't underestimate the power of basketball. Smith used to come out here with me every time he heard the ball bounce."

Ryan chuckled. "When he was nine. He's a young man now. He needs his space."

Ty smirked and glanced up at Smith's dark bedroom window. "No, I'm pretty sure he's figured out I did it on purpose."

"You're right. He's totally on to you, but I still think you get points for trying. Remember what Pop used to do when he wanted to manipulate us into spending quality time with him?"

Ty squirted water on his head. "No."

"That's because he never did."

"I saw that coming." Ty draped his arms over his bent knees. "The only time I spent quality time with Pop was when he was shooting pucks at me." He swore at the memory.

Ryan didn't know much about the abuse his older brothers suffered at the hands of their father. Ty and Wes made sure of that. Through the years, and with Wes gone, Ty divulged more and more about his tortuous childhood, and Ryan shared his perspective. He didn't make it out of the Firestone house unscathed. Neglect was its own form of torture.

"My favorite was when he sat on me and forced me to do push-ups. At midnight."

"Oh, yeah, that I remember. No push-ups, no dinner," Ryan snarled.

"Who the hell wants dinner after an hour of push-ups?" Ty leaned back, the grit of the driveway dug into his palms.

"But look who we are today." Ryan dropped his head back and faced the sky.

His brother always tried to find some explanation for his talent. "Don't give Pop that power." His voice hitched. "You would have been a professional hockey player no matter what. Your success had nothing to do with him." Their father didn't deserve credit for what they'd become. The older Firestones had endured many nights of impossible workouts while Ryan sat in his bedroom listening to the moans and grunts of his older brothers. The understanding between Wes and Ty included compliance with Pop's regiment as long as Ryan was left alone. They never considered the harm silence could do.

Ryan wiped his forehead. "He had something to do with it."

Raking his hands through his hair, Ty watched Smith's bedroom light snap on. "You're an elite player. You had that in you without Pop screwing with your head. Hockey lives inside you, and you found it, regardless. I know it."

Ryan's heavy hand slapped him on the back, rocking him forward. "Well, look at you, Coach, getting all feels on me."

"What the fuck is feels?" Ty looped a towel behind his neck.

"Jesus, Ty. You'd never know you were the parent of a teenager. It's warm and fuzzies," Ryan explained.

"Christ. I am not getting all *feels*." He wiped his mouth across his shoulder.

"You so are." Ryan's smile stretched ear to ear. "And I'm guessing, total shot in the dark, it might have something to do with—"

"Don't you dare say her name."

"Oooo, look at that. I didn't have to say her name. You're gone on her again."

Accepting defeat, he hung his head. Karis brought out every fucking *feels* he possessed. Three weeks had gone by since he'd actually seen her physically, but she haunted him every single day.

The night in her driveway was the memory he fell asleep to. Her warm body clenching him, her hands in his hair, her green heated eyes begging for mercy, but demanding more. She claimed him with her lips and thighs and moisture, and he dove right in.

"I know what you're thinking, and you need to stop." Ryan interrupted his thoughts.

The sky darkened. The mosquitoes buzzed, ready to feast.

"I'm good." Ty stared straight ahead.

"Liar. But I'm out." Ryan stood and offered Ty his hand. "Come on, old man. Let's go before the mosquitoes suck us dry."

Groaning with mock aches and pains, Ty jumped up and palmed the basketball in one hand and gripped his water bottle with the other. "You staying here tonight?"

Ryan had never gotten around to purchasing his own house. Hockey paid him plenty of money, but he'd never settle down in a place of his own. Understandable. Laying down roots meant commitment.

"No. I'm heading over to see what Pop's up to."

Ty started back to the house. "I don't understand what you have with Pop."

Ryan never minced words, something about Oprah and a short life. "I just think he wanted for us what he didn't have for himself, and it consumed him. He hated his own parents because they didn't push him the way he needed to be pushed, and when Mom left," Ryan sighed, "well, he just needed to make it worth it."

Both men stood on the back porch, needing to finish the conversation before donning their game faces and hitting reality.

"You're a good man, Ryan. A better man than me, on any given day."

"The ways of Oprah are amazing." Ryan held up his hands, but Ty knocked them down.

"All hail, Oprah," Ty teased.

"You should," Ryan confirmed.

Another Ryan mystery.

Ty had considered reading Oprah and anything else capable of helping him feel less burdened, but he just couldn't make it stick. "I can't find it in my heart to forgive Pop. It's not in me and I don't want it to be. I respect how you feel about him. I want to break his face for what he did to us. All of us."

"Well, there are times I want to break his face, too, but you feel strongly about that because..." Ryan swallowed past a thick pause.

Ty grabbed his shoulder. "Because I found Wes, I know."

Ryan spoke into the night. "I wish every day..." His voice cracked, and a shard landed in Ty's heart. "I wish every day that you weren't the one to find him. I wish it could have been me. Anybody but you. I think you've had your fill of crazy."

Imagining Ryan finding Wes made Ty's stomach roll with the need to purge.

He stared hard at his little brother. "No. It played out the exact way it needed to. If you would have found him, I would be more out of my mind than I am already, and we both know I'm way past steady." He sighed. "Karis is going to be the death of me." He pulled his hand down his face.

Ryan cracked a smile. "Nah, you can handle Karis, but you have to stop trying to protect Smith and me from Pop. We can handle it, plus he's too old and we're too strong."

Ty disagreed. "Words can cut as much as a punch. Pop's drinking is brutal, and I don't want Smith thinking that's normal."

"Ty, Smith knows. He's smart."

"I know." Ty gripped his hips, hung his head, and counted the lines on the planked floor. "God that kid. Emotions I put away years ago are back, and I know it's because of Karis, so don't even bother." He felt raw and worn out but kept those *feels* to himself. Ryan would just worry.

"I think having her back in your life is good for you." Always the optimist.

"Why?" Did it show on the outside? How much he needed her?

"Because it makes you think about yourself."

"I don't have that luxury," Ty whispered.

"Said every miserable parent on the planet. You have to deal with Karis. Face how she makes you feel, head-on. Don't pussy out on this."

"Jesus, Ryan. You just went all psycho, Doctor Phil, Oz, Oprah all at once. What the hell?"

"Don't even think of judging Oprah. I love that chick and every word in her magazine is quotable. So back the fuck off."

Ty didn't want to touch his brother's obsession with Oprah. If that worked for him, who the hell was he to judge?

"Hey, I get it. I don't understand it and I thought you were over her, but damn, whatever works for you?" Ty raised his arms in surrender.

"Oprah and I thank you. We appreciate it." Ryan opened the back door. Ty stepped into the kitchen just as Smith skipped down the stairs.

"Uncle Ty, I need you to take me somewhere."

Not the words he thought he would hear when Smith started talking to him again. "Okay, I can handle being used for a ride. Where're we going?"

"Lindsey's."

Ryan's head flew back, and his huge laugh boomed through the kitchen. Ty grabbed the counter, giving his hands something else to do other than throw knives.

He ignored Ryan's bouncing eyebrows and looked at Smith with as much indifference as he could muster. "Fine, let's go."

***

One bonding game of basketball and Lindsey wanted to play *every* night. The therapeutic dribble and the slight swish of rubber against the net, all combined for a sweaty mosquito fest of love and ignited a connection between aunt and niece. After dinner, basketball started promptly at six and continued until the ball slipped from their sweaty hands and their feet ached. The bond building offered more than a necessary escape. It offered family and an unbreakable tie.

Karis jumped and whacked the ball from Lindsey's hands. "Sorry." She raised her arms, palms up, above her head. The hit was a little too hard.

"Jeez, Aunt Karis. It's driveway basketball, not the WNBA."

Karis huffed and pivoted on the paved driveway, her mind replaying the conversation she'd had with her boss twenty minutes before. Basketball had been her go-to for stress relief since she could dribble a ball at age four. Tonight, she needed some hardcore dribbling.

"I know, too hard, sorry." She grabbed the ball from the long grass. When would she cut that? The honey-do list grew a mile a day.

"So, am I packing my stuff?" Lindsey snagged the ball and dribbled to the basket.

"Not yet. My boss gave me one more month. He's allowing me to set up virtual sessions with the players as long as they don't mind."

She would never understand how she lucked out with a boss like Mr. Lavitier. Realistically,

another month would do nothing for her. Hockey would still be in full swing, and Iona's doctor's appointments would still fill the calendar. She couldn't take care of any of it without a steady paycheck.

Chewing on her lips, she held her hands out for the ball. "I hope it works."

"We have jobs in Florida, ya know." Lindsey stole the ball and dribbled to the hoop.

All net.

"I know." Karis bit her tongue and took a shot.

Never in a million years was moving back home a consideration. Not with the money she made in NC.

"Aunt Karis?" Lindsey dribbled.

"Yeah, babe?"

"I want Grandma back the way she used to be."

"Me, too, and in my heart the right thing to do is to keep Mom, Grandma," she corrected, "in a familiar setting, but I have to work."

Lindsey shuffled around the driveway with the ball tucked under her elbow. "I can work at the rink, or..." She paused, her gaze floating off. "I can quit hockey, if that helps us stay."

One selfless act, and Karis' entire world shifted. No way, over her broke dead body, would Lindsey give up hockey. "Not happening. We can make it work as long as I have a job. We have hockey in North Carolina, too, ya know." She flashed Lindsey a smile.

"But my team's here," Lindsey countered, blocking her attempt to snatch the ball.

Not even close, thank you very much.

Lindsey laughed. "Man. I still can't believe how good you are at basketball."

She took a shot and, boom, landed it.

"Gee, thanks? Not sure that was said with 'I am so good' disbelief or a 'wow, you are the coolest aunt ever.'"

Lindsey dribbled to the edge of the driveway. "It's totally 'you are the coolest aunt ever,' and you would be the coolest/best aunt ever, if you take me to the rink tonight for stick and shoot." Lindsey shot and missed.

"Oh, here we go. You think missing a shot on purpose and letting me win is going to make me take you to stick and shoot? You can shoot pucks in the driveway." She swiped at the ball in Lindsey's hand.

"I'm not losing on purpose, and driveway shooting sucks. I need ice."

She tucked the ball into her hip and glared at her niece. "I took you to stick and shoot last night. It's twenty bucks a pop."

"Yeah, but it'll be so packed tonight we can get away with not paying. They won't even see me."

"Have you seen yourself play?"

Lindsey shot her a dirty look.

"You're not easy to overlook." But worth a try to save twenty bucks.

"Aww, thanks." Lindsey bumped her shoulder.

"You know I could get out there with you."

"Uh, really?" Lindsey's laugh put a warm pile of happy right in the middle of Karis' stomach.

Check making a teenager laugh off the bucket list. She nudged Lindsey. "Hey, I can skate. Who do you think helped your coach with his passing?"

"No way," Lindsey stuttered, her jaw dropping wide open.

"Yes way."

"Totally yes way." Ty stalked up the driveway. Smith strolled two steps ahead, showing the world they were still at odds.

"What are you doing here, Smith?" Lindsey snarled.

"You texted me you were going outside to play basketball. I wanna play."

Lindsey scooted closer to Karis. "Well, my text wasn't an invitation."

His brows bunched. "Why would I need an invitation? I come over all the time." Poor kid.

Ty pulled Smith back by the shoulder, but he shrugged him off. A battle of wills. Tangible tension snapped between them.

Ty tried to take the edge off. "Your aunt used to play ball with me all the time. Then we'd go to the rink to shoot pucks. She's a sports nut."

Those days were long gone. Karis wrapped her arms around her stomach, avoiding Lindsey's flicker of curiosity. He remembered. She swallowed hard and let her gaze breeze over to his. He held her stare, saying so much with so little. With his grip still tight on Smith, he flashed a half-hearted smile and dragged Smith back down the driveway.

Karis tucked pieces of Lindsey's blonde flyaways behind her ear. "Maybe you should take Smith inside. Play a game or watch a video or something." The argument between Ty and Smith, pursuing with sharp hand gestures and whispered tones, would not end well.

"I want to stay with you."

A little sweet and heart melting, but totally transparent. A teenager could turn in seconds. Where would sweet Lindsey be when she mentioned moving again? Every time Karis reached into her bank account, her palms morphed into pools of sweat, and her vision clouded, rendering her worthless for at least two minutes. Spending money was her worst trigger. Thank God basketballs were cheap.

"We can play later, but right now I think Smith might need someone to talk to. Other than his uncle." Karis gestured to the men standing against the car in deep conversation. Their voices rising to a combative level.

Lindsey tightened her ponytail. "Maybe you're right."

"Maybe I am," Karis remarked, hiding her smile.

"He's upset. Coach lied to him about his dad." Lindsey grumped and dribbled the ball between her legs.

"Did Smith tell you that?" She treaded lightly.

"Kind of. In his Smith way." Lindsey palmed the ball.

"Yeah, I think I know that way." She knew it all right. Smith was a mini-Ty.

"He's always been a health nut because of the way he thought his dad died. It was cool in the beginning. He was so healthy, but he got really crazy about it. And he's not gonna let the lying go," Lindsey confided.

The buzz in the air shifted. Ty and Smith sauntered up the driveway. A mountain of anger rising between them.

Ty clapped his hands and planted a fake smile across his face. "You guys ready to play?"

Smith grabbed Lindsey's shirt and pulled her up the steps and into the house.

Taking a deep breath, Karis faced Ty, not prepared for the amount of strength it took to keep her arms from wrapping around him. His creased brow and straightened lips tried to slide into a smile, but with sagging shoulders, he was all heartbreak.

Time for an outlet.

"How about some basketball?"

Ty jogged to the net and picked up the ball with fluid ease. Defined muscles flexed and bunched under his thin T-shirt. For a large man, he moved with grace. Cut thighs and a tight core, pure athlete. Covering most of the ball with his large grip, he dribbled her way. His light-blue shirt brushed his ripped flat stomach, and the sleeves expanded with every bounce. Every emotion crashed into her, and she boxed out the conflicting urge to run inside the house or climb him like a tree.

They could handle a harmless game of basketball. In school, they played all the time. If only she could forget how his tongue tangled with hers the last time they were outside together, maybe she could bring her body temperature down a couple of degrees and focus on the game. She peeled her sweaty shirt away from her stomach, fanning it to circulate some air.

"You think you can take me?" he clipped.

His dribble stumbled, but the ball landed in his hands, and he planted it against his hip with his elbow. A smolder flooded with shared memories lit up his eyes. He would always have this control over her. "That was stupid. Forget I said that."

"I can't." She caught the ball and dribbled. "Not sure this is a good idea." They were both suffocating in responsibility.

"I'm pretty sure it's not."

"So, game on, then?"

"Game on."

She darted around him, making moves like a swift ballerina. He was an athlete, true, but basketball was more her thing.

Swish.

"Nice shot, Aunt Karis."

Lindsey and Smith jogged down the steps.

Ty leaned in close. "I don't think she wants us to be alone."

Karis didn't want them to be alone, either. "You guys want to play?"

"We were hoping you could take us to stick and shoot," Lindsey chirped.

"Twenty bucks. So that's a no. Plus, you went last night." Her head cha-chinged like a cash register.

"If I take them, it costs nothing." Ty threw Smith a challenging look.

"Do you want to take them?" Karis asked.

The two men studied each other in a battle of wills. "Yeah, I can take them. I'll hang there while they skate. It's an hour, right?" He checked his watch.

"Yeah. I'll go get my stuff." Lindsey ran back into the house. Without a word, Smith headed to the car.

With some quiet time at home, getting a little work done was in sight for the first time in a long time. She could do a lot in an hour. "I'm going to check on Mom." She jumped up the first step.

"How is she?" Ty asked.

He didn't need the real answer. "She's fine."

"I want the real answer." He stepped to the stairs.

He read right through her. Like always. "She'll be all right. We have a few more doctors' appointments and we'll get more answers then." Her hands shuffled in the air, emphasizing each word. "They're trying to regulate her medicine and watch her diet."

"What can I do?" His voice cradled her thoughts.

So much.

Lindsey bounced out the front door. "I'm ready."

"I guess you can take them to stick and shoot," she suggested.

"I'll take them and then come back, and we can talk."

She wasn't about to spew her doubts to him. He'd want to fix everything, and he had his hands full with Smith.

Lindsey interjected herself between them. "Wait, you always stay with us," Lindsey stated.

Ty's brows drew together.

"Yeah, but he doesn't have to. We're fine. We've been there a million times without him," Smith lobbied, obviously not wanting Ty there, and Lindsey, just as obviously, didn't want him here. Poor Ty, if his ego wasn't healthy, this could be a problem.

"Aunt Karis, you'll be fine here with Grandma, right?" Worry flittered across her face.

Mutilating her lip between her teeth, Karis rubbed Lindsey's arms. "I'll be fine here. You go. Don't worry."

"You sure?"

It couldn't be healthy to have such a full plate. Thirteen-year-old's needed fun.

"Lindsey," Karis moaned. "Go." She turned, yelling to Ty as he stuffed Lindsey's hockey bag in the car. "She's ready."

Ty slammed the trunk a little harder than necessary and headed back to Karis. His dark hair hung over his forehead. She loved it when he didn't wear a hat. Hair like that shouldn't be covered.

Their eyes locked. Heat sizzled in the tiny space between them. Towering over her, she challenged the need to press her face against his chest and soak in every bit of pleasure and protection he offered. She shouldn't want his arms thrown around her shoulders, blocking out the world, or his words whispered into her ears, promising everything would be okay. She controlled her life, and could make herself feel secure, not a man.

He backed away. "You'll be fine here?" he questioned in a rough voice.

"Yeah, I'll be fine. It's better that you take them so I can stay with Mom."

"They're not in charge of us," he said. "I can drop them off. Come back and we can sit and..." He looked down the driveway at the two kids running around his car like five-year-olds.

"And we can what?"

Ty curled his fingers around his neck, massaging at the sides, no doubt filled with tension from the strain of staying away from each other. They smiled, and she wanted to laugh. A mother losing her mind, kids running around the car, and a million bills to pay. An unrecognizable version of Karis and Ty.

Stepping close, his words held promise and danger. "Honestly, if I come back here without them, there's no telling what I'll do. You make me lose myself."

She bit down hard on her lip, but there was no stopping the heat pooling between her legs. Her stomach did its part with a flip and flutter. He shouldn't say things like that.

He moved more into her space. A curse sighed past his lips. "I don't trust what we were, what we didn't become, and I can't be this. It's too hard for me." His voice deepened. "I want inside you every fucking time I see you, smell you, hear you. I'm on the downslide. Spinning out of control."

Everything she wanted to say shouldn't be said.

He pounced on her hesitation. "I'll be back in ten." He walked away, giving her the masculine width of his back.

She gripped her thighs, trying to latch onto something grounding because all she wanted to do was run her fingertips over his skin. "Ty," she called, stopping him.

Needing to keep her words private, she met him toe to toe. The scent of piney soap invaded every clear thought she possessed, but she pushed through.

"I don't think it's a good idea to leave Lindsey," she muddled.

He tuned in immediately. "What do you mean?"

She glanced at his car, making sure the kids were still busy chasing each other. Indeed, they were, but now they had a hockey ball involved.

"I think she's struggling with how to feel about everything. This is the first time in days she's been willing to be out of my sight."

"Really? What does that mean?" Profound concern filled his face.

"I've done some research and reached out to some of my colleagues. They suggest therapy, of course," she lowered her voice.

"Of course," Ty said.

Ignoring his jab, she continued, "She feels unsure, off-balance, and doesn't trust adults. I think she's nervous I'm going to leave her."

"Christ." Ty's features softened, and he glanced at the kids skipping around the car.

"Right, so I think you should stay. I mean, you've been her coach for two summers and she loves Smith, so maybe staying might help her see she can trust us."

Us. Oh boy.

"Sounds good. Then I'll stay."

They were two adults with fucked-up childhoods trying to prevent more fucked-up childhoods.

She shoved her hands into her hair. "I can't leave either of them alone at the moment. I know you have a lot going on with Smith right now—"

"No. We got this." He regarded her with warm sincerity.

She reached for the front door. "I hope you're right."

Chapter Fourteen

Karis handled her family like a pro. A trait Ty admired. She possessed a remarkable ability to shut out, hide, and run. All dangerous options. Dealing with Iona and Lindsey stretched her grasp on the one thing she put above all else: her independence. He could see it in her tired eyes, in her faded smile, and in her doubtful decisions. Harnessing the urge to call the shots took every ounce of his strength. She'd resent him even more if he tried to help, but seeing her struggle did him in. He wanted to wrap his arms around her and absorb all the pain and exhaustion taking over. After all these years, his innate need to take care of her continued to possess him. He knew better.

She'd hate him for that archaic thought.

He'd stay at the rink with Smith and Lindsey because if he didn't get his mind right, crazy would come calling. Next stop, the looney bin. His muscles clenched tight with every wrong he wanted to make right. He needed to murder some pucks. Fast.

Entering the rink, he tugged his hat down low. No one needed to see the heat behind his eyes. Because clearly, the lust he had running through his veins was visible on his face. It had to be.

Finding vacant ice was imperative.

"Hey, stop messing around. Go get dressed, and get on the ice," he projected.

"What number locker room?" Lindsey asked.

Even at the rink, Smith avoided him. Couldn't ask him a simple question, had Lindsey do it for him. Ty swore the two kids could read each other's minds. Scary teenagers.

"Read the board. I'll be on rink three if you need me."

Kids of all ages ran around shoeless. Parentless. Independence, ice hockey, and summer. A perfect combination.

Lucky for him, the grouchy rink owner kept rink three empty for professional players and coaches. Tonight, it belonged to Ty.

Booted up, he took to the ice. Each grounded dig into the frozen surface eased the pressure a little more. She rattled him. Altered his focus.

Slap!

The puck sailed, a blur of black.

Smith may never trust him again. No offense to Karis, but it didn't take a psych degree to see the armor Smith built around himself. Just like Karis, right before she sent him packing. Ty could specialize in fucked-up people. The need to take care of them ached deep in his bones. Was it that bad to want to take care of the people you loved?

Slap!

The puck flew to the net. Bar down. Boom. He rolled his clenched shoulders and rested his sweaty forehead against the gooey knot of tape at the end of his stick. Taking deep breaths, he opened his mind and prepared for the onslaught of thoughts. Smith wasn't talking to him because he lied. Karis left him because she thought he would be better off, brainwashed by his drug-addicted brother. Lindsey, Smith's only friend, had a grandmother who may not know her in the future and a mother who may never come back. Then there was Ryan. The sweetie pie of them all, trying to get Ty to love their father and build a "family." Insane. All of it. The pressure ripe for explosion.

"Uncle Ty."

Slap!

The puck flew to the net and Smith dove to the ice.

"What the fuck, Smith?" He raced to his nephew, dropped his gloves, and leaned over him, running his hands over his shoulder and scanning him from helmet to skate.

"What hurts? Christ, make some noise when you come on the ice."

"Jeez, Coach, you didn't have to shoot at him," Lindsey yelled from the bench.

Ty righted himself and offered Smith help up. Surprise and relief combined when Smith took his hand and stood. Ty waited for him to say something. One word and he would spill his guts until Smith understood the reasoning behind his choices.

Patience eluded him.

He took one lap around the boards, willing everything good inside of him to emerge with his next few words spoken to the one person he loved more than anything. The one person he could hurt the most.

Ice sprayed as he came to a halt in front of Smith.

"I would never, ever do anything to hurt you." Frigid air surged into his heaving lungs.

"I know," Smith heaved.

Ty coughed. "Everything I do, everything"—he couldn't keep his teeth from clenching—"all of it is for you. To keep you happy, to keep you safe."

"I know." Smith's voice floated quiet and small.

"Then why the cold?"

"You lied. We don't lie to each other. We were supposed to trust each other."

Ty caught the grunt before it exploded from his mouth. Smith recited the same words Ty had spoken to him a million times. Apparently, Smith *had* been listening.

"I know." He became the kid getting reprimanded. His whole body shook, wanting to grab Smith and wrap him in the un-manliest, un-hockey-like hug possible, but he didn't. He didn't have to.

In a flash, Smith wrapped his gloved hands around Ty's waist. The power, raw and hard, consumed them both. Three weeks of resentment and confusion released in one long grip.

He couldn't get his arms around Smith fast enough. He swallowed the emotion teetering on the edge of erupting. No way was he going to lose it on the ice. No way. Well, maybe. He held Smith as tight as he could without making them both fall on their asses.

Smith's grip lightened. Ty held his breath, waiting to see what would come next.

"Did he kill himself?" Smith stared at the ice. His words quiet and almost inaudible.

Defeat rolled over him.

A ton of questions had to be wrestling in his mind. Wanting answers, he was afraid of hearing, but needed all the same. It reminded Ty of why Ryan didn't leave Pop. The hope. The hope of family. Belonging.

Ty pinched his lips. "No way. He did not kill himself. He did not want to leave you."

"Then why?" Smith screamed, doubling over, his blades digging into the ice. Ty reached for him but thought better of it. Smith needed to get it out.

Across the ice, Lindsey jumped up from the bench, ready to skate their way. Anything to protect Smith. A perfect ally, but he and Smith needed to hash this out. He signaled an all good. Lindsey nodded and sat back down.

"My God, Smith," he released on a breath. "I wish I knew. Your dad was a good guy. A great hockey player."

"Not that great," Smith righted. Tears streamed down his face.

"Yeah, that great," he disagreed, holding Smith by the forearms. "He lived with so much anger and bitterness twisted inside of him, and he just couldn't kick it."

"So, he did it on purpose. I wasn't enough to make him want to stay."

"Not true." His coach's voice snapped back full force. Taking a thousand lashes, which he was sure he'd done in his younger days, would have been easier than seeing Smith fall apart.

Smith drifted toward the exit, but Ty cut him off, spraying ice against his skates. "You were more than enough to make him stay, but your mom never let him see you. She held you over his head to get money and then snatched you away so fast."

"Why didn't he try to take care of me full-time?"

"Oh man, Smith." *Goddamn it, Wes.* He leaned on his hockey stick, resting his mouth against the handle. Smith waited. The stillest Ty had ever seen him. He waited for the answers that would make everything okay, but those answers didn't exist.

"He wanted you so bad, but..." He looked away. Smith's sadness gutted him.

"But what?"

Ty shrugged. "He played hockey." A pathetic excuse. The silence and silliness of the answer hung over them. Stupid, but completely understandable to a hockey family.

"I could have gone with him. I could have stayed with Pop when he traveled."

Ty stretched his arm out, balancing his stick. "Pop? Really? I wouldn't do that to anyone." He grabbed Smith by the shoulder pads. "Listen to me, your dad was a great, great man. An elite hockey player, who loved you so much, but was blinded by the drive to be the best. Nothing could make him let go of that. Nothing."

"Except drugs."

Time to get real. "Except the allure to forget. He couldn't handle it. It was too much, and I hate him for that. I hate him for leaving you and me." Ty cleared the knot forming in his throat. The pain in Smith's eyes undid him. Looking to the rafters, Ty prayed for a pass from the hockey gods.

"How did it happen?"

Ty shook his head.

"Come on."

"No way. Forget it." He looked up, filling his lungs. "I am not going to discuss that with you."

"Uncle Ryan will."

"I'll kill him." And he meant every word.

"You lied to me." Smith's lips turned down at the corners.

It hurt like hell to break the one rule Smith and Ty had built their relationship on. No lying. Whatever the truth, they could handle it.

Smith stared into him. Trust, love, and admiration front and center. Ty breathed for the first time in weeks. His neck muscles released the residing tension.

"Please," Smith whispered.

Lindsey skidded to a halt next to Smith. "Sorry, but they said they need this ice."

Ty sighed, "Smith, I will tell you some day, but not today."

Chapter Fifteen

Lasagna.

Sweet red sauce, well-done Italian sausage, loaded with three types of white cheese released a wave of memories. Ty stumbled into the kitchen, letting spices and hot mozzarella take over his senses.

"Hey, Iona," he said gently, hoping not to startle her or himself if she didn't recognize him. It was just a matter of time before it happened.

"Hey, Ty, come in, come in. Sit." She pulled a chair from the kitchen table. The Hill family's giant table grounded their kitchen. He'd designed his setup the same way. Nothing yelled family like a kitchen table.

"You hungry?" Iona slung a dish towel over her shoulder.

Ty took a seat. "I'm always hungry for your lasagna."

"Sweet talker. Where're the kids?"

"In the garage." He stood and snagged a glass from the cabinet.

Iona wandered through the old kitchen. They didn't make kitchens like this anymore. Big and cozy. Intimate. New kitchens flaunted fancy open concepts, barstools, and counter-height bars he didn't fit at. Give him this old kitchen any day.

"More hockey?" she asked, opening the oven.

"Always more hockey. Where's Karis?" She tilted her head and looked out the window. Her slender fingers twisted the dish towel in a mechanical move too calculated for his liking.

"Iona?" Ty set his glass on the counter.

Her gray bob swayed with the shake of her head, and her slim fingers rubbed her hairline. "Is Karis upstairs?" he asked.

She plopped her hand into the sink, sloshing the water. Ty listened for the kids' commotion in the garage. He ignored the loud familiar thump of a puck hitting the connecting door. With no holes and no crying, he palmed Iona's elbow and guided her to a chair. "Sit for a second. I'll find Karis."

Her hands shook, but she did what she was told, thank goodness. The information he'd read regarding dementia cautioned caretakers about sporadic confusion and aggression.

Nervous to leave her, he shot up the stairs two at a time. The voice he heard when he hit the top step took his worry for Iona straight to WTF Karis?

He jiggled the doorknob.

Fucking locked.

A man chuckled from behind the door. Ty's heartbeat kicked up like a rookie on professional ice, and a wave of heat rolled through the pit of his stomach. He squeezed the doorknob a little tighter, and taking a page from Ryan's Meditation/Oprah's Live your best life-whatever bullshit, he counted to ten and visualized...*the beach*? Nope, not the beach, because that was Karis behind this door. With a man.

Angry waves washed over every gear churning in his mind.

Beach his ass.

What she did behind locked doors was none of his business. She didn't want him. He pinched the bridge of his nose, remembering how just a week ago, her ripe body told him differently, but every action since then had wedged a gap between them. A wedge he needed to keep there in order to function like a responsible adult in charge of a child.

She wasn't his, but the door had to come down. Before he could rip it from its henges, Karis stood in front of him, wide-eyed and raging. "What the hell are you doing? Are you listening at my door?"

He stormed into the bedroom. "Where is he? Really, Karis, you're almost forty and you're hiding men?"

Her face turned hard instantly. "Are you serious? And I'm *not* almost forty. You are."

He pressed on. "Why was your door locked?"

"I don't have to answer that. Where's Lindsey?" She crossed her arms over her chest.

Defensive. Definite sign of guilt. He gathered his control and peered around the room. "Lindsey's in the garage, thank fuck. How would you explain a man in your room?" She didn't look bedded, or flushed, or sweaty. She looked calm and warm in a red tank top and cutoff jean shorts. Jesus. He plowed his hands into his hair.

"There's no man in my room, Ty." Her hands gripped her hips, the move more turn-on than intimidation.

He checked the closet. "Then why was your door locked?"

Her stare narrowed. "Because I had a meeting with one of my athletes." She smiled sweetly.

That could be reasonable. "Oh," he chirped.

Karis raised an amused eyebrow. "Lucas is a client, and you're not supposed to hear those conversations. They're confidential, hence the locked door."

"*Lucas?* His name is *Lucas?*" Judgement laced his voice, but come on, Lucas? The man had her full attention behind a locked door, and that jabbed a little too intimate for Ty's taste.

"Yes, *Lucas*. You snob."

"Hmm, Lucas, the baseball player. I knew he sounded weak."

Her hands went up in the air. "Again. Snob."

"Probably, but you're working from home?" he asked.

"Um, yeah." She licked her lips in that nervous, *where's my lip stuff* kind of way.

"Why does that sound doubtful?"

"Well, I'm working here for now, but I'll have to go back, eventually." She chewed her lip and shuffled papers around her desk, clearly avoiding him.

"Do you think going back is a good idea?" His body buzzed to get close to her.

"I think having a job is a good idea. We both know my sister isn't sending any money my way. I only have so much in savings and it's dwindling." She pressed a hand to her forehead. "I'll take clients here until I can get back to North Carolina."

North Carolina wouldn't happen any time soon, but he didn't have the heart to lay it out. Any sign of losing her independence, she'd come out guns blazing with sharks in the moat. There were more imminent problems to solve.

"When I got here your mom was making lasagna. Now she's downstairs with a blank look on her face. She didn't know where you were, so—"

Karis hustled out the door and Ty stumbled to keep up.

"Mom," she called, with no answer.

Black smoke billowed from the center of the kitchen. Fire flickered around the perimeter of the old range. A dish towel, on the stove, glowed in bright orange, and Iona stood next to it with a small glass of water shaking in her hand.

"Karis, stop!" he shouted, catching her by the waist and pulling her behind him.

"Mom, move. Ty, under the sink," Karis called.

He pulled Iona away from the flames and handed her to Karis. He didn't have time to think about the pain in Karis' eyes, or how she wrapped her arms tight around Iona, both women shaking.

"Get out of the kitchen." He reached under the sink, pushed all the cleaning supplies aside, and grabbed the fire extinguisher. He pulled the plug, his arms clenched, preparing for the kick. White foam covered the stovetop, dousing the wagging flames. His lungs sifted the air. A quick cough cleared his chest.

Smoke floated to the popcorned ceiling, cloaking the tall white cabinets, above the stove, in a sheen of black soot. This wasn't safe. Not for him, Smith, or any of them. Iona had some questionable behavior, but this act went straight to dangerous.

"What happened?" Smith and Lindsey stood in the doorway; their sweaty faces plastered with panic.

"Where's Karis and Grandma?" Lindsey asked but left the kitchen before getting an answer.

"Smith, out of the kitchen." Ty's voice was thin but demanding, and as usual, Smith didn't listen.

Instead, he lunged hard against Ty's chest, his arms circling beneath his shoulders and gripping the back of his shirt. Ty dropped the extinguisher and held Smith for as long as he would let him.

They would always have each other's backs, no matter how much they fought or destroyed each other. Smith dropped his arms. Ty stood back and smiled. His heart lightened.

"Smells like something's still burning," Smith mumbled.

"Shit." Ty jerked Smith aside, turned the oven off, took four potholders, and threw the charred pasta into the sink. RIP. They hovered over the sink, mourning the loss and surrounded by white foam and pillows of black smoke.

Smith opened the back door. "Pizza?" he asked.

"Looks like it," Ty relented.

"Awesome, I'll call it in."

Smith pulled out his phone and left the kitchen as Karis entered it. The hair on the back of Ty's neck stood ramrod straight. Even in the smoke's aftermath, he could smell her. A definite sickness.

She surveyed the damage of what was becoming a regular occurrence of disasters. His fingers longed to smooth down the tightness in her shoulders. The energy between them flowed in a comfortable current. She stepped into his open arms, and he absorbed her, soaking in the feel of soft curves pressed against his pounding chest. He wanted to take care of this woman. An urge so deep and raw it knotted his insides worse than Iona's twisted dish towels.

"Where's your mom?" A small ripple of fright vibrated into his fingertips. He widened his fingers, refusing to let her back away. Even though he should.

"She's upstairs in her room, pretty shaken." She moved out of his arms, leaving him wanting and tortured.

He scratched his jaw. The five-o'clock shadow had doubled within the past twenty minutes. The Hill women still sent him reeling. All of them.

Lindsey beelined straight to Karis, on guard and wary. "We ordered pizza."

"We're gonna turn into pizzas. You guys hang in the living room while I clean this up." She reached for the window, but with a wink, Ty beat her to it.

"I'll help clean up," Lindsey offered, all defensive and final.

Ty glanced at Karis and swallowed his *I told you so*.

"I think we got it, Linds. I don't want you in here with the smoke," Karis said.

With an unhappy huff, Lindsey moped her way out of the room in perfect teenage fashion.

Karis worried her bottom lip. "I think you're right."

"I'm right about a lot of things. Can you be more specific?" He flashed his widest smile.

She pinched her lips closed, cuffing the beautiful smile he needed to see in order to breathe again.

"Ha, ha," she finally said. "You know what I mean."

He did, but he wouldn't be a jerk about it. The entire house felt as edgy as Karis' fake laugh, and even though he relished her attempt at happy, he cursed himself for wanting to make it real. For wanting to reach out and turn the corners of her mouth up with his fingers.

No matter his intentions, they all led to trouble. But he could solve her problems. All she had to do was give him the word.

***

The poor kitchen had seen better days, and so had Karis. Cinderella didn't do this much scrubbing. She held the rag under the running water and scanned the cleaning products littering the floor. One of them had to take soot off the walls, and, at least, hide the smell of charcoaled lasagna. All life's messes should be cleaned up with a wipe of a rag and some type of spray.

"I think it's wet enough."

"What?" Her brain moved through cotton.

"The dishrag. You've been holding it under water for five minutes. It can't get any wetter." His perfect eyebrows shot up and he smiled wider. Light humor dripped from his voice. She wanted to laugh. For real. Surrounded by smoke, cleaning products, and a drenched lasagna, she wanted to crack open and just laugh with him.

Impossible and irresponsible.

"I think you're right about Lindsey not wanting us to be alone together."

He snagged a rag from the kitchen drawer and picked up a spray bottle from the floor. "I know I am."

Swiping a finger across the stove, he held up a greasy black tip and moved around the kitchen, surveying the walls. "I think we need professionals to clean this."

"I can't afford professionals, so start scrubbing."

"Karis," he pushed.

"Don't even offer." He had a point though. She'd never get rid of the smell or clear out the corners still stuffed with flour, without some type of serious scrubbing and maximum cleaning products.

More money.

She deflated against the sink. The pressure poked her aching muscles but didn't dissuade the underlying urge to run away from trouble. And that's what all this amounted to. Trouble. Insecurity nudged her heart. Scrubbing for hours and still having to hire someone to come deep clean stole every ounce of confidence she'd built over the years. Time and money. She was short on both.

"Do you know someone that can clean this up? And get the smell out."

Ty clapped his hands together. "Yes, I do."

"I want the name, number, and the bill."

He tilted his head. "Yes, ma'am."

"I'm serious."

"I know."

He knew. He also knew chaos ate away at her. They'd spent too much time together for him not to. Exposed and vulnerable. The two traits she'd spent years removing from her life covered her.

People abandoned homes because of disasters like this. "If you can get me the names of the professionals, that would be great. This place needs to be spic-and-span if I plan to sell."

"You're selling the house?" The previous humor gone.

The place was a dump. Even if she were sentimental, this house still wouldn't qualify for one night of remorse. It was the shack her mother had settled on when her supply of men dried up.

"I am. My mom can't keep it up and goodness knows it needs too many updates and repairs for me to deal with, so it's going on the market with minimum repair."

Deep concentration lines crinkled across his forehead. "Do you think you should sell? I mean, your mom knows this place."

"True, and I have thought about that, believe me. There's no easy answer, but I need my job." The bills were relentless. In her dreams, in her shower, in her sessions.

"North Carolina isn't the only place with jobs. You can get a job here." His tanned lips curtained the straight white teeth sparkling on his sincere face.

Ty had a history of cleaning up messes, but never hers. He always tried, but she was no better than her mother if she let him. Right? The theory lay loose in her head, jingling around, unable to plant itself. Her mother had changed from the woman she grew up resenting, but the shift couldn't be trusted.

"Oh, that's easy." She laughed and opened the curtains. "I like my job, and few teams take a sport psych on staff. You know most teams outsource."

"You can *like* jobs here. What about another company? Another field?" Another field?

"What? I like my field. I work in sports. Hence, sports psych."

"Yeah." He shrugged, no big deal. "But to stay here, and give your mom and Lindsey stability, you might have to look elsewhere." He stood cool and casual across the kitchen, changing her life plan like it was a play on his miniature whiteboard.

"It's not that easy, Ty. We all don't wake up and have opportunity banging on our door. I waited for this job. I went through more school for this job. Why? Because this was the only one offered. I'm a female shrink looking to get into sports, on a team. It's nearly impossible, and I don't have my pick. I don't roll out of bed and fall into choices."

He pushed off the counter, his blue eyes narrowed in fury, and the fluid ease of his large frame shifted to stock-still and rigid tight.

"Is that what you think?" His words floated across the room. Soft and scary.

"Um." Not everything needed to be said out loud. When would she learn that lesson enough to make it stick?

"You think I rolled out of bed and landed on a hockey team. Jesus." He linked his fingers behind his head and glanced at the floor. She knew more than anyone that answers didn't grow there.

"No, I know you worked for that." Panic surged, but he didn't give her a chance to explain.

"I worked for us. For us, Karis. Not...*that*."

"I know, I didn't mean to—" She sounded pathetic, but she wouldn't apologize. He had ample opportunity. She didn't. Whether it was because of money, connections, or whatever.

"For years, I didn't even play when I made the team, and you think–" He moved closer, crowding her, rattling off stats and setbacks.

She pushed against his chest, holding him away.

He may have endured the physical torture of professional hockey and the mind games that came along with it, but, in the only way she knew how, she had withstood them, too.

"I think you sat on the bench for a month before you got your first fifteen seconds on professional ice." That shut him up, but she wasn't done. "I think you worked out every off season in Quebec, never giving yourself a break. I think you scored your first professional goal, your second game, second period, thirteen seconds in. I think you've done just as much for the league off the ice as you have on the ice. I also think you're still the biggest hockey snob, and maybe coaching has made you worse."

A small smile appeared across his lips. "I thought you didn't follow me?"

The room shrank, squeezing her with immense pressure, but she owned her weakness. "I watched every game for the first two years, but then the girls came, and I couldn't." Her throat tightened, and she shook her head, refusing to let him see her tears.

He stalked across the kitchen and braced his hands on the counter, framing her in. He rested his head on her shoulder. His breath filled the room with a frustrating calmness.

"Let me help you get a job here." He had to know her response.

"No," she whispered. "I can't give up my job. I've worked too hard." Heated air, too thick to inhale, curled around her. She slipped out of his muscled barricade and ambled across the kitchen, leaving a safe space between them.

A low growl pushed through his lips. "It's not about you anymore."

"I know that." She was motivated, not a moron. True, her mother and Lindsey were depending on her, but she'd spent years perfecting her independence. It wasn't as easy to give up as he made it sound, and foregoing the money source could be dangerous.

"Lindsey is all on you," he continued. "Her mother's gone, and her grandmother's losing it and don't think she doesn't see it, because she does. Moving would be detrimental to all of you."

"Losing the income would be detrimental."

He pushed off the counter. "I didn't know shrinks put money before mental health."

Ouch. "Low blow. At the moment, money is sacred to my mental health." Pathetic, but true.

"Do you hear yourself?" He gripped her hand in his. "Let me help you."

Taking a man's help, even if it was Ty's, had the powerful potential to turn her in to her mother, and the sad, shocking reality was she didn't mind. But her brain didn't accept the archaic philosophy, and years of anti-mother training kicked in, settling the issue.

"I know that look." He inched closer, blocking her escape and pulling their clasped hands into his chest.

"What look?" she questioned, butting up against the counter.

"Your *I got this* look."

"I have an *I got this* look?"

His lips hovered above hers. "You do, and it kills me when I see it and it's not directed at me."

How could she take care of herself and her family with him in her life? He consumed her and things were so out of her control she feared she might she let him.

Chapter Sixteen

The spider crack ripped and stretched across the gym's mirror. A haunting reminder of what she could do to him. Ty's cell phone lay on the blue mat, shattered into a million pieces. His self-control lay right next to the tech mess, doubled over and laughing.

He deserved it. Stabbing his hands through his hair, he sucked in an unsatisfying breath. All huffs and puffs and no oxygen. A shitty end to a pummeling workout.

"What the fuck? Go shower. You've been nothing but a tyrant the entire session." Ryan jumped off the treadmill and swiped a towel down his face.

If Ryan thought he had it bad, he should check in on Smith. The poor kid had been dealing with his anger for a week. Ryan had it for an hour.

Massaging his temples, his brain clouded in a haze, Ty floated to the locker room. Without a care, he stripped down, leaving every stitch on the floor. Aching to destroy something, his hands flexed and clenched in time to the bunching of his muscles and the fucking twitching in his jaw. For the millionth time within the last hour, his mind ticked off reasons she wouldn't be picking up her phone, and why he shouldn't care. Down to his shorts, he screeched to a halt. He needed the anger to go away. A sucker punch to the ribs could do the trick.

"Talk. Now," Ryan demanded, blocking the path to his locker.

One-word sentences. Scary. In the league, they were men who didn't mince words, and when it came to talking to each other, the same rule applied. Minimal words. Maximum trust. Brothers.

Ty wrapped a towel low on his hips and dropped onto the closest bench. He jabbed the top of his knees with his elbows, giving an extra twist of deserved pressure. Dropping his chin to chest, he stared at the carpet. Second-guesses swarmed his mind all day and capturing one, on demand, to give to Ryan wasn't happening.

"Not sure what to say." He steepled his fingers and counted three stains on the carpet.

"Hmm. The cracked mirror in the gym says plenty, but I want to hear it from you." Ryan slapped him on the back and plopped down on the bench.

A million words flashed in his mind. None of them made sense, just clogged his head and made his stomach queasy. A light-headed, gut-wrenching remorse he couldn't name had him stuck between broken and lost. How would he say that to Ryan without sounding like a complete pussy? He was the big brother. The head coach. The one who should know better.

Ryan stood and leaned all calm and easy against the lockers. His body locked in his perfected defense pose. Arms folded across his chest, his *let's chat* stance in full force. He needed a punch in the face.

"Let me make this easy for you, since you seem to be struggling with words, which would lead me to wonder, yet again, how in the hell you ever landed someone as hot and smart as Karis to begin with."

With white clenched knuckles, Ty ignored the bait and settled on an eloquent, "Fuck you."

"Ah, another use for Karis, so I'll pass."

His nerves jangled on the cusp of explosion, a level he didn't pass often considering his stamina for bullshit. Surviving beneath the demeaning strength of Pop had at least taught him to recognize his limit and control it when necessary.

He rammed his fist into locker number seventy-nine. Bone and skin hit metal.

Ryan never flinched. "Does she know she's gotten to you like this? Again?"

He grabbed his towel from the bench. "How the fuck would she know? She hasn't answered her phone in a goddamn week." He threw the towel across the room.

"So, she's dodging you? Ignoring you? Blowing you off?" Ryan smiled. Loving it.

"Are you trying to die today?" He sat again and rolled his shoulders. Old wounds clicked and cracked.

"Why? You going to throw your phone at me?" Ryan sat.

"Jesus, shut up." He needed some type of outlet. "She hasn't called me back in a week."

"And?"

"And?" He might as well turn in his man card. "I can't do it again. It was so easy for her to leave the first time. I was a mess."

"You were more than a mess."

"But I played great hockey," he justified, trying to keep some dignity.

"Yeah, psycho. You played great hockey because no player wanted to deal with your shit. But you don't play anymore, and now you have Smith, and coaching responsibilities. You can't Hulk around, breaking mirrors and punching things."

Smith.

He'd lost it again. With every doubt she had about them, herself, her family, she made him insane when she pushed him away. And not answering his calls was a clear shove. "She's not gonna stick." He took a deep dive into his head, thawing thoughts better left frozen. "A week ago, we felt different, stronger. I thought she felt it." Idiot. "And now she's ghosting me. She's on and off like a fucking goalie net."

"I knew this would happen. I knew she'd throw you." Ryan took a steady breath. An oak of a man. "But in her defense, which I don't come to easily, she has a lot on her plate right now."

"She still wants her mother and Lindsey to move to NC." Proving she didn't want to build a life with him.

"Ouch." Ryan smarted.

"Exactly. Smith would go crazy without Lindsey."

"I wasn't ouching for Smith. Have you offered to help her get a job here?"

"Yep."

"Shit." Ryan scrubbed his jaw. "You didn't tell her, did you?"

Ty shook his head. He'd thought about telling her. Hell, he'd had nightmares about it. Tossed it back and forth like a hockey puck until the truth lodged in his throat, threatening to drown him in guilt. No. Like the many other manipulated truths holding his life in check, this one had to stay hidden until it faded. "She had an interview with the soccer team downtown, sometime. If she'd answer her phone or show up at practice, I'd know how it went."

"You already know how it went. That team sucks to work for. They've been through a million people in every position. Why don't you get her a job with our team?"

"Yeah, okay. We have two head docs on staff." He held up two fingers.

"And you don't think they'd add another one for you? That's some pull you got around here, *Coach*."

He ignored the jab. "She doesn't want my help. She loves her job in Carolina with her baseball players. Baseball, can you believe that?"

"Yeah, it's as far away from hockey as you can get, but let me remind you—"

"Fucking stop. You don't have to remind me," he yelled behind him as he stepped into the showers.

The warm water fell against his skin, softening tight muscles, and quieting his mind. A couple of deep breaths he never had the balls to take in front of anyone gushed from his lips and deflated his remaining tension. So what, he'd done some things in his career he shouldn't have. Everyone did.

If she didn't want his help with finding a job, fine. In fact, better than fine, because it kept his focus on Smith, which is exactly where it should be. Who needed the stress of contacting asshole sport executives and making small talk to land an interview for her? Why bother to call in favors when she didn't want them?

He dug his nails into his scalp and scrubbed hard. Moving to NC might solve money problems, but it would double Iona's health issues, and fill Lindsey with resentment. That may not matter to her right now, but it would eventually. Kids had a way of sneaking into your life, grabbing on, and never letting go.

He dropped his shoulders, rerouting the water to sluice down his back. Karis would murder him if she knew what role he played in helping her accomplish her beloved independence. But how could he not? She would never understand his deep-seated need to provide for her. Half the time he didn't get it. Years later and he still burned to make her happy.

The sad reality slithered between his toes and down the drain. They both had more than they could handle, and the last thing they needed was a mediocre version of their younger relationship.

Ty twisted the shower to freezing, stood under the harsh spray, and forced his mind to concentrate on business. The league had called him an hour ago, confirming his annual "All In for Hockey" fundraiser.

After rallying friends and family for over ten years to create a night of unforgettable fun, and those same friends dropping tons of cash to support local hockey, the professional hockey league decided to back his efforts.

Ten years later.

Assholes.

Where were they when all he could serve was pizza and beer?

Annoyed, he snagged a towel, cursed the league, and started a mental list of things to do that didn't involve Karis. He rubbed his hair dry, dropped the white towel in the basket, and air-dried back to his locker. Drops of punishing cold water dripped from the hair curling at his neck. A haircut was not on the to-do list, but it wouldn't be long.

And damn if thoughts of her fingers didn't float through his mind, moving up his neck, pushing into his hair. She loved it long and wavy.

A haircut was out of the question.

Chapter Seventeen

All ice rinks smelled the same. A strange blend of clean ice, dirty hockey socks, window cleaner, and fried food. A comforting combination.

Karis massaged her aching cheeks. Who knew smiling throughout a Pee-Wee hockey game used so many muscles? Forty minutes of teeth-showing action. Ty looked sexy as hell behind the bench, but Lindsey held her attention. Light on her skates. The kid knew where the puck was going before it did. She ripped the puck across the ice, scoring multiple times and solving the mystery of holes riddled in the garage drywall. A well-practiced shot.

Smith dominated as her wing, playing like the other men in his family. He had a future in the sport and lacked the aggression the other Firestones were penalized for. He kept up with Lindsey and could grab a pass from two hundred feet down the ice. Tape to tape.

The best surprise was Iona. She glowed with excitement from the puck drop to the final whistle. Screaming over the glass at Lindsey, yelling at Smith and the other players, calling them all by name and jersey number. Each period, the poor refs gave her a polite, but stern, reminder to behave. Parents laughed, flocking to her in greetings and hugs after the game.

With each familiar hug her mother received, the pit in Karis' stomach tightened, and it didn't get any better when she spotted Ty, shooting her a death stare, and passing her mother a loving smile.

How could she take her mother away from everything she knew? It was responsible to stay and responsible to go.

The soccer interview was a waste. The guy had been a total prick, and she said as much before walking out. She was desperate, not stupid. She must have been impressive. Somehow the horrible interview resulted in a job offer. Weird. Less pay than the baseball team, but it would keep her family put. The thought of pulling her niece and her mother from the things they loved sent spirals of nausea into her gut. But losing her salary and risking the loss of her independence hurt just as much.

Karis held out her hand, hoping her mom would take it before stepping off the bleachers. Yeah, right. Iona smacked her hand away. Message received.

The loose clank of the board's door opening shot sharp memories to the forefront of her mind and for a fast second, she wanted to break down the wall she'd secured around herself and not be so damn solo.

Dodging Ty's phone calls for a week fastened an airtight foundation around her heart, but attending the game chipped away at the progress.

She couldn't fall for him again. Opening wounds sealed up years ago would hurt them all, and she'd already risked too much by indulging in his touch. Family had to come first. An act her own mother had never done.

Scanning the skaters exiting the ice, in a sea of sweaty, red-faced, adrenaline-induced smiles, she spotted Lindsey sporting the biggest grin of all. So happy. Despite everything, they'd made a life here.

As the kids shuffled into the locker room, Iona grabbed a couple of helmet cages, and leaned into sweaty spaces to let each kid know she was proud of them. Karis' heart both ached and sang when most of the players acknowledged her with a shy "thanks, Iona."

"Good game, Linds. You nailed it. Number twenty-two on the other team needs a spanking, but you were awesome." Iona grabbed Lindsey's shoulder pads and pulled her in for a hug. Smith waited his turn to get off the ice and probably snag a hug from Iona as well.

"Thanks, Gran." Lindsey wrapped her gloved hand around Iona, accepting the hug before entering the locker room. Smith didn't get off so easy.

Iona leaned in. "Why would you let twenty-two get her like that?"

"Mom, easy, killer. At least let him step off the ice before you yell at him." Poor kid.

"What? He's aggressive and fast. He can do it. And I'm not yelling." Her stare never left Smith's and her smile shined a mile wide.

God, she probably should take the soccer job. Dick bag or not.

"It's all right. She's right," Smith chirped. Such a sweet boy.

In skates, he towered over Iona, with the body of an athlete, gifted with grace and strength, like his uncles.

"You had a great game, Smith." Karis nudged her mom, looking for support. A week's worth of canceled practices rarely resulted in a win.

"Of course, he had a great game. He would have had a better game if he'd stopped twenty-two. Smith, go change before you catch cold." Goodness, she was demanding. But he took it like a young man raised with the kindness of a gentleman and the brute of a hockey player.

"Yes, ma'am."

Ty followed the players off the ice and leaned down and kissed Iona on the cheek. Another knife to the heart.

"Good game, Coach." Karis cringed at the awkwardness.

"Yeah, thanks." He shuffled off the ice, balancing water racks and whiteboards. His hockey jacket snug in all the right places. What kind of parent ogled the coach?

There had been a time when he would have dropped those water bottles and had her against the wall, covered in licks and kisses before she could get that jacket unzipped.

His gaze hit the embroidery stitched above her heart. Recognition and confusion played across his face. A flicker of heat singed her resolve. She covered the emblem.

"Lindsey played great." He focused on Iona.

Karis butted in. "She did. She's got speed."

"I'm glad she's feeling better. I thought she'd be a little sluggish on the ice."

"Sluggish? Why?" She wouldn't be sluggish if he wouldn't have canceled practice, and she felt fine all week.

He slammed the half door closed, and set the case of water bottles down, mumbling hi to kids passing by. "She was sick last week and missed all the practices."

Iona peered at the locker room doors, a guilty avoidance tactic she'd done a million times when trying to hide something. Sketchy little woman.

"Mom?" Karis questioned. "Lindsey wasn't sick last week."

"Uh-oh." Iona glared at Ty, pinning him with an accusing stare.

"Uh-oh?" Karis exhaled, hoping the release of pressure would prevent the oncoming headache.

"She wasn't sick?" A deep crease etched above Ty's brow. "She missed practice all week. I called you, but you never answered your fucking phone." He accused, so comfortable and confident in himself, he could bottle it and sell out in seconds. The man coached teenagers in hockey sweats and professionals in suits, looking good in all of it.

Understanding clicked. "She wasn't sick. She told me you canceled practice."

He jerked upright, his relaxed composure gone. Every muscle flexed with precision. Each ripple shot a hot reminder straight to her greedy fingertips. He bowed over her, squeezing into her space. "You believed her?" he asked too close to her ear.

Heat bloomed in the dormant corners of her body. Backing away, she adjusted her purse strap, pulling it taut across her shoulder. "Of course I believed her. Why wouldn't I?"

"Because it's *hockey*. We always have practice." His teeth clenched behind tight lips. "If you'd pick up your phone instead of sending me straight to voicemail, you would have known." His square jaw didn't budge. Except for the slight tick jumping on the right.

"Is that why you've been calling? My cell—"

"Sucks," he finished.

She backtracked through the past week. Shit, her cell did suck. Most of the time she couldn't find it and when she did, the thing was dead. Truth be told, the few times he called, she sent him to voicemail. Iona wasn't the only master avoider.

"Confident, aren't we? How do you know I wasn't ignoring you?" she said, digging around in her purse.

"Were you?" he dared. The hurt on his face a log to the quiet fire kindling between them.

"Maybe," she admitted, "but only twice."

He ran his hands through his hair, a boyish move considering how intimidating confusion made him look.

"I called you all week," his voice strained.

"Oh boy." Iona shuffled away from the ice.

He blocked her escape route, and Karis barricaded the back. Iona had intel, and it was time to spill. He winked, and the tag team ensued. "Iona, what's going on?"

Another worthless scuttle, prevented. "No chance, Mom," Karis warned.

"All right, you two big bullies." The last words a simple sigh.

"No name-calling." He teased with a sweet smile. This man. Good with kids, executives, athletes, and grandmas. She'd swoon if she wasn't rolling her eyes.

Iona batted her hand. "So, um, wait—" She peered around the cold rink, sucking her teeth. "Move away from the locker room." She motioned them down the hall. This little spitfire of a woman held massive power over all of them. They did exactly what she asked. "Here's the short of it." Her change bag dangled from her wrists.

Ty leaned in, his face pure seriousness. Karis steadied her heart at the sight of his respect and adoration for her mother.

"I'm sorry, Karis," Iona said.

"For what? Exactly?" she questioned. Not liking the unhopeful start.

Iona's small green eyes darted between the two of them.

"Lindsey sees everything. All kids do. She knows seeing Ty upsets you, so she didn't want to make you come to practice. She lied and said it was canceled. On top of that, she doesn't want him hogging you, or making you want to move to North Carolina even more."

"Oh." Karis let out a breath and avoided his heavy gaze. Her thoughts tangled. Did kids really think such intense thoughts? No wonder they were moody.

He reached for her hand, and she held it like a lifeline.

Iona babbled away. "She knows you two have a history, and she knows you two still love each other."

She pulled her hand from his. "No, we don't."

Iona poo-pooed. "Oh, please. We know. You two" —she wagged her finger between them—"don't." The old wisdom, far from cute and sweet. "Fools," she muttered.

Smith emerged from the locker room and joined the group. "Uncle Ty, am I still going to Pops?"

Ty took off his hat and speared his fingers into his hair, grabbing every curl he could get his hands on. "Yes"—he dragged his fingers down his face—"you are. Are you good with that?"

"Yeah, Uncle Ryan will be there, but I'm gonna shower here." He headed back to the locker room.

"You don't have to go."

"No, it's good. I just want to be done with hockey for the day." No one could miss the sadness in his voice, or the worried look passing between them.

"Me, too. I'll be in, in a second." Ty sent Smith on his way.

"Why let him go to your dad's when it clearly tears you up?" Karis dared, hating the pain blanketing his face.

He paused, hanging his head with a heart-wrenching stillness. Iona cracked under the quiet tension and left for the lobby. Thank goodness she stopped outside the glass window to sit at a table as if she'd done it a thousand times.

He shrugged. "Simple, I have to."

Impossible. He didn't do *have to*.

"Well, he's an abusive bastard and doesn't deserve to see him, or you." She threw in her two cents, wishing it could be more.

He stepped close. A masculine musk swarmed her senses. "I always loved how you could feel what I'm feeling. How protective you were of me when it came to him."

Her brain tripped over his admission. "He hurt you and I don't think Smith should have to go." Any man who hosed his naked kid down, in the freezing cold, after losing a hockey game, didn't deserve to have visits with his grandson.

"He doesn't do to Smith what he did to us, so I'd like to keep the peace between my dad and me, plus Ryan—" He glanced behind him.

"Ah, Ryan." Her inner shrink appeared, but hell, she couldn't help it. "He always had a soft spot for your dad."

"Yep, and I'm still trying to figure that out."

"That could take years." She smiled.

"Yeah, you could probably study him for a lifetime. His brain is like no other." He flashed a perfect smile. Heat stirred low in her belly. The caged butterflies flickered to life.

"Are you offering him up to science?" She nudged into him.

"Not yet. I need him to chaperone Smith's visits, and he's a fucking great defenseman."

A laugh escaped her lips. A soul-clearing chuckle hiding so deep she feared she'd lost it. Locking eyes, a familiar charge surged between them.

He rocked back on his heels. "So, looks like I'm kid-free tonight."

"Cool." Happiness drifted like a smoky illusion. Grasping it couldn't be done.

"How about dinner?" The smoke thickened.

Toeing the line. "I'd love to, but I don't know how I feel about leaving Lindsey with Mom at night."

He glanced at Iona. "She seems fine today."

"Right now, but how long will fine last?" She couldn't ignore the sleep deprivation on her mother's face.

"Karis," Ty sighed. "Go to dinner with me." A sweet plea from an exhausted man.

"I just," she started. God, she wanted to.

"We'll be back early, or she can come with us?"

A laugh escaped her. "What? No." In the worst of times, they could always laugh.

"Sure. She can sit at another table; she can bring Lindsey," he said, dead serious. He reached for her hand, pulled her glove off, and laced his large, warm fingers with hers. He put them inches apart with only intertwined fingers between them. Every muscle tightened in warning and the butterflies flapped double time.

"Your hands always froze, even in gloves." His whimsical words took her back to when he was hers.

"Okay." She stared down at their hands. Thick tan knuckles tangled with slim fingers.

"Okay?" he questioned.

"Dinner." His face brightened with the word. Anticipation pulsed around them. Her teeth dug into her chapped bottom lip.

"Are we bringing your mom?" His smile confirmed her decision. The throb in her heart echoed into her stomach and buoyed her thoughts between doubt and disaster.

"No," she pushed at him. "But we have to be done early."

"We will. I have a meeting about the hockey fundraiser. It should be about an hour, and then we're on."

Handing her glove back, he leaned close to her ear. "I'm dying to kiss the hell out of you right now."

Provoked heat surged through her, and for sure, everyone could see it. Confirmation lit up Iona's glowing face.

Chapter Eighteen

The sexy restaurant had been impressive with its fancy plates and sparkly glasses, but Ty's house stole her breath. Filled with masculine lines and old Florida dark-wood furniture, a definite tribute to being a native. The walls were tastefully covered in his hockey life and highlighted the progression of his stellar career, including all the teams and charities he helped make successful, both in and out of Florida. On and off the ice.

Running her fingers over every shining framed sports clipping and family candids hanging on the walls, regret wormed its way into her heart and kicked her in the stomach. He'd changed over the years, but his love of family and game never wavered.

"I remember this game." She covered her smile with her hand.

He stared, pulling her hand from her face. "Don't you dare cover that smile. I've waited too long to see you like this." His lips formed an O, and he tilted his head to the side.

"Like what? Surprised?" He was too close. She needed to move, but her feet wouldn't budge.

His dark, heated stare met hers. "No, like mine."

"Ty," she whispered, nervously glancing back at the framed pictures. She wasn't ready to dive into her all-consuming want for him or start a deep reflection about all the pieces of his life she'd missed. Pain would take over. Stepping away from the people she loved, to "find herself" and release them of a burden, was the glaring pathetic theme of her life.

Keys landed on the hall table with a loud clunk.

"Karis?" He inched closer. His chest brushed against her back, heating her spine. Facing him would be fatal, but she needed to touch him like she needed air. Surrounded by every minute of his life without her, she needed more of him. Wanted to be filled to the top with nothing but Ty.

"I always loved to watch you play," she admitted. His light touch on her arm was a hesitant question and a shivering invitation. Would this be more than she could handle? Would one night change them into another regret?

"What?" His lips hovered over her ear.

She read the framed newspaper clipping in front of her before meeting his undressing stare. Dark hair fell over his brow. Her fingers twitched, eager to rub his square jaw, dusted with the slightest sexiest stubble. The need lay heavy against her. Inside of her. Around her. Consuming and frightening.

"I never stopped watching you. I watched almost every game you played." Tears slid down her cheeks, and her heart thudded with the confession. She'd wasted so much time watching him from afar. They could have been so much more, if only they were strong enough.

"Why?" The word dripped from his lips, tinted with fear and anticipation. Her body tensed under his tortured inspection.

She'd searched for that answer for years until realizing she'd have to be content without one.

"I needed to see if you were happy." Surrendering the truth, she looked away.

He reached up, placing one calloused finger under her chin. "You were in my life, and I didn't know?" His voice cracked.

"I had to know your dreams were coming true. I couldn't just take Wes' word for it. I had to see it." She placed her hand on his cheek, relishing the feel of him without hurry or confusion. She stared at every line. It didn't matter that his shoulders blocked the world. She wouldn't have seen it anyway. Only him.

His hand widened on the small of her back, fitting her into him. The sliver of space between them disappeared. His fingers skated up her neck and into her hair. "This dress is going to be on my floor in seconds. Is that good with you?"

"Yes," she breathed.

He pressed his lips to hers in a hungry, growling need. His warm tongue slipped between her lips, hot and demanding. He pressed into her outer thigh and notched her knee to his hip. Rough hands on smooth skin.

Long fingers grazed the inside of her thigh, burning a familiar trail, and bunching her dress up to her waist. Hot, impatient lust surged through her, and she burrowed into him, needing the closeness. Needing more.

"I got you," he said and eased her back against the door, with their lips still sealed in a consuming wet kiss. Pressure pushed her from all sides.

Fisting her fingers into his shirt, she held on, opening her mouth wider. She met his tongue stroke for stroke. Caged against the door and framed within his thick arms. Her fingers roamed over his shirt, tracing the contours of every muscle she'd given up. A cry escaped her lips, and he released a thick moan that had her unbuttoning his shirt and lost in the ridges of his shadowed stomach and steel chest.

"Jesus, once this happens, I'll need you more. I can't do once. It won't be enough." He painted raspy words. Harsh and true and riddled with accepted consequential regret.

Her hands shook, roaming over his silky back muscles covered in smooth burning skin.

He leaned his forehead against hers and stepped back, leaving her wanting and cold. His hand drifted down her face, down her neck, between her breasts, to the knot at the front of her dress.

With one pull, the fabric draped open. "Fuck me," he breathed. "You're so beautiful, I don't know how to not have you," he bit out.

"Have me." She closed her eyes to the softness of his fingers.

"Do I?"

"Always."

***

Inside her.

It was raw and savage and all he wanted. How in the fuck was he going to take this slow? How was he going to make it matter to her?

Black boy shorts and lace, holding her soft white skin, made him a weak man. The need and surrender in her eyes cut him to his knees. Reason left the building.

He pulled her to his bedroom and unbuckled his pants. They hit the floor with his briefs and shirt. He needed her skin on skin.

The king-sized mattress bent to his weight as he lay along her curves and, just as he remembered, she was made for him. Their legs tangled until he lifted one of hers over his hip, opening her. Her scent clouded his head with desperation, and greed. All the things he taught himself never to be.

Kissing the sweet skin on her neck, he eased down to her soft, warm breasts. Drifting over sheer lace, his tongue drenched her nipple. She lifted enough for him to strip her down. Her nipples puckered making his mouth watered. He latched on, sparked by the pain of her nails clawing down his back. He drenched each velvety bud with sucks and tugs. She squirmed beneath him.

He ran his fingertips down her flat stomach and gripped the boy shorts at her hip.

"Off. Now," he growled.

She raised her ass, and he slid the lace down the smooth curves of her legs. His hand flattened on the dark curls covering her mound.

"I need to watch. I need to watch you come undone."

Bending his elbow, he propped his head on his hand, adjusting his body to the side of hers. She was so going to remember what she took away from them years ago.

"Ty, please." She dug her heels into the mattress. Her hips pushed against his hand. Score. He still knew how to satisfy her desires.

He teased the folds of her moist heat. The throbbing flesh thick with need for him. Swept away, he stopped, hoping to catch his breath. Taking a moment, he steadied his dominating body, willing it to slow down, but it cruised on.

His finger entered her easily. Not enough. A second finger slipped into her warm entrance. She threw her head back, releasing a gorgeous moan. Giving him permission to taste her throat and drink from her mouth as she pulsed around his curved fingers.

She pushed him to the brink. Waiting was over. He needed to feel her clench around him. He moved over her, and she opened her thighs. Wide and wet. Slick and sensuous. A perfect fit.

Just for him.

A sweet invitation.

"I'm clean." He lay between her legs, gasping for air and desperate for release. His body seizing for a second of coherent control, he adjusted his elbows, trying to keep from crushing her, but shaking from the want to melt into her. Shifting to his knees, his mind rode on a one-way track. Urgent.

Her hesitation murdered him, but no way would he pretend she was some puck bunny, giving him a quick release.

Praying for patience, he slipped two fingers back inside her, and absorbed every shiver each thrust created. He never thought he would see her flushed face or ride between her thighs again. He would never have survived without it.

He hooked his fingers, caressing her walls. "Karis, I'm not fucking doing it. I've never been inside you with a condom, and I'm not doing it now. You're not some lay off the street." He panted like a teenager, desperate and eager.

"I'm clean." Her eyes softened, and her fingers sifted through his hair.

"You're mine." His fingers pumped into her creamy channel. Her heavy lashes fluttered trying to stay open. A small smile pulled at his lips, amazed he could still do this to her. His stare locked on hers and he brought his fingers to his lips, licking her from each soaked digit.

"You taste"—his words hitched like a fucking high schooler—"like nothing I've ever had and the only thing I'll ever need." His shaft stood ready at her entrance and her silky moan whittled at his patience. Her hips rolled and her small fingers circled his wrists, gliding him in and out.

"Karis?" he questioned, beneath a choked moan. He gripped the sheets and hunkered onto his knees.

"Please," she whispered.

She raised her hips, meeting him. He stroked his cock and slowly slid inside her.

Wet heat slipped over him. Tight. Pulsing. The world dropped away, and he pushed in deeper, his body threatening to collapse onto hers. Hip to hip, fear of crushing her flickered, but his body ruled him. He gripped for control. A lost cause.

She wrapped her arms around his shoulders and her long legs clasped behind his ass, urging him deeper. He pulled out just enough to feel her heels push him back in.

"Oh," she cried.

"Do you feel that?" he said on a winded breath, his hips rolling in hungry thrusts. Her cries spurred him on. He twisted his fingers in the sheets above her head with the facade of taking his time. Their stares locked in silence. He drove deep, losing himself to her.

"Yes," she cried.

"Karis." With a hard push, her nails scored his ribs.

"I need you." The weep in her voice and the shaking of her body convinced him this meant more than sex, and it always would for them.

She surrounded him. "I'm right here, baby." He eased out and inched inside her slowly. Her legs widened, and her hips tilted, angled just right. She contracted around him, the friction an unbelievable rush. His tight balls pounding between her cradling thighs.

Long gone.

Her long hair lay covering her naked skin. Her body moved fluid and hot. Each time she moved, he teetered on the verge. She clenched. Milking him. Their fingers threaded, knuckle to knuckle, gripping the disheveled sheet.

Her body bowed to his will. His name tore from her lips and into his ear, pushing him to the edge of his release. He held her tight, beginning his sinuous leave of her warmth.

Her arms gripped him. "Don't you dare think of pulling out."

And she was serious. He pulled his head away from her neck, needing to see her face. Needing to see she knew what she was asking. What she demanded of him, because he was strong, but not that strong.

His fingers dug into her back. He dared her to look away while he claimed her as his, for always, no matter what.

Chapter Nineteen

Karis lay in his enormous bed, in his enormous house, a fraction of his enormous life. A past piece. A small girl weighed down by life and nothing close to what he deserved.

Her thoughts branched off into paths of equal confusion. A nervous rumble vibrated low in her stomach and her brain spiraled into a deep dive. Lying in bed, thinking of someone other than him produced all kinds of turmoil. He used to be the only one to consume her.

"Oh, I know that look." Ty pulled her close. His crooked nose sucked in a breath and his blue eyes squinted with concern. He knew all her looks.

She snuggled deeper into the pillow they shared. "Weird to be thinking about Lindsey when I'm lying here with you," she offered unguarded. Almost guilty. He did always have a way with breaking down her walls.

"Twenty-year-old me would be offended, but almost-forty me gets it."

She tucked the sheet to her chest, and just as quickly, he tugged it down. His lips curved into a small smile. She sighed in surrender, trying to claim this one night as her own without remorse. When she walked out the front door, she had to be right back to survival. A promise pinned to the board in her mind.

His calloused hand roamed over her hip. "It's the parent inside you," he said, bringing her back from the deep decline.

"What?" His touch set her skin on fire.

"Thinking of Lindsey right now, it's part of parenting, you'll get used to it." His lethal smile grew and burrowed into her heart.

"I'm not so sure about that." She rolled onto her back and stared at the ceiling.

He propped himself up on his elbow, studying her like a new play scratched on a cocktail napkin. "Why? It's a good thing. Lindsey's only ever had your mom thinking about her. She deserves someone good in her life."

"I've missed so much of it."

And so much of his.

"No one's condemning you for going after what you wanted, plus, you and your mom needed to be apart." He smirked, shaking his head. "Some of the knock-down fights you guys had were brutal. Iona wasn't exactly mother of the year most days." He whistled, twirling a strand of her hair between his fingers.

"Yeah, but I should have been here more. Even after graduation I—" She pressed her dry lips together. "I just got so caught up in the money and trusting myself." Money equaled security, and she needed her own security, but even with it, life was so unpredictable and always throwing reminders at her. No one here was really in charge.

"You're here now."

"I know, but—"

"No." He cut her off. "Life's too short for buts, Karis."

"Oh-my-God." She pulled a pillow from under her head and clocked him in his beautiful smile. How dare he throw her own words back in her face?

His laugh lit up the room. He snagged the pillow and tossed it to the floor.

"You always said that to me and I hated it," he revealed.

"And now?" she asked, surprised he remembered the mantra.

"And now it has its moments," he admitted, sliding close.

Naturally, she placed her head against his muscle-knitted chest and soaked in his piney scent. Too perfect. "Lindsey came clean about the cell phone." She cleared her throat, hoping to distract her greedy body. "She doesn't want you to take me away from her or force me to move back to NC. Just like Mom said."

It had been tempting to cancel the date after her talk with Lindsey, but the way she felt, lying on his chest, canceling would have been a mistake.

"Lindsey has a lot going on."

"I think she's embarrassed and scared." His brows creased in concern.

She swiped her own brow. No amount of wrinkle cream would save her. So unfair. Men got sexy with lines; women got old.

"Yeah, but kids are resilient, especially Lindsey." He settled against the headboard. She tried sliding to her side of the bed, but he pulled her back against him.

"Resilient, yes, but I want to be cautious. I need to take her concerns seriously." Nothing like honesty to make a person feel vulnerable.

"Pulling out the psych 101, huh?" He winked.

"No, just some basic aunt stuff. She's concerned about hockey." She rubbed the corners of the soft, one-thousand-count sheets between her fingers.

"Why?" His fun-loving smile turned business man.

Oh, why not give him a full confession? "We have a stack of bills a mile high, and hockey isn't cheap, ice is expensive." Damn frozen water.

"Yeah, it is. Let me help you with hockey." This time, she did pull away from his silky skin.

"No way. Don't even suggest it." Taking money from him equaled a big fat no. She leaned over the bed, feeling around on the floor. She had to get her clothes before all the air left the room. *Shirt or underwear, please.*

"Why not?" His tone defensive, he threw his legs over the side of the bed and planted his feet on the floor. He was in his underwear in seconds.

She rubbed her empty hand under the bed, still searching for any scrap of material. "Do you offer this to all your players?" He didn't, of course, and she would rather rob a bank than take his money.

"No, but Christ, it's Lindsey. She needs to play. Smith needs her to play." He shrugged like every kid needed hockey for survival. "I've helped out before." He glanced around the room, picked up her black boy shorts, and slid them into his pocket.

Seriously?

She pulled her legs beneath her, adjusted the falling sheet, and gave up on ever getting dressed again. "I'm sorry, what?"

"Forget it." He stood, all beautiful muscles and oozing confidence. The contours of his shoulders and neck, a brief mouthwatering distraction.

"Uh, no, I'm not going to forget it, so spill. And"—she drew out the short word—"give me my underwear."

Ignoring her request, he scrubbed his jaw, stalling. She wanted to punch him in the same spot.

"What?" He shrugged a no big deal. "Your sister never sent a dime, Iona can't cover it, Lindsey's a great kid, Smith loves hanging with her, so I offered to help."

He made it sound like nothing.

"And my mom took it?" The swinging hammer in her head grew three times larger.

"Yes," he confirmed.

There wasn't enough namaste in the world to calm her down. "How much?"

"Unimportant." He stared her down, and she rose to her knees.

She would not lose this. "How much?"

"Not sure." He stepped closer to the bed. His tussled hair was sexy as hell, and the dare in his gaze even more so.

"Right," she steamed. "How many seasons?"

He scrubbed his hands down his face and relented. "Three."

"Three? A year and a half of million-dollar hockey?" Her voice rose, cracking between syllables.

He pulled at his hair. "About." He toggled his head. "Listen, they were meant to be friends," he spoke fast, "I never worried about him as long as Lindsey was with him, so to guarantee she stayed playing, I offered to pay for it. I wanted Lindsey in Smith's life. He needs her, and now I think they need each other."

Her heart broke at the lengths this man tore through to make his family happy.

"You are not going to pay for hockey. We got it." She attempted to climb off the bed. Every moment in her life did not happen so she could take money from an ex-boyfriend to clean up her family's mess. No way, but as usual, Ty saw it differently.

His abs blocked her view, and when he put his hands on her shoulders, pushing her back onto the bed, her damn thighs spread on their own, eager to feel the pressure of his weight. He maneuvered between her legs, hard and hot. His intensity burned through her. Heat soaked into every submissive corner of her body.

"You're not going to let me help you?" he muttered.

"No," she breathed.

He caged her beneath him. She curved her fingers around his thick wrists.

Hanging his head low, his nose grazed her skin from neck to chest. "At least take the soccer job."

"What?" Living in Florida was supposed to be relaxing. The heated energy lay thick and bubbling around them. The ticking of his watch chirped loud, reminding her of years gone by. "How do you know they offered me the job?" she ventured.

His wrist flexed beneath her fingers, the cage his body created became stifling and still. Smooth shoulders bunched and the tick at his jaw jumped double time.

"I didn't." He buried his face into her hair, his lips heating her skin.

"I don't believe you." His gaze snapped to hers and she knew. Fighting for her own air, she asked, "How do you know?"

He looked away, his profile tight.

"Answer me," she whispered.

He eased off her. His face etched in confusion, and to Karis' dismay, regret.

"Don't go," he swallowed.

With shaky fingers, she gathered the sheet around her and stumbled from the bed.

"Just let me explain." He watched her every move. "Please."

His explanation didn't matter. "I'm not taking that job." She rushed through the room, snagged her dress, and threw it on.

"Jesus. Why the fuck not?" He raced tight on her heels.

How could he? He knew she had to do it on her own. She wasn't proud of debilitating independence, but damn it!

"Because it's not *my* job. It's the one you got for me. I worked too hard for too long to get my own job, Ty. I don't need you stepping in. I got this." How could he not see? Independence was all she had. Was all she'd ever owned.

"I know you got this. Christ, Karis. Taking help doesn't mean you don't have it together." Barefooted, he marched across the carpet, loose jeans slung low on his hips. Half naked, he looked all business and in control.

"Help me?" Unbelievable. "I'm not taking a job I didn't earn on my own. How dare you." She rounded on him, her finger in his face. "You didn't think I could do it?" Hot blood stormed through her veins, burning her from the inside out.

"That's not it and you know it," he countered. His face went all sharp edges and dark shadows.

"Yeah? Then why?"

"Because I want you to stay."

"Well, I can't without a job. A job I earn. Not get because I'm friends with the local professional hockey coach."

He shoved his hands into his pockets. His fight for patience evident in every move. "What the fuck? Your mom won't survive a move."

The sharp truth stabbed her in the heart. "I have no choice at the moment."

"There's always a choice," he countered.

Yeah, at twenty.

"No. I have to take care of them, and right now, care means money. My organization has been more than kind." She couldn't let her feelings for him cloud her discipline.

"They better be." His wince faint, but obvious.

"What does that mean?" Everything always came easy to him. How would he ever understand the struggle?

He stepped closer, never one to back down. "It means you gave up on us for them. This is the least they can do."

He didn't sell it, but she didn't have the strength to push it. Heading to the front door, hoping to find her shoes along the way, she gathered her thoughts.

"Wait." He blocked the door. His chest bare, his pants zipped and unbuttoned. His six-pack stretched tight, diving into a V past the waist of his jeans. Thick corded sinew lined his hips, and a pulse pounding under his jaw called to her. Her mouth buzzed wanting to taste him from hip to neck.

Her dress fell to the floor. He guided her back down the hall and into the bedroom. Falling onto the bed, his warm tongue assaulted every part of her.

Angled against her, his long thick fingers slid down her neck, slowing between her breasts, pressing deep into her skin. His intense blue stare followed every stroke. Her stomach clenched wanting more even while her mind warned against it.

Her body won. She dug her heels into the bed, pushing up to meet his hand pressed against the juncture of her thighs.

He hooked his fingers inside her slickness. "Wet and ready for me." He panted inside her mouth.

"Always. Now what are you going to do about it?"

Challenge accepted.

In one move, he flipped her over, moved between her legs, and urged her onto her knees.

Pulling her back to his lap, his erection throbbed. His chest hot against the sensitive skin of her back and his silky engorged cock teased the top of her ass. He pressed her into the mattress, and she adjusted herself to him. Opening her legs, she pulled her knees to her shoulders.

"I'm gonna come just looking at you on your knees, waiting for me." He leaned over her curved spine. Close to her ear. "Do you see what you mean to me?"

"Ty?" She arched up onto her elbows.

"Years, I needed you. Dreamt of you. Played for you. Fucked other girls trying to forget you."

Her fingers white-knuckled the sheets, and his voice poured into her soul. Her body burned, wanting him fast and hard.

He sat back on his bent legs and scooted her hips like they weighed nothing. Lined up to her depth, he rolled into her. A hiss escaped his lips. He slipped inside of her, filling her, until his name tore from her lips and became etched onto her heart.

Chapter Twenty

"Ty, wake up, your phone's ringing." Her body instantly responded to the warmth of his bare chest. The urge to rest her cheek against the smooth skin crucial. Stretching out, Karis reached across him to the nightstand. The noise had to stop. Why in hell would a jackhammer be someone's ringtone?

Wide fingers gripped her arm stopping her momentum and scaring her to death. The unladylike shriek flew from her mouth. Damn if the man didn't still have stealthy skills. For everything.

"I got it." He sat up, the white sheet slipping low on his hips. She demanded her body to chill out and return to its side of the bed. But before she could crawl back, he pulled her onto his chest, leaned against the headboard, and raised the phone to his ear.

Letting her eyes drift close, she snuggled into him, and inhaled the sweet scent of a man fresh from sex. Her fingers hovered up and over his long torso, reaching his neck, the prickles of his jaw, and almost into his thick dark hair.

Almost.

"Smith, calm down, where's Uncle Ryan?"

As fast as she tried to get off him, didn't matter. He bounced from the bed, putting his phone on speaker, grabbing his pants and shoving his legs into each side. Sans boxers.

Panic spooled low in her gut. She covered herself and glanced around the room trying to focus on something other than his frantic tone. Pieces of clothing lay scattered on the floor. A light lamp. A long mirror. All things ignored hours ago.

The pitch-dark world outside matched his jerky gestures. What time was it?

On speakerphone, Smith yelled and lapsed into crying. Her heart picked up speed and a sick wave crashed into her. Oriented, she picked up Ty's shirt and shoved it into his hands.

Her gesture brought him back from panic, but Smith's voice reached uncomfortable levels of loud. Her stomach clenched with helplessness and a need to call and check on Lindsey.

Smith's breath pumped through the phone. "Ryan left and Pop's gone nuts. Uncle Ty, come get me."

The pounding on the door coming from the phone was something out of a horror movie.

"Jesus Christ, Smith. Don't open that door. Do you hear me?" The desperation in his voice, an alarming blanket of terror.

"Hurry. I'm scared," Smith yelled.

Ty slipped on slides and raced to the door. "Smith, don't hang up. I'll be there in five minutes. Do not open that fucking door." He snagged his keys and faced her. "He promised me. He fucking promised me, Karis." His eyes blazed wild with fury. Haunted by the past and what could happen if he didn't make it there in time.

Imagination was scarier than *Jaws*. "Just go get him."

Ty slammed the door. Two pictures crashed to the floor.

Ryan better run and hide.

Chewing on her lip, she dressed fast, not replaying the way Ty's touch sent her reeling, or the familiar way he roamed her body. No. She replayed Smith's voice, and the way each word sliced into Ty. She should have gone with him. What was she thinking? With Ryan gone, he might kill his father.

Down the hall, she scanned the contents on the small table in the foyer. No keys.

She scooped her purse up off the floor, snagged her phone, and headed to the leather couch.

The screen lit up with a million bubbles of missed calls. Sliding her shaky finger across the glass, Karis gripped the cold metal rectangle.

Without a ring, Lindsey's voice came loud and fast. "Aunt Karis, where are you? Are you with Coach?"

Damn she wished she had keys. She wished she had a car, a bike, anything to get her to Lindsey. After hearing Smith's plea for help, she needed to wrap her arms around the protective girl and never let go.

"Lindsey." Her voice held steady. How much did she know? Did she register the fear in Smith's voice?

"Smith needs help." She was frantic. Not listening and way past panic.

"Lindsey, Ty's on his way to get him—"

"On his way! He should be there—"

"Calm down." Not gonna happen. "He's with him now. Smith's okay. He's safe."

The heavy breaths coming through the phone would make an entire hockey team light-headed. What the hell did parents say to their kids in times like this? All Karis wanted to do was make it better. Her brain blanked and her vision tunneled. Definite signs of stress, with no end in sight.

"Linds, is Grandma okay?"

"Yeah, she's sleeping."

"Did you check on her?" Karis checked her watch. A little past midnight. Midnight. How did that happen? This date had been a bad idea. Guilt arrived and took its place in line right next to selfish.

"I've checked on her twice."

Reasonable.

Good to know. When panic sets into a teenager, change the subject. Give their crazy mind something else to think about.

Karis gathered her hair around her shoulders and pulled her legs beneath her. She needed a car. Next date, she would drive. "Did you talk to Smith?"

Her silence screamed.

Stay with me girl.

"Yeah," she finally answered.

Karis' heartbeat knocked around her chest like a wild bird fed up with being caged; her stomach curled with worry. "What did he say?"

"He was screaming," Lindsey's voice shuttered. "He was screaming that he needed help. He wanted me to take the car and go get him."

Knots pulled tight in the pit of her stomach. "Did he say where Ryan was?"

"Smith told Ryan he could go out, and that he would be fine with Pop, but they are not fine. Pop is not fine. He's never fine. No matter what they all say. Pop is not fine, and I hate it when Smith has to go over there." Her voice revealed high levels of anxiety and anger, and rightfully so.

Karis jumped up from the couch, pacing like a wild beast eager to get to her young. The desperation to see Lindsey crawled over her like nothing she had ever known. Her mind spun in a million different directions searching for a solution.

"Wait. Why does Smith *have* to go over there?" Puzzle pieces locked into place.

"He said Coach has to take him over to Pop's at least twice a month. It's like a court ordered thing. Smith overheard Coach and Coach Ryan talking about it. I told him to ask about it, I even told him I'd ask about it, but he said no."

Court ordered? What the hell was going on?

"Aunt Karis, can you come home?"

Her heart broke wide open. "Aww, honey I don't have a car."

"You could Uber?"

Uber?

Oh goodness. She hardly talked to strangers much less drive with them. In a vehicle with no way out except the hard rolling road. Sure.

"Ya know what? I'm gonna Uber." Sounded easy enough.

"Nice."

"Can you tell me how?" Good thing she didn't care about cool points.

Lindsey chuckled and the flapping bird in Karis' chest simmered down. After a quick lesson and a rock-solid promise, given about fifteen times, she hung up the phone and Ubered her first ride.

Who needed a car when Uber was arriving in five minutes?

The pounding on the door rattled her tattered nerves and pushed her to the edge. Uber said they would text, and she certainly did it right. Shrugging her purse over her shoulder and slipping on her shoes, Karis answered the door. Hopefully they'd wait while she jotted Ty a note.

The woman on the other side of the door could seriously use a sandwich and a shower.

"I see he's got himself another one." The twig sauntered in on shaky legs. Clearly familiar with her surroundings. She headed straight for the kitchen.

"Come on in," Karis clipped.

Opening the fridge, the bag of bones ignored Karis. Her sunken eyes roamed the cool shelves while her bony fingers gripped the stainless handle. Large-rocked rings graced her wrinkled hands and earrings climbed up and around both ears. The nose ring was nothing compared to the two hoops in the center of her bottom lip.

The woman closed the fridge empty-handed, all loose skin and long limbs. The cutoff shorts and tank top, an open view of the obvious abuse done to her body. Also, obvious? How much she resembled Smith.

"You know Smith's in trouble tonight, right? Certainly, you meant to go there instead of here." The woman flinched.

"What do you mean in trouble?" Surprisingly, the words held a hint of concern, but her shifty eyes didn't follow through on the sale. Concern for a child murdered you from the inside out. It didn't make you hungry and needing your next fix.

"Why are you here?" Karis questioned, keeping the current situation under wraps.

Smith's mom leaned over and placed her elbows on the center island. She pursed her lips and sized up the situation. The purpose of the visit became obvious.

"You must be Karis?" Hard lines deepened around her mouth.

Well, that was a little unsettling.

"I am. And you are?"

"You know who I am." Super-Mom tossed her purse onto the counter.

"Ty's not here. He went to get Smith." As if she cared.

The woman held up a hand. "Listen, do me a favor. Tell Ty it's time." Skinny fingers reached behind her back and patted for her phone.

"Time for what?" Karis asked.

A sharp, soulless laugh ricocheted around the kitchen. Bouncing off the stainless appliances and landing like an empty echo on the tiled floor.

"He hasn't told you? Interesting." She pursed her lips, deepening the wrinkles that grew on an addict's face.

Karis ignored her cell phone signaling Uber had arrived. As much as she wanted to run out and take the car all the way back to North Carolina, she forced herself to stay. "I'll relay your message."

The woman pushed off the counter and swayed toward the door, her flip-flops flicking with each step. "You do that. Tell him Tish came by and time's up."

Tish. Yeah, okay. She'd tell him more than that.

Sympathy cut as much as concern. Did Smith know her? Did his idea of family include her? She wrestled with asking Tish to stay. As unpleasant as she seemed, the woman could use a bed, and she *was* Smith's mother.

Another cackle escaped through Tish's pierced lips. "Don't go all soft on me. I don't need your help. I need Ty's payment. From everything Wes said about you, I'd think you could handle delivering a message."

See ya, toots. Karis opened the front door.

"Subtle," Tish smirked.

"Sorry, didn't mean to be. I think it's time for you to go." Smith was better off without this lady.

"So it is." The woman's disgusted gaze drifted over her. A grinchy smile slipped across her lips. "Good night, Karis. Tell Ty to be in touch, or I will."

***

Smith slouched in the passenger seat, white as a ghost, and silent. Fucking silent and staring at the dried blood cracking on Ty's knuckles. Ty adjusted the weapons to the bottom of the steering wheel, but blood covered every angle.

The scene at his father's house made his stomach coil and his childhood memories gurgle back to glass seats. He shut that shit down. There was no room for a stroll down the haunted memory lane. God only knew what scenes were flashing through Smith's mind. It was never supposed to be like this for him.

Never.

Fucking Ryan.

He squeezed the steering wheel. Even though Ryan had been protected from all the horrible blows of one of Pop's tirades, he knew the story, and had become well versed in his role as Smith's bodyguard.

Triggers from every direction assaulted Ty's stability when he'd entered the house, climbed the stairs, and zeroed in on Pop's meaty fist banging on the bedroom door. Smith's breathless screams ignited the beast Ty had quieted years ago.

Without wasting a second, his fist connected with Pop's jaw sending him spiraling to the floor. He never gave it a second thought. There would be no discussion. No reasoning. The empty vodka bottles on the table, on the couch, and stacked in the garage were a definite sign that things had gone south.

The door opened as soon as Smith was calm enough to comprehend he was safe. Ty wasted no time grabbing the kid and bolting, never to go back. Ever. Not this time. No matter what Ryan said. Pop didn't deserve any more chances, and to hell with all his threats to tell Smith the truth.

Smith deserved a normal family, not one doused in alcohol and hate. Hope was a huge chance not worth the risk. Having no family was better than having this one. Ryan could Oprah-ize all he wanted. Pop was never going to change because people didn't change.

He landed the car in the curve of the driveway. The house lay dark. Cold. Not one beam of light glowed from any window. Empty.

"Come on, Smith." He reached for the door handle praying Smith did the same.

He didn't.

Ty got out, slammed the car door, and ripped his fingers through his hair. Heading around to Smith's door, he glanced up at the sky, and swallowed the scream trudging up his throat. He bowed his head and steadied his breathing, compartmentalizing his anger and helplessness into open files for later review. He had to be levelheaded for Smith.

He'd bank his anger for Ryan.

Smith flew out of the car and landed square on Ty's chest. He pressed his face tight against Ty's shirt. Small shudders shook his boney frame, and thin muscled arms anchored around Ty's waist.

"I don't want to go back."

Ty broke into pieces.

"You will never have to go back. Never. I am so sorry. Did he hurt you? Did he hit you?" They clung to each other. Ty's eyes and fingers searching for wounds.

Smith shook his head, but trauma liked to play hide-and-seek, and days would pass before he would feel the full effect of a Pop episode. Ty had to be ready for the nightmares, the lack of trust, and the anger Smith would feel toward them all. A sliver of resentment for Wes wormed into Ty's heart, but he locked it away, staying focused on what Smith needed and what Wes couldn't give him.

He guided Smith up the front steps, opened the door, and surveyed the quiet.

She was gone.

His fists clenched to take out a wall, but one shiver from Smith's shoulder and Ty's composure locked in solid. Smith had seen enough violence from the adults in his life for one night, and every inch of the blame sat square on Ty. One night between Karis' warm creamy thighs and his reality became her. He couldn't risk it.

Ty blew out a breath, trying to be thankful she was gone. Smith needed him, and Karis held the power to negate all his life's responsibilities. Weak, but true.

With Smith safe in his room, Ty scanned his texts and drifted to his bedroom down the hall. Still not a peep from Ryan. The sorry dick.

The paper sitting on his dresser sent his heart racing. Innocent and lovely, with curvy lines and dark dots, it lay propped up, luring him to the slaughter.

Thanks for the roll in the hay.

Nice lay.

Still killing it between the sheets.

He scanned the words and stuffed the note in his pocket. There would be no sleep in his future.

"Smith, you good?" he called out, and with no answer, stalked back down the hall.

He pushed the door open. "Smith?" The shower running in the connected Jack and Jill bathroom laid a suspicious repetitive beat against the eerie quiet.

Tossing the cell phone on Smith's bed, he entered the bathroom. Dark memories flooded his mind and cut off reasonable thinking. Survival had to be self-centered.

Behind the curtain, Smith lay hunched on the floor of the shower, water streaming down his back. His shoulders bounced from the thick sobs released with each cry. Jesus, parenting encompassed the best and worst of everything. What could he do to take the pain away? What the *hell* could he do?

Karis' note forgotten; he pulled Smith to his feet. He snagged the towel off the rack and wrapped it around the boy's waist. Smith kept his head down as Ty directed him to his bedroom.

"Talk to me." Ty sank onto the bed, hoping Smith would do the same. When he did, Ty sucked in a thankful breath.

Smith stared at the floor. "He wouldn't stop. I was so scared."

Ty wrapped Smith in a gripping hug. His family. His responsibility. His life.

"Smith, listen to me." He had to at least try. "Right here, right now, you are home. You are safe, and what happened tonight will never happen again. Ever. *I promise.*" A promise carved in the blood of his heart.

"What's wrong with Pop?" Smith shivered.

A good question with too many unsettling answers.

"He's not right. But honestly, I thought there was hope. I mean, listening to Ryan, which I should have known better, I thought Pop was recovering," he confessed, pissed at his awful judgement.

"He's not."

Ty squeezed his fist. "No, he's not. Do you know where Uncle Ryan went tonight?"

"He went out with people from New York. Said it was important, so I thought it was fine."

Ty steamed. Ryan Mr. —All About Family— left his nephew to go wine and dine with another team? Douche. Why didn't Ryan just say he couldn't be there? He would have canceled his date. At least, he had to believe he would have.

"I don't know what I did wrong." Smith sobbed and covered his face with trembling fingers.

Ty centered his control and clutched Smith by the shoulders. "You did nothing wrong. This is all Pop. Don't you dare think you're the reason this happened or that you could have done something to stop it, because you couldn't, and you can't. It's just Pop. I wish it wasn't, but it is."

"Did he do this to you?"

The world froze. "Tell me what happened?" Ty pushed the words between his teeth. Never in a million years did he think he'd be sharing Pop rampage stories with his nephew.

"We were shooting pucks and he was telling me what I had to do better. How to put my arm back to get more power, and then before I knew what was happening, he was banging his stick on the ground and then against the garage door and then on the car." Smith swallowed and looked up. "On the car. His eyes looked crazy, and he started coming toward me with the stick, so I threw my stick at him and ran into the house."

"Jesus." Ryan was a dead man. Pop was a dead man.

"He chased me, and caught me on the stairs, and bent my arm back," Smith rambled on. Words quivering.

With a worthless breath, Ty clenched his knuckles. The ache to punch something grew strong, but he searched for words to help Smith cope instead. Words never whispered to him when he had been the teenager running upstairs.

"You got away from him," Ty encouraged.

"Yeah, he squished my face against the stairs, but I flipped over and pushed him off. I ran to my room and locked the door. What if my phone hadn't been in my pocket?"

"Your phone was and you're okay." He squeezed the mattress.

"I don't feel okay." Smith stood and grabbed shorts from a drawer.

"I know, but you will be." He'd pray every night until it happened.

Within five minutes, Smith dove under the sheets, and filled the room with small, exhausted snores. Ty cracked his bedroom door. At least one of them would get some sleep.

Chapter Twenty-One

He couldn't wait any longer. Karis hadn't reached out, and fuck if he'd spend the rest of the afternoon waiting for her to text him back. Clearly her phone was off, like always. Ty hated to think Lindsey had it again, but damn, he didn't put it past that girl.

Smith beat him to the front door.

"Smith, doorbell." The kid froze, the doorknob clutched in his hand. Ty stepped onto the porch, bracing himself for a clash.

"It's Lindsey," Smith whined. For all the hell Smith suffered last night, he looked good. Amazing what a shower, some sleep, and pancakes could do for a kid. Resilient beasts.

"I don't care. This is not your house. You don't walk right in." He straightened Smith's hair, like he swore he'd never do.

On cue, Lindsey opened the front door. "Hey, why'd you ring the bell? You normally just come in."

Smith stood ramrod straight and sent Ty a death stare. These two. He would never understand their relationship.

"Apparently, the rules have changed, and now I'll be ringing the bell." Cutting sarcasm bounced off Ty's uncle armor.

Lindsey's brows drew together in a look she certainly got from her aunt. "Uh, okay. Hey, Coach. Come in." She hesitated. "I'm not sure where Aunt Karis went."

Karis slid up behind her. Sun baked and flushed. "Lindsey, I told you I'd be in the backyard." She shot Lindsey a puzzled look. The air between them snapped with friction.

"Smith." Karis stepped past Lindsey and pulled Smith into a big mom hug.

"Aunt Karis," Lindsey laughed.

Karis dropped her arms and stepped back. "Sorry, I was just worried." She bit into her lip, and Ty wanted to fall to his knees. "I was worried about you and it's good to see you smiling." Her long hair was strapped up in a mesmerizing ponytail, with messy chunks falling around her face. The look, paired with her concern for Smith, stole Ty's breath in the most uneasy way.

He fisted his fingers and ran a quick scan down her legs. Tan and long. Short ratty jean shorts paired with a tank top and muddy rubber gardening boots. A healthy bronze graced her nose and brightened her cheeks. Outside looked good on her, even if she did spend all day planting things she could never actually grow. Her lips glistened, making his own tingle to rub against the sensitive skin.

He pulled in a steadying breath before he lost his mind and acted on his need to fall into her. He yearned to pull her hair out of that ponytail, slide his fingers up her thighs and dive inside those shorts. An all too real and inappropriate thought.

She moved aside, letting the kids escape to the garage, no doubt to shoot pucks. Her tongue slid between her teeth. "That was probably a little too much with the hug, but I just—" Her white teeth nibbled on her lip.

"No worries." He swallowed a groan and stopped himself from ripping out his heart. She could be good for Smith, but he couldn't handle it.

"I'm working in the yard. You want to come out with me?"

Not really, I'd like to go upstairs and have my dirty way with you, but outside is good.

"Sure." He might need to douse himself with the water hose.

A loud thud banged from the garage. "Nothing better than garage hockey."

"Yeah, well, how good are you with drywall? Those holes need patching before we sell the house."

The issues between them stirred in the air, and she just dropped another one. "Still planning on making the move?" He followed her out the back door. His jaw tight as hell, and his gaze glued to her ass. The fringe of the jean shorts framed the back of her thighs. Pieces of grass stuck to the curved muscles.

"I mean, it's still a possibility. I'm choosing between two evils so there's really no win. My mother's health or the ability to pay for my mother's health? The money thing doesn't go away unless I win the lottery. You didn't win last night, did you? 'Cause if so, I'd like to borrow some cash." She laughed, and it lightened the heaviness for a fleeting moment.

"I didn't win, but you can still borrow cash. How much? You name it."

A tired frown burned across her lips. "I'm kidding, Ty. I don't want your money."

"Said no girl ever." Total fact.

"You keep sketchy company. I'm a girl and—"

He held his hands up. "Stop, you're not a girl."

Karis looked at her chest and sent him an evil grin. As much as she teased, the unanswered questions between them grew heavy.

"You know what I mean," he clarified, hoping the distance he felt was one-sided.

"Indeed, I do. I'm not borrowing money from you, so stop offering. No cash. No hockey payments. I have money, and I'm going to find Leah." She exhaled and rolled her head back from shoulder to shoulder. "But that's a hunt for another day."

"And now?"

They stepped through the open slider and into blue skies. She grabbed a ball cap, doused her lips with balm, and closed the door. He wouldn't make it one more minute without touching her.

"Now, we go outside and do something physical before I lose my mind, so"—she shrugged—"I'm weeding."

Ty smacked his head. "Of course, weeding. Who goes for a run or to the gym or talks for stress relief? Weeding, yeah." He gave a thumbs-up.

She offered a soft smile. Points for him. How long were they going to dance around the note she'd left him?

"Here, you need a bag."

"Awesome. Do I have to get on all fours, too?" He sighed, remembering the gardens she'd made him pluck back in Carolina, *just for fun and good mental health.*

"Of course, man. We do it right around here. You have to get good and dirty." She handed him a plastic bag.

"Don't look at me like that when you say those words." His body hung on the edge. The words a jab at the past he couldn't forget combined with the turmoil of wanting her, Smith safe, and a normal family he could love, provide for, and protect all meshed into one dire want. "Walk away from me. Now." Tension tightened between them, pulling their bodies closer.

"I'm not sure I can." They couldn't skirt around the issue any longer.

"You did last night," he jabbed.

"I had to, but I left a note."

Another cold splash.

"You want to talk about it?" She softened.

Good question.

He scanned the yard. Grass stretched from fence to fence, and familiar green crawlers with purple flowers covered two huge hilly flower beds. The same purple flower she tried to grow in North Carolina but ended up settling on hydrangeas. He knew way more about flowers than any hockey player should.

"Come on." She headed to a light-blue-and-white shed. Wooden flower boxes, overflowing with thirsty plants, clung to small windows. Inside, the shed reeked of character and comfort. Rugs covered the plank floor and baskets filled with greenery flanked two lamps. It didn't look ready to sell. It looked permanent.

"Holy shit, Karis. You always had a thing for plants." He closed the door.

She switched on an old, rusted floor lamp. "Too bad I can't grow them."

"Yeah, but you never give up. It looks great in here."

She stepped around the small couch, straightening things. Avoiding him. A heavy sadness radiated from her, hitting him hard.

"Thanks. I need a private space to have some counseling sessions. Ya know, the bedroom office doesn't provide much privacy." She thumbed over her shoulder. "I remembered this old shed and spent the week cleaning out Leah's junk, and voile. My 'she shed.'" Usually, people were pretty thrilled with a completed project, not unsure or worried.

Her attempt at happy included potted plants, framed pics on chipped bookshelves, a workbench, and a couch. A permanent adjustment.

Before he could ask, she flew into pieces. Tears rolling down her cheeks. Unable to resist, he welcomed the shudder of her shoulders against his chest. The need to shield her from the hurt of her world overwhelmed him, but he couldn't condemn it. The soft clicks of the shed's AC buzzed in a comforting hum. He never wanted to leave. *Dangerous thought number one million.*

"We got this, baby."

She coughed through her tears. "No, *we* don't. Why didn't you tell me Tish was in the picture?"

She pulled away from him. His body resented her absence, and anger surged quick and thick. He waited, watching carefully. Her arms drooped down her sides in defeat. She looked tired, confused, and pissed. He looked like that every day. He called it parenting.

Gritting his teeth, he jumped right in. "Tell me what Tish told you."

"First, tell me how Smith's doing?" She sniffed and wiped her face.

"How is Smith doing?" The question baffled his brain and grief broke wide open. He turned to the closest wall and sank his fist into it. Repeatedly. The tin of the shed wall stood no chance against the power of his anger and grief.

He heard her shriek, but she didn't stop him. Smart girl. Punch after punch. He ignored the sting in his hands, and the blood on his knuckles oozing from his reopened wounds. Until hot, slim fingers gripped his biceps, jerking him back to reality.

What about Smith?

Fuck.

Yeah, Ty, what about Smith?

All he could do was grab her. Just grab her and hang on while the storm moved through him.

"It's okay. He's okay." Her fingers sifted through his hair. Her lips close to his face.

His body kicked into high alert. And what he was about to do was no good for anyone, but he was out of his head with the need for comfort and control.

His lips crashed into hers, hard and desperate. His tongue wasted no time capturing her warmth and wetness. Her moan meant everything except no.

She landed on the workbench with as much grace as a hockey player could muster at a time like this. He needed to sink into her. A simple goal. He slid her to the edge of the bench. Her thighs spread. The thin jean shorts could be torn in seconds, but his fingers reached her center without the macho bullshit.

In fast need, he edged her shorts to the side and brushed his fingers against silky panties, drenched and ready for him. Wanting him. Letting him do whatever he needed to come back from the chaos spinning around him.

She opened wider, and her head fell back with a soft sigh.

He slid three fingers past the elastic on the inner thigh of her panties and slipped deep inside her warmth. She arched in his arms, gripping his hair and holding tight.

"Jesus, Karis. Need you now." His hands splayed across her back. Gripping as much as he could.

Her garden boots flopped to the ground. She pushed him back and jumped off the bench. Her shorts and a creamy scrap of lace dropped to the floor.

He grabbed a handful of her ass and set her back on the bench. Uncovered and open, she was fair game. His stomach tightened with each pass of her sweet fingers, trailing over him, setting his skin on fire. His constricting shirt landed on her boots, and her tank top followed. Before he could blink, she sprawled out long in front of him. Her body arching off the table, giving him the green light.

His pants puddled to the floor.

"You're beautiful," he surrendered. Sliding his fingers up the curve of her neck and into her hair, he released her thick waves, catching them all in his hands. Her scent ignited his soul. Lavender. Long limbs encouraged him to rid the guilt and pressure built up overnight.

Her heels balanced on the edge of the bench. He worked his cock and teased her wet core. Fanning her knees out, her scent stronger, he had to have a taste. Needed to lick her from front to back, in and out. His dick had other plans.

Leaning over her, he entered her in one slow slide, hitting deep. His breath hitched and his elbows gave. Their stares locked. He stilled, resisting the want to thrust hard, and then harder again. She was always down for the physical, but she was nowhere near ready for what he had in mind. He blinked, breaking their soul-touching contact.

"Karis?" Her name a gasp. Unrecognizable to the Ty he had become without her. The Ty he still needed to be.

"Ty?" His name was a fallen sob. Her fingers fastened around his wrists.

He leaned close to her ear. "See what you do to me?"

"Ty," she cried.

"Don't come." He pulled out of her. "Not yet."

"Don't." She looked straight into him, and they became the two lovers they once were.

"Don't what?" He stroked in and out of her in long, deep rolls.

She shook her head. Her eyes glistened. If she cried while he was inside her, he would lose it. "Talk?" he cave-manned.

"No 'don'ts.'" She inched her fingers into his, bonding their hands.

He stopped mid-thrust and pulsed centimeters at a time. Patience lost. Picking her up, he laid her on her stomach across the back of the old red couch opposite the workbench. Lifting her hips, he entered her from behind.

Letting his fingers run down her warm back and wrap around her hips. He found the bud that would make her scream. And scream she did.

He leaned over and whispered through her hair. "Let me feel you let go. Give me that, at least."

She shook her head. "Not without you." She pushed her ass against him.

"Jesus," he hissed.

"Please," she begged, her thin voice wispy. Her head fell back against his shoulder.

With her release, he grabbed her hips and painfully pulled himself away from her warmth, twisting her around, needing to see her face.

"Ty?" Her body dripped hot and pliant in his hands. Her feet hung from the arm of the couch, and his body pulsed from the skin-to-skin contact. Their foreheads touched, and he soaked her in.

His tongue dove maddeningly deep into her hot mouth. Licking the soft inside, and with one push he entered her, coming like an out-of-control high school boy.

Trouble became a slight fade on his lost sanity.

Dammit, Karis.

Chapter Twenty-Two

In silence, he handed her each stitch of clothing, looking everywhere but at her. She slipped on her boots. A sliver of light drenched the floor as Ty opened the door. Hockey pucks still smacked against the wall in the garage.

She was a horrible aunt, but so help her God if he stepped out that door. He was restless to escape. She recognized it right away.

He pulled his shirt over his head. "I'm going to go check on the kids." A tempting excuse to dismiss him, but she passed.

"No, you're not. Hear that? They're fine. Sit." She jabbed at the couch.

He followed her directions and leaned over, taking a small sniff of where her body had just been.

This man.

Behind her belly's wild somersaults, she rallied her composure. "Talk to me about Smith and did you find Ryan?" His family had always been his weakness, binding him to a desperate search for love and acceptance. She had no right to offer either.

He pulled her close. His head lodged into the curve of her neck. His breathing, pumping puffs of warm air. "Why would I let Smith go there? When will I get it? Pop will never change."

"Oh, babe." She held onto him, wanting to take it all away. "Don't be mad because you had hope. How were you to know?"

He stiffened. "How could I not know? Both my brothers are dicks, but I'm the idiot asshole. I believed them. Believed them when they said he changed. Believed Ryan when he said he'd stay while Smith visits the dick of a grandfather he's so fucking unfortunate to have."

Ty pushed off the couch and paced to the hole in the wall. Evidence of his lost control. Ty liked control.

"Smith is fortunate to have *you*." She angled up behind him, her arms aching to hold him.

He slipped around, facing her, but backed away. "My one condition is I can't be there when Smith visits Pop. It triggers an uncontrollable downward spiral and takes days to overcome. But Ryan promised me he'd stay. Always. Never leaving them alone."

"Where was he?" So much hurt shadowed his face.

"That's the question, isn't it? I'm hoping I don't kill him before I find out the answer."

"You haven't seen him?" The AC unit clicked, attempting to dry the sweat trickling down her back.

"No. He hasn't responded to a text from me or Smith."

That explained the unraveling composure. He couldn't find Ryan.

He doubled over, bracing himself on his knees. "Don't look at me like that."

"Like what?" She ventured closer.

"I've seen that look a million times. It's the *Ryan is a grown man* look and I need to let him be, but I fucking can't when Smith's involved."

"Maybe you shouldn't let your dad see Smith for a while." She reached for an idea to assuage the hate filling the room.

He shook his head no.

"Why not? What's going on?" she pressed.

"You don't want to know. You don't like complications, remember?" he snapped, distancing himself.

"Don't." The sting angered her more. She would not cry over this. "Don't take this out on me. On us."

He laughed. His demeanor shifting. "There is no us. You don't get to know about my business anymore. You didn't give a shit then. Why would you give a shit now? I needed you then, and you bolted. I needed you now, and you bolted."

She flinched at his words. Fire blazed in his icy-blue stare. "Yet you have no problem fucking me. Not fair." As a hockey player, he was an emotional beast. As a coach, she thought he might have chilled a little. That theory was a bust.

He huffed, lashing out. "No, it wasn't fair, and it still isn't."

She plowed over his rage, refusing to give in to the hurt from their past. The hurt he kept throwing in her face.

She narrowed her focus. "Smith's mother walked into your house like she'd been there a million times. Why?" She clenched her emotions. A large feat considering she still tasted him on her lips and felt his pressure between her thighs.

"You have enough to handle without knowing my shit." His bulging shoulders and heaving chest disclosed his stance. He was ready to throw down.

"Wanting to know what happened to Smith isn't shit. He's Lindsey's friend and I need a heads-up about whatever it is he might be telling her this very moment."

He stopped. "Careful, you sound concerned for something other than your career."

"Fuck off, Ty. I just want to help you." Succumbing to the burning need scorching her inside and out, she calculated the volatility of their actions and his words, refusing to log them as a mistake.

Her body was good enough, but she wasn't?

His laugh was bitter. "Why? You don't let me help you, and confiding in you would just scare you off."

She reached for the door. He could stay and sweat his balls off for all she cared. She'd prepared herself for his defensive play and harsh words. It was how he worked through things, but she'd reached her breaking point.

He moved fast, pulling her against him, wrapping his arms around her stomach, her back flush with the tense muscles of his chest. They breathed as one.

Breaking away, she rounded on him. "A strung-out woman in flip-flops and stripper clothes showed up at your house last night looking like a dead ringer for Smith. I was not going to hang out while Lindsey sat at home freaking out."

His eyes softened, but his shoulders dropped only an inch. "Fair enough." He rubbed his temples and pulled his hands down his face. "But I needed you." He breathed.

Her heart kicked to break free. "I didn't even think about that. I just had to leave. Between Tish showing up and you bringing Smith home, I didn't know what either of you needed, and thought you'd want privacy."

"What we needed was you," he threw out, sharp and cutting.

But nobody ever needed her.

"So did Lindsey, and I'm here now," she offered. They needed her and she ran. A desperate need to make it right pulsed through her.

Ty pushed off the wall, passing her on his way to the door.

"You know my dad, hockey coach, trainer, AKA psycho. He thinks we all got into professional hockey because of him. Little does he know, having him for a dad meant there was no way in hell we would take no for an answer. We had to get out of that house and hockey was our best chance."

She swallowed hard, remembering the plot of this conversation.

"And you did," she encouraged.

"Yeah, we did. But Ryan always, *always*, had a soft spot for him." His jaw twitched. "But I can't forget the late nights with Pop rifling ninety-mile-an-hour pucks at me. Body checks in the garage more brutal than anything we'd ever encounter on the ice. The screaming, the hitting, the fighting. Hockey sticks slashed across the back of our legs. Wes and I got it more than Ryan ever did." He bit his bottom lip. "But last night it was Smith."

Dizzy with worry, she searched for something missing in his story. "Then why let Smith go there?"

He released a breath. "I have to. If I don't let Smith go, Pop will tell him I'm the one keeping him from his mother."

"What?" Puzzle pieces bounced around her brain, near missing every connection. The hum of the wall unit sputtered along. Still, no air reached her lungs.

Ty dug into his pockets. His lips tight with exhaustion and lined with worry. "Wes paid Tish to stay out of Smith's life."

She couldn't have heard that right.

"You heard right." His foot brushed at the floor. "Once I met her, I knew why. Wes was fucked up, but she was worse. I wanted Smith. She recognized a payday. Smith didn't need more losers in his life, so I continued to pay her."

"You didn't?" Karis covered her mouth.

"Don't look at me like that." He white-knuckled his hips.

Somewhere, this made sense.

He stepped forward, frantic to explain. "You saw her. She's a junkie. She ruined my brother, and she could just as easily ruin Smith. I can't let that happen. I can't sit by and let him live with a fucking addict." Anger ripped up his voice.

The missing piece was so close. "Why'd she show up at your place last night?"

"Now and then, she makes an appearance."

"She wants to see Smith?"

Ty laughed. "Fuck no. I paid her a small fortune, and she blew through that. She wants more money."

Shame covered his face. His shoulders drew up tight, and his chest rose with a deep inhalation.

She hesitated. "And you give it to her?"

"I do," he responded with quiet embarrassment.

"And what does Smith think happened to his mom?"

He hesitated.

No matter how awful the women were, every kid wanted to see their mom. Karis leaned against the couch, trying not to look like a shrink. She crossed her arms a million times in a million different ways.

He licked his lips and clasped his fingers behind his neck. "He thinks his mom gave him up for adoption."

"What?" Right versus wrong warred inside her head.

"I pay her to be out of his life and she stays away. It's her drug money." The heavy confession floated between them.

She reined in her shock. "Has she ever wanted to see him or be with him?" Her voice cracked. She wasn't Lindsey's mother, but she couldn't imagine a day without her.

"Never." Cold remorse for Smith ribboned the word.

"And your dad?" She could venture a guess at how he played into this madness.

"Ryan told him," Ty spat, disgusted.

"Shit." And so much more.

"Yep, Ryan's soft spot. He tried to bring Pop into the fold several times, but Pop just uses us as ammunition to get what he wants. Which is to create another hockey player in Smith."

"But you're doing that, and Smith *is* a hockey player," she countered. The corner of her lip flared from gnawing. Families like Ty's kept sports therapists in business. It broke her heart.

He shot her a dangerous look. "I am, but according to Pop, he could do better, and if I don't let him see Smith, he's gonna spill about Tish."

"Do you believe him?"

"One hundred fucking percent," he sighed.

"Jesus, we have problems."

He moved away from the door and folded his body onto the old couch. Relief washed over her. With the absence of hockey pucks clanging against metal, the silence wrapped around them, and her thoughts shuffled between the kids, Ty, and her mother.

Lacing their fingers together, his large hands swallowed hers. He pulled their touch to his mouth. His warm lips rubbed across her knuckles. One kiss and he pressed their union against his forehead.

"Stepping into that house," his deep voice trembled, "hearing those noises again. The banging on the door. The same door Pop banged on when I lived there—" He squeezed his eyes shut and clenched her hands. She tried pulling away, wanting to wrap her arms around him, but his hands held hers strong.

"A bottle of alcohol in every room, and Ryan no-fucking-where to be found. Moving Pop away from the door was easy but holding him off was almost impossible. Poisoned rage lives inside him and he's set on destroying everyone."

"But you got to Smith," she soothed.

"Yeah." He tilted his beautiful face toward her, their hands pressing against his rough cheek. "I did. Seeing Smith in danger brings me to a level I never knew existed."

"Ty," she whispered, a soft hitch in her voice.

"Nothing can break that man." He released her hands, steepled his fingers, and hunched his shoulders. His face turned to the floor and his elbows rested on his parted knees. "Smith was screaming at us to stop. Through all the pounding, I heard him, saw his red face and the tears dripping down his chin. Fucking welts on the back of his legs. I thought I was going to lose my mind, and Smith knew it."

"But you left. You didn't demolish Pop, even though he deserved it." She finished, relieved. Bouts with his father tore him at the seams and putting him back together was a delicate task.

"Smith grabbed my arm and pulled me out of the house. Not sure how we made it home."

She should have been there for him, but the goddamn need to run consumed her. She threw her arms around him, and he clung to her. His fingers dug into her back. Like he needed more of her. His face burrowed against her neck. Fear and exhaustion hummed on the surface of his skin. Holding him, she absorbed every ache.

A strong need to solve the problem and cut away his misery kicked in. Stunned, she watched him, waiting for the desire to fade. It didn't. Three words flashed through her mind, but she settled on, "It's going to be fine."

Whether she believed it or not didn't matter.

***

Ty stared at the phone lying on his lap, his stomach growing hotter with each text cascading down the screen. The majority from Pop, and none from Ryan. The most important one telling him five minutes until pizza.

"I got it," Ty called, pushing off the couch, and heading toward the door. He reached for his wallet, and no surprise, Karis met him in the hall.

"You're not buying dinner." She held out cash.

"Put your money away." He shoved her hand away, taking a second look at the mass of hair draped over her shoulder lying soft against her black T-shirt. Tempted to ignore the pizza and take her upstairs, he swore, remembering he had kids to feed.

"Here." She thrust money into his palm. He threw it on the hall table.

She puffed her cheeks and stalked back to the kitchen. He didn't care. He and Smith would devour most of the pizza anyway.

Ty opened the front door, and pizza became the furthest thing from his mind. His fist met Ryan's face with a fierce crunch, knocking the traitor away from the door and onto the porch. Ty had enough space to get a good run and torpedo the scumbag, sending them both down the steps and rolling into the grass.

"Fuck. Ty, stop," Ryan spat.

"Not a chance." He covered his brother, straddled him, and let his fist do the work.

"Uncle Ty!" Smith's voice floated somewhere near his head.

"Aunt Karis!" He was sure that was Lindsey screaming.

"Ty, get off of him." There was Karis.

Everyone coming to sweet Ryan's rescue.

"Tyson," Iona's stern voice cut through his rage. He stopped clobbering his brother who pleaded guilty by just sitting there accepting the pummeling.

Ty never lost a fight.

"You left him. You fucking piece of shit. Where were you?" His chest heaved, begging for air. Looking at his brother's face, he wanted to scream. Here he was, doing exactly what he was afraid his father would do to Smith. Fear and disappointment, trimmed in anger, coiled tight around his body's cocked muscles.

Ty jumped up and stumbled into the dusky night. The world housed betrayal. Disgust pitted in his stomach, and a rush of loss seared down his spine. Taking a step away, he gripped his hair, doubled over, and cupped his pulsing hands over his bent knees. A sharp roar, full of desperate despair, exploded into the air. How could he do this? How could he lose it?

Bruised knuckles glowed with rage as the air sailed in and out of his lungs. Insanity slipped and rattled. A loose vibration ricocheted through his body.

"Ty, don't think about it." Ryan patted his back, but the contact was too impossibly brutal. He bounded upright, flinging off Ryan's hands. Meeting his gaze, Ryan's bruises and swollen skin had Ty's stomach knotting up, and yet, one glance at Smith had him right back to needing to beat the shit out of his little brother. Ryan looked unruffled, but Smith was changed forever.

Catching Karis' look, Ty watched her shuffle the kids and Iona into the house.

The door slammed, and the brothers squared off. "Where were you?"

Ryan hung his hands on his hips, his eyes sad and swollen. "I'm sorry, I fucked up."

"You did, you fucked up. I hope she was worth it because you are out of here."

"What? There was no she."

"You left our nephew there with that lunatic." There had to be a she. Some chick popping up on his arm covering media platforms. Ryan's one un-Oprah-like vice.

"What did he do?"

"Jesus, I just want to fucking pound you." They stood, brother versus brother. Ty taller. Ryan wider. Both broken.

"You did that all ready," Ryan snarled. "Now, tell me what the fuck happened because I couldn't get anything out of Pop."

The thought of Ryan and Pop sitting around talking about what happened instead of Ryan coming to find Smith, raked on Ty's nerves. "You spoke with Pop and are just now getting here? Getting to Smith. Jesus, Ryan, you know how this goes."

"He was fine when I left," Ryan mumbled.

"Yeah, because Smith knows what wrong looks like on Pop?" he mocked.

Ryan's words slipped past his tight lips. "Like I said, Pop and Smith were fine. They were playing hockey, getting ready to have dinner. Smith said it was cool that I go, and he'd call if he needed me. You were going to be coming to get him soon anyway."

He shook his head. "No, Ryan. He was staying the night because you said you would stay. Does that ring a fucking bell?"

"Fuck." Ryan's shoulders sagged.

"Yeah. Remember when I told you Pop used to corner Wes and I in the net in the garage and shoot pucks at us?" He gasped for a breath. "Hard?"

Ryan's eyes went huge. He gripped each side of his face. His breathing rivaled the crickets chirping a symphony in the yard.

Ty skated over Ryan's grief. "Remember? Yeah? Cool. Remember when Wes and I told you about how Pop would get so drunk, he'd hold a beer in one hand and a hockey stick in the other and knock the shit out of our legs if we refused to drop and save a puck? Remember?"

"Stop," he begged, but Ty was short on compassion.

"Remember when we had to run into our rooms and barricade ourselves inside while Pop banged on the door? Well, you could have seen all that happen live, you asshole."

"Jesus Christ." Ryan paced in a circle. His hands clasped behind his head. He marched straight up the porch steps and entered the house. Ty followed close behind.

"Smith," Ryan called out.

Smith answered from the kitchen and by the time Ty crossed the threshold, Ryan had Smith wrapped in his arms, locking him tight against his chest. Large sobs shook Ryan's shoulders and Smith clung tight.

Karis led her mom and Lindsey to the living room, leaving Ty leaning against the counter, watching Ryan and Smith overcome the new gouge in their relationship.

"I'm so sorry, Smith." Ryan pulled back, grabbing Smith's forearms in a tight hold. "Are you okay? What can I do? Fuck." Still on his knees, Ryan looked at Ty. "What did I do? How do I fix this?"

Ty pushed off the counter and knelt down beside his family. "You're doing it."

Smith grabbed both brothers, pulling them together. His arms wrapped tight around each bulk of shoulder.

This was his family, and he would do whatever he had to do to make sure it stayed that way. Even if it meant giving up what he wanted most.

Chapter Twenty-Three

Something was off, for sure. The buzz in the house hummed low and haunting. Karis threw the covers off and padded to her mother's bedroom. Nothing made a calm night light up with an emergency like an empty bed where just two hours ago her mother slept tucked in tight.

Hustling downstairs, she spread her fingers over her stomach and tried to yoga breathe her way out of panic. The house lay too quiet; even the cicadas went radio silent. No slamming of pots, pans, or oven doors. No life whatsoever.

In the living room, the front door's chain dangled. Separated from the latch that she'd connected right before going to bed. Her mind slid sideways, presenting one awful scenario after another.

"Mom?" she screamed throughout the house.

Nothing.

She stumbled into the abandoned kitchen, her focus locking on the keys still hanging from the hook on the wall.

She took the stairs three at a time. Upstairs, her mother's cell phone lay on her bedside table. Confusion and turmoil battled for reasoning. Her mind attempted to comprehend and create some type of sensible plan.

Running to Lindsey's room, she sighed with relief. Lindsey lay in bed, her chest gliding up and down with quiet breaths.

Flying back downstairs, she pushed through the front door, halting briefly to adjust to the thick humidity. The yard sat empty. The closest neighbor an acre away. Where the hell would she go? Panic-induced indecision flared before coiling like a snake at the bottom of her stomach.

"Mom?" Karis called again, heading to the backyard. The edges of her vision blurred. *Oh God.* She choked on panic. Thinking was impossible.

Inside the house, she picked up her phone. Trembling fingers tapped his name.

"Karis?" Ty answered, his voice groggy with sleep.

"My mom's gone." Her chest tightened, the words barely making it through her contracting throat.

A creak came through the phone, and something fell hard to the floor. "Fuck," he groaned. Maybe not the floor, maybe his foot. "Gone?" Sleep drained from the scary word.

"Yes. I checked all over. She's not here, Ty." Her voice rose amongst the quiver. Fear surged through every limb.

"Where's Lindsey?"

"In bed asleep. What do I do? Where would she go? The keys are here?" she rambled. Unable to lock down a coherent course of action.

"Well, that's a relief."

"It is?"

"Yes."

Keys rattled on his end.

"I'm on my way. Stay there," he mumbled.

"I need to go find her." Yes. Good plan. She needed to go look for her wandering lost mother.

"Karis, don't you dare leave that house. I'll be there in ten minutes."

"Bad things can happen in ten minutes."

"Karis, stay with Lindsey," he commanded.

Cheap shot.

"Do you hear me?" he softened.

"Yes." She ended the call.

"Aunt Karis?"

She slammed her hand over her heart. "Jesus, you scared me."

Lindsey stood on the threshold in her pink-and-yellow pajamas. Her eyes puffy. Her hair wild. Adorable. Karis pulled her into her arms and gave a tight squeeze.

"What's wrong?"

"Nothing, go back to bed." But she didn't mean it. Would it be super detrimental to interrogate a teenager about the whereabouts of her disappearing grandmother? Probably. She skipped the idea but still wanted Lindsey to stay close by.

Lindsey plopped in a chair at the kitchen table and rubbed away the sleep. Looking no less worried than a yoga coach, she flipped her head to one side and brushed her hair back with her hand. "What's going on?"

A good parent would try to hide emergencies. Forget that.

"Grandma's not in her bed, Linds."

"She probably went to the swing set."

Was that code?

Karis sat, swinging her own wild hair to one side. "What's the swing set mean?"

"You know, the one down by Martha and Benny's house. Our neighbors."

Of course, the neighbors. She pressed hard against her temple and swirled her fingers. "We don't have neighbors. Martha and Benny live two miles down the road. They're an acre away."

Still, cool as a cucumber, Lindsey pulled the hair tie from her wrist and put her hair up. "Yeah, that's crazy. Anyway, sometimes Grandma goes there. She likes to swing."

She likes to swing.

"Jesus." It sounded so normal. Karis breathed like Vader and jumped up from her chair, swiping her car keys. Second-guessing herself, she hung them back up and tapped her fingers on the table.

"I'm gonna walk that way. When Ty gets here, will you tell him where I went? He's on his way."

"Yeah, he'll know where she is."

Reaching for the doorknob, Karis' hand stopped mid-grab. A few more wrinkles took up residence, and she paused, trying to recenter. "What do you mean, he'll know where she is?"

"He just knows." Lindsey shrugged, pulling pieces of hair out of her messy bun.

Karis fisted her hands and tried to calm the regret of Ty knowing more about her family than she did.

Ten minutes later, he stepped through the back door and took her straight into his open arms. He kissed the top of her head and for a quick second she allowed herself the luxury of his care.

"You know where my mom is?" she asked, looking up at him. Her chin resting on his chest. His hands pressed against the small of her back.

His words were careful and soft. "I might."

"Can you take me to her?"

He shook his head. "I'll go get her." He pulled his cell phone from his pocket and tapped it twice. His one arm locked tight around her waist, and she let it burn into her side.

"Hey, Ryan, Iona's missing again. Can you come?"

No one should have to handle her family emergencies but her. How humiliating. Frustration clobbered her rationale, and her embarrassment surged. She didn't do incompetence.

"Hey, Linds, you good?" Ty took a seat next to Lindsey.

"Yeah," she snapped and crossed her arms. An uneasy competition crackled between them. Their relationship had shifted to more than coach and player, and Karis had to show Lindsey she could love both her and Ty.

Love?

Worse timing ever.

She sat across from Lindsey, holding her hand, and listening to Ty make two more phone calls to both his pro goalies, mortifying her to the bone. "Please," she groaned. "I'll go find her." Karis stood, anxious to take care of this before he called the military.

He shoved his phone back in his pocket. "Karis, sit down. We've got this."

At that moment, she understood. "You've *all* done this before."

In front of her, he went down on one knee and crooked a gentle finger beneath her chin. "This is what family does."

"Just go find her." She leaned her head on his shoulders. Surrender and fear swarming inside her, mixing with the overwhelming hint of his warmth and sincerity. Escaping him, she replaced his heat with the cold counter. He was more connected with her family than she realized.

Ty stepped behind her. His mouth hovered over her ear. "We'll find her."

"How often were you called to look for her?" She focused on the black night outside the window.

"Lindsey called me a couple times." He spoke too fast for it to be true. It had to be more than a couple, but she let it go.

She leered at him and glanced over at Lindsey still sitting at the table. Her head cocked down like a girl in trouble. Heartbreaking. She'd been through enough because of the incompetent adults in her life. It had to stop.

Karis released a heavy breath. "What do we do to these kids?"

Ty shrugged. "The same thing our parents did to us. We fuck them up."

"I think you might be right."

Pounding on the back door had Lindsey up and Karis jumping out of her skin. Three enormous men squeezed into the house. The only recognizable one was Ryan. He kissed Lindsey on the cheek and wrapped an arm around Karis.

"Hi, honey." His voice filled with concern.

"Hey, Ryan, thanks for coming." She leaned into his hug.

"That's enough." Ty cut in between them.

"Are we going to the usual places?" one player asked straight through the tension.

They had usual places? She curled her arms around herself and waited for the urge to run to take over. Men in her kitchen. Her mom gone. A sad girl used to this crazy turmoil. All motivation for running away.

Ty tucked her into his side, holding her steady. "Yeah, check your normal places and call when you find her." He kissed the top of her head.

With that, the kitchen emptied.

Karis considered sending Lindsey back to bed, but she'd been alone long enough.

***

Iona sat on the swing in her pink bathrobe, moving side to side, her bare feet digging in the dirt. He had found her here a dozen times and questioned the necessity for backup. But better safe than sorry.

"Hey, Iona." Ty sat on the other swing just like he always did. He finished sending off the texts to the search party and twisted his swing toward her.

"You didn't need to come tonight. I'm fine," she grumbled, looking down at the ground. He believed her.

"We've talked about this. You need to tell people when you need to get away," he said the words carefully. Remembering not to make her feel incompetent.

She laughed like a teenager. "Why would I tell someone now? It's late and everyone's sleeping."

Right. Who would she tell at two in the morning? So what if she hoofed it two miles down the road to sit on the neighbor's swing set? No, that wasn't crazy at all.

"What's on your mind?" He dug his feet into the ground.

"I can't sleep."

"Fair enough. I can't, either. Neither can Lindsey and Karis when you're not there."

She smiled and shook her head. Gripping the chains, she gave the swing a push. "My daughters are lost, Tyson."

Oh boy.

"They'll be okay." He hoped at least one of them would be.

"Both my daughters left me and for good reason. I was a terrible mother." She pushed the ground with her toes.

He'd heard stories about a wild young Iona, but never from the legend herself.

"Not terrible." He couldn't argue it but wasn't about to let her think the worst of herself. Those days were gone.

"No, it's true."

"But you've changed." The thought connected to everyone in his life, making sense to why he pushed it aside.

"I am so thankful for you. What would have happened if you hadn't come back to Florida?"

"But I did come back."

She nodded and continued to float back and forth, her pink-and-white moo-moo swishing with her slight sway. Slight or not, he watched her carefully.

"Karis came back, too. You love her," she stated it as if it didn't punch him in the gut or twist the screws in his brain.

He sighed from every corner of his heavy soul. He didn't deny or agree. Iona knew either way. He stopped her swing and fit her soft wrinkled hand into his. "I love her more than I love breathing," he admitted on an exhale of relief. "I always have. Since day one."

A grin slipped across her face. "She's difficult to love."

Ty laughed. "Yes, she is." But he always had.

"She's too goddamn independent. Too many years we spent depending on others." Tan, wrinkled fingers rubbed her temple. "That ruined her, and that's my fault, not hers. She's done well, financially, and I don't think that's as comforting as she thought it would be. She's alone."

"She didn't have to be," he rebutted. They'd shared a life. Made plans. But she guarded independence like he was there to take it away.

"She's an idiot for letting you go."

He chuckled. "Thank you."

Iona looked at him. Her shoulders hunched in disappointment. "She doesn't want to depend on anyone, and she doesn't think she can make anyone happy. That's why this thing with Lindsey is making her nuts. She doesn't want Lindsey relying on her because she thinks she's not good enough."

"She's so good for her, better than—" Shit. He better stop. Hill women were loyal to the bone. He'd experienced Iona's mean side once, and that was enough for him. *Thank you very much.* He'd screeched into their driveway, urging a sobbing Karis to get out of the car. The next day, he returned to apologize. Iona grew into a mama bear protecting her college girl from getting tossed inside out by the likes of him.

Iona's lips turned up at the corners. One blink and he would have missed her smile. "Go ahead. You can say it."

No, he didn't think he could. "Uh-uh."

With a laugh, her eyes crinkled at the corners. "I thought hockey players were all big and bad."

"Coaches have a little more control. We know who not to cross."

"Ha!" She reached out and patted his knee. "I always liked you, and you're right, Karis is a much better role model than her sister. Much better than me."

"I'm not believing that for a minute." It went against everything he believed about people, but here she was. Living proof against his oldest theory. People can change. If he believed it about Iona, why not others? Just before going down that scary street, his phone buzzed.

"It's Karis. We should get back." He held the swing still for Iona and answered the call.

"Ty? Is she all right?"

The worry in her voice sliced through his heart. "She's fine. We're just talking. She's swinging, so—"

"She's swinging?" Karis interjected. "I'm freaked out, and she's swinging? You're talking?"

It was unarguable, ridiculous, and important. "Uh, yeah."

"Awesome."

It didn't sound awesome. "We'll head back now."

"I would appreciate that." Her voice ran cold.

He studied his phone, reading a text from Smith, who, yes, should have been in bed. He wanted to know why Ty was taking so long getting Iona back to the house. Smelled like a Lindsey question.

The pressure of the last few minutes rolled off his back. He dropped his phone on the metal picnic table and sat back on the swing. They didn't make swings for men his size. When he finally looked over at Iona, she had a knowing smile brushed across her face.

"What?" he questioned softly.

"Nothing."

He knew better. Something stirred in that mind of hers. "I've seen that look a million times. The last thing it says is nothing."

She giggled. "Okay, you tell me."

Mothers had superpowers. Ty sobered. "She's bound to pull away. I can hear it in her voice. She holds her independence like talons hold a feast."

"Don't let her pull away." Her smile faded.

Impossible. He'd spent years proving she'd have her own life no matter where they landed. He offered to stay until she graduated because he wanted to build a life together. She didn't think she was worth the wait, and he failed to show she could be independent and in love at the same time.

"It's not that easy." He gazed at the stars, wishing it were. "I don't know if I can do this again. I don't know if I can trust her to stay and I need that. Especially with Smith."

"What about your job in Missouri?" The woman had a brutal cross-check.

He should have known. "How do you know about that?" One interview. But damn, he wanted it.

"I haven't lost my mind completely. Are you going to leave her?"

Good question.

Hell, great question.

Iona faced him, not waiting for his answer. "She's stepping up for Lindsey and me, and she'll step up for you, too."

God, he hoped so.

"She wanted what was best for you and that's what she thought she was doing when she broke it off, but now she's getting spooked by responsibility. Me, mostly. I'm becoming more expensive with each doctor's visit, and you know how she is about money. Her own money."

Eager to end the Iona rescue-gone-therapy session, he stood. "I don't think that's how she sees it. She's happy to be back, but I'm more involved than she expected."

"You guys aren't exactly young chickens anymore, and you both carry a ton of baggage. That girl's self-esteem drops as fast as your goalie when he's trying to make a save." Iona chuckled, taking his hand from the chain.

"You follow my pro team?"

Her smile widened. "I always have." She stood, clearly ready to go.

He dug for his keys. "Iona, you're pretty great."

She headed to the car. "Yep." She nodded. "I am."

Chapter Twenty-Four

Karis snapped the cap back on her lip balm and waited for the click to satisfy her over-taxed nerves. The sprawling hockey arena hosted too many places where a person could hide or get lost. There had to be a hundred corridors, a thousand bathrooms, and a million people hidden behind windows, ramps, and escalators. Brilliant. Her anxiety shot through the roof.

Iona could slip into the labyrinth within a matter of seconds, a dilemma not considered when Karis agreed to attend Ty's fundraiser game with her family.

Too late now.

Clutching her mom's hand, Karis followed Lindsey, Ryan, and Smith through the throngs of lighthearted people laughing, with their beautiful drinks and money to spare. If she had money to spare, it wouldn't be for drinks, or tickets.

Thank you, Ty, for the comps.

Maybe she should snag a pretty drink to calm the worry plaguing her ever since the swing debacle three days ago. The entire episode, a hardcore lesson, reinforcing how unprepared she was to take care of her mother. Lindsey racked up better qualifications, but Karis usually felt lacking where her mother was concerned. So, nothing new.

"Karis, you're squeezing the hell out of my hand." Iona pulled her arm free.

"You've got to stay by me. If you get lost, I'll never find you." Didn't they make leashes for people?

"You're not going to lose me in here. Geesh, I've been here a million times." Iona stepped in front of Karis, causing her to stumble.

The story of her life.

They should have stayed home, but when Ty invited them to his team's summer scrimmage fundraiser, Lindsey and Iona's faces lit up like they'd won the lottery. Apparently, they hadn't missed a game in three years. How could she argue?

So, here she was, moving through a crowd, trying to steady her hyperventilating, while watching the happy pair skip down the corridor. She stayed behind them with Ryan, trying like hell to process the words pouring from his mouth while spotting all the exits and stairways. Her brain activity skyrocketed past overload.

"Aren't you playing in the game? Don't you have to get ready?" She appreciated the extra chaperone, but if Ryan was anything like Ty, he needed ample time to get ready. And she needed silence to concentrate.

"I still have time. It's a fundraiser and I'm not nearly as superstitious as Ty." He guided her into the swanky lounge area.

"So you get the babysitting job, while superstar gets interviewed?" She gestured toward Ty, standing across from the lounge, surrounded by bright lights and reporters shoving questions his way.

Ryan smiled wide. "Yeah, that's it. It's PR. He loves it, and I hate it."

She released a chuckle and stopped short. Pristine white high-top tables dotted the lounge. High-heeled women dripped over the arms of older, giant-watch-wearing men. White ice glowed beyond the balcony. Oblivious to it all, Lindsey, Iona, and Smith claimed a smaller table by an ice cream cart in the courtyard. She'd rather be with them.

Large TV's, stationed behind the bar, highlighted players warming up on the ice below. A phone number floated across the bottom of each screen, reminding viewers how to support the cause. Ty had come a long way since the smaller rinks of their college days.

"This is great. Does Ty orchestrate all of it?"

Ryan adjusted his hat and cast a glance at Ty's circus. "Yeah, with our head coach, Sebastian. They tag team. They both played in NC for the Rapids, connected, and Seb became another brother."

"Like Ty needs another brother," she joked.

"Smart-ass. They connected in a quagmire of broken family issues and started the Take to the Ice Foundation locally. After about five years, the league noticed Florida hockey and decided to help them out." Ryan snapped his gigantic fingers. "'*Voila.*' Total success."

She gritted her teeth. "What's the charity for?" She meant to research the organization prior but was too worried about crowds and losing Iona. Glancing behind Ryan, she checked on her crew. They sat, laughing and licking their ice cream with deserved giddy abandonment. More people filled the arena and the usual, anxious heat pooled at the base of her neck.

Ryan leaned on the table. "Karis, you good?"

"Yeah, great." Sweat dripped down her back. Awesome. "The foundation?"

"It's a nonprofit Ty set up for kids wanting to play hockey in Florida. Hockey's expensive, so it isn't an option for many families. A ball and a driveway are much cheaper than ice. So, he created Take to the Ice to offer opportunity. It's been about eight years now, I think." Ryan hummed, squinting an eye.

Ty gave hockey credit for his fortunate life. In college, he always talked about how he would give back. Had notebooks filled with plans and ideas.

"And do you always play in it?"

"I do. I've only ever played for Ty and Seb, so I'm kind of obligated, plus, I love the cause. No matter where I played, I do it."

"Do you plan on playing for another team?"

"Nope."

A slapshot answer, with none of her business written all over it. Ryan was a family guy. She could see him staying in Florida with Ty and his dad, but the hitch in his voice said other plans were possible.

"Heard you had an interview with the pussy soccer players. How'd that go?" He jostled the table.

What was it with hockey players thinking they were the best athletes?

"Awful, but you already knew that. Ty scheduled that interview, and I'm declining the offer." She pulled her jacket around her shoulders. The more she observed the top-notch patrons, the more inadequate she felt. The last game she watched live was a college game in a dumpy arena with rust stains on the ice and mold on the ceiling. Nothing like this.

He lived far from those days. Regret stabbed its evil knife into her ribs and gave a quick twist, reminding her of what she had thrown away and how far apart their lives had become. Here, women dripped in jewels and stood on swanky high heels. Men wore suits and shiny shoes. Where she came from, hockey wore a blue collar.

"Why don't you let him help you?" Ryan asked before taking a sip of water.

"No," she mumbled, shifting her focus over to the camera crew packing up.

With a brief smile and a glance at Smith and Lindsey's ice-creamed faces, Ty sauntered toward her, all fresh business, sexy hockey coach, and out of her league.

His heated gaze studied her from fuzzy boots to alma mater scarf, starting a hot buzz beneath her skin. Finally, rubbing his jaw, he addressed Ryan. "What are you still doing here? You should have been gone already."

She cleared her throat in total *I told you so.*

Ty forced a quick smile. His stare hardened and bounced between them. "What's wrong?"

She shook her head and scooted her chair, allowing more patrons to pass. "Nothing." *No job, mother's losing her mind, guardian of a teenager, not good enough for you.* What the hell could be wrong?

Ryan agreed, his voice rising to conquer the growing roar of the crowd. "Yeah, nothing. Karis was telling me about her interview."

"Ah, with the pussies." Ty glanced around the room and tossed a piece of gum in his mouth.

She dropped her chin to her chest. Firestones were impossible.

"Karis?" He leaned close to her.

The building's capacity had to be at max. She inhaled, forcing her breathing to equalize. "This place is pretty crowded—" she scrambled.

"Easy," he whispered into her ear, moving her arms beneath his jacket and around his waist.

She pulled away and sat on her hands. "What if I lose her again? There are so many people here."

"You won't lose her. You're at club level. Everything comes to you, and the crowd will die down when everyone heads to their seats."

"You've got it covered." She wished that made her feel better.

"For you. Yes." He kissed her nose.

Her insides oozed, and a million lights flashed. "You should go." The curious stares added to the jangling nerves already hanging by a thread.

"Not until you're good."

He never believed her. "I'm good." She smiled wide and looked him straight in the eye, uncomfortable with all the handling he thought she needed.

He slid his hands in pockets. "Fine, I'm going. I'll meet you after the game."

"Sounds good." She spotted the section numbers hanging from the ceiling.

"Go that way." He pointed left, a small grin pulled the corners of his mouth.

A million people flowed the same way. "Nice. More people." She gave him two thumbs-up and jazz hands.

He bowed his head and pinched his nose, but the smile showed his patience. "Karis, it's nice. Good food, and good seats. Enjoy it."

"We could have had regular seats."

"Yeah, because you'd love sitting in that crowd. Now shut up and go." He nudged her left. She started through the crowd, grabbed her party of three, clenched her mother's hand, and headed for their fancy seats.

***

What a mess. Cheers from the fans heightened Ty's rising blood pressure. His players passed the puck through the blue line in a synchronized effort and changed shifts as smooth as the ballet. Lights blazed throughout the arena, advertising beer, raffles, and upcoming concerts.

Ty saw none of it.

He scanned the crowd, thankful for the support, and in a blink, focused back on his team. Back on Ryan, the hothead. Two hundred feet of ice and his brother stayed right on top of his rival.

"Ryan, it's a scrimmage, for fuck's sake. A fundraiser. Do *not* drop gloves or fuck with Corsiconiva, again."

Ryan dropped onto the bench, his breath heaving. His plastic shield steamed from sweat, heat, and anger; his posture set to kill. Players slid down the bench, giving him ample space to huff and puff. Anxiety stretched among the team. So much for a night of fun.

A month ago, he warned Ryan. Corsiconiva was playing on the opposing team. He took it like a champ, but all along had obviously planned to blast the poor bastard on the ice.

"Why the hell is he here to begin with?" Ryan spat, his concentration glued to the action on the ice.

Why did he put up with these divas? "Because he's a hockey star. He's a donor, and people pay to see him play." The crowd roared with the anticipation of a fight. The shit Ty would get from his best friend and fundraiser opposing head coach, Sebastian, would be never ending if Ryan threw a punch.

"I'm a hockey star," Ryan huffed.

Ty blanked from the game and zeroed in on his brother. "And look." He raised his hands in the air. "You're playing the game. The fundraiser game. It's not the playoffs. You missed those."

The entire bench smirked, and half let out oohs and aahs.

"Indeed, I did...*Coach*," Ryan sneered back.

The players on the bench got smart and turned their attention back to the game.

"Ryan, you're up, and stay out there until you puke." The team snickered.

Ryan hopped over the boards and sped down the ice. He snagged the puck and slipped into the offensive zone.

Bam.

Lamp lit.

Score.

The team cheered and Ty flicked Ryan off as he skated along the bench, high-fiving his teammates. Hopefully, the bigwigs from the Missouri team he was trying to land on watched the game and not his hand gestures.

He banked on sliding into the top running for the head coach position. Missouri wanted a well-rounded community guy. A sellout and a win proved he was that guy. Every seat held a fan, including the one filled by the thinned-faced woman behind him.

Tish's hallowed cheeks battered Ty's solid stability. Her skinny, drug-addicted frame sent a guilt punch square to his gut. His money contributed to her demise. Oh, she deserved it, but Smith wouldn't see it that way.

Living without a mother could slay a boy, but knowing the issues Tish had, keeping her from Smith was worth it. A mother so easily paid off had no right in her son's life.

The game blurred, his focus shot. Her presence rattled him and so did the bloodshot grin coming from Pop, slumped in the chair next to her.

"Ty, I didn't know." Ryan's voice pulled him from the rabbit hole. He stared at his brother, recognizing an agreeable truth. Evil lurked under Pop's skin and swam like poison to his brain. Thank God Smith wanted to sit with Lindsey this year instead of on the bench with his uncles. Ty considered himself strong. Except with Smith, a different level of emotions ruled him.

He leered at Tish and his red-faced father. They stewed in addicted vices. Gritty smiles stretched across their faces. As if they had every right to be there.

"Ty," Ryan called, snapping him back into the game.

Ty flinched at the concern and hopelessness on Ryan's face. It didn't belong there. The guy believed in their worthless father. He wielded enough faith and strength to hold them all together. He looked broken and defeated.

The last few minutes of the game ticked by without them, both brothers thinking about something more than taped sticks slapping black rubber. The buzzer squawked and cheers erupted. Ty studied the scoreboard for a good two minutes, trying to land his bearings. A win.

"Hey." Ryan leaned in with a hug, catching his attention. "We won. Missouri's gonna love that."

"Yeah." Excitement bubbled from the fans and the players. Pop and Tish's location stayed hazing on the margins of his vision.

"Let's get them escorted out of here," Ryan said, ignoring the whoops and yells from his teammates.

Ty scrubbed a hand down his face. "No, it's over. I want to know her game and we don't need a scene."

"You know what she wants." Ryan picked up his water bottle and headed to the handshake line.

"It's gotta stop." In an absent state of mind, he followed Ryan onto the ice, shaking hands and thanking players.

Through the glass, Tish and Pop made their way up the stairs.

How could these two people control his life for so long?

Chapter Twenty-Five

Club level was elbow-to-elbow sports' reps loaded with money. Sports produced millionaires with large egos and heavy wallets. Including the creepy ego with the octopus hands from her soccer interview.

Fancy food topped every linen-covered table. Plush recliners formed straight rows in sizable sections. Clearly, the invited sports organizations had donated a fat penny to Ty's cause, making their presence almost tolerable. *Almost.* Luxury dripped from the rafters, and yet Scott Marks and a few of his buddies had misplaced their manners.

Her family's cheers and boos made it easy to ignore the Masters of the Universe. With every goal Ty's team scored, their excitement filled the room and gave the worry in Karis' heart a night off.

The brand-new trying-to-improve, selfless, responsible-for-others, Karis knew she had to take the soccer job to care for her family with minor disturbance. She'd rather swallow hockey pucks.

But moving her family to North Carolina was inching out of her reality. The closer they became, the more moving hit like a betrayal to her tribe.

Lindsey's small, warm hand slipped into hers. A gesture she started without warning or reason. Shocked at first, and only briefly uncomfortable, Karis grew to love the new habit.

"Good game, right?" Lindsey popped her gum.

How in the world could a healthy girl stomach so much candy?

"Right, but I'm not sure how you saw any of the game as many times as you went to the candy bar."

Lindsey smiled at her partners in crime. The three of them bounced around, all hyped up and jittery on sugar.

Karis monitored the craziness and pulled out her buzzing phone. She studied Ty's text. He wanted Smith out of the building as soon as possible. Not so easy with everyone leaving at once.

"Mom, let's head downstairs. I have to use the restroom and then we can meet Ty at home." She reached for her mom's hand.

"The bathroom lines are too long downstairs. Use this one," Lindsey suggested.

Some fans were clearing out, but some, like Karis and Ty used to be, stuck around until the very end, maximizing a free-food opportunity.

"You're right. Hang here. I'll be right out." What in the world could happen in two seconds?

Pants down, the knock on the door felt just like at home.

Seriously?

"Someone's in here," she called.

"Grandma walked out. Smith and I are going to get her. We'll meet you downstairs."

"Oh-my-gosh, I can't even pee," she whispered.

"What?" Lindsey replied.

"Nothing. Yes, go get her. I'll meet you downstairs." At least downstairs put Smith closer to the exit.

She flushed, washed her hands, and skipped a glance in the mirror. Primping had to wait; she had a mom to catch.

***

They should be gone. Ty checked his cell, confirmed the text had gone through, and forced himself to believe no news was good news.

A sweaty-faced, half-geared-up Ryan insisted on escorting him down the crowded stairs. Both men amped up and struggling to handle the slow pace of spectators.

"I'm gonna find Pop and figure out what the fuck is happening, or do you need me to take Smith home?" Ryan offered.

Ty doubled up on his steps. "Karis is taking him. They should be gone."

Ryan lifted his chin, gesturing across the atrium. "Not yet, Bro, she's right there."

What the fuck?

Off the stairs, Ty picked up speed, and struggled to keep his pace at a decent speed walk. Making his way straight to her, he gazed from left to right, not computing why she still stood in front of him.

"Where the fuck is Smith?" He couldn't help himself.

She turned in a circle, and he grabbed her arm. "Karis, where's Smith?" Panic churned in his stomach and inched up his throat. Sharp heat hammered against his chest. He'd been dealing with Tish for too long. He knew better than to underestimate her end game.

"I was just in the bathroom," Karis screeched. Her worry matched the punching of his heart.

"They have to be close." She jerked her arm free.

"That's fucking comforting," Ty spat. "Ryan, go look around the elevators. Text me if you find anyone."

"Got it."

He didn't get very far before fans swarmed, clamoring for an autograph. Ty raked his fingers down his face. Frustration shredded his composure. "All you had to do was get them from point A to point B. There are exits on every wall." Agitation swam in his gut and bled into every word.

He stared over her head, and when she didn't move, he risked a glance at her pasty face. She never liked crowds but could usually handle it. The urge to take care of her boiled beneath his skin. He wrestled with the innate part of himself that always put her first and mentally placed Smith in front of her. Smith had to get home before Pop took things into his own hands, but she looked ready to vomit.

He took her hands in his. The quake of each finger a dead giveaway. "Talk to me."

"My mom," she spoke fast. "She left the suite. The kids went after her. I thought they would be down here." She sucked in a shaky breath. "I don't know where she went."

Ty pulled his hands out of hers, but her tightened grip stilled him.

"Christ." Pulling her behind him, he stalked to the security room, his mind on autopilot. The security booth was quiet. It's only occupant, Mac, stared hard at a wall of computer screens.

Ty pushed Karis into a chair with little reluctance. "Stay here."

She shook her head and tried to stand, but he caged her body to the chair. "Stay here. I cannot look for them and worry about you."

Her fingers wrapped around his wrists. "I can help."

"No, just stay here. Please." Giving the guard a warning look, he darted out the door. He checked his phone and scanned behind a curtained entrance.

Empty.

With one buzz, he answered his phone. "You find 'em?"

"No, but I just escorted Pop and Tish out of the building. She's lovely, not sure what you have against her. All wasted and trashed out of her mind, she's the picture of perfect motherhood."

He stalked down the corridor, looking in every corner, his phone cracking against his ear. "Yeah, she's awesome, but gone, right? Any sign of Iona or the kids?" He wanted the intel why Pop and Tish showed up at the game but had to move to emergency number two. Great night.

"No, but did you check the bobblehead line?"

Ty stopped short, his dress shoes screeching on the buffed concrete. "Holy fucking mother of hockey. She's got to be there."

Chapter Twenty-Six

Iona carried on from the back seat of the car. "I wanted the bobblehead. They ran out of them upstairs, so I wanted to see if they had extras downstairs."

Karis heard every word her mother said, and yet comprehension of wanting a bobblehead just didn't register. "Mom." She made her words slow and deliberate. "It's fine. You wanted a bobblehead, but you needed to tell us you were going to get it."

She pinched her lips closed. Elaborating on what she was really thinking would only cause the car to explode. The night had gotten the best of her, and when Ty suggested they all stay the night at her house, she couldn't argue. He was clearly more capable of taking care of her mother than she was.

Staring out the window and into the black night, tears rolled down her cheeks. Iona hadn't lost her mind. She wasn't confused. She wanted a bobblehead. A toy. Ridiculous and innocent.

The car rolled to a quiet stop outside her house. She sat up, brushed her hair away from her face, wiped her cheeks, and focused on the slamming of car doors. With each person out of the car, Karis breathed a little easier and tried to gather her strength. An impossible task.

Letting go of the fight for a minute, she surrendered to weakness, and worthlessness pounced. Allowing Ty to stay the night sparked relief and shame. He would take care of them. She couldn't, but he could.

Ty spoke to Ryan across the cars parked side by side in the driveway. They agreed on something; at least, she thought they did. Their words sounded muffled and faraway. The kids escaped with Iona inside the house, laughing about her stupid bobblehead.

"Karis." Ty's whisper tore into her heart. He'd opened her car door and kneeled down to face her, but she couldn't look at him.

How would she ever get the hang of this? How was she supposed to know when her mom was doing something normal, or when her mind had clicked time off, erasing people who cared about her and places she was familiar with?

Karis ripped her hand from Ty's, using more force than he deserved. Glancing at his concerned stare, her mind shifted into flight mode, and the need to escape swirled inside her. He closed in trying to read her, but she denied him access.

Cornered by her own thoughts, teetering between responsibility and her highlighted inadequacies, Karis' lungs twitched for air, and her ego hummed to run from his scrutiny. Darting from the car, she jetted into the yard. The side sensor light flickered on, exposing her.

"Karis, wait," Ty called.

There was no point in running. With one step, he'd catch her. Panting, she faced him, shocked by the understanding lingering in his hard features. She needed him, breaking her life rule to need no one.

"I can't do this." She tore the band out of her hair.

"Yes, you can." He erased the space between them, but she backed away. Touching him would melt her into a pool of nothing.

"I'm the worst person for people to rely on, and now I have these two beautiful people in my life, counting on me, and I don't know how I'm going to do it." Fear blazed. The lights in the house came on, highlighting her priorities.

The cicada's humming raked across her nerves. Her jumpy thoughts tried to set anchor. Stars dotted the black sky and helped center her attention, but a mocking of her inadequacies danced within the stars. When the tips of his shoes touched hers, she rooted herself to the spot.

"I did things all wrong. I should have tried to help my family sooner. I could have prevented all this. My mom, maybe my sister?" She shrugged and shuffled back. Her heart ached from the distance.

"That's quite an ego, thinking you could have controlled your mom and your sister. And dementia."

The truth weighed heavy from soul to toes.

"You can know everything about Iona, but tonight still would have happened."

He was right, of course.

She wanted the night to swallow her whole. "I lost her." She cupped her hand over her mouth.

His fingers dug into her waist, and she welcomed the pressure. "No, you didn't. She went to get a fucking bobblehead like any fan."

"That's the worst part. How in the world am I supposed to know that? How do I learn the difference between a memory loss and a normal disappearance when I don't even know my own mother?" She swallowed hard. "It's going to drive me crazy."

His lips pressed into a straight line. He backed away and thrust his hands into his hair. Pacing in quick jabs, his hands covered his face and tore down his cheeks, ending with a pull at his chin.

He came back full force, gripping her shoulders, his blue eyes hidden in stormy shadows, colliding with hers. "A lot can happen in our life no matter what decisions we make, Karis. What you think you could have done is different from what you actually could have done. Believe me."

Regret bounced between them. Success wasn't always about the money or the dream job. In this moment, for them, it centered on people. Family. The people who were once second thoughts in the lives of Karis and Ty were now first.

"You were taking care of yourself, and you'll learn all of those things about your mother now," he challenged.

"Yes. My ego, like you said." She heaved. Once again, stricken by all the time lost.

Anger flashed across his face. "Don't put those words in my mouth. That's not what I meant. Your sister fucked up from the beginning and she would have gone south no matter what."

She tried to speak, but he plowed on. "You're not doing this tonight. You're not taking the blame. You wanted to take care of yourself because you thought it would help your mom and sister, giving them one less mouth to feed. You and your mother couldn't stay in one room without breaking into an argument. You saved all of you. That's what people do."

She pushed at his chest. The closeness too suffocating. Too real. She didn't deserve it. "You didn't. Your dad sucked and you still let him stay in your life."

"That's all Ryan and Wes, not me." He hung his head between his shoulders, but he didn't stay down long.

"Right, and now I have Lindsey." A surge of pride shot into her heart.

"Which is great." He shifted her closer, his hands resting on her hips.

Family persevered even after everything his dad put them through.

Could she let herself buy it?

"No, it's not, Ty. The only thing I can do for my mom and Lindsey is help financially. That's it, and that's dwindling." Ignoring his shaking head, she stumbled a beat, hating the emptiness he created by stepping away from her. He flashed her the same look he always did when he thought she was out of her mind.

He pressed his lips together, and the words barely slipped past his locked jaw. "Yeah, that's a no." He glanced at the house and back at her. "You think all you offer your family is money?" His brows narrowed.

"Believe me, right now, that's a tremendous bonus. You don't have my mom's medical bills, my mom's health issues, and Lindsey's heartbreaking offer to give up hockey." She held up her hand, waylaying his pity. The reality of her life hovered like the stars. She existed in impossible situations. The algebra all one-sided.

"If you wouldn't have found her—" She swallowed the weak sob sneaking up her throat.

He squeezed the bridge of his nose. "But I did, and she's fine." He ignored her hand and reached for her. "It was normal. She always wants a goddamn bobblehead, and *I* should have known." A smile tugged at his lips, but it didn't curve his cheeks or erase his concern.

Iona was her mother. "*I* should have known." Her voice grew. She slapped the tops of her thighs, emphasizing the point clearly alluding him. "I don't even know that she collects bobbleheads, Ty."

He blocked her escape. A calloused finger brushed against her cheek. The connection calmed her racing heart and quieted her need to run. His forehead met hers and his fingers pressed into her arms.

"Aunt Karis?" Lindsey stood in the center of the driveway, hands on her narrow hips. Smith, as always, stood beside her. Behind them, Ryan leaned out the front door.

"I tried to keep her inside, but she's super strong when Smith helps." Ryan paced to the edge of the porch, flashing the kids an evil stare.

Karis cleared her throat. Her gaze locked on Ty. "It's fine."

Without a word, Lindsey snuggled up to Karis and laid her head on her shoulder. A sweet strawberry scent surrounded them. Ty stayed close, guarding it all.

"You didn't lose Grandma, did you?" Karis whispered.

Lindsey squeezed and giggled. "No, we tied her to a chair."

Karis pulled back. "Don't laugh. We may have to do that one day."

Chapter Twenty-Seven

Stretched thin and pulled tight, Ty surrendered to the wash of adrenaline pumping beneath his skin. Another successful fundraiser, one of the best, and here he sat waiting for the drainage to start. For the exhaustion a Tish and Pop encounter always ignited. He'd handled it. The dangerous memories. The loss of childhood and family. All punches to the face he took like a champ. But Karis brought a whole new sequence to the pain, and the crushing pressure of heartbreak shredded his insides. Suckered him like a bully. As an adult, he had more to lose. He wanted more than the job. More than a normal life for Smith. He wanted it all. And an appearance from Tish and Pop, so close to Smith, threatened the goal.

Tish ruined her chance to be a part of their family. Years ago, even when she went days without seeing Smith, they welcomed her back whenever she showed up. She acted like she wanted to be there and be a family. But mothering turned into quick leverage, which, for a brief stint, allowed her to stumble into one of Ty's practices, demanding a "small loan" for a quick fix.

Never again.

Staring out the kitchen window, he hung his head, stretching his jarred neck muscles. The outside flood lights clicked on, illuminating the Hill's backyard basketball slab.

Ryan had something on his mind, the hard bounce and tight slump of his shoulders a dead giveaway. Pain induced by his confrontation with Pop and Tish tore at him. Ty had ignored Ryan's silence, took his help to settle everyone for the night, and expected him to bolt at lights out.

The half court was the best of upgrades. He'd made sure of that when he had the new slab poured last summer for the kids. A secret he'd remind the kids to withhold from Karis for the rest of his life.

The harsh pound of the ball echoed through the lit-up yard, and Ryan's scrunched, sweat-drenched face coerced Ty to the court.

"Hey?" He snagged the ball midair.

A fearful look covered his brother's face. His arms hung loose, hiding all of the confidence he always displayed.

"Talk to me." There wasn't an ounce of Coach in his tone; he was all big brother.

Ryan scrubbed his hair. A deep frown shadowed his brow. "You're not gonna like what I have to say."

Riddles. His fucking literature-loving, poetry-reading, brother always talked in riddles.

Ty swallowed. "Say it anyway." He did *not* talk in riddles.

Using the hem of his T-shirt, Ryan wiped the sweat from his face. "Pop's drinking problem isn't something he can overcome on his own."

No shit, but they had never discussed it. Drinking remained the underlying secret in the Firestone household.

"We need to put him in a program."

"Why?" Throbbing knots pulsed at Ty's core.

Ryan dribbled the ball. "I think it's obvious."

All the upstairs lights in the small house flickered off. Except one. He wanted to go to her. Touch her until his fingers burned and the world lifted from his shoulders. Not yet. "I've suggested this a million times and you've never been on board." He pushed out the world, focusing on Ryan.

"He's sick." Ryan's voice hitched.

"What do you mean?" In his peripheral, Karis' room went dark. Peace rolled through him. She needed the rest.

Ryan palmed the ball. "You know what I mean." The brothers squared off.

"Jesus. I've only been telling you this since you played juniors, and you've fought me every fucking inch of the way."

"I had to." The words were quiet and airy.

Ty watched this mountain of a man doubt himself. "What? Why?"

"Because if I sided with you, he'd stop paying for hockey." Ryan's shoulders fell two inches.

Ty's control hit the ground. "You're fucking joking? *I* could support your hockey." He stepped into Ryan's space, poked at his chest, and hit a wall of muscle he'd go through if he had to.

"I knew you'd say that, but you'd been through enough. Pop had put you and Wes through hell, and I got off easy." Ryan stepped back.

"Thank God," Ty choked. He stood by his decisions.

"No, not thank God. I feel guilt every day for that, Ty," Ryan snapped, and slammed the ball into the cement.

Ty snagged the bouncing ball and chucked it across the yard. "There's nothing to feel guilty about. We're brothers, that's what brothers do."

Ryan shifted, looking uneasy in his own skin. "No. It's what you two did, and I was not going to burden you with my hockey bill after what you'd been through. We're all fucked up, but we can't let Pop get his claws into Smith. I don't need him to support me anymore. I've done my damnedest trying to be a family for him, but after tonight, I sure as shit won't give him any more money."

Aw, there's the guilt. The sky went red. "I told you to stop giving him money."

"I have, but it just makes him meaner and drunker. He doesn't deserve to see Smith, and I sure as hell don't want him hanging out with Tish. I want to get him help."

Ty looked to the stars. "You were always the softy for Pop."

"I had to be, but not anymore. Not after what he did to Smith, and not after what he's planning with Tish."

"What's the plan?" Ty gritted his teeth, waiting to hear what he already knew. It was just a matter of time.

"Sucking you dry. Taking your money. Holding Smith over your head until you give in." Ryan shot him a defeated look. "You're going to have to tell Smith the truth."

"I know. I've done just as bad raising Smith as Pop did to me. Mentally, of course." He sighed and rubbed his hand over the burning hole in his chest. "I'll be the fucking bad guy."

Ryan shook his head. "No, you won't."

He disagreed. "I lied to him. Took away his mother. Made him spend time with his wasted grandfather. I'm not parent of the year here."

"He'll understand once you explain it." Ryan swatted a mosquito.

"I'm not so sure about that." There were too many ways this could all go wrong. People with family on the line were unpredictable. Even teenagers. *Especially* teenagers.

"Sure he will. He's levelheaded. Clear. But we have to get Pop help before he does serious damage." Ryan paced the white line and bounced every third step. His fingers pinched his waist. A restless energy rolled off him.

"It's not going to stick," Ty laid out. "People don't change, especially people like Pop, but I'll do whatever you want. You find the place and I'll support you. I think between you and me, we can get him there. If he admits he has a problem."

"He knows he has a problem. He just doesn't care, but that's why you have to tell Smith the truth, so Pop doesn't have leverage."

Another kick to the gut. "This is going to suck."

"Yep," Ryan agreed.

"Off-season isn't supposed to be this hard."

"Nope," he finished.

The floodlight's timer clicked off, covering them in darkness. Neither of them moved. They were used to the dark.

***

In the quiet of the living room, Ty pushed back on every scene filling his head. Fear, doubt, and greed. The wicked hat trick possessed the power to ruin lives. He'd battled them for years. But Ryan's desperation to fix their family presented a new twist.

Ripping his shirt over his head, he sank onto the springy pullout and let the deep breaths stretch his lungs. The old sofa bed's thin piece of foam promised an uncomfortable night of jabs and pokes. No problem. The only comfort he needed was knowing all the people he cared about were safe, asleep, and close by.

Ty tossed his watch onto the end table. His body hummed tighter than laced-up skates before a game, knowing Karis slept a small flight of stairs away. Stairs he could take two at a time, skipping the squeaky one.

But he wouldn't.

He had to go lights out on this night and stop the wheel churning. The quicker he escaped to sleep, even shitty sleep, the quicker his composure could glue back together. The people he loved were sucking him dry. Pretty sure it wasn't supposed to work that way.

Knotted up and tied tight, Ty stormed into the bathroom and splashed water on his face before the cobwebs took root. The mirror confirmed a tired life, but parents didn't have the luxury of sleep. Neither did coaches, brothers, boyfriends, or guardians. All lonely jobs, requiring twenty-four-seven attention. He reasoned with his exhausted reflection. Smith and Ryan needed him to be at the top of his game. They had to be his priority.

If he hadn't found Iona at the bobblehead line, he'd still be looking. Back-burning everyone else. Goddamn it. Karis was a tethered complication, pulling him away from the people he needed to take care of the most. This evening, he dropped his guard, and it almost cost him. Pop and Tish should have been on his radar long before the end of the game.

He swore again and dipped his head under the cold running water. The splash didn't erase his desire for her. The urge to hold her beneath him, her body bowed for release, overwhelmed his good intentions. Skipping the shower, he stalked to her room, determined and hard. Opening the door, his clothes hit the floor.

He slid the covers down her body, exposing every tan inch of her smooth skin. Possession had him by the throat. Her lashes parted. She lifted her arms, welcoming him against her soft chest.

In surrender, he claimed her mouth, controlling the tempo and wanting only a taste. A small taste to quench his thirst. Catching her sleepy moan, he licked and scooped her sweet warmth. His knees nudged her thighs apart, and his body dropped perfectly to hers.

Her arms snaked around his neck. Tight. Real. Her gentle fingers curved around the back of his head. Her heated green eyes filled with sweet concern, captivating him. Owning him.

He fucking needed her.

Simple.

His hungry lips crashed onto hers. The electric touch smoked all hope of walking away after a good-night kiss fell to the devil. Soul-shrieking want seared him. His fingers tangled in her long hair, exposing her slender neck with one pull. So much hot skin needing to be licked. He laid his tongue flat against the column and tasted her in tiny strokes.

Her satiny pajama shorts slipped down her legs, leaving her open and bare. Perfect for his fingers to roam the curves of her hips, slide along her bikini line, and find her silky heat.

"So wet, for me." He took a breath, pacing himself.

"I was wet the minute you opened the door."

His cock rested against her mound, demanding friction, and a squeeze from her warm muscles. He'd settle for a slip of her fingers against his cock. Out of patience, he hunched onto his knees, moved her long legs, and flipped her onto her stomach.

"Ty," she gasped.

"I need to be inside you." He leaned close to her ear, straining for control. Her back rubbed his chest. Skin to skin. She hissed into the mattress. Her tight ass positioned high. Hips bent just right, cocked against him. His fingers roamed between her thighs. He pressed wet kisses down her arching spine, his balls heavy and gunning for release.

He licked his fingers and swiped through her folds, finding her bud. With one flick, she pushed back hard, sliding onto his cock, moaning his name into the pillow.

"That's it, baby." Hot heat surrounded him. He pushed into her, their fingers laced together, tangled in sheets, holding tight. Her fleshy walls milked him hard. With will of steel, he eased out. Every limb shaking to possess, but she held him hostage. He calmed his nerves with a deep breath. Quick sparks spooled low in his spine. He gripped his cock and fed it slowly into her entrance. "Again," he begged, slipping the pillow from under her face.

"I can't." She squirmed.

She'd scream his name again if it killed him.

"You can." Her muscles contracted around him. He pressed her into the mattress, pulsed in and out of her slick channel with slippery friction. The sight of her curved and on bent knees devoured him. He aligned his tip to her threshold and slowly sank inside her. Her body liquid in his hands. Her soft mews a cry of submission.

He took his aching cock away. Torturing them both.

"Please," she cried with mercy.

He steadied himself, inhaled her scent, and skated his fingertips over every inch of her skin. He tried to abstain long enough to clear his head. His heavy sex throbbed to fill her until all she could think of was him. A quick thrust had him planted right where he needed to be.

Her.

All her.

Only her.

His weakness.

He slid in and out with a slow roll. His hips pumping in the same rhythm they had always used. His body fell to all fours, caging over her. No matter where they ended up... No one would ever fit him like she did.

A fierce groan crawled up his throat. He pulled out, and in one move, had her on her back. Plunging inside her, her wet thighs notched to his hips. Her feet locked around his waist. Balls tightened; his release imminent. His arms shook with the effort needed not to crush her. Even that wouldn't be close enough.

"Karis, look at me." She did what he demanded, giving permission and love.

"Ty," she cried. The thick emotion in her voice took him to the edge.

Don't say it. He wasn't ready.

His hands splayed wide on either side of her head. Her gaze sank into his. "Karis?" He fought for control. Fought to do what was right but had to give up the illusion of doing it alone.

Her arms tightened around him. "I got you," she breathed.

He entered her hard and released the years of tension waiting for her had built up. She did indeed have him.

Chapter Twenty-Eight

A night inside of Karis tore Ty's nerves into fringing strips. She'd refused to let him stay another night, and almost laughed in his face when he asked her to the charity ball, capping off the fundraising weekend. But with Ryan's very charming, double-triple, tons of convincing offer to stay with Iona and the kids, Karis conceded to the ball.

Ryan was all too happy to get out of the formal event but continued to bitch about it being called a ball instead of a puck. They circled this topic every year.

Ryan stepped up and took the kids and Iona to Ty's for an afternoon in the pool, a sleepover —pending Iona's mood— giving Karis time to get ready for an evening of schmoozing, handshaking, and her body tucked into his.

All night.

She'd refused the gown he'd offered to purchase. Refused the makeup, the pedicure, the manicure, the facial-cure or whatever the hell else gorgeous women did to get ready for a ball. Her independence clobbered his good will, and she bid them all farewell from the porch, clearly relishing having the house to herself for the first time all summer.

A quick shower, a few phone calls, and he was back on his way to pick her up with a giddy smile stretched across his face. It lasted a whole five minutes.

Chucking the phone onto the passenger seat, pissed that he even answered it, Ty adjusted his bow tie. *Damn thing might as well be a noose.* Over his dead body would Tish get one more penny, and her threats to tell Smith the godawful truth proved she knew he meant business. Family made him a sucker, not an idiot.

Thank you, Ryan.

Tish, the calculating bitch, thrived on causing havoc as long as it gave her a payout. *Goddamn it, Wes.* Out of all the puck bunnies, he had to get wrapped up in the most conniving one of all. What mother threatened to destroy a family who adored and took care of her son? A mother too far gone and self-medicating to overcome loss and regret. And using his money to do it.

Pulling in a breath, Ty's M6 took the curves a little too fast. Tish's threat turned his fresh tuxedo into a brick oven. He cranked the air and pushed the pedal flush to the floor.

Years ago, it seemed legit to keep Tish away from Smith, but just as Ty raised him, Smith considered family the most important thing in the world. Paying off his mother to keep her distance was not congruent with the "family is everything" theory. When she threatened to tell Smith, again, Ty ended the conversation with a nice "fuck you" and a fast tap on the end call button.

Just for the phone to ring again.

"Tyson?"

Ty squeezed the steering wheel. Fucking hell. He'd been home all day fielding phone calls. It never ended, and all he wanted to do was pick up Karis.

"What do you want, Pop?" He should just let the bow tie put him out of his misery.

"I want to thank you for paying for my treatment." No hint of a slur, but Ty knew better. The jackhammer went to work between his temples, creating a masterpiece of a headache.

"Pop, that's not me, that's all Ryan."

Silence. That could not be a surprise. Pop had to know better.

"Oh, Ryan said—"

"Not me, Pop." Ty cut him off. "You need the help, so I am glad to hear you're getting it, but Smith is not up for negotiation. You won't see him for a long time and not without me."

He'd decided days ago. Ryan begged to be responsible for Smith again, and maybe someday he could, but Ty and Smith had talked about it and Smith wasn't into it. Case closed.

"You can't keep my grandson from me."

"You're wrong. I can and I am."

"You forget yourself, Son."

"No, Pop. I haven't." His finger hovered over end call.

"I gather you haven't spoken to Tish?" Wilson asked.

His heart threatened to blow from his chest. This man was evil, and no amount of rehab was going to help him. *Sorry, Ryan.*

"Yeah, Pop, I spoke with Tish. Nice touch by the way, you and her at the charity game together. That was sweet. Loved that."

"Son, you need to tell Smith the truth."

"You're giving me a lesson on truth. That's fucking awesome." The tension tightened in his jaw and he stretched his mouth wide open. The loud crack released some of the angst his father always put there.

"Smith is gonna find out. Tish will not keep quiet, especially if you go to Missouri as the head coach. You make more money, she's gonna want more money."

"How do you know about Missouri?" He gritted his teeth, waiting for the obvious answer.

"Ryan."

"Jesus, that kid." Ty took a breath.

"No big deal. Your secret's safe with me. I get it."

Bullshit. Ty pulled onto Karis' street and started to end the conversation.

"I wasn't much of a father," Wilson grumbled.

Ty almost laughed. He swerved to the side of the road, his pulse raging. His emotions skirted the brink of explosion. "You're going to have to say that again." It was more a dare than anything else.

"I'll say it again, but I'd like to do it in person. So when you have some time, I think we should talk."

Every muscle in his body tightened, and still he wanted to say yes, but it'd take a grappling hook to get those words out. He leaned his head back against the seat, counting to ten with a Ryan-suggested visualization in his mind. Something had to help.

If Karis could patch up and handle Iona, then maybe he could find the strength to do the same. "Fine." He squeezed his eyes shut, thinking of Smith.

"When?" his dad shot back. The heavy word laced with emotion.

"I'll have to call you tomorrow about that. I'm on my way to the ball now."

"No problem. I'll talk to you tomorrow, Son."

"Yep." Ty didn't feel one bit of relief jabbing end call.

He pulled back onto the road and raced to Karis' house. Within minutes, he stalked to the front door. His shoulders still worked up and bound. His back knotted with worry, like an old man with too much on his mind. But she answered the door and, Jesus, that dress.

The black lace wrapped around her neck and skated down her sides, showing the skin of her curves. When she turned, letting him in the house, he praised the open back of the dress and the puckered material starting at her ass. The cut so low if he put his finger underneath the hem, he'd feel the heated skin of her cheeks, and that's exactly what he needed to do.

He grabbed her arm and tugged her into the hall bathroom. The one he'd pulled her into a million times back when they came home from college. The decor hadn't changed and he still didn't give a shit.

"Ty," she yelped, stumbling into his arms. His hands went immediately into her perfectly set hair.

"Karis, please."

Her warm understanding threatened to knock him to his knees. With one look, she knew, and heat flamed behind her eyes.

He braced himself against the door, locking her against him. The pulse on her neck doubled, giving him the permission he wasn't asking for. Pressing his forehead to hers, he slid his finger over her pulse and drew a line down her side. The warmth of her skin mixed with the lace of her dress was a wicked combination. She melted farther against the door. Fluid and expectant.

Her leg hitched to his hip.

"Yes. Yes. Thank you. Thank you." His lips crushed hard onto hers after every word. Their tongues dueled with urgent need. His greedy strokes demanded more. All the responsible thoughts playing in his head on a twenty-four-hour reel slipped away. Her silky thighs, warm and wet, cradled his hips.

Hot, sparkling green heat met his gaze. He pressed his palm into the door, searching for stability. "No panties," he hissed.

She shook her head, her hair, coming loose, tumbled around her face. "Not tonight." She rested her long leg on the counter. Black lace and beads slid up her silky thigh.

He wasted no time and slid a finger inside of her, cupping her heat. Fucking drenched. "Goddamn it, we are never coming out of this bathroom."

She reached up to stroke his chin, forcing him to stop and look at her. A second finger thrust inside her slickness. Her fingernails dug into his shoulders, and she let him do what he needed to do.

"Ty," she whispered.

No, don't ask me. Please don't ask me. He shook his head, but she held his jaw.

"What happened? What's wrong?"

Her warmth clenched. Her fingers pummeled into his hair and clawed down his shoulders, pulling him close. He absorbed every shiver. Her head fell back against the door, giving him full access. The dress cut to a V between her breasts and his mouth watered, wanting to lick every inch of glowing skin.

"I just need you. I just need you," he begged. Her body started to sink to the floor. He crushed her against him. She held strong, moaned his name, and made him feel whole again.

His jacket gone, he stood back, letting her unbutton his pants and cradle his heavy cock. In one motion, she rose. He cupped her ass and steadied her against the door.

Her body tucked into him, her warm, elegant fingers tightened around his cock. He held her gaze, desperately needing to watch her face as he entered her.

"Karis." His rusty voice croaked thick with desire.

"I'm right here," she whispered between them.

Lined up, she guided him home. Soft gasps fell from her lips. A tight release mixed with overwhelming desire.

She parted his shirt. Cool air hit his chest. "I need to feel you."

In one powerful thrust, he rammed her against the door. "Sorry," was all he could get out. He held onto the doorframe. She had him. All of him. And he was scared to fucking death of losing her again.

He rolled into her, and she clung to him, hard and desperate. Her tongue tapped little wet licks against his neck.

He bent and licked her ear. "Do you feel what you do to me?"

"Ty." Her legs clenched around his waist so tight he could hardly move. So hard he didn't need to. A few inches in her wet folds and he was spent.

"Baby," he breathed, snaking his arm around her waist.

She studied him nose to nose. Soft heated air floated between their lips.

"Please." With one plea, he was lost. Released. Free.

"Karis." He couldn't get close enough.

Holding her. Dripping inside of her. Sweating from need and fear and —something he didn't have the balls to admit.

"Ty? Don't move," she murmured.

Her muscles clenched. His name tore from her lips. Clasping his shoulders, she pulled him close. Her thighs squeezed his ass, and he held her as she had the sweetest orgasm he'd ever heard, giving him everything he needed.

***

Ty sat unusually quiet, thoughtful, and focused on the road in front of them. His relaxed fingers maneuvered the wheel with elegant confidence. Flashes of color blurred behind him through the car window. Something heavy weighed on his mind, and she'd bet the rest of her once-robust savings account, it wasn't the same turmoil crushing her brain.

Karis clenched her thighs together. Lingering memories of him gliding into her with deep emotions wrestling across his face made her skin burn and her insides quiver. He'd entered her house on a dangerous mission. A mission to forget and let go. To get lost. She'd wanted to strip the minute she'd opened the door. Something lay amiss in this beautiful man.

The Take to the Ice Charity Ball seemed well in swing judging by the number of cars valeted in the parking lot. A supreme testament to his success and die-hard determination.

"You don't use the valet?" she asked as he sped past them, lifting two fingers in a wave to the young boy dying to park the M6.

He navigated them into a shaded spot. "Not tonight." His strained voice matched his dark mood. He didn't make a move to leave the car, causing her heart to somersault.

With an edged brow, he grabbed her hand. "Let me—"

She pulled her hand back. "Oh God, what?" Her senses reared up and stood ready.

His tongue flickered over his lips, a nervous twitch she recalled from their younger, less adult days. "Ty?"

"There's gonna be a lot of schmoozing in there." He nodded his head toward the venue.

"That's fine." She took in the peach-colored building. "You do you. Schmoozer."

Inside, floating lanterns covered with white flowers lit up the ballroom. White glassy pinprick lights dawned each window, making the room less sporty and more wedding.

Circling the hors d'oeuvre table, deciding what she could sneak home to her mom and Lindsey, Karis watched Ty make his rounds, thanking each donor one by one. Schmoozing nonstop. He talked with ease, laughing in all the right places, shaking hands and kissing cheeks. The ladies, dressed in provocative fine ball gowns, scanned him from head to toe. He moved through the room without a glance at any of them, and the disappointment showed across their pinched faces.

From across the parquet floor, a wicked, sexy smile burned across his lips. His heated stare drifted down her gowned body, stripping her with a twinkle and a smirk. Snatching a champagne flute tooling by, she took a sip, and made her way to the sexy heart thief.

She slid him a smile.

"Karis, this is Mitch Murphy, The Florida Currents, GM." Ty's wide smile didn't hide the nervous pinch at the corners of his mouth.

"Hello." She took Mitch's hand. "It's so nice to meet you."

"Hey, Karis, good to finally meet you." Mitch's voice held a surprised lack of business propriety, thank goodness. He looked too young to be a GM, but the few gray hairs at his temple said it was possible.

"Finally?" Karis questioned. Ty had talked about her? To his GM? Were they friends?

Mitch flashed white teeth. "I've heard a lot about you, so it's nice to put a face, especially one as beautiful as yours, to a name."

Ty palmed his sarcastic cough. Definitely friends.

"Oh, wow. Thank you." Her smile muscles ached. Who knew schmoozing could be so fun?

Mitch leaned closer, allowing Karis to hear him over the jazz band. "Sorry the soccer job isn't going to work out for you, but I understand. That organization isn't nearly as nice as your current position with the baseball team, but you've been there awhile. I'm glad *that* worked out."

"Mitch." Ty tried to intervene.

What?

Edges around the room grew hazy, and the sax from the band drilled into her ear. She bit into her lip, stared at Ty, but directed her question to Mitch. "And exactly how *did that work out*?"

She knew the answer. It was plain as day on Ty's face.

Fiery, blatant anger surged between them. The surrounding crowd stepped back into their small pockets of wealth and so-called friends, whispering hushed words and giving nosy glances. Even good old buddy Mitch mumbled his goodbye with an apologetic grimace and hustled from the room with an athletic haste.

She waited all of two seconds before she followed in Mitch's footsteps. The urge to escape consumed her and this time she didn't question it.

"Karis?" Ty reached for her elbow. His fingers burned just as much as his doubt for her abilities.

She tucked her arm into her side. "Don't touch me," she hissed. Storming past the bar and into the foyer, her mind churned, with bits and pieces of a life unraveling. Quick, determined steps stomped behind her. Seething, she rounded on him, caught by the unexpected sorrow and regret stirring in his eyes. She stole a quick breather, but it didn't soften her fury. It couldn't. His doubt for her was a heavy punch, followed by a faithless smack to the heart.

"Why?" The word squeezed past her lips. He flinched and took a step back. Good. He should step back.

"Karis." His rigid shoulders were all defense, waiting for her to strike.

"Don't, 'Karis' me. Is it true?" she demanded, unable to keep the squeak out of her voice.

"Fuck." He looked away. She stepped closer. He didn't deserve a reprieve. Tapping her foot like an impatient child, she'd stand there all night long waiting for him to spit out the truth. Waiting to hear her entire life was a farce.

"Yes," he breathed.

The single word hit her straight in the heart, singeing the frayed edges. "Oh my God." The words echoed through the empty foyer. Irritating tears ripped down her cheek. A sick emptiness sank into her bones. Her shaking hands shoved at his chest. "Why? Why would you do that? All this time, I thought they hired me for me. I thought I was doing something big, breaking the cycle my mother had created. On my own. How could you?" She could take care of herself. She didn't need anyone doing anything for her, but he'd never given her the chance.

"Listen to me."

She couldn't. Not for another second. Pushing at his steely chest, she planted her heels, willing to break a million bones to make him feel how she felt.

Worthless.

"No, Ty. No." She shook her head, desperation dripping from her burning soul. "You knew how much it meant to me to build my own life. It's all I've ever wanted. After coming from a lifetime of watching my mother depend on men to pay bills, control where we lived, make horrible decisions about me, my life." She jabbed at her chest and stepped out of his reach.

Finally looking at her, he inched forward. His face solid stone. "What the fuck would you like me to do? Watch you fail? After everything you'd been through? I wasn't going to do that."

"Oh." She burned, listening to his disbelief.

"That's not what I meant," he corrected as fast as his slapshot used to be.

"Thanks for believing in me. No wonder you and Iona get along so well." Her teeth gnashed behind dry lips. "Saving me from failing is not your call!" she screamed.

He moved with the agile speed of an athlete, grabbing her, his mouth cinched closed, making every breath loud and palpable. "It is when you love someone the way I loved you. The way I still fucking love you with every goddamn breath I take."

"No." She tried to jerk away. Her breathing struggled to remain calm.

He loved her?

Still?

Her brain shuffled through all the things she wanted to say, all the things she *should* say. The anger bubbling inside her slipped sideways.

He pulled her close, leaving no room between them. "I was not going to let you flounder after watching you work your ass off in school, dealing with your mom and your sister." The words blew out of his mouth, cold and protective. The honest confession jabbed at her anger.

She bowed away from him. "You knew how much it meant to me to do things on my own. To make my own way, to not depend on anyone else." The hurt in her heart ricocheted down to her ribs, looking for a way out. She held tight. None of this made sense. If he loved her, why did he hurt her so badly?

Releasing her, he stepped away and pushed his hands into his pockets, restless for an outlet. "How in the hell do you think people get jobs in our field, Karis? Sports jobs only come to people who know people."

"It doesn't have to be like that." It shouldn't be like that.

His fingers raked through his hair. "But it is."

He didn't get it.

"When you help me, you take away what I've worked so hard for, Ty."

His large, capable body, poised for protecting, stood inches from hers. "No, when I help you, it's because I love you. I wanted to take care of you. That's why I did it. All of it. The workouts, the crazy hours, the fucking degree you made me get, the hockey, the job. I never wanted either of us to have to go back to where we came from, and when you told me to leave," he seethed. "I wasn't about to let you go. No matter where I went or where you stayed, I was going to take care of you." His chest pressed up and down. With one step, he erased the space between them and pressed his fingers into her hips, pulling her close.

She huddled against him, letting him hold on to her. His breathing heavy and his body tense. For her. She understood the need to take care of the people he loved. Her mind reeled untangling everything she ever believed she had to be, because all she wanted to be was his. She loved him, and taking care of people was how he loved. Just like letting people go was how she loved.

"No matter where I go, I'm going to take care of you." The soft words were a mere mumble.

She searched his face. "What?"

"Nothing," he said with finality.

"It doesn't feel like nothing," she protested. "No more secrets."

He sighed. "I got a job offer in Missouri." His shrug downplayed the excitement flashing across his face.

"What job?" And why did it feel like cocktails were sliding up her throat?

"Head coach." He hesitated, watching her closely.

She glanced at the shiny black-and-white checkered floor for the first time. Head coach. "Your dream job."

The resentment never came. He led a charmed life, and she wanted that for him. She waited seconds for hurt to churn in the pit of her stomach, but happiness showed up instead. Even though she'd have to let him go.

Again.

The bar behind the large double doors shrank with every tug he pulled of her elbow. Dainty clips tapped against the shiny marble, and he maneuvered her onto a private balcony with little fight.

"You're leaving." She gripped her clutch, twisting it every which way. The poor silk bag didn't stand a chance.

"Make me stay," he whispered.

"What?" she swallowed. His size shrunk the tiny space and took all the air. How could she go through this again?

"I love you, Karis."

"No." She shook her head. He would not do this to her. She couldn't take it. She hated herself for it but knew herself all the same. Fear and doubt doubled down. This wasn't her choice. He had to do him, and she had to take care of her family. Their time was up.

His hands slid to her waist. Her fingers clasped his, trying to pry them off. Pressing his nose into her hair, he sucked in a breath.

"Don't you dare do this." His words were sharp. His hands tightened on her body. Her fingers did their damnedest to break free. "You're not quitting me again."

Tears streamed down her face. Why couldn't he see? He had everything, and she had nothing but a mess of a family. Her choices were not her own, and for the first time, she knew that was the point.

She dropped her hands and leaned away from the security of his strength. His familiar gaze, fierce with the determination he saved for dangerous opponents, pressed into her. Intimidating and lethal, but she wouldn't deter.

"I won't be the reason you bail on this opportunity." He couldn't expect her to. She pushed her fingers beneath his.

"I haven't taken the job." He brushed her fingers away and adjusted his grip.

"But they offered it?"

"Yes, and ample time to think about it."

She spun out of his hold. "There's nothing to think about. You have to take it."

The distance between them, a cautious shield. They faced off, and without words, a battle raged. Panic seized her. He deserved this job, but he'd want it all. No one could have it all, and her mess of a family would hinder his ability to excel as a head coach. He'd worry and contemplate and stew. His focus would thin with all the worry taking care of someone with dementia could cause. She couldn't let that happen.

He steadied his outreached hands. "There's so much to think about. It's not just me. It's Smith. It's Ryan, and as much as I fucking hate it, it's my dad." He shifted another inch closer. "It's you and Iona and Lindsey."

"No. We are not your problem." She couldn't take much more. He might as well pull her heart from her chest.

He loved her.

He loved her.

She ached to say those words back to him.

He blocked her escape. "I want your problems to be my problems."

She tucked a fallen strand back into her braid. "No, you don't. I have too much to deal with right now, and you need to focus on your next step."

"You're my next step. I love you, Karis," he repeated, stepping into her.

Swallowing tears, she whispered, "But I can't love you."

Chapter Twenty-Nine

She can't love him? Can't love him? She might as well stick a skate blade in his heart and slice straight down to his balls.

There was no getting around it. The Missouri job was an opportunity realized, but letting it go had to be considered. Something had shifted, and it wasn't the stick shift. He plunged the car into gear and took the curve, heading home.

What he valued had changed. What he wanted in life had changed, and he couldn't be sure the change included a head coaching position.

I can't love you.

I can't love you.

Karis sat in the passenger seat, strangling the door handle and killing him with her silence. What was wrong with him? He was a tough guy. Strong. Muscled. Convicted in his abilities. Yet she slaughtered him to the core.

Taking the last curve, he downshifted, and the tires gripped the pavement of the driveway. He wished he could take her home, cancel out the noise and focus on them, but everyone was at his place for the sleepover part two.

"Who's that?" She motioned to the black truck parked in the driveway.

His stomach soured. He ripped the emergency break into position. Couldn't he get one fucking night of nothing?

He headed straight to the front door, ready to confront the issue waiting for him.

Step one: deal with Pop.

Step two: kill Ryan.

With his heart broken and bruised, his stomach twisted and torn, Ty took in the scene and let the outrage seep into his bones. "What the fuck, Ryan?" The hate ran thick in his voice.

Ryan stood, full height and unapologetic. "Let me explain."

"Ryan, I'll just go," Pop spoke from the kitchen table.

Ty's blood boiled. The man looked right at home. In his home.

"Pop, I'll ride with you," Ryan offered. A nice extraction from the mess.

Ty pointed at Pop. "You leave. Ryan's staying and after I kill him, you can come back and get his fucking body." Fists throbbing to get a hit, he advanced on his brother.

"Ty." Karis' voice broke through his adrenaline. His gaze met hers. Huge mistake.

"You can go, too," he spat.

"What?" The hurt spread across her face, knocked him to another level of anger, but he was too far gone for reasons or apologies.

"Ty," Ryan warned.

Fuck his warning. "Shut up."

Karis' stony stare lay on him, and for the first time in a long time, he didn't care. Ryan would never get it. No one would get it. The trauma that came with being an abused child never died, never disappeared, never got better. What would it take for them to fucking comprehend that? His issues bled from the very man that stood in his house like a welcomed visitor.

"Ty, I can explain," Ryan attempted, moving closer to Pop and the front door.

"Explain what exactly? How would that go, Ryan?"

"Well," Ryan started, before coughing into his fist. No words could make this better. How many chances was his bleeding-heart brother going to give?

It didn't matter.

"Yeah, I don't give a shit. Our nephew is in this house. Lindsey and Iona are in this house."

"Oh, for fuck's sake, Ty. He's here to talk with me." Ryan's face tightened. A warrior against his own flesh and blood.

"Was this your plan? You brought him in here behind my back? Have you lost your fucking mind?" Ty searched Pop's eyes, unconvinced he hadn't had a drink. Even if the check he'd written to his father's program should be enough to sober up a few men, it would take a lot more than three weeks to convince Ty sobriety was in Pop's future.

He stepped closer to Ryan. He was older, taller, and flooded with hate. His fingers itched to strangle them both. Lay them out and make them bleed for all the pain they'd caused.

"Jesus, Ty. It's not like that. He's been here for ten minutes. Relax." Ryan squeezed the words between his teeth.

"Ryan, I'm going." Ryan handled Pop's pat on his shoulder without a flinch, something Ty had never accomplished.

"Yeah, I think that's best." Venom snaked from his voice. Ryan may have convinced him to open his checkbook, but Ty was far from convinced Wilson Firestone would ever be family.

Ryan stepped to Ty. Chest to chest. Seething. A look he sported on the ice when an opponent seeped into his head, and he couldn't wash him out. A weakness penetrated. Had Pop done that to him?

"Ty, he's trying." Ryan's words barely escaped his lips. "Pop, you stay here. Ty, in the kitchen," Ryan commanded, but he was no coach.

Pop dug into his pockets, no doubt looking for keys he shouldn't be using. He paused and gave a calculated look around the foyer. With a dagger-sharp stare and a quick guilty nod, Pop left, leaving an unsettling pang rolling up Ty's spine.

"Ty." Karis' voice and the touch of her fingers on his elbow stopped his train wreck of thoughts. "I'm going upstairs to check on everyone." Her soft face and tender eyes calmed him. She knew the pain rolling in his veins whenever Pop came around and could always bring him back to a better reality.

In that moment, he wanted to take back the night they'd had, and everything he'd ever done to hurt her. Even if it was in the name of love. She wouldn't let him love her the only way he knew how, and he'd have to live with the aching need for the rest of his life.

He put his lips to her ear. "I'm going to talk with Ryan. Listen." He cleared his throat. "I'm sorry about tonight."

"It's okay." Her words were airy. Her eyes watered, bound to break against the pressure crackling around them.

"It's not okay, but I need to deal with Ryan." He longed for her to drape her body over his, covering him in warm consoling comfort, and taking away all the hurt they'd gone through.

Understanding, she nodded and made her way upstairs. The nod should have been reassuring. Hell, her going upstairs should have been reassuring, but assurance was a luxury as fleeting as a championship.

"You're a prick," Ryan assessed. "You can't give Pop one break?"

The man had a million breaks. "I'm trying," he appealed, and rubbed the exhaustion from his neck.

"Well, fucking try harder. He came by with cookies and pizza, going out of his mind with AA meetings, and nothing else. Where are you going?"

"In the kitchen, I need a drink," Ty tossed back, throwing his jacket on a chair no one ever sat in.

Straight to the whiskey. Two fingers shot back easy.

Ryan downed his just as fast.

"I came in tonight with a piss-poor attitude and seeing him here didn't help." Bronze liquor splashed in the glass. Down the hatch. A toasty burn smoothed his edges. "You're giving him too much trust too soon."

"And you're not giving him enough," he countered, angling against the sink, arms folded, and, knowing Ryan, geared up with a million reasonable Oprah-inspired explanations.

The kitchen squeezed with tension. Insane, considering the spaciousness of the room, but filled with Firestone men, it shrank in a matter of seconds. Ty scratched off the counter and paced to the fridge. "I can't. I've tried." He had. The best he could.

"You can't? That's weak," Ryan shouted.

"Apparently I'm weak, because I can't be a lot of things tonight." Ty closed the fridge, twisted the cap off the bottled water, and slammed down another shot.

"You can be a dick," Ryan shot back, pouring his own shot.

"Wanting what's right for you makes me a dick? Fine, I'm a dick. Trying to help Karis get a job makes me a dick? Great. I'm a dick."

Ryan's eyebrows rose in question.

"It doesn't matter. You got balls letting him in here."

"You weren't supposed to be home for another three hours." Ryan toed at the table chairs.

"And that makes it okay?" Ty gripped the chair.

Ryan hooked his foot around the chair leg and ripped it from Ty's hand. "You're not in charge of me. You're not in charge of any of us. I want a family with Pop. We're all he has, and we can help him." Ryan's shoulders dropped two inches. A release of tension, not a white flag.

Glass shattered against the far wall, and not one of them blinked at the crash. Air pumped through his flared nostrils. Heat swarmed up the back of his neck. "Pop cannot be helped, Ryan." Ty jerked his bow tie and chucked it across the granite.

"Listen to me." Ryan moved closer. "People change."

Not this again.

He sighed, "No."

"Yes, they do," Ryan disagreed.

This old argument was a planted stake between them, and Ryan lived on the losing side with too much evidence stacked against him. Ty lived in reality.

"No, they don't. It's in their genetic makeup. They are who they are."

"That's kind of fucked up, considering you're a hockey coach, trying to make people better."

Touché.

"Save it. Pop's damaged to the core, and I don't need any of your Oprah bullshit."

"I'm thinking that's exactly what you need." Ryan pulled two beers from the fridge; shards of glass cracked beneath his boots with each step. Ty accepted the bottle and joined Ryan in a long pull of his beer. "You don't think Pop can do it. You think that's just the way he is. So, do you think that's who we will become, ya know, considering our damaged core?" Ryan lifted his beer, dotting the *i*. Too smart, with a mind that wouldn't quit, making Ty ponder everything.

"You couldn't control her, and you can't control Pop. You have this undying, unyielding belief that people can't change, that people will always revert, and they don't learn and grow and move on, and that sucks, plus, it's wrong."

He stood motionless, the unwanted words sinking into his mind, latching on to his heart. "I only believe that about people who have proved it."

Ryan pressed on. "Pop will change, but I don't expect you to buy that. Not anymore. But be careful, because your way of thinking is going to cause you to lose Karis again."

Attention granted. "What does that mean?" The pounding in his head increased with each theory Ryan introduced.

"Easy. You think all change comes from within, and you're right, but people need help getting there. Improving, changing, getting better is not a solo job. And change may not happen on the first try, but that's life. Life is, Pop's a bastard, and Karis did what she thought was right by you."

"That's a lie. She thought of no one but herself. Like Pop," Ty defended, taking another swig of water.

"Yeah, graduating with a degree so she can take care of herself and not be a burden to her withering family or you. That's incredibly selfish. I see that." Ryan's smooth voice dripped with sarcasm and "told you so."

"I'm not talking about Karis with you." His stress needle jetted past anger. Ryan's specialty, on and off the ice.

"And I'm not discussing Pop with you. You'll get half the bill." Ryan kicked back a swig.

During hockey season, he complied with Ty's every word. Summer didn't work that way.

Ty hated it.

"You would rather watch Pop drink himself to death, and pay Tish to be out of Smith's life, than try to help them get better. Be better for Smith. Not just write them off. Think about that."

Ty poured the rest of his beer down the drain. "You don't know what you're talking about. I've seen, firsthand, people 'try to get better.' I spent months getting Wes into rehab. Months," he hissed. "Only to be called night after night to be told he was unruly and didn't want to be there, and after every release, he went right back to drugs. Every time. Tish would be the same way. Pop would be the same way."

"We'll never know," Ryan said easily. "For someone who's so die-hard family, you sure know how to shatter yours."

Ty pushed Ryan into the stove and anchored his shaking palms on the cold stone of the counter, locking Ryan between his arms. The best way to teach him a lesson.

"Where were you in all this, Ryan? What part did you play in Wes' recovery? Oh, right, none." Ty spoke over the pain triggered on his brother's face. It shredded his soul, but he couldn't stop. "Why? Because I"—he jabbed his chest— "took care of it all while you played hockey. While you became you, I took care of Wes and Pop and Smith and Tish."

Ryan pushed away, cursing under his breath. He rolled right over the pain Ty unleashed. "You have to allow people the opportunity to change. Yourself included. Give them a chance. Love them and believe in them. Love changes people more than control. It takes time and more than one shot."

Such naiveté. Maybe taking the job in Missouri was what they both needed. They faced off in silence. Clenched fists at each side. Ryan would never believe it, but every word he'd said settled in Ty's mind. Locked in place like synthetic ice. There had to be a reason why, with every success he'd ever had, and there were many, happiness skipped over him.

"It's difficult for me to trust Pop, and I'll do whatever it takes to keep Smith safe. That's my foundation." The heartbeat of the issue. "That's just who I am."

"Smith is safe, and you're more than that."

Ryan shot his bottle into the recycling bin and charged up the stairs. Leaving Ty in the dim light of the kitchen, the argument on a never-ending reel inside his head.

Chapter Thirty

A movie blared from down the hall, and three voices roared with careless laughter. Karis paused outside the door. They deserved to laugh without interruption. She left them alone and escaped to Ty's room for a quick reprieve.

When Firestones engaged in a hot-tempered argument, glass shattered but ended in a respectful truce. How they managed that was beyond her. She couldn't even get her sister on the phone.

Karis sighed, sinking down onto Ty's oversized bed. With each breath, the disastrous night unfolded scene by scene. He'd tried to help her get a job, and she'd ripped him apart. He still didn't get it. If she couldn't support herself, the vicious Hill cycle would continue, and for Lindsey's sake, someone had to stop it. He didn't see it that way, but there could be no other way.

Protecting everyone kept Ty living his life behind walls. He'd refuse the job of his dreams to take care of the people he cared about. She wouldn't let her life impede his opportunity.

Her nerves shot to attention, hearing the thumps in the hall. Ty stomped into the room. His hair a ragged mess, his breathing strained, and his face a shade of too many drinks. The tuxedo jacket gone, and the white sleeves of his dress shirt shoved to his elbows. A door slammed from down the hall, and tension hooked into every muscle.

Gathering the folds of her gown, she headed for the door and out of the line of fire.

"Don't go." His request pulled at her core.

She stopped at the far side of the room. She'd stay but needed space. Every piece of their history churned between them, but she clung to her decision. Loyal to what was better for him, her mother, and Lindsey. If anyone could appreciate sacrifice for family, it was him.

He rounded the bed like he was on skates. His strong fingers cradled her elbows. "I let you push me away before. It won't be that easy again. I won't survive it." His voice hitched. Darkness swirled beneath his lashes.

His desperation sliced her armor. Whatever this was between them, she would never get over it and would learn to live with wanting him haunting her.

She would not be a burden. "I think it's best that we end this before it gets too big. You have too much. I have too much. You need to deal with your dad. I mean, we're going in different directions. Again." The sad truth.

He tugged his shirt from his waistband. "Of course we have too much. We're not in college anymore, Karis. We have a shit ton of baggage. Life happened, and we have to figure it out." His finger wagged between the two of them. "We have to figure out how to make it work. You and me," he pleaded with her.

A strong man on his knees.

"I won't be a burden to you or Smith." Sidestepping, she snagged her purse and headed downstairs to the front door.

Blocking her route, he held her forearms. "You could never be a burden to me."

She wanted it to be true, but she had lived her entire life as a burden and didn't know how to fix that except to be alone. Alone made the ache go away. A brand burned deep into her core. As much as she tried to redeem herself and believe she was worth the energy he put into them, something always brought her worthlessness back. She couldn't do it anymore.

She took the stairs as fast as she could without tumbling. The laughter from the theater echoed behind her. A cruel reminder that she'd have to come back to get her mom and Lindsey.

He stormed after her. Her focus narrowed and nothing could stop her, except the faces of the last two people she expected to see when she opened the front door.

Hadn't these two done enough damage? Dropping her bag, Karis stood in front of Ty, shielding him from the evil vibe rolling off Tish and Pop.

"Fuck me," Ty said under his breath. "Anything else?" He stretched his arms up to the heavens. She had learned a long time ago to never ask that question. There was always something else.

"Karis, go upstairs." Protective, he stepped in front of her.

"No, I think I'll stay right here." He'd have to tie her up and drag her upstairs himself.

His disgruntled glare collided with her resolve, and once again, they were Karis and Ty versus the evil family.

With a knowing smirk on his lips, he confronted his father. "Hey, Pop, back so soon?"

"I think it's time Smith met his mother, don't you, Ty?" The whiskey-drenched words poured from Wilson's lips. Bloodshot red laced the whites of his glassy eyes.

"Drinks again? Good to see rehab's working its magic. What'd you do? Run to the bar down the road? Ryan would be so proud."

Karis stepped forward, the scene, a haunt from their college days. He'd attack his dad and be hungover for days with grief.

"What do you mean, it's time to meet my mom?"

Fabulous. Teenagers. Perfect timing and ears like guard dogs.

Smith stepped off the staircase, his eyes glued to the tall skinny woman standing outside the threshold. Tish shifted from foot to foot, in what might be embarrassment, but then she stared back at Smith, speechless and tattered. An alternate, better version of her life realized as she looked at her hopeful son. Tish had thrown away the best part of her life.

Smith shuffled forward. Lindsey hustled down the stairs, having his back, as always. *Stop right there.* Karis snagged her, securing her from Ty's imminent explosion.

They should leave. Bypass all the trouble and protect Lindsey from what was sure to be catastrophic. But her body froze. Refused to run away from the pain and seek the safety of being alone. Instead, Karis' heart splintered, and a possessive need to protect Ty flickered to life.

"Smith." Ty blocked the line of fire between his family.

Smith attempted a sidestep, but mountains were easier to move. "Uncle Ty?"

The universe softened.

Ty took a deep breath and tugged Smith into a hug, scorched with promise.

"My mom? Pop?" Smith pulled out of Ty's hold. He studied his sauced grandfather and his sickly thin mother. Leaning sideways, he assessed them quietly, trying to make sense of the situation.

Lindsey squirmed, ready to intervene for the well-being of her friend, her family, but this was beyond her.

"He can do this," Karis whispered into her ear, and to her surprise, she listened. She didn't interfere but scrutinized the scene at the door.

"You're my mom?" Smith asked.

Tish swallowed hard, embarrassment settling in the lines of her young face. The dark circles and exhaustion showed every rough patch life had thrown her way. Pop, the roughest of patches, took a step, and Karis, once again, reached for Ty. These two would not hurt him anymore.

"Smith, this is your ma," Pop declared in a proud, juicy tone.

"What the fuck?" All heads turned as Ryan bolted down the stairs. He glanced at his brother. "Did you invite him back?"

Ty shook his head, hate and anger bouncing off his body. "Never." He slid between Smith and his mother. "I think it's time you two left."

"I actually think it's about time we stayed," Pop slurred.

Ryan planted himself behind Ty, forming a muscled front. "No, Pop, you take this trash and get gone, or I'll take care of it and you myself."

There weren't many people Karis had ever seen go up against the Firestone boys, especially when they doubled up.

"Smith deserves to know his mother." Bloodshot eyes drooped with deceit.

"She's not worthy of him," Ty spat.

"She's *back*." Smith ignored the tension and stared at his mother like she was a unicorn.

Ty swayed. Karis inched closer. Every wave of his rage quivered beneath her supporting fingertips.

"Oh, baby," Tish oozed, stooping low. "I wanted to be here, but your uncle didn't want me in your life." The hate and amusement in her voice sent nausea crashing through Karis' stomach.

"So you left?" Smith struggled. What kid could overcome this? Ty and Ryan stood like soldiers, but Smith needed more. He stood stunned and frozen.

Well, not on her watch.

"Smith, come on." The boy absently wrapped his fingers around her outstretched hand. Lindsey grabbed his other hand, and they led him to the kitchen. The ease with which he went proved his shock.

"We'll be in the kitchen." She glanced at Ty, fighting the consuming need to wrap her arms around him, and let him know he was strong enough to handle this.

***

Quick as lightning and mean as a snake, Pop pushed Karis out of the way, sending her tumbling to the ground. Ty reached for her, getting full-blown permission from her glare alone, to kick the deep dark shit out of his asshole of a father.

Within seconds, Pop had Smith in his evil clutch, lodging his arm into the middle of his back. "The kid belongs with his mother," he snarled.

"Pop," Smith screamed.

"Smith," Lindsey yelled.

Ty reached, needing to wrap his hands around his father's neck. For a drunk, he was quick on his feet, and backed away from the group, dragging Smith with him. Even Tish looked surprised. She was going to see what she was really up against.

"You gonna keep my grandson from me? You think you can do that? You think you're better than me?" Pop screamed, red exploding up his neck and landing on his cheeks.

Ty's sights locked onto Smith's twisted arm. In that position, with the right amount of pressure, it shattered in two places. Pressure his father knew exactly how to give. He'd done it to all his sons except Ryan, and Ty had the pleasure twice.

"You break his arm and I swear to God, I'll kill you." Ty stayed steady. His heart banged with a deep vibration, adrenaline geared up, preparing to take over.

"What the hell are you doing? Let him go," Ryan called out.

"Wilson, are you nuts?" Tish backed away from the chaos, her mothering skills clearly missing.

Pop wasn't bluffing. "Tell him. Tell the kid the truth." Smith struggled in Pop's arms, but even young strength couldn't outdo old and crazy.

Smith met Ty's stare. Only the truth would work. "Listen to me, Smith. What I did was for you. I did exactly what your father wanted. Even against my own judgement. I fucking stuck to my word." The air in the room thinned.

"What do you mean? I don't get it?" Smith replied, licking his crusted lips. A pasty-white sheen bled across his face.

"Pop, ease up." Ryan tried to make his way closer.

"You ungrateful sons! Ty, talk. Tell him," Pop yelled.

Smith cried out in pain.

"Ryan, don't move," Ty commanded, stretching his hand in Ryan's direction.

"The closer you get, the more I push," Wilson slurred.

"You're a sick fuck," Ty breathed.

"I'm sick? You paid off his mother."

The choice was made. The love he had given Smith all his life had to count for something. It had to be enough.

"Smith, look at me. I know your arm hurts. I've had it done to me twice."

"That's a lie," Pop spat.

"Smith, look at me. Don't listen to him. I did—" His lungs seized. The scene in front of him swirled sideways. "I did what was right by you, and I would do it again."

"What?" Smith asked, his voice quivering.

"I paid your worthless, piece-of-shit mother to stay away from you." Not as eloquent as he thought it would be, but true.

"Fuck you, Ty." Tish sucked a drag from her cigarette.

"Point made." He glanced from the waste back to Smith, determined to make him understand. "She was never going to take care of you. I wanted you with me. Your dad wanted you with me, and the only way she would concede was if I continued to pay her like your father did. It was supposed to be a one-shot deal, but she came back repeatedly. The more she came back, the more I wanted her out of your life, so I kept paying her." A disgusting cycle.

Silence.

He locked his lips, and let Smith process his upside-down life.

"I thought she didn't want me." A tear fell down Smith's cheek and that was the last straw. Old-school reflexes and muscle memory snatched Smith out of Pop's arms and flung him in Ryan's direction. Pop's jaw glowed for the taking, and Ty sent him spiraling to the floor. Knocked out cold.

"Smith, I wanted you. I just couldn't take care of you." Tish threw her cigarette on the brick porch and stomped it out with a rubber flip-flop. Mother of the year right there.

Ty reached Smith and hit his knees. "I paid her to stay out of your life because she wasn't fit to be your mother. I never thought much beyond that, I just wanted to take care of you. I wanted better for you." A pathetic excuse. All the adults in Smith's life, him included, stirred up chaos.

"You lied to me about my mom and my dad." Smith leaned into Ryan.

Ouch.

"Yes." He owned it.

"I thought no one wanted me."

Ty bit into his lip and held Smith's stare. "*I* want you."

"You bought me," he stated, his brows coming together like they did when he questioned something.

"I wanted to protect you. Your parents." Ty pinched the bridge of his nose. "Your mom and dad, they just—"

"Didn't love me?" Smith finished, desperate for answers. For truth.

"Smith," Ty pleaded. Every breath depended on forgiveness.

Smith gawked at his mom. "You sold me?"

Black globs dripped down Tish's bony face. "I," she tried, but her voice hitched with what should have been regret and worthlessness. "Ty, we'll talk," she finished. With only a blink in Smith's direction, she hit the road, her brake lights lighting up to take the turn at the entrance.

He knew better than to think this was over. The sick twist in his gut didn't lie. She'd be back. She always came back. The paralyzing need to protect started the adrenaline buzz from core to fingertips.

Warm fingers slipped into his. He held on and followed Karis into the living room. He moved easily, his body buzzing and his mind swirling with how to fix it. Pausing, he glanced back at Smith still clinging to Ryan's waist and staring at his knocked-out grandfather.

"Ryan will take care of him." Karis' voice smooth as silk and warm as comfort slid into his ears.

"I got him. Go sit down," Ryan said.

When he sat down, every muscle jellied with relief. It was out. It was over. Smith may never speak to him again, but he'd never regret any of it. The toxicity of Tish and Pop was clear to everyone.

Smith charged into the living room and locked his arms around Ty's chest. Ty absorbed every shake and held on as long as Smith would let him.

"What in hell's going on in here?" Iona strolled into the room, looking all in charge and coherent. "I can't even go to the bathroom without the world falling apart."

"Mom," Karis tried.

"Oh my. Karis. Ty's dad is lying on the porch." Iona studied the scene.

"Yes, he is," Karis confirmed.

"Well." Iona smacked her lips. "It's about time."

Chapter Thirty-One

"Any word from your sister?" Ty lounged on the couch, his thigh inches from hers. Every day he came over, without invitation, just to hang out. So he said. Really, he was checking on them and trying to keep Smith's mind off last week's Jerry Springer events. He came to take the kids and Iona to a high school hockey game. A combined idea to normalize their life.

The joke was on all of them. Normal didn't exist. Still, he put in a massive effort, and Karis implemented her own back-to-normal formula.

"No, I haven't heard from her," she confessed. "I left a message on her cell, but, as usual, she hasn't called back."

After Lindsey witnessed the debacle with Smith's mother, she began asking about Leah nonstop, and rightfully so. No matter how unfit, every kid wanted their mom. A psychological mystery. Good, bad, or lit up like a bachelor on the Vegas strip. The phenomenon couldn't be explained, but they all suffered the same wound.

"Lindsey's desperate to talk to her, so I hope she calls."

Ty laced his fingers together, propped his elbows on his widespread knees, and hung his head. Her psych-y senses bubbled.

"She's not going to call." Hopelessness edged on each word.

"She might." Karis hoped for Lindsey's sake.

"Jesus, you sound like Ryan." Folding his arms, he sat back, his legs stretched out in front of him, taking up all the room. Adjusting his ball cap, he rested his head against the high back of the couch. "She won't. She's selfish in the worst way."

Relief. Horrible relief swamped her. She hated needing to hear someone else call her sister incompetent, but she owned the ugly need. She'd been owning a lot lately.

Without a second thought, she snuggled into the crook of his neck and let her restless love for him show. So much had changed since the Firestone family showdown. Somehow, overnight and without her looking, a yearning to take care of the people she loved became her top priority. She'd waited for the need to fade. For the narrow-sighted woman she'd always been to return and take back the life she had so carefully crafted. But that woman never showed, and if she did, Karis would kick her ass because nothing made you covet your family's safety like watching them get torn apart.

So much repair still needed to be done, and every day she found the confidence to take care of her people. Everyone huddled in the center of her heart deserved to move forward. So, she released all the hurt and neglect living inside her and grew determined to help Lindsey do the same.

"I've never been good enough for you." The words hung in the air, highlighting her vulnerability. What a simple, shallow confession. Her entire life summarized in one heartbreaking pathetic truth. She loved him. Always.

He draped his thick arm across her back, pulling her closer. Tilting her chin, he looked straight into her depths. She didn't turn away. She deserved to be soul searched.

"Not true," he whispered.

"You deserve so much more." A painful stab of truth rolled over her stomach.

"There's nothing more than you."

Oh, he had too much on his plate to think clearly. The man was nuts.

She swallowed hard and dove into the reason she asked him to come by early. "Ty." She swallowed, trying to refrain from lip biting. "You have to help your dad get sober."

"What? Christ." Wrinkles scored the corners of his eyes and deep creases lined his forehead. He gawked like she'd morphed into Medusa, clasped his hands, settled them on top of his head, and sucked in a noisy breath, making his chest puff like a boa constrictor.

Yikes.

It didn't take a shrink to see the issues with Pop needed to be resolved if he wanted to create a happy life with Smith. Especially with everything out in the open.

"And there's more." Why stop? She was going to hand it all to him. "Missouri's going to want an answer soon and"—she gulped, but still didn't chew her lip— "you have to take the job."

"Karis." He shook his head and scraped his hands down his face.

She had maybe another five minutes before the kids barged in. "A new start somewhere else would be great for you, Smith, Ryan, and even your dad."

Ty paced away from her. "No way. Not happening. Not without you, and not *with* Pop." His words slid past clenched teeth, and his jaw muscles contracted with a grinding click.

Along with everything else, the idea of moving with him had tumbled around in her mind, giving her more sleepless nights and edgy days. She would bring nothing but mess into Ty's already packed life, and the well-being of her family had to be the priority in any decision she made.

She cleared her throat, the pain a stiff reminder that tears waited. "I think you should take the job and make a new start for you and your family." There she said it. Lips still intact. Her stomach coiled and her heart kicked with a steel toe, but she'd done it.

Ty stared hard. His brows angled in sheer confusion.

Or perhaps disbelief.

"You're trying to get rid of me." He stated it like a well-researched theory.

"What? No," she snapped. "I'm trying to help you see what's right for you without the hassle of me. I won't let you turn down this job, and I won't let my family consume the life you want to build with Smith." She had to do right by him. By all of them. She'd done for herself for so long. She had to do for them, even as her stomach churned at the absurdity of losing love twice in her lifetime.

Ty crossed the room and laid his hands on her shoulders. "The job is my choice, and you and your fucked-up family are not *consuming* me. I'm stronger than that." He looked away and back again. So much desperation flared in his eyes. "You are my life," he whispered. "It ends and begins with you and me. Always has and always will."

Oh, this man. "How can you say that when responsibilities pull us apart?"

Ty dropped his hands to his sides and backed away from her. The small space mocked their ridiculous efforts for a reprieve from each other. "Our responsibilities pull us apart because you let them, and I can't let you do that to us again. I won't survive it." He pulled her into his arms. Thrust his hands into her hair. His lips hit hers, hot and heavy. Needing. Possessing.

She couldn't help herself and didn't want to. She opened for him and accepted the happiness pouring into her heart. She wanted him. Not the job, not the money, not the responsibility. Just him. Did that make her weak? Irresponsible? A burden?

She held him tight. His splayed fingers pressured the small of her back. His dangerous tongue licked the inside of her mouth, diving deep, and waking up every dormant live wire.

With a groan, he pulled away. Need and desire burned behind his locked gaze.

Combining their lives seemed impossible and a sure recipe for explosion.

Could they do it?

Could *she* do it?

Could she let him in without losing herself? Her family was enough to drive anyone away, but not him. He *wanted* to be there, helping her care for them, and the only thing he wanted in return was her. Was she worthy of his love?

"Ty—" A commotion from the stairs cut her off, and within seconds, they were surrounded by a whirlwind of teenage laughter and some serious flowery body spray.

She stepped away from him, pressing her arms into her stomach. Pushing on the guilt. The silence hung thick. The teenagers swept in on a blast of energy and swirl of hope. They possessed such power with just their optimism.

"Okay, awkward adult silence." Lindsey smiled and stared at Smith.

Ty gave Karis a wink and clapped his hands together. "You guys ready?"

She could play along and ignore the itchy discomfort. "Where's Grandma? I thought she was going with you."

"She is, she's finishing getting ready." Lindsey shoved a piece of gum into her mouth.

"Jeans and a jacket. What's to get ready? It's the same every day." Karis sighed. The woman was impossible and ultra-complicated.

Lindsey shrugged. "I don't know. She's putting her boots on."

"No, she's looking for her black boots," Smith corrected.

Karis blew some stray hairs away from her face. The threadbare black boots were thrown away when they cleaned out her closet. "She has to wear her brown ones until we get her new black ones."

"We tried to tell her that," Smith remarked, taking his phone from his back pocket.

Ty's chest bowed and his shoulders bulged into a tense square. Smith didn't see any of it. His split-lipped grin, focused only on the phone he held up for everyone to see.

Karis was happy for Smith but super worried about that overactive tick pumping from Ty's jaw.

***

"It's my mom," Smith whispered.

Ty cleared his throat and reined in his anger-xiety. "She said she'd call once a week, and as long as she—"

Smith held up one hand, cutting him off. "I know. Any slur, curse, cigarette puff, or sneaky question and it's click goodbye."

Ty's stomach lurched. Spun. Kicked around like a broken Kenmore from 1970 trying to wash a chest protector. Agreeing to a weekly phone call from Tish took him to new and unknown levels of strength. Even he was impressed with his ability to concede to the phone call idea. Maybe her tears had been real.

He hoped.

Smith opened the front door. "Gonna take this outside."

"Cool," Ty said, and cringed at the lameness of the word. Fuck, he was old.

"I need to check on Mom. I'll be right back." Karis jogged up the stairs, leaving him alone with Lindsey.

An orange glow from the afternoon sun filtered through the curtains. Outside, Smith leaned against the car with that massive smile still on his face. Trusting Tish completely would take years, but he'd struggle through the task, because Smith asked him to. And...well, that smile.

"Smith's so happy you're letting him talk to his mom." Lindsey flashed a small smile.

"Yeah." He dug his keys from his pocket, unsure of what to say about the situation. Would Tish fuck up? For Smith's sake, he shoved the *hell yes* out of his mind and replanted the new belief that she'd stick to the agreement, remain drug-free, and, perhaps, one day, phone calls could turn into visits. But they were far from that. The unspoken gist of the agreement was if she fucked up, he'd kill her. Smith didn't deserve anymore heartbreak.

"I just want you to know." Lindsey gulped and glanced at the floor. "I'm fine with you and Aunt Karis dating."

Ty took in the skinny blonde in front of him. She looked more supermodel than hockey player, and she'd kill him if she knew he thought that. Her looks hid her quirky, rough-around-the-edges hockey personality, and he adored it.

He bit the corner of his mouth, hiding his amusement. "There's really not a 'me and Karis.'" The stubborn woman wouldn't let him in her life until he kicked down the door. And that door was bolted, barricaded, and sealed around the edges.

Lindsey batted her hands. "Well, whatever. At first, I hated it, but it's all good now."

"Wait, you hated it?" He swallowed the laugh climbing up his throat. "We couldn't tell."

She rolled her green eyes like a champ. "Yeah, you could. I thought Aunt Karis would like you better than me, even though most of the time you pissed her off so much, I thought for sure you'd make her want to move."

Teenage rationalization? No wonder they were so screwed up. "I think you're safe from moving."

"Yeah. Grandma likes the day rehab facility you found. I think once she gets comfortable there, Aunt Karis won't want to move her." Lindsey held up crossed fingers.

"Fingers crossed," he managed. Lindsey was right. Once established in the cognitive facility, Karis would be nuts to move Iona. Anywhere.

"Okay, you guys, she's ready." Karis bounced down the stairs wearing a different but familiar T-shirt. She'd pulled her hair back into some type of sexy-bun thing and a slight flush covered her cheeks.

"Oh, my stars. I'm not a child," Iona snapped, taking the stairs one step at a time. It took days for them to convince her to slow it down.

"Sorry, but you are ready. Right?" A smile thinned Karis' lips, and her gaze rested on his. Her patience stretched to capacity.

"Yeah, but *I* can tell them I'm ready," Iona growled.

Karis took a deep breath. "Okay. Sorry."

Points for Karis.

"You changed." That shirt, all loose and touching her skin, spiked his body temperature.

She pulled at the hem and dodged the accusation. "Deep in the back of my mom's very dusty closet were, shocker, more black boots." Her voice rose an unsure octave.

"I knew they were back there. I knew I had fuzzy ones," Iona mumbled under her breath.

"Right," Karis agreed, flashing him a *can you believe this* look. "Didn't realize the closet went back that far, so another room to clean tonight. Yay, me. Anyway, shirt got dusty, so I changed."

"That's my shirt," he pointed out.

A wicked smile curved across her perfect lips. "No, I don't think it is."

"I'm pretty sure it is." Ty stepped closer.

"Gross. We'll be in the car. Come on, Grandma." Lindsey slipped her hand in Iona's and dropped her purse strap onto her shoulder.

"Hey, Linds, what's with the purse?" He escorted his ladies to the front door, not missing the daggers Karis threw his way. And then it dawned on him.

He was an idiot.

Iona shook her head and swatted at his chest before heading down the front steps toward the car.

Lindsey stopped at the door and flashed her own teenage daggers toward her aunt. A light red bloomed across her face. Karis, cool as a cucumber, smiled and nodded in her direction.

"Coach, sometimes a girl just needs a purse," Lindsey recited, tugging on the strap.

A proud motherly look lit up Karis' face.

He held up his hands. "'Nough said."

The girls laughed. "See, Lindsey? No boy wants to talk about *that*."

"You got that right," he agreed before stealing a kiss from Karis' silky lips.

"Uck, I'm going to the car. Coach, let's go."

"Give me a second."

Lindsey bounced out the door.

"Iona seems good." He followed Karis into the kitchen, hoping for confirmation.

"She's sleeping better, and she likes spending the day at the memory center." She sunk her hands into sudsy sink water.

"That was a great idea." He tangled his fingers with hers. Water sluiced between their loose grip.

It had taken a week to talk her into letting Iona go to a day facility. Another week for her to adjust to the outrageous cost, swallow her pride with harsh convincing, and apply for a scholarship. Conference room athlete deals were easier to solidify.

"It was a good idea, and I really appreciate the scholarship." Karis held up soggy air quotes.

"What's with the air quotes?"

"I know what you're doing!" She arched an accusing brow.

He snagged a dish towel. "I don't know what you're talking about." Maybe if he looked anywhere but at her, it wouldn't be so obvious.

"I'm thinking you do." She gripped her hips with dripping fingers.

"Nope, I know nothing about it. It was a scholarship. Congratulations." He couldn't resist and gave her a wink.

"Oh, please." She plunged her hands back into the water and swished silverware against metal.

Standing there in his old T-shirt, ignoring the car horn, she was everything he ever wanted in his life. Distance and a young lifetime spent doing what he loved didn't change *who* he loved.

"I want you and your family to come with me to Missouri." He didn't expect a response. Never did. In his mind, a decision had already been made.

She laughed, and, with wet fingers, pushed him out the door.

He bounded down the steps. A flicker of maybe fluttering inside his chest. Every chance found, he attempted to convince her to move her family with him. What she didn't know was, if she didn't go, neither would he. A brewing fight he'd deal with, eventually. He had a date with the two best teenagers in the world and a very impatient Iona waiting to start.

"My gosh, Ty, it's about time," Iona chirped, slipping into the back seat.

He blocked her door from closing. "You're in the front. I've learned my lesson. Until you stop kicking my seat, or playing with my hair, you ride shotgun."

Crinkling his nose, she grinned, and poo-pooed his concern, but moved to the front seat anyway. "You're no fun."

"Yeah, and you're too much fun. Now buckle up." He glanced in the rearview. "Smith, your mom conversation go okay?" The boy's smile told him everything, but he'd always double-check.

Surrounded by what he considered his family, comfortable contentment settled into Ty's heart. How he recognized contentment, he had no idea. It had been gone for so long. With Smith and Lindsey arguing in the back seat about why she was carrying a purse, and Karis waving to him from the kitchen window, all was right in the world.

Chapter Thirty-Two

They needed her. They wanted her. No amount of money could replace the peace bubbling to the surface. Sure, the unfamiliar feeling itched and played with her confidence, but she held fast. Self-doubt wouldn't take away her prized possession. Something she'd missed and longed for.

A family.

Karis dropped to all fours, ready to scrub the bathroom tile like nobody's business. The entire house needed a deep clean, especially if she was going to make this her home once again.

"I always hated cleaning this bathroom."

"Jesus." She spun around and tumbled back into the towel rack. Bracing herself, she stared at Leah, not knowing whether to laugh, cry, scream, or kill her.

Leah reached over the toilet and pulled her up by the wrists. Her long legs wrapped in tight jeans. It was a miracle she could move, much less bend down. The black tank top exposed scrawny arms. Black mascara half-mooned beneath crusted lashes.

Theory confirmed.

"What are you doing here?" Karis pushed her sister's hand away and tore off the bright-yellow rubber gloves.

"Lindsey's called a million times, so, as usual, I had to come check on things." Leah huffed with textbook disgust.

With Smith and his mother attempting to reunite, Lindsey had reached out to her own mother. Tish and Leah needed a parenting class.

Karis swallowed her scoff. "We don't need you to check on things. Things are fine."

"We'll see." Leah smacked her lips. "Where are Mom and Lindsey?" Her red toenails inched out of her black stilettos. She leaned against the door, scanning the tiny room with uppity disdain. Karis had done that a few times herself, but Leah had no right.

She ignored the fiery anger racing through her veins. "I have a better question. Where've *you* been?" Over her dead substitute-mother body would she let her sister waltz in here and run the place. She studied the woman who left her daughter with a sick grandmother, no money, and no plan to return.

Needing all the confidence she could get, and standing in the bathroom just didn't provide it, she flung her rubber gloves into the shower and headed downstairs. Her sister's cheap perfume lingered, giving the dread of confrontation a scent all its own.

"So?" She leaned against the kitchen counter and crossed her ankles. Waiting for what had to be a doozy of an explanation.

Leah sparkled from earlobe to pinkie toe and looked every bit put out and annoyed. *Good.* Her disgusted stare followed Karis' to the stack of medical bills always on display. She butted against the counter, undisturbed by the absence of her child and the illness of her mother. The mom in the room wasn't Leah, and Karis hated her for that. Lindsey deserved better.

"You know where I've been," Leah said easily.

"No, but I know you knew Mom was sick and never said a word to me about it, and you've sent zero dollars to help support your daughter this summer."

Leah's flippant stare hardened. "You make a lot of money with that fancy degree of yours. Remember the one you left us for? What was the point of getting it if you couldn't handle a few bills? It won't hurt you to help out."

She wanted to throttle the clueless bitch. "The point of my degree was to support myself. I'm not the one with the kid." The words felt vulgar coming out of her mouth. She wouldn't change one minute of the summer she'd spent with Lindsey, but she would not sit here and take a tongue-lashing from her sister.

Glancing at her phone for the third time, Leah laughed. "Ooh, Ms. La-di-dah. You don't have enough money?"

"Not the point. You left Lindsey here with Mom, who is sick. I have plenty of money, but Lindsey's not my responsibility. For some odd reason, she wants her mother, and it's taken every extra dime to pay for her hockey, but I refuse to let her give that up."

Leah cackled and splayed her boney fingers over her chest. "Oh my God, she's still playing hockey? Hockey's expensive, and please with the 'Mom's sick.' I've been taking care of her for years without complaint. This is the least you can do."

"The least I can do?" She squeezed the counter, her fingernails scratching at the particleboard underneath. "You haven't taken care of Mom. You've been in and out for years. You have a child. A teenage daughter who needs her mother, not some aunt she hardly knows."

"Save the guilt. Why should you be the only one allowed to leave?" Her curled lips made Cruella look like a princess.

Unbelievable. "Leah, everyone's allowed to leave. The question is, what are you leaving for? I didn't abandon my daughter." Hate clogged her throat.

"Jesus, you sound like Mom."

"Somebody has to."

A brief softness moved across Leah's mouth. "Where is Lindsey?"

The obligatory question made her sick. "She's not here."

Leah reached into her bag, shuffling around, sifting through God only knew what. She pulled out a cigarette and lit it with trembling fingers.

She could use a cigarette herself, but for the first time in years, she was exactly where she needed to be. "What do you want from me, Leah?"

"Too late. I needed you years ago." Leah blew smoke, suffocating the poor kitchen.

"Well, I'm here now, and I'm not leaving."

Chapter Thirty-Three

Ty's shoulder muscles clenched tighter with each kid's whiny shriek about leaving the game early. Including Iona's. Karis needed him, and the Stanley Cup wouldn't keep him away. Well, that would be the only thing to keep him away.

"I don't get why we have to leave early. The game was just picking up." Lindsey dug around in her purse and pulled out her phone. The backseat lit up with artificial light.

"Yeah, finally." Smith narrowed in on his own screen.

"Karis wants us back, so we're going back." The urge to grab both phones and chuck them out the window was quickly dismissed. He'd just have to buy them new ones.

Something was wrong. On the call, Karis stuttered with hesitation, and her request for him to bring Lindsey home had him guessing Leah had returned. He squeezed the wheel, trying to crush one final horrible idea. With Leah back, Karis could leave.

Jesus fucking Christ.

He was going to kill somebody.

Ty slammed his car door and stalked into the house. Hot frustration smoking up his insides so much it was bound to come out his ears. Good. Let them all see what they did to him. Fucking Hill women.

Finding her in the kitchen, he steadied himself. Her eyes softened at the sight of him and didn't that shred his fucking guts.

"You're leaving?" he accused, skipping the whole Leah's-back-and-standing-in-the-kitchen thing.

"Yeah, she's good at that." Leah stood up, catching Lindsey in her arms.

"You're home," Lindsey yelled, draping herself over Leah's stiff shoulders.

Smith leaned against the doorjamb. Confusion haunted his face. Ty rubbed his chest, because something had to ease the pain he experienced every time he saw that look.

"Leah?" Iona took a protective stance beside Smith. "Have you been smoking in here? You know I hate that."

"Karis?" Ty hissed. Exhaustion covered her, but he denied his body's desire to grab her, hold her close, and offer restoration.

"Mom, Leah's back." Karis slipped strands of hair behind her ear and narrowed her gaze at the floor. A definite sign she was way in her head.

"Yeah, back to smoking in my kitchen," Iona smarted, huddling close to the kids. The three of them a united front.

"Mom," Karis tried.

"Karis, you're not leaving," Ty interrupted.

Her gulp echoed like a goal horn after lighting up the lamp. Turmoil and angst surged from his core. Losing her meant losing all of this. The craziness, the family-ness, the nutso-what-the-hell-are-we-doing-ness. And that, Ty knew, he couldn't let go of.

"I need a minute." He pulled Karis into the living room.

Jerking her arm free, she stepped away. Hands on her hips, face flushed, all sexy and beat, she cut him to his knees. If she would just allow him back into her life, he could take it all away.

"Ty..."

"I want to take care of you. I've always wanted to take care of you. To help you. Let me, for fuck's sake. I want this." He pushed his hands through his hair and shoved them into his pocket. A desperate man.

"This?" she questioned, her hands flew up, gesturing to the room.

Was that good or bad? Fuck if he knew.

"You are helping me. Leah coming back is just one piece of the shitshow you're asking for. You've got your own things to deal with. You have your dad—"

"Who will be fine." Ty moved forward, cutting her off. No excuse would work.

"You have Smith." She stepped back.

"I've had Smith for a long time. We have this down. I want you. You." No more chances. No more thinking.

Her small smile put a crack in his desperation. "Ty," she said, and took his hands.

"I'll beg all night," he whispered.

"I'm not leaving, but you have your life, big things. Plans. And I have just jobless me and the mess of my family." Tears, indecision, and, maybe, a tinge of hope appeared on her sweet face.

Relief flooded him. "I want all that with you. You are my big thing." When would she understand?

Lindsey's scream shifted them both into parent gear. Without a word, he pulled Karis into the kitchen, tightening his hold on her shaky fingers.

"What's wrong?" Met with silence, Karis rounded on Leah. "What's going on?"

She shrugged. "I can't stay."

"What? What do you mean?" Karis reached for Lindsey's hand.

Done with the hurt, Ty stepped in. "Why the fuck not?"

"Awww, the love birds reunite?" Leah slurred.

"Shut up," he snapped, his body moving to protect his family.

Heading to the door, Leah snagged her purse. Lindsey reached for her shoulder, but Smith stepped into action and wrapped his hands around her waist.

There was only one reason Leah would leave, but Karis always refused to see her sister for what she really was.

"Why would you leave? You just got here. We need to take care of Mom and Lindsey?" Desperation clung to her voice. "Leah?" she demanded. The air in the poor kitchen hung stale and tense.

"Fine." Leah smacked. "I'm married, and he doesn't want kids."

Lindsey froze, stock-still in Smith's hold. Karis' spine snapped ramrod straight. Ty grabbed her, keeping her clenched fists from pummeling into her sister's deserving face.

"Married. What about money, bills, Mom? Lindsey?" Karis screamed, fighting to get out of his hold.

"Karis, stop," he whispered against her ear, shifting her around to get a good look at a shocked and withered Lindsey.

Karis released a jagged breath.

Leah curled her lip. "Oh, spare me. I've supported Mom for years. It's your turn."

"But Lindsey is *your* daughter." Karis shook in his arms, her quivering voice full of rage.

Both kids watched wide-eyed as the sisters squared off. An imminent confrontation. The Hill sisters in combat were a scary sight, but he had lived through it a million times.

"And I was your sister. I needed you, and you took off. Now, it's my turn." Leah tapped a long fingernail against the counter, her words dripped with resentment, and she didn't spare one glance toward Lindsey.

"Oh please, spare me the broken-life story. You didn't need me. Mom and I couldn't stand each other. I could barely breathe living in this house. I did you a favor."

Leah's face fell. "You're wrong, Karis. I tried like hell to ease everything between you and Mom, but you didn't see it. You couldn't see it. You were so busy worrying about how you were going to get out of here. And now I have someone who wants to take care of me. Me!" she screamed.

"Mom hated me. I was an unwanted weight to you, your boyfriends, her boyfriends." Karis nodded in Iona's direction. She tried to peel away his fingers. Her confession explained so much, and he released his hold on her.

"Wrong," her sister insisted. "You wanted to leave and thought of no one but yourself when you did. We weren't good enough for you."

"That's enough," Iona scolded. Lindsey and Smith stood as her wings.

Ty inched forward, needing to help Karis overcome the vulnerability stretched across her face. Etched in her shoulders. Visibly shaken, he waited for her to escape.

Right on cue, Karis darted to the bathroom down the hall.

No more running.

Ty knocked on the flimsy door. Force would push her away.

"Take Smith and go. He doesn't need to see another family shitshow."

He leaned his head against the door, her sad voice a sucker punch, and his patience a total surprise. "We can handle this." He swallowed hard, covering the emotion in his voice.

"Is that true?" she asked, cracking the door open, putting their faces inches apart. Her eyes blazed beneath wet lashes.

"What? That you took off when she needed you?" He jammed his hands into his pockets, fighting the urge to get into the room and take her into his arms. Smother her with the protection she always ran from. He'd learned his lesson and knew how this worked.

"It's true, isn't it?" she whispered through the gap. When her tears fell, he steeled himself.

"Maybe it is. But you can't go back now, and you can't blame yourself for what's been done. It won't help anything."

"But she's right. I bailed on my family. Just like I did with you. I took the easy way out. I let everyone go and only focused on me because it was easy. Because it was no more yelling, and no more judgement, and no more not feeling good enough for my mom, or you."

"Don't do this, baby. You're here, now." He reached a finger through the door opening, catching a tear. "We can't go back, as much as we would all like to. You and Leah have to go forward. We all have to go forward." Words his Oprah-loving brother had said to him for years.

"I'm not sure I can." It was fear talking, but she opened the door wider, and he pulled her into his arms, absorbing every shudder.

"You can," he said.

"For Lindsey," she whispered.

He rested his cheek on the top of her head. "For Lindsey. For you. For all of us." Together, all their broken pieces made a whole.

She wiped her cheeks and laced their fingers together. A solid bond flowed between them as they made their way back to the kitchen with their hands locked and their hearts full.

Smith held a red-faced Lindsey tucked tight against his chest. Her bucking efforts and a headbutt to his chin broke his hold, and she darted out the back door.

"Leah left," Smith huffed.

"That girl's just gone, gone, gone," Iona chanted, heading out the door. Karis right behind her.

Lindsey chased her mother's car down the street. Smith shouted after her. Ty snagged his shirt, catching him before he took off after her. Leah's bright taillights rounded the corner, drenching the road in darkness seconds before Lindsey fell to the ground. Broken in the middle of the street, her sobs filling the night.

No kid should have to watch their parent drive away. He couldn't handle it. Ty ran. His heart knocking against his chest.

They all had to be all right.

They had to be.

He crouched next to Lindsey and rubbed her back. She sobbed into her elbow, not caring about lying in the middle of the road. That's what losing someone did to a person.

"She's not coming back," Lindsey sniffed.

"I'm sorry." Losing someone sucked.

He lifted her, and she lay, emotionally beaten, against his chest, her small body shaking with each jagged sob.

"I got you. We got you."

She cried all the way back home, breaking every piece of his heart.

Epilogue

"You're wearing that to your interview?"

Karis buckled her high heels and smoothed down her skirt. "Yes, I am. Why? No good?"

"Too good. Go change." Ty moseyed around the kitchen counter and wrapped his arms around her beautiful body. The black skirt clung to her curves, and the black silk shirt framed her breasts beautifully.

She was not making it to the interview.

He grabbed her ass and inched her skirt up over her hips. She gave a green-light moan but pushed his hands away.

"No. This is serious."

"Karis, you don't need to get a job." For the millionth time.

She pressed her hands into his chest. "We talked about this. When we moved to Missouri, I said I was applying for a position on a team, you caveman."

He couldn't take it. The tan lipstick. The flowery smell. He needed her naked.

"Strip it down." He pulled her down the hall, eyeing her heels. They'd be in bed for years.

"No. I have to go." Her tone didn't say no.

"No, you don't, and you have the job."

She balked. "They weren't supposed to tell you."

He picked her up and carried her to their bedroom. "Yeah, well, I'm the head coach. They tell me what I want to know, and I wanted to know."

"They've never had a team shrink before. I wonder why they decided to get one." She gave him a knowing look, but he didn't care. He'd do anything for her, and she needed to get used to it. Karis wasn't the easiest person to help, and taking care of a family made her more stubborn.

He fought her to the very end. Wore her down like a team did to a rookie goalie but was still convincing her down to the moving truck backing out of his driveway.

He didn't win entirely. She may be in the house. In his bed. In his life, but so was Pop. *Goddamn it.*

Offering his Florida house and marking family visits on the calendar didn't make one bit of difference to her or Smith.

Set Pop up for success, they whined. They were a family. Blah, blah, blah. They were in this together. Blah, blah, blah. And then Ryan chimed in with his Oprah insight, and Ty gave up. The entire family moved to Missouri, and they were one gigantic misfit mess.

He loved it.

His forehead touched hers as he worked the buttons on her shirt. Silk ran through his fingers before hitting the floor. One finger dipped beneath the black lace covering her perfect breasts. Her sweet gasp, a soft cry of surrender. A million hockey hits didn't bring him to his knees like her permission did.

"We can't do this now. I have an interview." Her breathy sigh said otherwise.

He kissed her neck, and her scent swarmed him. "You have the job."

She started to argue, but he was ready for it. He crushed his lips to hers, swallowing her weak protest. Her hands plunged into his hair, and she rocked her body against his. He palmed her ass, encouraging the roll of her hips.

"The kids will be home from school soon," she teased.

How in the hell did skirts like this come off? "No, they won't."

She pulled back. Leaving him empty and cold. "Don't do that, don't pull away from me."

"Where are the kids?" she questioned rightfully so.

Since moving to Missouri, she had grown protective of Lindsey, Smith, her mom, and even Pop. She worked around the clock, taking care of everyone and forgoing her own breaks. He knew better. In order to survive the long haul, salvation needed to show up once in a while.

Cue the job.

"They're going to visit your mom. They'll be back before dinner."

"You have it all planned." Her smile stole his breath. Her soft skin left him spinning and aching to push inside of her. The skirt, no longer a problem. He'd make his own zipper.

The tear of fabric cut through the room.

"You did not just rip my skirt."

"I did." He pressed his nose against her warm sweet-smelling skin.

Roses.

"Let me go. I need to get another skirt."

"The job is yours."

She paused on her way to the closet they shared, her long legs and nice ass giving him the best view in Missouri.

Her mouth formed a thin line. "I get my own jobs."

He knew better than to question her need for this. She had come around but still demanded independence.

Not anymore.

Picking her up, he carried her to the bed, needing to make one thing clear. "So what?" He shrugged. "I need to help you."

"Why do you *need* to help me? I'm not a damsel in distress." The desperation in her tone warned him. The ice was thin, and the other side far.

This woman. Those lips. Those eyes seared into him, no longer holding anything back.

"Because that's what husbands do."

Silence.

Not what he expected.

"Ty?" she whispered. "Whose husband are you?" She pulled her bottom lip between her teeth.

"Yours, if you'll have me."

The struggle warred across her face. The fight for love and independence. He was ready to bargain, to give her anything, as long as she became his.

"I come with a lot of baggage," she whispered.

He rubbed his thumb over her damp cheek. "I'll take it all."

"Why?"

"Because I love you." He swallowed hard. Wishing he had better words for her, wishing there was more to him than hockey and a fucked-up family.

"I love you, too. So much." She breathed.

"Marry me, Karis." He ached for her answer.

"Yes, Ty, yes."

Thank you for reading my debut romance novel, Baggage. Sending you a big hug. I hope you enjoyed Ty and Karis' craziness and are ready for book 2 of the Firestone Brothers Series. If you think Ty and Karis were nuts, wait until you read Ryan and Farrell's story.

Desperate needs lead to weak decisions, even in the strongest men.

Ryan Firestone's a driven man, determined to prove to the professional hockey world he deserves his own legacy. Faking a relationship with hockey highness Farrell Eaves was never meant to be permanent or mean anything. With her on his arm and his stats in the stars, Ryan's well on his way to hockey elite. Until the trade, where his biggest competition becomes his own heart.

She didn't expect pretending to love him to be so easy.

Farrell Eaves has fought for her freedom for the last time. She's not about to be Ryan's pawn. She's paid that back a million times over. Yet the passion between them pushes Farrell away from her dreams, and into his bed. He wants it all, but she can't lose herself again. There are too many lives counting on her. Including his.

Ryan and Farrell must come to grips with the passion pulling them together even if it means giving up the most important pieces of themselves.

Distracted by Mar Mills releasing in May 2024.

A Note from the Author

Family can be tough. It can ebb and flow in our lives, make an impact, leave us crying, breathless or giddy with laughter. I have experienced all these emotions with my family and as awful as the roller coaster can be, it can be just as invigorating and worth that insane upside-down flip sending your stomach flopping around your insides. I'm a fan of family and that's where my characters derive from.

Writing a book feels the same way and I have so many people to thank. Thank you to my wonderful tribe of authors, The Write Spice. These ladies get me and love me anyway. A special thank you to Ginny, who has plowed on with me during this roller coaster of madness and at times urged me to move forward and to take the time to celebrate the small wins. A big shout out to Addison and Nan at Wizards Publishing for loving my characters like I do and answering my emails no matter how silly.

Once again, the author world has pushed me beyond my introverted comfort zone, but I've learned to embrace it. I must thank all the readers who have reached out to me with encouragement and kind words to keep me going. Believe me, it makes a difference.

Thank you to Mom and John for teaching me to dream and go after it.

Thank you to my fab fam, for encouraging me and for being understanding when I said I must write and disappeared for hours. This book is what I was doing! Now you can see.

To my babies. I love you E, V and J. Keep doing what you're doing. Play hockey. Sing and dance. Play outside. Read books. Love each other.

Jeff, love of my life, thank you for believing in me and the wonderful dreams that live in our house. I love you so much.

To all the new writers out there, keep going. It'll happen.

Be Brave. Love Hard.

Want more love stories by Mar Mills? Including getting your hands on Distracted, Book 2 of The Firestone Brothers Hot Hockey Romance Series.

Easy

Stay Connected

Mar Mills Website: marmillsauthor.com

Facebook: @Mar Mills or Mar Mills author
Instagram: @marmills1

About the Author

Mar Mills is a proud Florida native, who spends her time lying by the pool, basking in the sun while her sexy husband rubs her feet. KIDDING. He hates feet.

A former teacher, Mar now absolutely loves wrestling with the characters living in her head and bringing them to life for readers who enjoy a witty-hot and salty romance. She penned most of her contemporary romance stories in the car parked outside of wherever she had to take her kids for some kind of practice or rehearsal. Currently, when she's not writing, which is rare, she's planning her next adventure to see her children who are now off making their dreams come true.

If you'd like to receive a notification when Mar has a new release or want to get to her know her (she loves meeting all readers) sign up for her newsletter and stay in the loop. Go to marmillsauthor.com to get all things Mar.

Don't miss out!

Visit the website below and you can sign up to receive emails whenever Mar Mills publishes a new book. There's no charge and no obligation.

https://books2read.com/r/B-A-MPOCB-NBYXC

BOOKS2READ

Connecting independent readers to independent writers.

www.ingramcontent.com/pod-product-compliance
Lightning Source LLC
Chambersburg PA
CBHW051308130726
47987CB00004B/1718